The Kitsune Stratagem

The Kitsune Stratagem

David A. Tatum

Fennec Fox Press

The Kitsune Stratagem

Printed in the United States of America
First Trade Edition, 2014

ISBN-13 978-0-9912844-7-4

Fennec Fox Press
Ashburn, Va 20147
http://www.FennecFoxPress.com

Cover art by Sensevessel Studio
http://sensevessel.daportfolio.com/

Dedication and Acknowledgments

To Keith R.A. Decandido, whose editorial work and advice was invaluable.

To Adirasa Enggar (a.k.a. Sensevessel), whose fantastic cover art has truly livened up this work.

To Allen L. Wold, whose advice and education has launched a thousand writers.

And, as always...

To my brother, Jonathan Ken Tatum, without whom this would never have been possible.

To my mother, Betty Jo Tatum, without whose financial and logistic support I wouldn't have had the time to write.

And finally to my late father, librarian extraordinaire and book expert George Marvin Tatum, who instilled a great love for writing throughout our whole family before he passed away.
I miss you, dad.

Table of Contents

I. A Vixen Outcast

It was just a succulent roast bird, waiting on the spit for someone to devour it. The chicken's owner had started the rotisserie before being summoned away by one of the human nobles on the estate, leaving the chicken behind. The strong, delicious smell had drifted for blocks around as it slowly turned on the spit, and it was now cooked all the way through. The counterweight and clockwork system designed to keep the spit turning while the chicken cooked had stopped, and if it wasn't reset or taken off the fire soon it would fall off and burn.

Letting the poor bird's sacrifice go to waste would have been a shame, or so the female fox that had been watching it cook for quite some time now thought. Glancing around to make sure neither the owner nor anybody else was coming for it, the vixen pounced from her hiding place and snatched the treat. She was no thief – she had a payment prepared, and delivered it before taking the roasted chicken – but staying hidden as long as possible would probably prevent any unpleasant misunderstandings.

Careful not to burn her fur, or her tongue, the vixen extracted both meat and spit from the fire and took off running. She was in a castle – a walled city, really, but with homes and shops and even small farms, as well as several parks and gardens to play in – but there were no woods thick enough to hide herself while she enjoyed her meal. Nevertheless, there were plenty of places in town where she knew she would be safe.

The castle had been built with four major redoubts inside the outer walls that were only connected through a series of easily guarded tunnels underneath. These redoubts were also connected to the King's Keep, which was heavily guarded even in the most peaceful of times. Additional tunnels led to barracks for the Royal Army, but no creature would be foolish enough to try sneaking into that building. Still more tunnels led to purely residential towers, built to house the King's personal retainers as well as visiting Ambassadors, Lords, and lesser nobles. Almost a century of work building the castle had riddled the grounds with more tunnels than even the royal family knew of.

In order to bring light and air into that large network of tunnels, multiple shafts were added, many of which ended up in buildings like the residential towers, the Keep, and the barracks. A few had originally even been built in the courtyard, but those were sealed tight once it was learned that heavy rains could cause the tunnels to flood from those vents. Doors leading from the redoubts into the tunnels were as heavily guarded as the doors to the Keep, itself, but the vents leading into those passages remained unguarded, as no human could pass through them. The vixen, however, could fit through passages that small, and with a little persuasion so could her meal.

Because of the heavy guard on one side of the tunnel, there wasn't much security on the actual entrances into the Keep itself. The vixen was able to slip into that heavily guarded building without the slightest bit of notice, thanks to that oversight. She continued running through hallways, cautiously avoiding any people, until she came to the set of residential suites inside the Keep intended to house the families of the King's personal guardsmen. She slipped into a particular room she knew was unoccupied, leapt onto a table, and dropped the chicken in a plate. Finally she stepped back, glanced around for a moment, and grabbed a small black ball in her mouth.

In but a few short seconds, the vixen transformed herself from a well-groomed young fox with brilliant red fur and an unnaturally white belly into a young human of the female persuasion, looking to be no older than twenty years old with remarkable red hair, a nicely proportioned bosom, long shapely legs, and a toothy, mischievous grin. The black ball was now in her hand, and while initially nude she formed clothes around herself with a mere thought. She had been born a kitsune, and as such she could be either human or fox, with special abilities in each form. With those abilities came the power to create illusions, which was what allowed her to clothe herself after changing form, but as a kitsune she only had two forms at rest: Human and vixen. And right now, she preferred being human... even if she did have to expend a little energy to create her clothing.

"I have to agree with my brothers – chicken has to be the best thing there is to eat in this castle," the kitsune girl said to herself. "But I wish they'd at least try tasting it in their human form. Things taste so much better cooked when you're a human."

"Actually, Kieras, you're one of only a very few kitsune your age who can make so complete a transformation that even their tongues taste food differently," a voice said from behind her. "Your brothers certainly couldn't do that before they left home."

"Eep!" Kieras shrieked, spinning around to identify the unseen person belonging to that voice. She still had nightmares from when she learned that the current King's youngest son would sneak into her bedroom to watch her change, since she wasn't able to immediately generate her clothing when she transformed. Her eyes settled on a tall, ageless red-haired man dressed in the uniform of one of the King's personal guards. With a guilty smile on her face, she said, "Hello, Papa."

"Hello, daughter," he replied in a gently mocking imitation of her tone. "I see you've found yourself some dinner."

"Heh heh," she laughed nervously. "I paid for it! Honest!"

"And what did you pay for it with? Actual money, or twigs and stones?" her father asked. "You didn't hide your journey here as well as you think. The guards will find you if you stole it, you know. That chicken scent is strong enough that even human noses can follow it here."

Kieras narrowed her eyes indignantly. "I remember your lessons, Papa. As long as we live in the castle, we have to pay for the things we buy with real, human, money. I gave the cook a whole silver piece, which is much more than this chicken is worth."

"And did the cook know you were buying this chicken when you got it?"

Kieras blushed. "Well...."

He sighed. "I knew it. I wish you'd remember our position in this castle and not abuse it... although perhaps that is a moot point. I'm not here to talk with you about a stolen chicken, after all. We have some extremely important things to discuss."

Kieras glanced at her cooling chicken regretfully, but knew her duty. Turning to her father, she said, "What is it, Papa?"

"Oh, go ahead and eat your meal," her father said, gesturing to the chicken. "I have a lot to say. Just remember to keep your ears open."

"Thank you, Papa!" Kieras immediately started to shred the chicken off the bone with fingernails that were still as sharp as her fox form's claws.

"This starts with a story from my past... from almost a hundred years ago," her father began. "King Heshka II's great-great grandfather – who at the time was little more than the lowly captain of the guard for this town, back before it became the capital of the Kassian Empire – heard news that his own king had fallen, and that the invaders were on their way to mop up the rest of the resistance in the countryside...."

Sir Kazdri, the captain of the guard for the township of Kassia, couldn't help but allow the frustration to settle on his face as he took in the orders given by the refugee nobleman in front of him.

"Lord Haan, there is no way that my small manor house would be able to hold even three hundred men. If you think we can billet three thousand soldiers within this town you clearly have no idea how small this place really is."

"We will set camp outside of town, and build temporary walls and buildings to support ourselves," Lord Haan said. "All we need from you and your people is enough provisions to last us through the winter, when we can strike back against those accursed Erixonites. Believe me, I would love to move to a larger, more fortified city, but with winter coming soon I think we would be buried in snow before we could reach such a place."

"We don't have near that much food, either," Kazdri said, though he understood the situation completely. He came to only one possible conclusion. "We have long winters and short hunting and growing seasons. It's hard to add to our stores beyond what we've already acquired. What we do have, however, is sufficient pickling spices and salt to preserve a great deal more, if we can find it. We have all of the grains and vegetables we're going to get, and we'll have to ration them *very* carefully in order to stretch them out that long for that many people, but I think we can manage it as long as we have enough meat to go with it. If you will loan me a hundred men, I can detail some fishermen to help them catch and preserve fish. Another hundred could even be used to collect enough water to last us all for the winter. We'll need more than that, however. I'll need every man in the village to go hunting if we even want to have a chance at collecting enough food. Most of the animals are at their fattest as they prepare for the winter, themselves, thankfully, but...."

"But?" Haan prompted.

"The common land Kassia's hunters usually use will have been hunted fairly clean, by now." Kazdri sighed. "I'll need to call for the hunt to take place in the royal game preserves."

Haan grimaced. "Well... I doubt that His Majesty will mind, any more. Few people care about much after having a foot of steel lodged in their heart."

"Were you with Kazdri while all of this was happening, Papa?" Kieras asked. She had finished her meal – picked the carcass clean and then some – and was now hanging on her father's every word.

"No," he replied. "I only know about this conversation because he told me about it some years after it happened. I was completely ignorant of what was going on in the human world, at the time, preparing myself for the approaching winter. I had just found a good spot for a den – a marmot had abandoned a burrow for the summer, and didn't return as winter was approaching, allowing me to claim it as mine – when I heard the footsteps of a creature I hadn't set eyes on in my two hundred years of living in that 'royal game preserve:' Human beings...."

The snapping of a twig alerted the three-tailed kitsune to the presence of another creature near his newfound den. He had been scouting around for dry leaves to bed down on, but hadn't gone too far from home. Unfortunately, until he got back to his den, the kitsune was only as strong as an ordinary fox, so hopefully he could make it back unnoticed... or at least the intruder, whatever it was, wouldn't be out of a fox's league.

Neither proved to be true. The creature was human, which made him very dangerous to the kitsune in this form, and it was standing directly in his path, making it impossible to approach without being seen. Nevertheless, the kitsune desperately needed something that was hidden in his den, and could not leave without it... nor could he let the human take it away.

Even though the kitsune's approach was completely silent, the human seemed to sense him. "Oh, hello." The human smiled blandly up at the fox. "I didn't think marmots lived around here nowadays, but this burrow showed signs of being recently occupied. And then I found this...."

With that, the human showed something he was holding in his hand: A small, polished ball of what appeared to be marbled red clay. It was more than that, however – it was the kitsune's *hoshi no tama*; the focus for his magic.

"That, daughter, is why I'm never happy with you leaving your *hoshi no tama* in your bedroom when you go out adventuring. It may seem like it is in a safe place while sitting in your home, but you never know if you're going to need it. Even if you don't, there's no telling who will come and claim it while you're gone."

Kieras protested. "But it's so hard to carry both the *tama* and a bite of food while I'm in my fox form, Papa."

"It's still much safer to keep it with you. I admit, carrying it in your mouth can interfere with your ability to eat, but you could always just hold it with your tail or something. If you can't do that for some reason and it becomes too difficult to hold, it's better to swallow the tama and deal with recovering it, later, than to be without it when you need it."

Kieras thought about that for a moment before wrinkling her nose in disgust. "Ew. No, thank you. Swallowing it is definitely not something I *ever* want to deal with. I guess holding it with my tail would be okay, though."

Her father nodded. "A wise idea. I've only had to deal with having swallowed my tama once in my life, and never want to again. Now, where was I? Oh, yes, the human – who was the same Sir Kazdri from earlier in my story, by the way – was holding my *hoshi no tama*...."

While he needed his *tama* to transform or to use his magical strength and powers, the kitsune could still talk in human tongue without it. "I need that ball, human. It will do you no good. Give it back to me!"

"Ball? What ball?" Kazdri said, glancing at it in his hand tauntingly. "Oh, you mean your *hoshi no tama!* You're right. It won't do me any good. But it will do you a great deal of good, won't it? I'm not going to give it back right away, though."

"What do you want?" the kitsune asked.

"First of all, I'd like to know your name. I feel it makes conversations between people so much easier. Don't you agree?"

The kitsune hesitated, but there was no reason not to give up his name. Unlike some of the more mystical creatures of legend, names held no power over a kitsune. "My name used to be Lahti, although I haven't used any name in almost two centuries."

"I see no reason to give you a different name. Well met, Lahti the Kitsune. I am Sir Kazdri, captain of the guard for the township of Kassia."

Lahti dipped his head in a foxy imitation of a bow. "Well met, Sir Kazdri. I am sure you are not holding my tama hostage solely to learn my name, however. What do you want from me?"

"The township I am in charge of is in something of a crisis," Kazdri said. "We have three thousand unexpected mouths to feed this coming winter, and so I and my fellow townspeople are hunting for whatever food we can find in these last few days before the snows hit. I desperately need the help of your nose to seek out food to hunt – otherwise, we will all starve."

Lahti was not entirely unmoved by the human's plight, but nevertheless felt it was not a matter of his concern. "Return my *tama* and I will help you."

Kazdri shook his head gravely. "I am sorry, friend Lahti, but I cannot do that. See, I have met your kind before. A family of purebred myobu kitsune comes to Kassia almost every spring, and they have taught me and my people how to deal with your kind."

"Mama was a myobu kitsune, wasn't she?" Kieras asked softly. Her mother had disappeared many years before, and Kieras' memories of her were somewhat vague.

"She was," Lahti replied wistfully. "In fact, she was one of that family of myobu kitsune who would visit with Kazdri in the spring. Strong and clever, with a beautiful white shining coat, that was your mother.

Tianhyu was a couple hundred years older than I was, and a lot wiser about many things, but she and I often had many an argument thanks to her myobu beliefs. She was always playful, however, and we loved each other very much. I wish she had stayed with us, but it was better that she left."

"What are myobu kitsune like?" Kieras asked.

"Since I'm a nogitsune kitsune, I don't know everything about them myself. My red fur marks me as a different breed, so no matter who my mate was the other myobu would never take me into their confidences. Nor would they consider you one of their own, either, thanks to the red fur you inherited from me."

"But you have to know *something* more than me," Kieras insisted. "I don't even know the traditions of the nogitsune, and I'm one of them!"

Lahti sighed. "It goes back to our origins as kitsune, when the great wizard Inari, then living in what we know today as the city of Norre, created the first kitsune – a myobu – from a white fox, in an effort to save his daughter's life from a snakebite. She became the first myobu. The nogitsune were created later, by a different mage, using a red fox. While we share many traits, such as our compulsion for deception and the inability to fully understand human morality, the myobu have endured a magical compulsion to follow the agenda of their long-dead creator, while the nogitsune suffer no such compulsion. Beyond that... well, your mother would know better."

"I wish she were around for me to ask," Kieras said. "Or any of the other myobu who were here back then, if they were so willing to teach people about themselves. What did they teach him?"

"That he could trust no deal made with another kitsune that was not freely offered, but that we would do anything to regain a lost *tama*. So, to regain mine, I helped him and his people hunt the forests for food, unable to get my revenge for the indignity, because of his holding my focus of power. He treated me well, and after a while I no longer cared for revenge. I decided I would continue to help him even if I somehow managed to get back my *tama*. And then we ran into something a bit too difficult for me to handle without it...."

"I'm not sure what it is, actually," Lahti said, glancing up at Kazdri. "I've never smelled a creature like it, before – certainly not in this part of the forest. All I know is that it has fur, and smells of blood. Whether that blood is its own or someone else's, I cannot say."

"It may be a wounded animal." Kazdri sighed. "Or it may be a predator. Either way, we should investigate closer."

They continued on for a few minutes in the direction of the unusual scent before Kazdri spotted something. "Hello, what's this?" Bending down, he began inspecting an impression in the dirt which Lahti immediately started sniffing. "Looks like a paw print of some kind... and it's big."

"It's the creature we've been following. I think it's fresh, too. And... I'm becoming more and more convinced that this animal is something dang—"

Lahti was interrupted when Kazdri's hand picked him up around the torso, tossing him back. A split second later, while Lahti was still in mid-air, a giant paw the size of an elephant's foot slammed down where he'd been standing.

The kitsune landed safely, but was stunned for a moment. He glanced up to try and figure out just what had happened and then froze. It was larger than a horse, with fangs that must have been at least a foot long and blood staining its white fur. Lahti had never smelled or seen such a creature before, but its reputation preceded it.

"Amarok!" Lahti yipped, frightened. It was the greatest fear that every kitsune had – to be stuck as a fox when facing a powerful wild canine predator. Typically found only in the snows of the far north, the amarok was the largest breed of wolf known, more than triple the size of its nearest relative, and sometimes weighed over four hundred pounds. Legend said it could grow even larger than this one, but Lahti found that hard to believe. It looked deadly enough as it was. The only advantage to facing one, if you could call it that, was that, unlike just about every other breed of wolf, they were solitary hunters and did not travel in packs.

"An amarok?" Kazdri repeated, watching it circle around sniffing the air. They had rolled into its blind spot, which gave them a moment to think, but it remained to be seen whether the great beast would come after them or would just move on. Amarok rarely hunted human, but it sure looked like that stomp was deliberate. "What's it doing this far south, and in this weather?"

"Whatever the reason," Lahti said, backing away from the wolf without letting his eyes leave it, "it's here, and I think it wants to eat us."

"In that case," Kazdri said flippantly, reaching into his pockets. The way the amarok was sniffing the air, it was after something. "Maybe we should eat him. I've never eaten wolf – it's probably gamey."

"Are you out of your mind?" Lahti snapped incredulously, unable to believe Kazdri's flippant bravado. "We can't fight that thing! It'll tear us limb from li— huh?"

Almost casually, Kazdri tossed something Lahti's way that he instinctively caught. It only took a split second to figure out what it was that he'd been given.

"It never felt right, blackmailing you into helping me and my people out," Kazdri mused, preparing a bow and arrow. He also wore a sword and other close range weapons, but if he got close enough to use one against the aramok he probably wouldn't survive the exchange. "I never felt I had a choice when this started. You, however, did everything I asked, with far fewer attempts to deceive me than I should expect from a kitsune. I'm sure a kitsune as clever as you could have stolen your *tama* back when I slept, or when I was inattentive, yet you never even tried. I figure you shouldn't have to die for my people, who I know don't matter in the slightest to you. So, run while you can – I'll take care of this thing."

Focusing his energy into the *hoshi no tama* that had finally been returned to him after weeks in Kazdri's service, Lahti changed into his human form. After several hundred years of experience, he was able to make that change in an instant. Once completely transformed, he was faster, stronger, and had better access to his magic, making pieces of leaf or twig into illusory but effective armor in a matter of seconds. The *tama* turned him from a fox that had much to fear from humans and larger predators into a mystical being with powers few still living could match.

Lahti stared at his *tama* for a long moment. "I must admit, I'm absolutely terrified of all forms of dogs and wolves. Even the tiniest of puppies can do things to my kind that no other animal can, and it's in my kitsune blood to want to run from them. To make matters worse, they don't come any scarier than the amarok. But I'm also not going to leave someone behind to die when I can help them. Foxfire!"

A small ball of fire shot out of the hand that was now holding the *tama* and crashed into the amarok's eye. The giant wolf howled, staggering back, but unfortunately was not blinded as Lahti had hoped. Instead, it was merely angered. With a loud growl that shook the kitsune to his core, the great beast leapt into the air. Lahti's eyes widened as he saw it approaching, clawed foot first. The wolf's powers over his kitsune blood made him faint before a blow even landed. Just as everything was going to blackness, a human arm appeared between them... and then nothing.

He had no idea how long he was unconscious, though it didn't feel like it was very long. He was alive, however, which was astonishing enough, and the aramok wasn't. Instead, a very tired-looking Kazdri was leaning over the corpse, panting heavily.

"Sir Kazdri?" Lahti moaned, trying to make sure he could still speak.

The human glanced over at him and smiled just a little bit before pitching over himself. It was then that Lahti noticed he was missing an arm, and that his blood was starting to coat the ground around him. In mere moments, he was by Kazdri's side, looking him over. There wasn't much he could do about the arm other than stop the bleeding, but at least he could do that. And, with all the magical power he could focus into his *tama*, he might even be able to save his life.

"And so I did," Lahti finished to his daughter. "It took a while, but I healed him enough that he survived the battle."

"And then what happened, Papa?" Kieras asked, now so drawn into the story she had forgotten it was her father's actual memories, and not just a bedtime story of the type he told her when she was much younger.

"The man gave his right arm to save my life," Lahti said. "So I swore to protect him and his kin for the next one hundred years. Together, Kazdri and I saved Kassia from starvation that winter, and joined the armies of Lord Haan to restore their kingdom. Haan was eventually killed and the effort failed, but it was successful enough that the Erixonites settled on a treaty with Haan's surviving forces, allowing Kassia to become its own kingdom with the lands it still held. Sir Kazdri's efforts in that war earned him the title of king after it became clear that the old nobility had been wiped out. He ordered the construction of a castle that would eventually turn Kassia from a humble township into the great city it is today. He lived to see it largely completed – though it took almost a decade just to lay the foundation with all of the tunnels that were built into it, and another several decades to build the walls and gatehouses. It was during this time I discovered the foolishness of my promise to Kazdri: He was a good man, and if given the choice I would gladly have served as his protector again. His kin, however, weren't so worthy. Kazdri was usurped from power by his own children – a fate I could not interfere with, as I was bound to protect both father and son – and they turned his kingdom into an empire desperate to 'reclaim' the lands taken by the Erixonites in a war few of them were alive for. With Kazdri gone, the family of myobu kitsune who used to visit these lands every spring felt the need to leave as well, forcing your mother away from us."

Kieras gaped. "But... why did I not know of this, before?"

"It has been ninety five years since I made that oath." Lahti continued speaking as though he hadn't even heard her question. "And for the last several decades, I have regretted it. The only good thing left from my meeting with Kazdri all those years ago is that it eventually led to me finding my mate, and having you as my daughter. I fear I am about to lose even that."

Kieras' eyes widened. "P-papa? You're scaring me...."

Lahti looked his daughter straight in the eyes. "Kieras, you have proven to be an exceptionally powerful kitsune for your age. So powerful it will cause us problems with the royal family."

"I'm not that powerful," Kieras said quickly. "I can't even generate clothes when I transform!"

"No, but you're still only forty-seven years old. By the time you're a grown kitsune at two hundred years of age, you'll well surpass me in strength, both magical and physical. Even as a babe, while we were still weaning you off of your mother's milk, you were able to transform into a human. Even more significantly, you look completely human when you transform – no fox ears, tails, fur in places where a human girl would have bare skin, or anything of the sort. There are some kitsune *my* age who still aren't able to do that."

Kieras shook her head. "I... I suppose I've never been around kitsune my age, so I wouldn't know, but what does that have to do with anything?"

"You haven't grown into most of your powers, yet," Lahti said. "But your ability to make such a complete transformation at such a young age is putting us in a precarious position."

"How?" she asked desperately.

Lahti sighed. "Since you look completely like a human girl when you transform, King Heshka II knows that you can be married to a human boy. And have children with them."

Kieras flushed. "Well, I've flirted with a few of the squires and pages who are about the same age as my human appearance would indicate, but I never really did anything with them, and never took it that ser—"

"He intends to order you to marry his son," Lahti said before she could finish. "I was in my fox form, resting in a sunny spot near one of his private chambers, when I heard him discussing this with his councilors. I told you before, it has been a thousand years since there were true mages... but when a kitsune and a human have a child, that child often inherits odd magical abilities. That is what he wants, and he hopes that by tying you to his son with bonds of matrimony, he can continue to hold me in his service. If he succeeds, he's probably right – I would not abandon you, nor any grandchildren you might give me."

Kieras' blush deepened until her skin was almost as red as her hair. "But I'm much too young for that! I don't want to be a mother, or to be married. And while the Prince is a good friend of mine, I think of him as an annoying younger brother, not as a possible mate."

Lahti shook his head. "You are technically a subject of the king. As long as I am in his service, we are both bound by his decrees. He could force you to marry his son and I could do nothing to stop him."

"Then... then what do I do, Papa?" she asked, chewing her lip.

Lahti grinned, though there was no humor behind it. "Well, fortunately he forgets that while I am bound to him as his protector, you are not. Nor are either of us his slaves." He glanced at the long-forgotten chicken carcass. "Also fortunately for us, you've inherited some of the more mischievous parts of your nogitsune heritage...."

"Where are we?" Kieras asked, glancing around. They were in the tunnels underneath the castle, but she didn't remember ever seeing this particular passage before. They had entered it through an old, unguarded storeroom, through an access vent they could only pass through as foxes, and this tunnel was clearly not as well maintained as the others. It was very dark and musty. There was garbage and debris lining the path, and several puddles of stagnant water that they had needed to walk through. Kieras had nearly screamed when a swarm of rats had run past, though her father had anticipated it and covered her mouth with his hand. She had held her tongue ever since, but her curiosity wouldn't let her stay silent any longer.

"During the construction of the castle, Kazdri insisted on maintaining his residence at the old manor house that had been his seat of power prior to being named king," Lahti explained. "He believed that, after the castle's completion, the manor house could serve as a family retreat that was near the castle, but not in it. So, he had the same tunnels built into the foundation connecting it with the King's Keep as were built throughout the castle to keep the barracks and residential towers all connected. His descendants, however, found it too small and rustic for their tastes, so that tunnel was sealed when they finally moved into the King's Keep, and the old manor house has been abandoned and left to rot for many decades, now, sealed up so that none may enter. Fortunately, when they sealed the tunnel, they failed to seal the vents, so we can pass through it with ease, while they have likely forgotten its existence entirely. It's a good thing it's not raining, though – this tunnel was closed down before they figured out how to fix the flooding problems."

"But no orders have been issued, yet," Kieras said. "Why are we leaving in such secrecy?"

"No orders were issued at the last time I checked," Lahti admitted. "But that doesn't mean the King hasn't issued orders since I last talked with him, or that his guards would let us depart from the city walls unchallenged. Besides, there are a couple things in the old manor house I would like to show you."

"Such as?" Kieras asked.

"You'll see them when we get there," was all Lahti said.

They continued on in silence for nearly two hours. A few small cave-ins had to be cleared up along the way, but weren't too difficult for the pair of them to handle, or alternatively to pass through in fox form. Finally, however, they reached the end of the path, where a poorly constructed wooden wall barricaded the way further. There was a large gap in that wall that had been broken through many years before.

"Come on," Lahti said. "We're almost there."

Kieras followed her father through the hole in the wall, stumbling into a large room highlighted by streaks of light illuminating decades of dust, both on the ground and in the air. The walls were covered with an oddly honeycombed wood construct she couldn't identify through all the rot, as well as a few glass bottles completely buried in dust. The oddest thing about the room, however, was a bed of straw in the middle of it, covered in blankets, the floor dusted clear around it.

"Where are we?" she asked again.

"The old manor house's former wine cellar. I don't think all of the wine was taken when this place was abandoned, but I wouldn't recommend any of the wine bottles you might find – Kazdri had terrible taste. The first thing I want to show you is right here, however." Lahti led her down the path to the pile of straw, and for the first time she saw that a man appeared to be sleeping on it. Closer inspection revealed that the man was missing an arm, although a wooden replacement for the appendage appeared to be resting on the far side of the bed.

"Is that—"

"King Kazdri, as I'm sure you've guessed," Lahti answered before she could finish asking. "Myobu kitsune can extend the life of a chosen human for some time, as long as they live themselves, and your mother did so for Kazdri. He was badly injured in the coup attempt, and he was beyond the help of human medicine, and even with my kitsune abilities I couldn't heal his wounds. It was my belief that one of the haltija, a veden vaki, could heal him with their water magic; they have the strongest healing powers of any of the mystical races. I don't know where one is, however, and due to my oath I may not leave the city of Kassia to seek one out. Together, your mother and I were able to preserve Kazdri by putting him into a deep sleep and hide him here. It was our hope to extend his life until some cure could be found." He sighed. "It is perhaps a futile gesture, keeping him alive, since there is no way he can reclaim the throne after all these years. Still, I can draw some comfort from it. As long as he continues to draw breath, I know that my mate, Tianhyu, remains among the living."

Kieras sighed. "I wish I had known mother. Is she ever going to return?"

Lahti turned an appraising eye on his daughter. "You may have guessed by now that the story we told you when she first left us was a lie. She and I may have had our arguments, most due to the differences between our respective breeds, but we never would have separated because of that. In truth, your mother was forced to leave because there was the possibility that someone might discover we were keeping King Kazdri alive. If that was revealed to the Kassian Royal Family, they would order her assassinated so that Kazdri would die. The only safe way for her to return is for Kazdri to be healed and awoken, so that she would no longer be needed to support him."

"Then... is she looking for a veden vaki for him?" Kieras asked.

"We never discussed it." Lahti sighed regretfully. "I didn't think of consulting the vaki until after she left. She may be looking for one, or she may not even know to look. Not everyone knows of their healing powers, not all of them have such powers, and they are not a very common race. I just don't know what your mother might be doing, though I would think she could have found one by now if she had tried."

Kieras sighed, saddened. "I see."

Lahti's eyes lingered on his daughter for a moment while he was almost lost in thought. Finally, he said, "But this is only one of the things I wish to show you. Come with me."

He led her to another room, the path almost as clear of dust as the area around King Kazdri had been. They went up a flight of stairs that had apparently been crudely repaired some time after the building had been abandoned, and then down several hallways until finally entering what Kieras figured must have been the cleanest, best-kept room in the whole manor house. There were shelves lined with books – real books of the codex variety, not scrolls – and stacks of papers on unusually sturdy tables. There were also a few locked displays with glass doors – a remarkable sight, as glass doors of that size would have cost more money than many Kassian citizen's life savings.

Lahti strode over to one of the locked cases and opened it with a key. He reached inside and pulled several items out, taking them to a table to sort through.

"This is the old Kassian Royal Library, which once was open to all of its citizens. King Kazdri wanted his subjects to be literate, and built this library with that in mind. His usurpers, however, much preferred the ability to control what knowledge was given to their people. Nevertheless, this collection was much too valuable to simply destroy, so they ordered that it be put into storage. I've been, uh, 'rescuing' these volumes from that store room for several decades, and now have restored the library to much of its former glory. These books, however, are not why I brought you here." He selected one of the items he'd been sorting through and considered it carefully. "That should do... I hope. Put this on."

He handed her an intricate ladies' choker, lined on the inside with a padded satin silk and made of a soft, braided leather, a buckle of some extremely durable metal plated with gold on the ends. While not showing many signs of wear and tear, there was a great feeling of age to it, and maybe a bit of magic besides. Following her father's instructions, she put it on her neck, but needed his help to get it properly fastened.

Once her father's fingers left the buckle, the choker started burning sharply. Kieras yelped, and for one panicked moment Lahti started reaching to take it back off, but she stayed his hands before he reached her. The burning sensation was dying down fast, and shortly dimmed into a pleasant warmth.

"Well, clearly this is a magical artifact of some sort," she finally said, running her finger under the lining to check how tight it really was. "But what is it?"

Lahti, still concerned, examined his daughter closely to make sure she wasn't really in any pain. "It was left to me by your mother. I cannot wear it because I am a nogitsune, but since you have some myobu blood in you I thought it might accept you. I wasn't expecting it to hurt you, though."

"It didn't really hurt," Kieras assured him. "It just startled me. But that doesn't answer my question – what is it?"

Lahti hesitated. "In truth, I have no idea. Your mother wore it while she lived with me." Lahti showed Kieras a beautifully carved wooden box that held an ornate bracelet, a simple silver brooch, and a few other pieces of jewelry. "These were several items she left me, before she had to depart, to give to you when you got older. She explained that they would be 'beneficial' to you, as long as your myobu blood was strong enough for you to wear them. She never explained what they were capable of doing, however. The only thing I do know is that it should be able to change size as you change forms. You might want to try that before you leave, though, just to make sure it works."

"Okay," Kieras said, shifting into her vixen form almost instantly. She twisted and turned her head as far as it would go, and felt no discomfort. She glanced at her reflection in one of the glass panes and thought it vaguely resembled a dog's collar. "Seems to work."

Lahti let loose a breath he wasn't aware he'd been holding. "Well, that's a relief, but change back. I have more things for you."

Kieras looked up at her father, waiting patiently. Finally, she barked, "Papa, turn around!"

Lahti flushed. "Oh, right," he said, turning to give his daughter some privacy.

"Okay, I'm ready, now."

Lahti turned around, and the first thing he noticed was that somehow her clothes and the new choker were attached. Whether this was something Kieras intended or not, he decided not to ask.

"Now, since we have an entire library to ourselves," Lahti said, "I think we can do a little research for your upcoming journey."

"Research? I thought you just wanted me out of the reach of King Heshka, which should be easy enough with what I already know. What kind of research do you think I need?" Kieras asked.

"You know that isn't the only thing I want you to do," Lahti said. "As much as it will be our cover story, I think it would be a wise thing for you to undertake a mission to learn more about the human world outside of Kassia's walls, as well."

"Aw, papa, I don't want to—"

"However, that's not the only thing you'll be doing while you're gone," Lahti continued, hoping to keep that particular argument from reigniting. "You weren't supposed to inherit these pieces of jewelry until you got your second tail, so you know there's a reason I gave you that choker to wear so early."

Kieras cocked her head at her father. "Well, then, what is it you want me to do?"

"I would think the idea would have come to you, yourself, by now," her father said. "I gave you that choker so you could prove to any myobu kitsune that you are who you say you are. I would like you to find your mother, and with her help locate a veden vaki."

King Heshka II, the reigning Emperor of Kassia, was impatiently pacing back and forth across the floor of his throne room. Pacing was an extremely difficult thing to do in his full royal accoutrements, which included things like his ceremonial armor (that was completely useless as armor, yet was significantly heavier than the real thing would be), a royal crown (which didn't fit properly, and tended to slip off Heshka's head), and a pair of incredibly stiff boots that no one in their right mind would *choose* to wear. Yet despite all those things slowing him down, Heshka continued to pace, back and forth, as the members of his court looked on with varying degrees of concern and anxiety.

"Why hasn't anyone found that blasted fox, yet?" he suddenly exclaimed. He had sent word throughout the castle to summon Lahti over an hour before, and every few minutes he'd ask about him again, his temper rising each time.

"Calm yourself, Your Majesty," his majordomo, Gedig, admonished. "This is not a pressing matter, after all. This is a very large castle for your men to search through, and as a fox he often spends time in places the servants you sent to summon him cannot go. He will show up in time."

With a frustrated sigh, Heshka stormed over to his throne and slumped down into it, catching his crown before it fell off and repositioning it on his head. "Well, I might as well get something useful done while I wait. Send for my son, and that blasted fox's daughter as well – we need to get this taken care of."

"At once, Your Majesty," Gedig said, rushing over to the servant's doors and passing the orders along to the people waiting inside. After a brief discussion, he returned to his king with what he hoped was good news. "The word for your son and the Lady Kieras has been sent, Your Majesty. Meanwhile, the Honorable Kitsune Lahti has arrived."

There had been a lot of discussion, in the early days of Kassian independence, about just what Lahti should formally be to the king. Some felt he deserved a title of nobility, but as he wasn't always thought of as being entirely human, that didn't sit well with many of the King's advisors. Others – for either spiteful or thoughtful reasons – felt he should not even be formally acknowledged at all. Not having a title would both put him out of human minds and allow him a greater degree of secrecy in his efforts to protect the king.

The debate was never settled, and Lahti never received any title more formal than "Guardsman of the Royal Family," but over time people had come to address him as "The Honorable Kitsune" while they worked at the King's Court – a title some felt was spoken in irony, considering kitsune nature.

King Heshka, at that moment, was far too frustrated to care about the formalities. "About time! Bring him in."

Lahti stepped into the court, looking just a touch tense but otherwise fairly normal. It was not unusual for those who were summoned before the King to feel a little apprehensive, even if they were familiar with him, so no one thought much of it.

"Forgive me for the delay, Your Majesty," Lahti said, bowing respectfully. He may have lost his respect for the men on the throne since Kazdri was deposed, but he would always treat the office with dignity. That said, due to his unique station he did not have to observe as many formalities as the rest of the court, and could address the throne without being spoken to without impunity. "I was not in the Keep when your summons went out, and only just returned."

Heshka grunted, leaning forward on his crown. "Whatever. It doesn't matter. My business is actually with your daughter, not you, and I've already sent out a summons for her, too."

Lahti cocked his head. "My daughter, sire? What do you wish with her?"

At that moment, the King's son, Czerniak – who would be the third king of that name, if he ever took the throne – entered the throne room. "I am here, father."

"Good, this concerns you, too," Heshka replied testily. "Now come here so I don't have to shout across the room at you."

"Your Majesty," Gedig cautioned. "Please try to remember that your court is present. Certain formalities must be addressed."

The king's face twisted as his temper rose yet again, but then he took a deep breath and sighed. It was obvious even to Lahti that Gedig wasn't actually as concerned about the following of procedure as he was about Heshka's temper causing him to speak and act in a less than royal manner, which was something Heshka knew he still had to work on. "Yes, you're right, of course, Gedig. Proceed."

Gedig cleared his throat. "His highness, Prince Czerniak, is recognized. Please approach the throne and honor your King."

Czerniak stiffened into a more formal bearing. He had not been properly groomed for the role of royal heir from birth, but an illness that had swept through the castle claimed two of his elder brothers, and a third had been executed for attempting to assassinate his father. For that matter, Heshka's entire line was on the throne unexpectedly, as the same disease which claimed Czerniak's brothers had also killed Heshka's reigning cousin, who had left no heirs of his own. The entire surviving royal family was still adjusting to the unexpected upheaval. Still, it had been four years since the execution of his treacherous older brother made Czerniak the heir apparent, and while he had learned most of the formalities expected of him they didn't come naturally.

With the measured stride that had been drilled into him through those four years of training, he marched across the room to his father's throne. He knelt down, kissing the ring on his father's right hand – the wrong ring, but no one would complain about that while the court was still present. Done with that, he stood, looking a little indecisively around him. He still had not been in very many formal sessions of court, and wasn't quite sure where he was supposed to stand. With a brief cough, Gedig motioned for him to take the heir apparent's place at the throne's right hand side.

Carefully schooling his features, Czerniak gave his father the more formal greeting that he had demanded.

"Forgive me, father, for my rudeness. I am here to answer your summons. Command me as you will."

He winced, remembering that he wasn't supposed to use the word "father" in a formal setting, but at least no-one commented on it. Czerniak didn't think he was really suited for being royalty, despite actually being one.

Lahti watched all of that, including the mistakes, with a stoic expression on his face. That expression, however, was entirely illusion – underneath that tiny bit of magical artifice he was trying not to let anyone see his amusement. He'd been in Royal Courts for nearly a century, and none of them had as much trouble with the formalities as Heshka II's immediate family. Even Kazdri's first couple of years, when there was no one left alive from the older royal lines to teach proper court behavior, wasn't this incompetent. Czerniak was an adult now, with four years of training to master proper behavior, and he was clueless. Heshka had been in power another three years on top of that, and had been given extensive training in court behavior for years beforehand, yet his temper and his refusal to have the crown re-sized for his own head made him something of a laughingstock to anyone who had attended a *real* Royal Court. If there was anyone Lahti felt sorry for in the current Kassian Royal Court, it was Gedig, whose job it was to get these sorry excuses for royalty to behave like royalty. Gedig was actually a very good instructor in that regard – he just had lousy students.

Schooling his real expression, Lahti dropped the illusion over his face so he could speak. "Now that the formalities are out of the way, Your Majesty, may I ask what it is you want with my daughter?"

Heshka tried to turn on a smile Lahti was sure he intended to be friendly, but it came out more like a grimace. "As you know, the twentieth birthday of my son, Prince Czerniak, is coming within a few months' time. It is an important age, as that is the year in which he is permitted to take office as king without the need of a regent in the event of my death. His true coming of age, if you will."

Lahti nodded slowly. "Yes, Your Majesty. Those of us in your court are well aware of his highness's upcoming celebration. I have been spending a great deal of time working with your majordomo to ensure the safety of the event while still preserving the enjoyment and dignity of everyone who attends it."

Lahti knew the king had never trusted him, but Heshka could never say the kitsune failed to do his job. As a guardsman, there were none better, although Lahti had become understandably less co-operative in the years since the unfortunate events surrounding the removal of Kazdri from the throne. At one time, Lahti had been the chief strategist of the Royal Armies, as well as a powerful fighter and leader of men in the field of battle. Now, however, he was decidedly less significant. He was, in theory, the only one of Heshka's subjects who did not have to obey Heshka's laws. His only directive was to keep the king and the royal family safe. He would no longer help in any of the Kassian Empire's military plans, and as long as there were anyone of royal blood in the castle he would never leave the city of Kassia.

His value, however, was unquestionable: Inside the castle, there had not been a single assassination even attempted unless it was one member of the royal family against another. Lahti would always discover the plot well in advance and stop it before it even could get started. He was even largely successful at preventing violence within the family, although there he was hampered by his own oath. However, since the reign of King Kazdri ended, there had been nine successful assassinations of Kassian kings, all of them outside of the city walls. It was enough to make anyone on the Kassian throne never want to leave the castle, except there were a number of functions that even a king could not avoid attending.

With the coming of age celebration taking place in the King's Keep, Lahti had agreed to collaborate with Gedig on making the arrangements. It was one of the first major events Lahti would participate in as anything other than a guardsman since Kazdri's death.

"I am hoping to add one more element to that celebration," Heshka said. "At the age of twenty, it is time and past time for the heir apparent Prince of this kingdom to be wed. I have considered many candidates as his bride, some of whom would bring a great dowry, or cement political alliances that would benefit the entire Kassian Empire. However, my son is clearly infatuated with just one person, and so to her I will betroth him. Lahti, your daughter Kieras is to become the Princess Consort by marriage to my son, Czerniak."

Lahti had to make sure to register his shock at the suggestion, but it wasn't that difficult. He knew the announcement was coming, but it still hit him hard to hear it officially. In a way, he felt sorry for everyone involved. Heshka was being a lot more politic about his announcement than Lahti had ever expected him to be. Just looking at his face, it was easy to see that Czerniak was practically radiating happiness at the proposal. Kieras herself was close friends with Czerniak, and while she didn't want to marry him, she likely would be saddened to learn that she was breaking his heart.

Still, his daughter's welfare was involved, and she'd be a lot less pleased to be forced into a political marriage whose sole purpose was to control her father than she would be to break the heart of a boy she was merely friends with.

Lahti had other things to consider, as well. He knew that the King didn't trust him, and with good reason. While Lahti didn't dislike King Heshka, he wasn't very fond of his policies, and certainly would never have chosen to ally himself with the man if he had a choice. Heshka was a very weak king, with a quick temper and no real concern for the people he ruled. He relied too heavily on two particular advisors Lahti decidedly hated. Lords Devane and Kobach, who fortunately were not permitted to speak during this audience, had manipulated the king into policies that had his people think him a tyrant.

Heshka was not nearly as cruel as his advisors when acting alone, nor even as most of his predecessors since the end of Kazdri's reign. He was ill-tempered and quick to anger, however – a problem which allowed his enemies to manipulate him far too often – and Heshka would probably not take this next piece of news very well.

"I am afraid, Your Majesty, that such plans are impossible."

Heshka's eyes narrowed and he leaned forward in a threatening manner. His voice chilled into ice, he said, "Remember that you are my subject, fox. You have no say in the matter. If I wish your daughter to marry my son, she will have no choice but to obey! It would be in both of your best interests to agree."

Lahti didn't feel threatened in the least, but he did put on an embarrassed smile before answering. "You misunderstand me, Sire. I am not refusing your order." This was a blatant lie, which Lahti had to struggle to say without revealing his deception. To people they had sworn to fealty it was very hard – though not impossible, it seemed – for a kitsune to lie so directly. Lying to everyone else was fine, but not to those with whom they had made an oath. So far, most of the deception he had employed when dealing with the royal family was in using half-truths, incorrect implications, or simply talking around a question. This conversation would stretch Lahti's ability to resist those kitsune instincts further than he had ever dared try. "I am saying it is not possible. My daughter has left town, and probably will not be back for at least another year."

Heshka frowned, but at least didn't slip further into anger. Sitting back on his throne, he considered what Lahti had said, trying to place it into any reports he might have heard but ignored at the time. Finally, he said, "My guards are required to inform me of the comings and goings from this town. Unless I have missed something, they did not inform me of your daughter's departure."

Lahti looked even more embarrassed, this time genuinely so. "I'm afraid, Your Majesty, that I've recently discovered that my daughter can go just about anywhere she wants without being seen. It is for this reason I sent her away."

A couple people smiled knowingly, but the king himself did not seem amused. "Explain."

"Last night, I found my daughter in her room consuming a cooked chicken. Upon questioning her, I found that she had 'purchased' the chicken without the owner's knowledge, slipped through all of the guards in the castle – including those protecting the keep itself – and into her bedroom without being seen," Lahti said, adding a lie to that truth with the amused frustration only long-suffering fathers could really express steeped into his voice. "To make matters worse, she followed a rather... disreputable nogitsune kitsune tradition to make this payment, which is to leave twigs and leaves under an illusion spell to make them appear as coins. Those 'coins' would change back to twigs and leaves about one hour after they were touched by human hands, making them worthless even as counterfeit currency. I tried to teach her that this trick should only be done to punish price gougers, con men, and extortionists... but while my daughter inherently learned the skill, she did not take to my lessons on when to use it."

"And so... you exiled her for a year because she stole a chicken?" Heshka asked. That made it sound harsh, especially for someone with Lahti's reputation. Lahti knew it would not be believable without more of an explanation.

"Not exactly, no." Lahti sighed. "This wasn't the first incident of this nature. I feared, should I not train her otherwise, it would not be the last. I have explained to her the nature both of my people and of humans, trying to get her to live properly in a human society, but I have been growing increasingly frustrated of late with her refusal to understand the necessity. The guards, knowing our position in your household, look the other way on her crimes, and other humans indulge her. She needs to experience life with humans who are not so forgiving. So, as my father did to 'civilize' me, and his father did before him, I sent her out into the world in order to learn just why the rules I have imposed upon her need to be followed."

"It still seems to me that you exiled your daughter for a year because she stole a chicken," Heshka said dryly.

"She is not exiled, Your Majesty," Lahti replied. "She is in training. If she ever needs to return home for fresh supplies, to ask questions, or for any other reason, it is perfectly acceptable. I doubt she will, however."

"What will her training consist of?" This question did not come from the King, but rather from a rather anxious Czerniak.

"Manners, Your Highness," Gedig cautioned quietly. It wasn't proper for the prince to speak in this inquiry, although no-one could blame the young man.

Lahti turned a sympathetic expression on Czerniak. He really did feel sorry for the boy in all this mess. Without better training in politics than he was currently getting, Czerniak would be just as weak of a king as Heshka when he came to the throne, but he was also a lot kinder in general. He had also been a good playmate and friend to his daughter for many years, and clearly had real feelings for her that he'd never expressed. The king was raising the boy's hopes up for something to come from those feelings. Lahti just hoped Czerniak didn't take it too hard when it became apparent those hopes would be dashed.

"The training, your highness, is in relating to humans. To that end, I have required that she follow in her father's footsteps, although perhaps not to the same level that I did."

"I don't understand," Czerniak said.

"She is to put herself into the service of a human for a period of one year, employing her magic on his behalf," Lahti said. "Not to a serf – that would complicate matters too much, should the serf's lord learn of her presence. And not to a nobleman, either, because she has lived her whole life with nobles and learned little. Not someone living in a castle, as she has lived in this castle her whole life, but also not someone in so rural an area that the next nearest human is miles away. A freeman, someone with a strong character who is worthy of honorable service such as that a kitsune can provide. Think of it as a... a dangergeld, if you will; a rite of passage like that of a squire seeking knighthood."

Neither Heshka nor Czerniak looked pleased, but at least the Prince looked as if he were willing to accept Lahti's explanation. The King, however, wasn't as understanding.

"She will have to forgo her so-called 'training.' She has duties here, in the castle, as the betrothed of my son."

"It is too late, Your Majesty," Lahti said. "She left last night."

"We will send word to every city, village, and town for her, then," Heshka proclaimed, slamming his armor-clad fist down on the arm of his throne. "She is to return to the castle as soon as she receives my summons. Or if she returns on her own, all here will know to explain to her that her year of training has been canceled, and she has other duties to attend to. If worse comes to worse, we will simply wait the year out and have her marry my son then."

Lahti wasn't quite sure whether to feel relieved or concerned. The King hadn't yet made any threats against Lahti should Kieras not be found, which was a relief. He also had yet to do anything Lahti hadn't planned for. However, it was clear that the largely true tale he had told would only buy Kieras a year's time. If she was unable to locate both her mother and the veden vaki in that time, she most likely would have to marry Czerniak after all. If she could at least complete the ostensible reason for her journey, and actually spend a year in service to another worthy human, other possibilities might open up, but Lahti couldn't count on anything at this point. It was all out of his hands, now.

"Very well, Your Majesty." Lahti bowed formally. "The next time I see her, I shall tell her of your commands. If I may take my leave?"

Heshka nodded. "Yes. And Czerniak, go with him – it would do you well to spend more time with your future father-in-law."

"Of course, fa— Your Majesty," Czerniak said, remembering to use the title only when Gedig caught his eye. Walking to stand by the kitsune, he bowed to his father before he and Lahti left the room.

With Lahti gone and the audience officially over, Lords Devane and Kobach could begin their work on the King again. Gedig sighed, watching them come over to bend the King's ear. He and Lahti shared a dislike for these two favored advisors.

The first of these, Lord Devane, had Heshka's ear with regard to the course of the military campaigns. Under his direction, the Kassian Empire was expanding at an alarming rate. Gedig was not against wars of expansion, provided there was additional cause behind the war – as the founder of their kingdom, Kazdri himself had ordered the re-conquest of several cities when he found that his late kingdom's people were being used as slaves by the Erixonites. However, even Kazdri would be against wars with the sole purpose of expansion, especially when done at such a rate that it stretched the armies so far out that there was no possibility of defending the territory being taken.

Then there was Lord Kobach. Despite his title, he was actually a landless knight, whose claim to power rested in the fact that he was the treasurer of the kingdom. He expanded the coffers of the state treasury, that was certain, but at the cost of oppressing its people. He instituted taxes on every good or service, taxes on income, even taxes against the inheritance of the dead. He also demonstrated a complete lack of compassion for the elderly or infirm with a number of his policies.

For example, if a commoner grew too old or ill to work in his chosen field and was deemed unsuitable for any other, instead of being permitted to retire to his family he was required to forfeit all of his worldly goods to his nearest heir (less the inheritance tax, which had grown to be almost three quarters of all the person's estate) and surrender himself to what was euphemistically called a "retirement villa." There, it was claimed, he would be given medical care and food until the day he died. One law Kobach had proposed, which thankfully even Heshka found too extreme, was to execute these people rather than spend the money to look after them.

Gedig suspected Kobach of enforcing a form of this policy on at least one occasion despite Heshka's opposition. Kobach had gone to "inspect" one such retirement villa. Lahti had told Gedig, after his return, that Kobach smelled faintly of arsenic, ostensibly so that Gedig would know to monitor any food or drink given to King Heshka for a time. An "outbreak of cholera" shortly thereafter resulted in the deaths of almost every one of the retirement villa's residents. Given the similarities between arsenic poisoning and cholera, Gedig had a fairly good idea about what really happened.

"I'm not quite sure I believe him, sire," Devane said.

"Of course I don't believe him," Heshka snapped. "He's a kitsune – his race does nothing but lie!"

Gedig, always wary at these conferences, sighed. "Your Majesty, that is unfair. Even if only due to his promise, Lahti has been nothing but loyal to this throne for almost a century. If he did nothing but lie, you likely would not be alive to sit here, right now. In fact, he usually tells the truth."

Heshka rolled his eyes in frustration, but conceded the point. "True. But that doesn't alter the fact that kitsune relations are almost universally based on deception, and his half-truths can be worse than lies. You heard him admit as much, with his discussion about the nogitsune instincts his daughter was showing."

"Lahti has never been known to lie to Kassian Royalty in his entire ninety five years of service to it," Kobach said. "Since Kazdri's death, however, he has become quite secretive, even to the point of hiding information that would be useful to our armies. I believe he told us the truth, Your Majesty, but I do not believe he told the *whole* truth."

"Why would he not?" Gedig asked, feigning confusion. He wasn't entirely sure what Lahti's plan was, but he suspected it would be better for the kingdom than anything Kobach desired. "His daughter clearly isn't in the castle – that would be too easily disproven if that were a lie. He couldn't have known about the King's plan to betroth her to his son. Even if he did, why would he go to these extremes to object? He likes Czerniak. Czerniak is clearly in love with his daughter. It is a good match, and he should know that. So why would he be making all this fuss?"

Devane and Kobach looked at each other in concern, but before they could voice anything Heshka himself, surprisingly, gave the explanation. "Lahti's service ends in five years," he said. "With the marriage of his daughter to my son, he would be obligated to continue overseeing the protection and welfare of me and my children until the last of my son's line dies, as we would become clan."

Devane flushed slightly. "And he may have heard our plans for that. I was discussing the matter with the King yesterday morning. I didn't see anyone else present when we were talking, but Lahti might as well be invisible as easily as he can hide in this castle."

Gedig frowned. "So... this betrothal is simply a scheme to enslave Lahti, a man who has provided your family with almost a hundred years of extremely valuable service, to your family?"

Heshka appeared somewhat ashamed, unable to meet Gedig's eyes. "I wouldn't call it 'enslaved.' All I wanted to do was ensure he didn't attempt to get revenge on my family for any slights he might feel he had received, real or imagined. And I genuinely felt that his daughter and Czerniak would be a good match. So did you, if you'll recall."

Gedig nodded slowly. "I did... though I have no idea what Lahti's daughter's thoughts are on the matter. I suspect that, if she might have considered it once, any thought that it might be used against her family would prevent her from ever entertaining the idea of marriage to your son, however."

"If he heard us, he heard us," Heshka sighed. "But for now we have no proof either way. Which leaves us with the question of 'what do we do, now?'"

Gedig closed his eyes, rubbing his forehead in thought. "Well, it is too late to talk you out of this folly – you've already declared your intentions to wed Prince Czerniak and the Lady Kieras. It would destroy the Prince, at the very least, if you were to go back on that now. It would not be a wise idea to antagonize the Honorable Kitsune any further by pushing the idea, now, however, or else he really *might* attempt some form of revenge when he is finally released from his oath. We should table this discussion until the Lady Kieras is found, I believe, Your Majesty. At most, suggest to Prince Czerniak that he approach Lahti on his own, as you have done once already this evening. Perhaps some amicable arrangement can be made between the two if they become friends."

"I agree," Kobach said. That drew the eyes of everyone listening in to the conversation. Kobach and Gedig had agreed on precisely one thing in their entire time as advisors to the King, and that was merely on a particular beverage that they both enjoyed. "At least as far as tabling the discussion is concerned. Until the vixen is found, there is no point in discussing this matter at all."

Heshka sighed wearily. "Well, if the two of you agree on something, that means either the world is about to end – in which case I fear any further discussion of this matter will be moot, anyway – or I should obey your advice. So be it. This matter is closed... for the moment. Now, Gedig, please get my chief steward and send him to my chambers – I fear I need to lie down for a bit after this."

In a measured pace the King left the room, as did most of the lords and guards. Gedig slipped out of the room to attend to his duties, but lingered at the door. Devane and Kobach were the only ones left in the chamber, and it might prove valuable to hear what they had to say to one another.

"I am sorry, Kobach," Devane said sincerely. "I didn't check close enough before approaching the king about this matter. I didn't think Lahti could overhear us."

Kobach laughed. "Don't worry, friend Devane. I was expecting one of us to be overheard talking to 'King' Heshka about this."

"I don't understand," Devane replied.

"A thoroughly true statement," Kobach said, smiling darkly. "But you needn't concern yourself. Our plans are working out perfectly, and that's all you need to know."

II. The Tyranny of the Blacksmith

The young hostler for the township of Ekholm's largest roadside stable almost couldn't believe his eyes when he finally was able to make out the horseman slowly approaching his town.

"Rider ho! It's Torkki! Torkki's back!" he cried, alerting several nearby villagers.

Ekholm was something of an enigma. It was too large to be considered a village, or even a town, yet too politically and militarily unimportant to be thought of as a city. It was centered on the crossing of a major road and a major river, and was thriving on the recent increase in trade brought about by the cessation of the latest series of Erixonite raids. Its economy was growing fast enough to make it a reasonably cosmopolitan center of commerce, yet it still held the personal familiarity among its people commonly associated with small towns.

Ekholm once had been affiliated with the Republic of Eskesa, a large city-state that had been destroyed during the Erixonite wars of expansion almost three decades ago. By the time their founders' capital city fell, Ekholm had its own farms, blacksmiths, tanners, seamstresses, carpenters, and so forth, and could sustain itself quite nicely even without Eskesa's help.

What Ekholm lacked, however, was the ability to defend itself. It had a militia that could be called upon to fight local bandits, should the need arise, but not enough to take on the armies that had sacked Eskesa.

Fortunately, the people of Ekholm had friends among the rising City-State of Norre, which headed an alliance of a half-dozen other countries in a mutual defense pact. Norre agreed to provide Ekholm with protection, and Ekholm was allowed to retain its complete autonomy. In return, Ekholm paid a tribute to Norre and the other members of its alliance.

If a citizen of Ekholm felt the call to join the army, they had two options: They could join the Ekholm Militia – which was hardly the same thing as a 'real' army, lacking both the sense of adventure and discipline that many younger army recruits sought – or they could travel to Norre, and join the Armies of the Norre Hegemony.

Torkki was Ekholm's favorite son – a young man who went to Norre and made good. Just six months into his tour of duty with the Norrish Armies, word had reached Ekholm that he had won recognition for meritorious service. Six months after that, it was announced that he had been made the captain of a unit in the Elite Brigades. The Elite Brigades were notorious for success even in the face of overwhelming odds, but their actual missions were often a closely guarded secret. Any rumors of their activities were squelched by the Norrish government, and only after a campaign was successfully completed were their members allowed to contact their families. With all of the secrecy surrounding the Elite Brigades, it had been well over a year since anyone had heard from Torkki. His unexpected return was a call for celebration, and as word spread a growing number of people began to congregate at the stables.

By the time Torkki himself got close enough to really discern what was happening, a crowd had gathered and was milling about noisily. Some of the younger, more excitable peasants even began chanting his name in welcome. "Torkki! Torkki!"

The man they were all chanting for, however, was rather bewildered by the reception. "Just what is going on here?" he bellowed, silencing the crowd in an instant.

A young man with a familial grin stepped forward. Torkki thought he looked familiar, though it was hard to recognize the face behind the scraggly beard and wild hair, and the only person he knew who fit that face was a smaller, thinner man. "Tales of your exploits have reached even here, and most of us believe you deserve a hero's welcome to your own home town."

Torkki recognized the voice in an instant. "Mathis! Is that you? I expect you have a tale or two to tell yourself, to look at you."

"Of course," the wild-haired man snorted.

A twinkle in his eye, Torkki joked, "I dare not ask if you are one of those who believes I deserve a hero's welcome or not."

"A hero's welcome?" Mathis shrugged, laughing. "Perhaps, perhaps not. But I'll welcome my brother home, hero or no."

"I'm afraid I don't have any wine," Mathis said, dusting off the surface of the table. It had the kind of tabletop that needed to be flipped over to go from work surface to eating surface, but as Mathis rarely needed it as a work surface the table remained unturned from his last meal. "Would you rather have beer or tea?"

Torkki used to hate beers, and preferred sweet wines over just about any other beverage. However, he had believed that upon joining the army he would find it socially unacceptable to avoid drinking beer, so he trained himself to tolerate it before leaving Ekholm for his military training.

His fellow soldiers wouldn't have felt less of him if he hadn't, however. Torkki had proven to be such a natural as a soldier, and so valuable of a teammate in exercises, that they would have forgiven any such quirk.

But while he could stand to drink beer when necessary, he opted for some other choice when given the option. "I'll take tea, if you don't mind."

"Coming right up," Mathis said, scratching an itch on his beard.

Torkki watched his brother fuss around the brick oven that had been his own responsibility before leaving for Norre, expertly working with an iron stand and a fire ring to bring a pot of water to a boil. Torkki used to keep a fire going all day in the winter. It looked as if Mathis did the same even in the fall, when he was home. Mathis was a hunter by trade, and would often be out of the house for a week or more, so the fire pit had to have some rest.

There was something bothering Torkki about Mathis, however. Usually, his little brother would have been all over him, asking stories about his time with the Elite Brigade and what things he had done in training. Now, nothing. And then there was his physical appearance, which looked ragged to say the least. Torkki had never known him to appear so unkempt.

"I thought you hated growing out your beard," Torkki said. "And I must say, looking at you right now, you were better off without one."

Mathis grunted. "My razor is chipped and dull, and I lack the tools and skills to re-sharpen it. Otherwise, you'd better believe I'd have it off. When it becomes too unbearable, Uncle Savard lets me use his shaving kit, but even his kit is getting dull."

That statement raised Torkki's eyebrows more than the beard itself had. The tools to sharpen a knife were fairly commonplace, and even if one didn't own a set the town's blacksmith would typically fix a problem like a dull razor free of charge – or at least the one in Ekholm had before Torkki left, and the one in Norre had done the same.

Deciding not to pry, but still wanting to help, Torkki joined Mathis at the oven and took out one of his service knives. As a soldier, he had been issued several blades of the type, from weapons like swords and axes to kitchen knives. The one he pulled out was intended for close combat, but due probably to some defect in the steel did not feel balanced enough for Torkki to want to wield as a weapon. It was incredibly sharp, however, and would likely hold that edge for a great deal of use. "It's ugly, and I want it off if I'm going to be staying here for a while. It won't do my image any good to have a brother walking around with some odd furry animal clinging to his chin. When you're done with the tea, take this and shave it off."

Mathis took the knife, but raised his own eyebrows at Torkki's statement. "You're going to be staying with me for a while? I figured you were just on leave, but this sounds more serious than that. Have you resigned your commission in the army?"

Torkki laughed. "Not much chance of that! But no, I'm not here on leave, either."

"Why are you here, then?" Mathis asked.

Torkki hesitated. He hadn't really wanted to explain his presence in Ekholm if he could avoid it, preferring to let people form their own conclusions. This, however, was his brother, and was probably the person he would need to trust the most to help him get things settled. If anyone was owed an explanation it was he.

"I'm on assignment," Torkki said. "Volunteered for it, actually. I have a mission to do while I'm in town that should take several months time."

Mathis frowned, a twinge of something dark in his eyes. "But Ekholm is not part of Norre territory – we're merely a tributary power. Norre would never send you here on a mission... unless we are in danger, ourselves."

Torkki caught his brother's eye, his face expressionless yet somehow conveying a fierce intensity. "Exactly."

There was a prolonged pause, interrupted only when the water boiled over and Mathis had to rush to save it. "Ow! Hot!"

The moment over, Torkki returned to the dining table and sat in one of the rough-hewn stools surrounding it. In Norre, he had become accustomed to better, but while in action with the army he'd made do with worse. "Who is the current Archon?"

Back when Ekholm was still formally part of Eskesa, it had been represented in the government by one of several Archons. An inherited title at the time, the Archons formed a council that set taxes, passed laws, and made treaties with foreign powers.

When Eskesa was destroyed, so were the Archons and their heirs. Ekholm had maintained ever since that they were still the Eskesan people and followed Eskesan laws. To that end, Ekholm contacted other former Eskesan outposts – the closest being the fishing village of Finch and the mining town of Sugden – and invited representatives to join a new Council of Archons. No Archons arrived, however, though several of them later signed on to the same tributary treaty with Norre that Ekholm did. Faced with the impossibility of rebuilding the Eskesan government as it had been, Ekholm adapted the government to its current circumstances.

It was decided that the clan chiefs would meet each year to select one Archon who would formally head the government for a one-year term. Ostensibly, the Archon would be operating with all of the powers of the former Eskesan Council of Archons. It didn't work out that way, however, as the Council of the Clans, which elected the Archon, held most of the purse strings for Ekholm. Still, the Archon was always the most powerful member of that council and if one needed any action done he was the man to approach. Considering Ekholm's actual size and importance, most outsiders figured it was just a pretentious way of referring to the ruling mayor of the town and his town council.

"Well, Archon Abney returned to the council shortly after you left, as you know," Mathis said carefully. "Since then, we've had Archon Kuralt for two years running."

Torkki looked over at Mathis sharply. "Two years? But that violates all precedent! There has never been an Archon to serve consecutive terms. Some have been called back into interim service after having left office, but—"

"Archon Kuralt has influence, being the only master blacksmith in town." Mathis came over with two mugs and a pot. As he talked, he carefully poured the pot of hot tea into the mugs so as to prevent as many tea leaves as possible from joining the liquid. "Those of us who did not support his second term have not been able to employ his services since, and any apprentices who want him to teach them aren't safely able to go behind his back. The one or two journeymen who will still provide services to the people on his blacklist charge exorbitant amounts of money, and don't produce very good material. And they simply won't provide some services at all... such as sharpening razors."

Torkki winced, and not just because of the temperature of his drink. "The council should have stood up to him."

"Many of us did," Mathis replied, shrugging. He blew on the surface of his own tea to cool it. "Just not enough of us."

Torkki shook his head reluctantly. "Well, internal politics aside, I'm going to have to see Kuralt, both in his capacity as Archon and as a master blacksmith. And I'm going to have to see the head of the militia. And while there is no immediate need for me to rush over to their houses right now, I should probably have both meetings fairly soon."

"Well, Captain Hesketh – he took over the militia when old man Fornier retired last year – should be easy enough to get a meeting with," Mathis said, taking a very cautious sip of his tea after blowing on it once more. "Archon Kuralt, however, will be something more of a challenge. He's let the title go to his head in more ways than one. He's actually on a pilgrimage to the ruins of Eskesa right now, hoping to find one of the 'symbols of the office' that the Archons of old used to wear."

Torkki rolled his eyes. "Oh, great! Who's in charge while he's gone?"

"Councilman Cizikas. Abney, as the last Archon, should have been named Kuralt's regent, but he was among those who sided against

Kuralt in the last Council's vote, so I guess that disqualified him."

Shaking his head, Torkki took an unconscious swig of the tea. It burned his tongue, but he didn't flinch at all. "Sounds like the politics around here got uncomfortably interesting while I was away... and if I don't miss my guess, you're right in the middle of it."

Mathis grinned. "Well, I certainly wasn't a silent member of the minority. However, Uncle Savard took over our clan's seat when Kuralt ruled that my appointment to the council was 'in error,' as with you gone the line of succession should have fallen to our father's brother's family."

Torkki gaped. "But that's a complete falsehood! The rules of succession—"

"Are meaningless right now," Mathis interrupted. "Not with Kuralt playing at dictator. I don't really mind – Uncle Savard's proven even harder for Kuralt to control than me, and it's given me a great deal of time to spend in my trade."

"How is the hunting this time of year?" Torkki asked, deciding to change the subject to more pleasant things.

"Good," Mathis replied. "Not the best year I've ever had, but certainly not the worst, either. I've been a little hampered by my equipment, however."

"How so?"

"I've used up all my good arrowheads," Mathis explained. "I bought some new ones from Chiarot, one of the few journeyman blacksmiths willing to deal with the people on Kuralt's bad side, but his arrowheads are, um, not the best. They don't always deliver a clean kill, and even when they do they'll often chip if they hit a bone just the wrong way. It's hard to recover them even when they do survive intact. I figure only one out of every three I shoot can be re-used."

Torkki's face tensed fiercely. "Something needs to be done about Kuralt. In fact, something will. I'll send a dispatch to Norre right away, requisitioning a master blacksmith as the one in this town is 'unavailable.' I'll also be getting in touch with Captain Hesketh and Councilman Cizikas right away."

Mathis stared at Torkki for a moment. "I haven't heard you that determined since you defied Uncle Savard and Archon Abney both, insisting that it didn't matter if you were supposed to be the head of the clan – father promised you that you'd be able to join the army, and join the army you would, their blessing or no."

"Hmm." Torkki studied his brother, nodding slowly, but the look never left his face. "Well... it's time and past time that something was done about this mess. It will take someone with the connections to get a master blacksmith here... and I just happen to have those connections. You can't expect me to have served all this time in the Elite Brigades without it changing me some. It's my duty to my home, and to our clan, and to my family, to help in any way I can."

Mathis nodded. "I know. It's good to have you home, brother."

"It's good to be home."

"Mathis!" Hesketh cried, seeing who was entering his room. Unexpectedly thrust into the role of Captain of the Militia, Hesketh was an elderly man only a few years younger than his now-retired predecessor. He was also one of the few men in Ekholm who had experience in a real military, having been a decorated member of the Armies of the Eskesan Republic decades in his youth. One of his arms was twisted and unable to move properly, broken and improperly set during a large battle against the Erixonites. His arm made it impossible for him to properly hold both a shield and a weapon at the same time, making his value as a regular soldier nil. He retired from the army, returning to Ekholm where he became the drill instructor for the militia. He'd served in that role for forty years, never expecting a promotion until the very day that Fornier had formally handed the mantle of command over to him.

When not working with the militia, Hesketh spent his time tending a small tavern. It was not the only tavern in town – Ekholm had two others, both much larger, complete with serving girls and the occasional musician – but it did enough business to supplement his pay as the head of the militia.

"Captain Hesketh, sir," Mathis said, snapping to attention. He was always nervous around the old soldier, and combated those nerves with extreme formality.

"Bah! I get enough of that 'sir' stuff when we're drilling on the village green. I'm off duty, and you're in my tavern. Unless you're here to explain why you've missed the past two training musters? If our militia were a real army, you'd be in serious trouble for that!"

"I'm not a soldier, sir, but a hunter," Mathis replied stiffly. "And I was training in my own way – by hunting game, sir."

Hesketh shook his head sadly. "Yes, yes, I know. The militia's all volunteer, anyway, so it doesn't matter if you're there or not. I wasn't really asking for an explanation."

"I'm actually here, though, sir, to introduce someone who *would* like to talk with you in your capacity as the head of the militia," Mathis continued. "Torkki?"

Torkki came through the doors, giving a Norrish salute to his former drill instructor. "Captain Torkki of the Elite Brigades, sir!" he snapped.

"Reporting in as a formality, eh?" Hesketh laughed. "Don't worry, *Captain* Torkki. I knew you were here the moment you arrived. It was pretty hard to miss, after all."

Torkki grinned slightly. "Actually, Captain Hesketh, we have things we need to discuss. I may need to employ your militia, soon."

Hesketh's grin died in an instant, and Mathis no longer saw a tavern owner, but instead the old drill instructor that so terrified him. "How soon?"

"I'm not sure, yet," Torkki replied. "Possibly never."

Hesketh was old, but his wits were as solid as ever. He knew that an answer like that meant trouble. "Okay, what's going on?"

Torkki sighed and took a seat at one of the tavern's many tables. "Got any wine? This is going to be a bit of a long story, and I haven't even told Mathis most of it, yet."

"The local rot-gut okay, or should I offer you something imported?" Hesketh asked.

Ekholm made its own series of wines based on a wide variety of local fruits – salmonberries, mulberries, lingonberries, elderberries, gooseberries, hackberries, currants, and even sheepberries. Every variety of wine, though, seemed to have some problem. The salmonberry wine was insipid, the mulberry wine was too sour, the elderberry wine was too sweet, and so on. There was a decent export market for each of the wines – especially the lingonberry wine, which was the preferred drink of a certain species of clientele – but none of them were considered high class by anyone.

"I'll have some of the local elderberry wine," Torkki said, his face serious but a twinkle in his eye. "It's been a while since I've had some of that good home-grown wine so sweet it makes your teeth hurt."

"Local for me as well, but the lingonberry," Mathis said, grinning sheepishly. "The elderberry's a bit much."

"Coming right up," Hesketh replied, checking his shelves for the appropriate drinking vessels. "Now, why don't you start that 'long story'?"

Mathis could see Torkki mulling over what he was going to say. When he did finally start to speak, his tone was rather grave. "I am aware that you served in action against the Erixonites in their last great war of expansion. Those wars began well over a century ago. My question for you is, are you aware of what prompted the Erixonites to begin their expansion so long ago?"

"Not really." Hesketh shook his head. "I do remember that the initial Erixonite Invasion was one of the weirdest things I'd ever heard of. They were an incredibly powerful nation, capable of demolishing just about anything in their path. They would buzz through a land, taking as much territory as they could. Once anyone organized a somewhat effective campaign of resistance against them, however, they would immediately sue for peace, even if they had more than enough strength to push through that resistance. They were fast and powerful conquerors without the stomach for conquest, in other words."

Torkki nodded. "Yes, when I was training to be an officer, I was instructed in Erixonite strategy and tactics and noticed that pattern, myself. It wasn't until just a few months ago, however, I began to understand their motives."

Hesketh finally served the wine to both Mathis and Torkki before sitting down to join them at their table, his own mug of ale accompanying him. "I'd wondered about that, but my career as a soldier was over before I could find out."

"The Erixonites were invading everywhere they could because they were being invaded, themselves," Torkki said. "They were perfectly content inhabiting their own lands as a loosely-organized nomadic people when they found themselves faced with a large enemy, known to them as the Haula, who were probably more powerful and definitely better organized than the Erixonites were. Now, *most* organized civilizations would have mounted a defense against such an attack, but not the Erixonites. They were capable warriors, and probably could have matched the Haula if they had chosen to, but when they were faced with such a powerful opponent they chose to uproot their entire civilization and move elsewhere.

"The Erixonites did everything they could to put distance between themselves and the Haula. They salted the fields behind them, burned any bridges they crossed, started avalanches to bury any roads they could, and so on. They pushed westward, crossing leagues upon leagues of uncivilized territories and unsettled lands, before finally arriving in our corner of the world. Upon discovering that there were civilizations out here, and that these civilizations were strong at arms, they made a decision.

"They would test these newfound civilizations. Carve out land for themselves from those who were weak, and build a secure border with those that were strong. Slowly, they would encourage the ones they deemed worthy to expand, until all of the Erixonite territory was surrounded by nations they felt were strong enough to provide a challenge should the Haula ever hunt them down. Their new neighbors might not be happy to have them around, and would build up their own armies to defend themselves from the Erixonites – making any Haula invasion that much more difficult – but the Erixonites keep themselves powerful enough that none of these neighbors can challenge them directly. In case one of these countries seemed to be slacking off too much to fend off the Haula, they launch a new war to 'encourage' them to stay strong."

Mathis frowned in thought. "There's the Kassian Empire in the north, we're to the east with the Norre Hegemony, the Republic of Vincour is to their west, and to the south... well, there isn't really a dominant power in the former Skorran lands, but the constant warfare breeds strong warriors, and the mountains are a pretty effective natural border as well. I'd say the Erixonites plan succeeded."

"It did, indeed," Torkki said.

Hesketh took a deep breath. "So, since you're telling us all of this, does that mean the Haula are actually on their way?"

"Not that I've heard, though I imagine it's a possibility," Torkki replied. "Like I said, the Erixonites ran westward, leaving the Haula to their east. We're their east, so if the Haula come the same way the Erixonites do...."

"We would be the first in their path," Hesketh said grimly. "But you say you haven't heard anything of their approach?"

"No," Torkki replied. "Actually, I'm here because there's *another* power attempting to do the same thing the Erixonites did, and they're probably going to hit here first." He paused, letting that sink in. "The kingdom of Knodel was recently assaulted by the Kassian Empire. As expansive as the Kassians have been in recent years, I imagine the surviving Knodelian armies look upon them the same way the Erixonites looked upon the Haula. They intend to launch probing strikes into the weaker areas protected by the Norre Hegemony, and re-build Knodel in those weak areas while putting the stronger parts of the Norre Hegemony between the Kassians and themselves. As much as my pride as a citizen of Ekholm would rather not admit it, there's not many areas weaker than the lands surrounding my home town."

Hesketh growled in annoyance. "So... you mean Norre expects my militia to fight off these Knodelian armies with the aid of just one soldier, who happens to be a local boy himself?"

"Not at all." Torkki raised his hands as if to ward off the accusation, though Mathis thought he detected a flicker of guilt in his brother's eyes. "Since this was my hometown, I volunteered to come ahead of the rest of the forces Norre is sending this way and start setting up the defenses. With all the other towns that need protecting, though, Norre can only afford to send one company of soldiers for our defense. They'll all be from the Norre Elite, but even so a hundred men can only do so much. The militia will have to be a part of the defense, at least. We are getting more help than just my company of soldiers, however – Norre will also provide any technical support we need in the form of engineers, specialists, trainers, and so forth, and will foot the bill. At least some of the money Ekholm has spent over multiple decades of paying tribute will be returning home in the form of what may become permanent fortifications."

Hesketh snorted. "Like that'll matter if we're going up against a full scale invasion."

"If it helps, Norre's spies seem to think that the Knodelians will not send a full strength army straight here, but instead will break up their forces into campaign armies a little larger than your standard raiding party. They will be accompanied by a portion of their civilian population, but the Knodelian civilians aren't expected to engage in any fighting. This is probably the best-case scenario in this situation, though admittedly it is still quite worrisome," Torkki said. "And we have time to prepare. The estimates are it will take the Knodelians almost a year to prepare their assault. It'll take that long just to organize the evacuation of those towns and cities they still hold."

"It's not like it needs to be a full-scale army to deal with us," Mathis said, quaffing much of his remaining wine. "I don't envy you two this challenge." By keeping himself out of this discussion, it was going a lot smoother than it would have if he had laid out all of his fears. To calm his nerves, he reached into a pouch on his belt and pulled out a handful of mud. Inspecting it, he thought it a little dry for his purposes and poured the remaining wine onto it.

In their youth, the parents of Mathis and Torkki had taught them the art of making *hikaru dorodango*. Basic *dorodango* making was a kid's game done to pass the time and to teach young children to focus, but creating the *hikaru dorodango* was an art form – taking a ball of common mud, and forming it into a perfect, shining sphere. Mathis was such an enthusiast that he always made sure to have a few handfuls of the right texture of soil with him at all times.

Technically, you were supposed to use water, not wine, when adding liquid to the mud, but Mathis didn't have any water handy. It would be interesting, he supposed, to see how it turned out with the substitution.

As Mathis focused his nervous energy on his artwork, his brother and Hesketh talked through their initial plans for the defense of Ekholm. Mathis caught few details, but he still picked out the gist of their discussion. Fortifying Ekholm wouldn't be too difficult, they decided, as it was built upon a hill backing up to a large river. With some effort, Ekholm could be turned into something resembling a hill fort in very little time. The debate raged, however, over exactly what form that hill fort should take. Hesketh favored a simple outlying barricade that could be constructed without any outside help, while Torkki wanted a much more elaborate structure closer resembling more modern fortifications. His plan involved several layers of defensive earthworks, stronger barricades, and external ditches that would hamper any horse-drawn attempts to cross into the town. They would require extensive help from Norre to enact Torkki's plan, and it would be more time-consuming, but all of them recognized that it would make Ekholm defensible even without the Elite Brigade troops. Torkki's plan also had the side benefit of perhaps removing the power base from a certain would-be dictator who was persecuting both his brother and, as Mathis knew but Torkki didn't, Hesketh's family as well.

Torkki turned to his brother to ask for his input on a certain matter and almost gaped. Mathis was focusing on making sure his ball of wine-soaked mud was a perfect sphere instead of paying much attention to the conversation. For the first time since their reunion, he was actually disappointed in his little brother.

"Doesn't this matter to you at all, Mathis?"

Mathis flinched, which was enough to send his still-in-progress *dorodango* into a thousand pieces. "Ack! Um, sorry. What was that?"

Torkki continued to glare at him incredulously. "This is a very serious matter, and I thought you came with me because you wanted to help. We're talking about a possible invasion of Ekholm, here, and you're playing around with those same mud balls we used to make when we were children."

Hesketh sighed. "He's like this in militia drills, too. He doesn't come nearly as regularly as he should, and he often seems pretty distant when he does."

Mathis reclaimed his mud, stuffing it back into his *dorodango*-making pouch, and wiped the table with his sleeve. He refused to meet the eyes of either his brother or his militia captain. "I am not a soldier, brother. I never was. I would help defend our people if I could, but I know I'm not cut out for it. The only reason I was ever in the militia was because I wanted to be there to help you fulfill your dream and become a soldier, and since you left I've felt no compulsion to remain in it. Since I've already long since put in my mandatory year of service, attending training is voluntary, so... I guess I just don't volunteer to go that often. The only reason I haven't formally left is because I feel obligated to stay in for you. I am worried about this invasion, but I had nothing to contribute, so I decided to try and work off my nerves."

Torkki was silent for a long moment, staring at his brother as if he were a stranger. He knew his brother would follow his own path, but the Mathis he thought he knew wouldn't have completely ignored a life-and-death decision-making conversation. As untutored as Mathis was, Torkki still expected him to contribute his own observations on their plans, just as he had in their tactical discussions in their youth. Had something happened while he was gone to change his brother so greatly?

"I don't understand you, Mathis," he said finally. "You have a lot that you can contribute to the defense of our home."

Mathis finally met Torkki's eyes on that comment. "Truly? Name one thing."

"Well, to start with, you're a better archer than anyone I've ever seen, both here and in Norre," Torkki said.

Mathis laughed bitterly. "I know enough about how Norrish armies use their archers to know that the difference between your average bowmen and a bowman of my skill would be practically worthless to any Norrish strategy. They just gather archers together in a group, and have them all let fly with cloud after cloud of arrows... until the enemy soldiers get close enough that the archers have to retreat. I suppose I could do that, but I don't really think my one bow would matter much if we were attacked, and it's not like Ekholm can produce hundreds of archers to join me out of nowhere. My talent, in that regard, is fairly useless."

"You're decent with a sword," Hesketh piped up, though he didn't sound convinced of it himself. "Better than most raw recruits in the Norrish armies, at any rate."

"If that's the standard, then I suppose so," Mathis said, bemused. "After spending years as a sparring partner for my brother and then still more years in training, first under old man Fornier and then with you, my skill with a sword is indeed marginally better than your average raw recruit. I still wouldn't trust it in action against a trained enemy soldier, would you?"

Hesketh coughed. "Well... perhaps not. I still think you undervalue yourself, though."

Torkki tried one last time. "I recall many a day, when I was getting ready to leave and join the Norre armies, when old man Fornier would give me tactical problem to study. I'd come home, ask you to play the role of the enemy tactician for my first attempt at the problem, and then we would switch roles just to give me a different perspective. You were very good, tactically. Better than me, to be honest. Don't you think you could offer that much, at least, considering what's at stake?"

Mathis stood up from the table. This was something he desperately wished they didn't have to talk about. "Not really, brother. I just can't do that, anymore." He started to head out of the tavern doors, stopping at the entranceway. "I'm planning to leave this afternoon to start a week-long hunting trip. Feel free to use my house as your own until I return." With that, he was gone.

Torkki stood to pursue his wayward brother, but Hesketh grabbed his arm to stop him. The older soldier shook his head at the younger. "Let him go, boy. He's got to work this out on his own. If the possible assault is as far off as you assure me, we don't really need him at this stage. Let him get it out of his system before we *really* need his help."

Torkki continued watching the tavern door, as if expecting Mathis to return. "I don't understand. What happened to him?"

Hesketh sighed. "Well... I think Fornier was pushing him too hard to follow in your footsteps. He actually tried, for a while, but lacked adequate skills as either a swordsman or a pikeman. He begged for the chance to fight as an archer, instead, at least up until Fornier explained what the duties of an archer were in the Norre army. I think that... disheartened him. The one skill he felt he had to offer to an army was given so limited a role that he felt useless. It's a shame – I always felt that, while his skills as a swordsman weren't the best, he would have made a good captain, even if he limited himself to the militia. He's only attended five of the weekly militia training sessions these past three months, and he just shuts down whenever people try to talk about militia training, military tactics, or anything at all in that area."

"He was a pretty decent student of unarmed hand-to-hand combat, too, if I recall," Torkki mused. "It's just, put a sword or a spear in his hands and he can barely stand on his own two feet. Honestly, I don't care if he joins the army or not – just that he cares when the village is about to be assaulted."

"I think he does care," Hesketh said. "I think he cares a great deal. You know, he was actually talking with Fornier, at one point, about developing a standing army for Ekholm. He felt we shouldn't have to rely solely on being a tributary to Norre for our defense, but Fornier – properly – said it was entirely impractical."

Torkki frowned at that. "Immediately after the fall of Eskesa, it would have been suicide, but Ekholm has grown considerably since then. We're at least the size of a mid-sized castle town, by now, we just don't have the walls or standing army you would expect of a city this size. It might be possible, now, especially if we construct the defenses

I'm talking about."

Hesketh nodded. "I agree, actually, despite wanting something simpler. In fact, I wanted something simpler to help prove to our people that yes, we *can* defend ourselves on our own, if we just try. But Mathis... I think over time it just grew in his head, more and more, that he was worthless as a defender of his home and his people, especially when all of his plans kept getting rejected."

Torkki bit his lip thoughtfully. "I know the average archer rarely uses his skills beyond draw-and-shoot in large-scale battles, but someone of Mathis' capabilities would have opportunities the average archer wouldn't. Like I said, I don't care if he becomes a soldier or not, but I don't like how he just shut down when we were talking about defending our home. He has to be convinced he can help protect himself and those he cares about." He paused. "Perhaps I could bring in some more unconventional weapons; if we could find something he could use in close quarters, maybe we could bring his confidence back."

Hesketh considered the suggestion for a second. He wasn't exactly an expert in anything other than the sword or spear, himself. "What did you have in mind?"

"Well, I had expected we'd need to call in further assistance from Norre, regardless. I already want to bring in some craftsmen to help fortify Ekholm, and a master blacksmith to help arm it. I happen to also know of a couple other experts who just might be rather useful, if they could be persuaded to come...."

III. The Vixen and the Hunter

Kieras found herself wishing she still had some of the beef jerky her father had insisted she pack even though she absolutely hated it. While she'd been fairly well stocked with supplies when she left Kassia, that was more than a month ago. She found her foraging skills somewhat lacking, and her father had made her promise not to steal anything from the humans while she was on this journey unless it was absolutely necessary. If she didn't find something to eat soon, it would actually be necessary just to avoid starvation, but so far she was only hungry – not starving – and even if she were in such desperate straits, she didn't know where any humans were that she could steal from.

Kieras and her father had talked some time about where she should go. To the west was an uncrossable mountain range, and to the east was the war front. North was largely uninhabited due to the cold, which left just one direction. As soon as she had left the ruins of Kazdri's old manor house, she ran to Kassia's nearest border in the south. She crossed into Erixonite territory, but didn't find the idea of living in that land a very comfortable one. After a few days travel further south, upon hitting a wide river, she turned east. She wasn't sure when she had crossed the border leading out of Erixonite territory, but she knew it must have been within the past week. She hadn't been able to find any trace of human civilization since.

She wished she'd had more experience in the wild. In the castle, it was easy for her to distinguish among the smells she was familiar with, but here in the woods everything smelled unusual. She didn't know how to tell the difference between what was a possible source of food and what was, for example, just a different type of tree.

It wasn't as if she hadn't found any food, fortunately. About two weeks after she left, she had encountered a basan – a sort of oversized, fire-breathing chicken – and managed to dispatch it after a brief fight. Whatever it used to fuel its fiery breath must have been cooked into the meat when she roasted the bird, because after cooking she found the basan meat to be juicier and more flavorful than any chicken she'd ever eaten.

The basan meat was now just a drool-inducing memory, though, and her current food supply had grown monotonous. She had recently found a clear stream feeding the river from which she'd been able to drink and refill her canteen. Thanks to the fish she had been able to catch, she'd been able to sustain herself for a while, though without proper fishing equipment catching them was difficult. However, a pack of wolves tried to make a meal out of her, which drove her away from the river. She was able to give them the slip, but now had lost her way back and was beginning to despair.

As a fox, her eyesight was absolutely horrible in the daylight compared to what she could see in her human form, but her night vision was spectacular, and her sense of smell was much better. Trying to sniff out some provisions she had turned herself into a fox, but so far had no luck.

Fortunately, her hearing was excellent in either form. A distant rustling in the bushes told her there was some kind of animal was nearby... but her nose couldn't distinguish it from the surroundings.

With a mental sigh, Kieras transformed herself back into a human, taking a moment to generate some clothing afterwards. Hopefully, she wouldn't scare any potential prey off with her sudden change in size and shape... and hopefully it was prey, not predator.

It didn't take her long to spot the source of the noise. It was one of the many varieties of horned rabbits local to the area. Horned rabbits were a common sight for Kieras – in Kassia, people often kept them as pets. Once domesticated, people called almost all varieties of horned rabbits "jackalopes," just like almost all varieties of domesticated canines were called "dogs." In the wild, however, they were called by different names to reflect each different breed, often distinguished by their fur and horns.

This particular horned rabbit appeared to be an al-mi'raj. They were bigger than the usual horned bunnies – almost two feet in length – and their yellow fur was distinctive, but the most unique thing about them was that they were the only wild breed of horned rabbit to have just a single horn. Medicinally, those horns were quite valuable, often used to treat rheumatism, but even more importantly as a component in several antidotes for poison. However, that horn also made the al-mi'raj the most dangerous of the wild horned rabbits, as it was straight and extremely sharp.

None of the varieties of horned rabbits attacked humans very often, though if they were provoked their horns could seriously wound even the largest of creatures. There had been plenty of times an al-mi'raj had attacked smaller animals, however, including predators such as foxes or even small wolves. In her human form, she had little to fear from it, but as a fox she was in great danger.

Horned bunnies of all types made good eating, though, and Kieras was desperate. She started to pull out her *hoshi no tama*, intending to use her magic to help her hunt the creature down, when the need to do so was taken from her.

The al-mi'raj was dead almost before she heard the twang of an arrow leaving its bow from a hundred feet away. Glancing at the twang's source, she didn't think that she had been noticed. Her first instinct was to hide and avoid the strange hunter's presence, but then an inkling of a plan came to her mind. There was a skill she had been honing with great success against many of Kassia's castle guards, and it just might prove useful here.

Mathis grimaced at his catch, deciding not to pull the arrow out of its hide until he returned home, just like with the last three. It was too solidly embedded to retrieve... and might not even be worth the effort, considering the quality of his arrowheads. He supposed the al-mi'raj was about average sized for its breed, but it still felt like a waste to use his last arrow on such a small creature.

"Well. That was a good shot," a feminine voice said from behind him.

Mathis nearly jumped. He had seen someone out of the corner

of his eye before he shot but he hadn't heard their approach, and as a hunter he could usually hear even the slightest of noises. Turning to face her, he found the most striking thing about her was her very deep red hair, which was left wild and untamed.

The girl was dressed in clothes which might have once been fine for a merchant-class girl on a ship, but were now a little too threadbare to be considered so. There were a few small holes in the shirt and the pants were fairly ratty, with strings hanging down around her heels. They also seemed just a touch small for her, clinging to her skin tighter than should have been comfortable. Despite all that, both clothes and girl looked as if they were freshly washed, with no visible mud or dirt anywhere.

In addition to her carefully groomed appearance, she appeared to be standing in something of a pose. Her arms were held behind her back, which was curved upwards as she leaned slightly forwards. The effect was to enhance the sight of her generous bosom.

From that pose, and the all-too-bright smile on her face, Mathis thought he knew just what type of girl this young woman was. He had seen many in his day, though it was rare that one would pay any attention to him. She didn't smile like a world-weary prostitute, thankfully, but rather like the idealistic girls who always hoped for the favor of one of Ekholm's most prominent residents... such as his brother. Such young women would fall all over themselves around his brother, almost always for naught. Almost. Unless something had changed while he was in Norre, Torkki was still unmarried... and he was by no means *completely* immune to their charms.

Neither was Mathis, but while it was rather flattering to have a girl fawning all over him he couldn't help but be disconcerted by a complete stranger giving him this kind of attention... in the middle of the woods... several hours away from the nearest village. Not to mention she spoke with a foreign accent, something from the Kassian region. Which might mean Knodelian, as well – Mathis didn't know if there was a difference.

"Good day," he said, nodding his head warily at the girl. "And who might you be?"

Her smile softened into something a bit less flirtatious and a bit more apologetic. "I'm sorry, that was rude of me. My name is Kieras. I'm the daughter of a merchant who was traveling up the river. We had stopped to camp out for the evening, but while preparing dinner we were attacked by wolves. I managed to get away, but I also got lost. I was hoping you could maybe help me find the river. If I could walk up and down the river bank, maybe I'd be able to find my father's barge."

Mathis paused to consider this. Some parts of her story were... plausible, perhaps. It was not unheard of for barges to stop for the night at a safe river bank, if there was the possibility of crossing one of the rockier portions of the river, and wolves were fairly common in the area.

There were several problems with her tale, however. Any barges traveling along this part of the river would go ahead and make the rest of the journey to Ekholm or Kinch for a night rather than stop on one of the rocky river banks. Then there was her accent – the river trade ran from the mountain border of the Skorran peoples to the city-states of the Norre Hegemony, with occasional stops among whatever temporary settlements the nomadic Erixonites might set up on the river. It wasn't possible for any ships from the Kassian Empire or its neighboring states to come up that river – most trade with the north came through ancient and well-traveled roads such as the one that ran through Ekholm. The fact that her clothing would never be that clean should she be telling the truth was the clincher, however.

While it seemed possible she was a spy for the Knodelians, Mathis saw some sense in helping her, anyway... though not in the way she was asking. It was easier to keep an eye on a possible enemy when you knew where they were, after all.

"I have a better suggestion," he said, trying to sound helpful rather than suspicious. "My home town is only about a couple hours away. It is a port of call for just about all of the local river traffic. If your father is looking for you, he will undoubtedly stop in town. It will be a lot easier and safer for you to look for him from there."

Kieras hesitated. "Well... I don't know. Suppose my father starts looking down river from you?"

"Then he'll spend several days traveling south until he hits the Sointu Sea," Mathis said. "And then a few weeks fighting the current back north until he gets to Ekholm, again. It really is the best place to meet your father, if he's looking for you along the river."

The girl flinched slightly. She looked uncomfortable with the idea, but Mathis knew she had no way out of it... short of admitting that she lied.

"Oh, very well," Kieras finally said. "I'd really like to look for my father, myself, and not just wait for him, but I suppose patience is the better way to go. Which way is your village?"

By the time they reached Ekholm, Kieras had figured out where they were. Ekholm was an important trading town, since it was where the Orrpars Road – a major trade route to the Southeast of Kassia – met the Knapp River. From Ekholm, trade would either follow the road south into the heart of the Norre Hegemony, or would take the river leading from the Sointu Sea to Skorran lands. Kieras recalled, from snippets of conversation overheard in those not-so-infrequent occasions when she was invited to state dinners at the Kassian Royal Court, that Ekholm was considered a burgeoning city. It was in a very strategic location economically, but it was politically and militarily unimportant, clinging to an archaic model of government and making itself a tributary state rather than a fully independent power. In any war launched from Kassia or its neighbors against Norre, Ekholm would be among the first set of targets.

For all of its economic potential, Ekholm was very slow growing. With only a few thousand people inhabiting the town, Kieras worried that the presence of a strange girl with unusually colored hair who was "lost" and "looking for her missing father" would surely cause something of a stir. If there was one thing Kieras didn't want to do, it was attract attention. Should King Heshka learn of her whereabouts, he could quite easily dispatch soldiers to retrieve her from a largely undefended town like Ekholm.

Yet she had no choice. The young man – who had eventually remembered his manners and introduced himself as Mathis – practically forced her to come along. Not only that, but he was using her as labor, insisting she carry several of the (already field dressed, thankfully) carcasses from his hunt on the way. He could have carried them, himself, but he was too busy playing around with a ball of mud to bother with it, which infuriated Kieras to no end.

No, she was not particularly impressed with her new hunter "friend." About the only positive thing she got from meeting with him was a share of the few scraps of food he had with him, which weren't enough to fill her empty belly.

When they arrived in town, she found that Ekholm was actually larger than she had expected – perhaps she wouldn't cause as much of a stir as she feared. The Kassian Royal capital held something over eight thousand people, and was considered very small for its importance. Ekholm was certainly smaller than Kassia – it maybe boasted half the population – but it was large enough she should easily be able to lose herself in the sprawl when the time came. She had been concerned that her hair, which was an extremely exotic color in Kassia, would cause her to stand out, but Ekholm appeared to be a fairly cosmopolitan settlement with several people whose hair color was a close match to her own.

That much she was able to take in as she – reluctantly – followed Mathis through the town until he came to a large building. That building didn't smell very good on the outside, but once the door opened Kieras started gagging. Her sense of smell was duller in her current form than as a fox, but she still had a much stronger nose than any normal human. The odors coming from the furrier and tannery shop were enough to almost knock her out. If her ability to transform into a human wasn't so complete, she might have done what most kitsune her age would have been forced to do and retreat into her fox form, which would have made things even worse.

While never quite fully unconscious, she did lose all sense of awareness for a while. She started regaining a few minutes later to find that Mathis was helping her to an area with a much more delightful scent – perhaps somewhere near a bakery, as she distinctly smelled fresh bread.

"Sorry about that," he finally said, looking more amused than sympathetic. "I know most people don't like the smells from a tannery, but I didn't expect it to affect you that much."

Kieras wheezed a little bit, but found she was able to talk. "I just wasn't prepared for it, that's all."

Mathis studied her for a moment, and then shrugged. He handed her a few coins. She didn't recognize the denominations, but it looked like one silver piece and a few coppers. "Well, as thanks for helping me carry that load, you get a share. I'll also treat you to a meal and a drink at a local tavern, which is run by the captain of the village militia. If anyone has come into town looking for their lost daughter, they'll have contacted him. With any luck my brother, Torkki, will be there, too –

he's a soldier in the Norre Hegemony, and he'll probably have some other alternatives for finding your father. He has better resources than any I might have, anyway."

"Thanks," Kieras said hesitantly. It was looking more and more like her story was going to get her into trouble, once Mathis got his friends involved in looking for her 'missing' father. She was beginning to worry that the deeper she got into it, the harder it was going to be to get herself out. As a kitsune, she was quickly losing her pride in the deception.

After a brief walk, during which Kieras' nose was able to make more of a recovery, they arrived in a very small tavern right next to the village green, which had several tents currently set up inside it. The smell of coals burning hot wafted through the air, and it looked to be coming from the fire pit set up in the middle of that encampment. Mathis shot a curious glance over at the tents and their occupants, but ushered her in to the tavern after a brief moment.

Inside, the smells were almost as strong as they were in the tanner's shop. Fortunately, these odors were easier to withstand – stale sweat, beer, wine, smoke, and food all combined into one slightly unpleasant odor, but by focusing on separating the scent into its more tolerable component smells she was able to ignore the full effect.

"Mathis! You're back earlier than I expected," a young man, not much older than Mathis, called. He was a powerful looking man with a sharp smile and intelligent eyes, his hair trimmed military-fashion. Undoubtedly, this was Mathis' brother, Torkki. "And you managed to shave off that horrid beard."

"I'm back for two reasons," Mathis said. "One, I ran out of arrowheads. I tell you, Chiarot's arrowheads are practically useless. I might as well go and find one of the local tinkers and get them made of tin – they'd be almost as lethal, they'd last just as long, and they'd cost quite a bit less."

Torkki smiled secretively. "That may not be a problem for you, much longer. But never mind that – what's the other reason?"

"Well, I found this young woman in the woods." Mathis gestured to Kieras with a subtle wink. "She says she was attacked by wolves and got separated from her father in the ensuing chaos. Her father is a merchant, she says, who is traveling the Knapp River, but they had been camping ashore some miles downstream. I figured she could stay in town until he was found, and we could take very good care of her in the meantime."

Kieras wasn't sure how to react to what Mathis said. She could tell from the way Mathis winked that the 'very' was meant to convey something between the brothers, but not whether it was simply an expression of some amorous intent, or if he was already suspicious of her. The way he was weaseling all his words, though, she almost suspected him of being a kitsune, himself.

"I... see," Torkki said, and the confusion evident in his voice told her that he wasn't quite so sure, either. "Well, we'll certainly do everything we can for her."

"She did help me bring home my catch, however, so I promised her a meal and a drink for her troubles," Mathis added.

"Of course," Torkki said, now much more sure of himself. "Hesketh?"

Kieras jumped at the name, initially mis-hearing is as a slurred form of "Heshka." A quick moment was all it took for her to realize that Torkki was talking about someone else, however.

"What'll you have, missy?" said a much older man, who Kieras hadn't paid any attention to until that point. He looked nothing like her erstwhile king. In his late sixties, possibly early seventies, he looked big and strong despite his age, and had the presence of a military man. One of his arms was badly twisted, but that looked to be a very old injury that he paid no mind to as he worked.

"What can you offer?" Kieras asked tentatively.

Hesketh frowned slightly when she spoke, but hid it quickly behind a subsequent boisterous grin. "Well, to eat, I can offer only two choices. First, there's a fine beef stew that I've been cooking all day and should be just right by now – while my grub isn't usually as varied as what you can get from some other taverns, my stews are the best in town. Second, Reiter – an old buddy of mine who makes salt fish for a living – sold me a barrel full of salt cod today. I've made a few fish pies with it, and most of my customers seem to come away happy." He paused and turned to Mathis. "Knowing your tastes, I'm guessing you'll want the stew, yourself."

"Of course, sir," Mathis said with an expectant grin.

Neither meal really appealed to Kieras. She loved chicken and other forms of poultry, and rabbit made a nice meal, too, but beef never really appealed to her. Then again, she had been living off of fresh fish for over a week before she found Mathis, and all he'd had for her to nibble on was some *dried* fish.

"I think I'll have the stew as well," she said.

"Good, good." Hesketh walked over to a wall of shelves where several types of bowls and plates were kept. "As far as drinks are concerned, we have a wide range of beers and wines. I have a few imported wines – most from Norre, since the shipment of Skorran wines I'm expecting hasn't arrived yet – but most of my stock, including all of my beers, are local."

"I'm afraid I don't like beer, very much," she said, a little embarrassed at the mention – most people she knew found her distaste of beer strange. "And I'm not too familiar with your local wines."

Hesketh laughed, now serving his bowls filled to the brim with stew. "Our big, tough, soldier boy over here doesn't like beer, much, either, so pay it no mind, miss," he said, gesturing to Torkki. "As far as the local wines go, we tend to play around with fruits other than the standard grape in our wines. The favorites for most strangers are usually gooseberry, elderberry, or currant wine, but we also have salmonberry, hackberry, lingonberry—"

"Lingonberry?" Kieras exclaimed excitedly. "You actually have lingonberry wine?"

Hesketh was momentarily taken aback by her sudden outburst. "Yes. Have you ever had it, before?"

"Once," Kieras said. "It was a special treat for one of my recent birthdays. I liked it a little too much, I'm afraid. I drank myself sick off of it, and since then my father's forbidden me from having any."

Hesketh grinned, grabbing one of the stone goblets from his shelves and filling it from a large barrel. "Well, your father isn't here, so drink up. But only the one cup full, missy – I'll be keeping an eye on you."

Kieras took a careful sip and swallowed. The wine tasted even better than she remembered, and just that one sip full raised her spirits more than they had been since before the night her father sent her away from Kassia. Perhaps there *were* some advantages to spending time in Ekholm, after all.

Mathis was burning with curiosity, but it wasn't safe to ask his questions right away. He'd successfully kept all conversation about the pending invasion by the Knodelians at bay since arriving in Hesketh's tavern, and he wasn't about to break that confidentiality while Kieras was in earshot.

Clearly, things had already been set in motion by his brother in the defense of their home town. Strangers were camped out in the village green, and those people could only have come from Norre. It wasn't the Elite Brigade soldiers he had been expecting, however. He couldn't ask who they were until Kieras was out of earshot, however, and even then he would have to brief his brother on the potential danger she posed before he could ask any questions of his own.

Noticing that she was *finally* done with both her stew and her wine, Mathis felt it was possible to send her away without alarming her.

"Well, now that we're all done eating," Mathis said. "Why don't we see to this young lady's other needs? Captain Hesketh, sir, could you escort Kieras to the seamstress' shop across the street and arrange for her to get some new clothes for her stay here? I would take her, myself, but that shop is run by Madame Oberta. I'm sure you remember that she follows Kuralt's blacklists...."

Hesketh opened his mouth to say something, but then closed it and nodded his head reluctantly. "I suppose I can do that. Will you and Torkki look over my shop while I'm gone?"

"You can count on it, sir," Mathis replied stiffly.

"Well, let's go get your measurements, girly," Hesketh said, helping Kieras to her feet, but shooting a significant glance Mathis' way. "That'll take about fifteen minutes. I doubt Oberta will be able to get your clothes done before tomorrow, however, so we'll come right back here, afterwards."

As soon as the door slammed shut behind them, Mathis breathed a sigh of relief. "Finally! I was beginning to wonder if I would ever get a chance to speak with you alone."

Torkki grinned sadly at his brother. "Then you *do* know she's a spy, right?"

"Of course!" Mathis snorted. "Or at least I suspected it from the moment I first met her, and I'm pretty sure Hesketh suspects, too. She's certainly lying about where she's from and how she got here, but I'm not so certain she's really a spy. She's not a competent enough liar to really pull off that cover story she's pushing, and a real spy would have had the details worked out better than that."

Torkki shrugged. "You might be surprised at just how poor spies are at this kind of thing. You may be right, though."

"Even if she isn't one, I figure we'd better keep an eye on her." Mathis paused, taking a deep breath. He knew this would require something of an explanation, and he wasn't looking forward to it. "Spy or not, I think she's a kitsune."

Torkki's eyes widened. "A kitsune? Why?"

"Several reasons, some of which I'll go into when we have more time later tonight," Mathis said. "Her nose is overly sensitive, for one thing – she nearly fainted at the tannery – and then there was her... uh, affinity for lingonberry wine."

"What's so suspicious about that?" Torkki said, somewhat puzzled. "We both like lingonberry wine and neither of us are kitsune."

"True," Mathis admitted. "But remember, lingonberries are often called foxberries for a reason."

"So, any other reasons for suspecting she's a kitsune?"

"Honestly, I more than just suspect it," Mathis said, rubbing the back of his neck in embarrassment. "Like I said, we'll talk about it more, tonight. At the moment, there are a few questions I want answered before Hesketh brings her back here."

At this, Torkki grinned. "Well, I think I can guess a couple of them, but ask away."

"First off," Mathis said. "How goes the fortification project?"

"So far, it's been going well. Hesketh and I reached a compromise plan where we build only one permanent wall, and when that is complete we'll set up additional impermanent defenses to help handle the immediate threat. I've already got local workers started collecting the construction materials we'll need for when the engineering team from Norre arrives to complete our plans. It's going to be tough to get it done in time, but I think we can handle it. We'll start with some quickly built wooden walls and trenches, so we'll have something in place soon in case they attack early, but then we'll start reinforcing or maybe even replacing those wooden walls with stonework from the local granite and marble quarries, and whatever soil and clay that can be re-used from the trenches we dig. Throw in a couple towers as archery platforms, a gatehouse, and other little things like that, and we should be well protected... as long as they attack the town from this side of the river. I'm afraid we don't have time to sufficiently fortify the outlying areas or anything on the other side of the river, which means we'll be susceptible to flanking maneuvers that involve crossing the bridge, but there's only so much we can do before they're supposed to get here."

"You won't have any defenses on the other side of the river?" Mathis asked, surprising even himself with his interest.

"A few," Torkki sighed. "We'll be able to put in a small wooden wall, maybe, but no trenches, no stone or brickworks, no towers or platforms from which archers or machines can safely assault any attacking armies, nothing like that. Thankfully, there's not much over there, so at worst we could always destroy the bridge. I'm actually much more concerned about the outlying farms and fields, which will have no protection at all."

"It wouldn't make sense for them to attack the farms," Mathis mused. "Their goal is to find themselves a new homeland, and having ready-made farms available would be a great boon to them. They would probably be satisfied with just shutting down the supply lines between Ekholm and its primary food sources.. We need to make sure that we have enough food to last for at least a brief siege, and hope they don't go so far as poisoning the Knapp."

"Yes, I know. I haven't had a chance to deal with that, yet. We'll need to build a warehouse, first, and then send a trading mission to the town of Arsene so that we have enough salt to preserve that much food." Torkki pulled at his hair in frustration. It was the first sign Mathis had seen that might indicate his brother was starting to feel overwhelmed, but it didn't surprise him in the least. "They've got the closest salt-works in the area. The problem is they'll need just as much salt, themselves, for much the same reason we do. It may take some careful bargaining."

Mathis almost volunteered to make the trip, but held himself back. He would be stuck looking after Kieras, most likely, so just about anything he might want to do outside of town would have to wait for a while. Letting the girl leave town now that she was inside it was not an option.

Instead, he turned his attention to the other question that had been nagging at the corners of his mind since his return. "Yeah, maybe we can talk more about that, later. I have a few ideas that might convince them to help us. Right now, though, I have another question: Just who are those people camping in our village green? They certainly aren't the Elite Brigade soldiers you promised us, but they're clearly from Norre. Your doing?"

The stress from planning the defense of Ekholm left Torkki's face in an instant after that. Instead, it was replaced by laughter. "Yes, entirely my doing. The soldiers are still mustering and won't be here for at least another couple weeks, but I brought in a few specialists from Norre to help Ekholm prepare. I needed an engineer and his workers to help design and build the walls. I needed a quartermaster to help plan out how much billeting and warehousing space we would need to support my men. And perhaps of most interest to you, since our local master blacksmith was out of town I sent for a team of blacksmiths to make sure everyone would have all of the swords and armor we might possibly need."

Mathis started to ask another question when the realization overtook him. "Wait a minute... has Kuralt approved of *any* of this? Especially the part about bringing in your own blacksmiths?"

"How could he have?" Torkki asked with feigned innocence. "I didn't have time to wait for him. He *still* hasn't returned from his pilgrimage to Eskesa. You know the custom. In the absence of the Archon, any of the council members – not just the regent – may authorize emergency action provided it requires no funds from Ekholm's state treasury. The law only states the regent must be informed when another councilman makes this kind of decision – there is no need to wait for his approval. The Norre Hegemony is footing the bill for all of this, so nothing is coming out of the state treasury. Uncle Savard was more than willing to help authorize it as a member of the council, and I slipped a letter under Regent Cizikas' door to officially inform him of the decision, so..."

"Archon Kuralt hasn't exactly been following the customs *or* the laws since coming to power," Mathis warned. "He almost certainly will cause problems when he returns."

"Let him," Torkki said, the humor in his voice replaced by steel. "His sole claim to power is that he is the only master blacksmith for Ekholm's nearly four thousand citizens. That is no longer a concern. There are now three additional master blacksmiths in town. All three of them have been certified by Norre – which means they're better than Kuralt will ever be. Two of the three swore their allegiance to Ekholm's flag four days ago, in the presence of witnesses, and will be opening up shop as soon as the current crisis is over. Their apprentices and several teams of journeymen came along and made the same oath, too. I'd wager many of the journeymen are better than Kuralt, too."

"That seems a bit unfair," Mathis said, though he really wanted to agree. "I always thought Kuralt's work was pretty good."

"It's decent," Torkki admitted. "But I was amazed at how shabby even his finest work seemed next to what I could find in a journeyman's wares in Norre. I think, however, he's waged a pretty vicious campaign to keep himself on top in this town. He no longer trains anybody. He keeps his apprentices busy, so no one suspects, but those apprentices never seem to advance. In fact, since being named the Archon, it seems as if he's had them doing all of his work, but no one of them does any more than a single part of the job. I was talking to one just a few hours ago who told me he had been doing nothing but stoking fires for Kuralt's smithy in five years, but had never been taught any other part of the trade. Another said he did nothing but sharpen blades. Another said he only prepared molds for casting. Each apprentice is now at a master's level for one small part of the craft, but none of them have any experience doing anything else. Working together, they can and do manufacture all of the goods that Kuralt sells, but alone none of them could handle the job alone. He rarely lets his apprentices learn enough to become journeymen, and those that do wouldn't pass muster as journeymen anywhere but Ekholm. You said yourself that Chiarot's steel arrowheads aren't even as good as your average tinker's tin arrowheads – that should tell you something."

"That may be true," Mathis said, not entirely convinced but definitely receptive to the idea. "But he is still the Archon, don't forget. He still holds authority over Ekholm... unless you intend a coup, as well?"

"A coup?" Torkki snorted. "Hardly. Well, not unless it comes to that – which it shouldn't. No, you see, I found out that the reason he's been looking for whatever 'symbol of leadership' he's after in Eskesa is that he wants it for his re-election bid. I know you haven't been in the political loop, lately, but you do remember when the election is supposed to be, right?"

"Of course I do. It's...." Mathis checked the current date in his head. "It's just six weeks away, isn't it? His term's almost up, and suddenly his power base is gone. All he'll have to go on is some worthless token from Eskesa and whatever genuine support he would get otherwise. That might give him a few votes, but as long as there's a good candidate to oppose him, he's done."

"And guess which one of our favorite uncles is going to run for Archon?"

Mathis started laughing, but stopped the moment a loud bang crashed into the front door of the pub, as if someone had stubbed their toe into it... or kicked it.

"That hurt!" Hesketh's muffled voice groused. It was clearly a warning of his imminent return.

Mathis still had other things to talk with his brother about, but they could wait. Things in Ekholm were finally starting to go right, again.

Things in Ekholm were finally starting to go right for Kieras. The elderly lady who took her measurements – Oberta, if she remembered the name right – said she would have a simple dress available the next day, and several nicer outfits in a week or two. Kieras didn't think she actually needed normal human clothing, but it would be easier having them around than explaining their absence when people were in her room, at least while she stayed in town.

And people did seem to enjoy sticking close to her. First it was Mathis, who pawned her off on Hesketh, who gave her back to Mathis and his brother, who took her to one of the larger local inns and paid for her to have a room, there, for at least a week. The people at the inn, though, were supposed to allow her some privacy, finally... or would once the chambermaid quit fussing over her room, at least.

"Why are you doing all this?" Kieras asked, yawning. The yawn wasn't entirely play-acting to get the girl to go away – it had been a very long day, which had followed a very long week, which had followed a very long month, which left the kitsune vixen quite worn out.

The girl flushed, giggling slightly. She looked just a little younger than Kieras' human appearance led others to believe, and had the appearance of a real heartbreaker.

"Forgive me, mistress," she said, giggling again. "But this *is* my job."

Kieras narrowed her eyes at the girl. She had lived for decades in the royal castle of what was one of the most powerful kingdoms in the known world, and she had never seen this much attention provided even to the King. "I wasn't aware it was your job to light the fire and every single candle in my room, dust every piece of furniture twice, and fluff each of my pillows four times... all in one night."

The chambermaid blushed even more, now looking almost sunburned even though she had a very pale complexion. "My apologies, mistress. I... I just wanted to find out something from you, and couldn't work up the courage to ask."

That softened Kieras up dramatically. She certainly understood curiosity, just as much as the next person... or kitsune, for that matter. "Enough of this 'mistress' nonsense. If we're going to be having a chat, we should call each other by our names. I'm Kieras, by the way."

The girl hesitated for only a split second before sketching a bow. "I'm Ziani, mistress."

"None of that 'mistress' nonsense, I said. Now, what is it you wanted to know?"

If Ziani's blush could have gotten any deeper, Kieras suspected it would have. She couldn't even meet Kieras' eyes as she spoke. "Well, um, I saw that... that you were brought to the inn by Torkki, himself, and the word is that he's paying for your room and everything...."

That just confused Kieras. What did that have to do with anything? "I don't understand. What are you asking?"

"Well, if *Torkki* is bringing you to this inn and paying your way, he must know you very well," Ziani continued. "I just have to ask – what's Torkki like? I'm dying to know!"

Kieras had been friends with some of the girls her apparent age around Kassia and fully understood the concept of gossip. However, the idea of partaking in said gossip was completely alien to her.

"I hate to disappoint you," she began. "But I really don't know him that well. His brother, Mathis, rescued me when I got lost and brought me to this town to help me find my father. I've never really talked with Torkki."

"Oh," Ziani said, crestfallen. She started to fluff a pillow – again – but with much less enthusiasm than before.

Kieras felt bad for the girl. Ziani had *very* clearly wanted to talk about Torkki, though whether it was just hero worship or something more Kieras couldn't tell. Well, maybe she could do something for the girl and figure more out about her benefactors at the same time.

"Why don't you tell me about him?" Kieras suggested. "And his brother, too, of course. I'd like to know more about the people who rescued me."

"Well, Torkki's handsome, to start with," Ziani began with a lustful sigh. "The most handsome man I've ever seen. He's very strong, and everyone says he has a good head on his shoulders. He's older than me... though not by too much! I like older men, anyway."

Kieras held back a smile that was quirking around her lips. "I can't really say a man's age has mattered all that much to me."

Ziani laughed. "Torkki may only be a few years older than me, but he's experienced a lot in that time. He's always been one of the most courageous men in Ekholm... even before he came of age as a man! In fact, my first memory of him was when I was seven years old. A large tree came floating down the river and struck a bridge, breaking the supports all along one side. It collapsed in two places, stranding most of a merchant train in the middle of the river, on the bridge's lone surviving platform. Most of our townspeople were too afraid to attempt a rescue. They feared that their very weight could cause the rest of the bridge to collapse taking the merchants with it, and the fishing fleet was out of town leaving almost all of our sailors and most of our boats gone, but Torkki saw the folly of inaction. He got his father and his brother together, took a pile of rope, and went out to the bridge...."

Ziani continued to talk about Torkki, describing how he had managed to hastily construct a rope line from one broken part of the bridge to another, until he got all the way to the other side of the river. At that age, he and his brother were still small enough and light enough to walk across the damaged section without causing any more of it to collapse, and once they were on the other side it was possible to send additional rope lines safely. Eventually, the stranded merchants were able to return to dry land using Torkki's rope line system.

Once the fishermen returned with their boats, the bridge had been repaired and reinforced so that such an incident would never happen again, but a potential tragedy had been averted by Torkki's quick thinking.

Ziani continued to describe Torkki's adventures growing up, as well as his early entry into the militia. Torkki turned out to be something of a prodigy with a sword or a spear, and wasn't half bad with a bow and arrow (although Mathis was unquestionably the best shot in Ekholm). Kieras was learning quite a bit about Torkki, but only a very little about her "benefactor," Mathis. Information was information, however, so she'd take what she could get.

After his parents died, Ziani explained, Torkki left town to become the soldier he seemed destined to be. In Norre he excelled, quickly rising in rank, winning awards and earning a position in the most coveted of Norre's military divisions.

Kieras wasn't very familiar with Norre's military, but even she knew that it was quite unusual for a man of Torkki's background to get that many accolades from a major power like the Norre Hegemony. As Ziani continued to describe him, Kieras grew quite impressed.

It was true that Ziani was viewing him with biased eyes – the girl's infatuation with Torkki couldn't be more obvious. Distinguishing the facts from Ziani's opinions wasn't too hard, however, and the picture those facts painted were of a courageous young man who had achieved much in his life already.

"I'm a little concerned he may have bitten off more than even he can chew with this latest mission he's undertaking, though," Ziani said, her storytelling finally coming to the present.

"Oh?" Kieras asked.

"Yes. I overheard him arguing with... oh, what was his name? L-something. Laing! That's it. Laing is one of the engineers Torkki brought in from Norre. He and Torkki were discussing who should be in charge of some massive building project. Eventually, I gather, Laing will move on to another town, leaving several other engineers behind. From what I could tell, Torkki insisted on taking that responsibility once Laing left." Ziani frowned. "I don't know what it is they're building, though. I thought he came home for a vacation, but that doesn't seem to be the case after all."

Kieras frowned. Her father had strongly recommended she find a human to spend a year in service to as a part of her cover story. If their plan to revive King Kazdri fell through, it would be wise to have a witness who could say that she really was out doing what her father claimed. This Torkki sounded like he would be perfect for the role – he was neither noble nor serf, with what appeared to be the sort of character her father would approve of, and – if Ziani's suspicions were correct – a mission that she might be of use for. She'd need more information on just what it was Torkki was doing, though, and she would need to make her own judgment of his character separate from what one besotted girl's opinions might be.

Realizing that Ziani was waiting for a response from her, Kieras decided to think on it some more, later, while still looking for other potential candidates. "Well, I certainly wish him the best of luck, and I may try to see if I can help in any way. But you've talked all this time about Torkki. What about his brother, Mathis? He's the one who actually rescued me, you know."

"Mathis?" Ziani repeated uncertainly. "Well, he's a nice enough guy, I suppose. A hunter by trade, though he also earns some money fletching arrows for other hunters – not that he's done much of that since he was blacklisted by the Archon. He's a little older than me, as well. Not a bad looker in his own right, I suppose, when he cuts that damned beard of his off, but... well, I hate to say this, but he smells when he comes back from his hunting trips."

"Really?" Kieras asked, unsure of how to respond to that one. She had a keener nose than most humans whatever form she was in, but she didn't sense any unexpected odors coming from Mathis on their brief journey to Ekholm. Perhaps a slight blood smell coming from his efforts to field dress his catches, but nothing too offensive. She had no idea why Mathis had been blacklisted, or even what that meant, and he didn't have a beard when she met him, but those were questions for another time. She was pretty sure he didn't "smell," though. Was Ziani talking about the right person?

"Well, I haven't really gotten close enough to smell him," Ziani admitted. "That's just what the other girls tell me. I haven't really seen much of him since Torkki left town. He used to follow Torkki around a lot when they were younger – he even joined the militia at the same time Torkki did, but had absolutely no talent for soldiering outside of his skill with a bow and arrow. When I *have* seen him away from his brother, he's been kind of quiet, but Torkki tends to liven him up a bit." Ziani frowned. "He's hard to describe, really. He stops training with the militia because it's too difficult for him, but then sticks to his principles to defy the Archon even after having been removed from the council. I really don't know what to tell you. I will say, though, that many in the militia are disappointed with him. They had hoped that he, too, would become a possible officer candidate in the Norre Hegemony's armies, but now... well, they're looking elsewhere for their next 'favorite son.'"

Kieras nodded slowly. A man who was the disappointment of an entire town wasn't worthy of the boon of her service, so she ruled Mathis out as a possibility. It sounded like her options would either be to sign on with Torkki or to move to another town.

"But enough about boys," Ziani said with a large grin. "Let's talk about you."

"Me?" Kieras exclaimed, unprepared for any change of topic. She was expecting Ziani to go on about Torkki all night.

"Yes, you," Ziani said. "You told me that Mathis rescued you when you were lost in the woods. Where are you actually from, anyway, and how did you get lost?"

For some reason – perhaps it was just the other girl's friendly nature arousing certain feelings inside her, or perhaps it was merely the need to find a confidant in a strange place – Kieras found she didn't want to lie to the young woman. She didn't want to tell the girl the same story she told Mathis and Torkki, but she also didn't want to have everyone in town talking about the kitsune from Kassia who had run away from the castle, either.

"If I tell you, will you keep it a secret?" Kieras asked.

"Oh, this sounds juicy," Ziani said slyly. "Of course I will."

"I want your word on this," Kieras insisted. It was unfair of her, but there was a bit of kitsune magic she could inflict on the girl if she gave an oath, binding the secret inside her. It wouldn't harm the girl, or even prevent her from breaking her word in a crisis, but it would reinforce any natural reluctance to break that vow.

"Fine," Ziani said, lips quirking slightly in amusement. She wasn't taking this seriously, but the magic Kieras was weaving would correct that. "I give you my word that I will not discuss this with anyone else."

Kieras worked the magic from the oath. She was having a great deal of trouble focusing it into her *hoshi no tama*, which she was carefully holding behind her back. It wasn't a big deal – she was probably just tired, which made focusing magic harder – but she couldn't be certain that her spell had succeeded. Still, she felt confident enough in her abilities to continue.

"Well, first off, I have to admit I lied to Mathis and Torkki when they asked me that same question," Kieras began.

Ziani gaped at her new friend. "Why in the world did you do that?"

Kieras sighed. "Well, I didn't really intend to come to Ekholm when

I met Mathis. I was just hoping to be able to beg some food off of of him, and get directions to a certain landmark. I didn't want anyone to know where I was."

"Why not?"

Kieras wondered how much she should say. Even with her magic reinforcing Ziani's oath, there was still the possibility that the girl might reveal what she was told, but she wanted to keep the girl's interest.

"Well, there's a long story behind that," she began. "And it starts in the Royal House of Kassia...." This time it was Kieras with the long story. She did not reveal that she was a kitsune, but she did explain how she was fleeing from an arranged marriage, traveling in secret to find her long-lost mother. She emphasized the importance of keeping it all a secret, as it was possible that the Kassian King would be sending people out to hunt for her. She concluded her story by adding that she regretted lying to Mathis and Torkki, and hoped that her secret brought no danger to their doorsteps, but in the end she didn't know how to get out of the lie.

Unconsciously, Kieras gave a jaw-cracking, tongue-curling yawn. That caught the attention of Ziani, who had been riveted to her story. Apparently just realizing how long they had been talking, she quickly glanced out of the window, noticing to her distress how much darkness had fallen.

"Oh, no," she cried. "I've been here way too long! I'm sorry, mistress Kieras—"

"Drop the mistress, already!"

"I'm sorry, Kieras, but I have to go! I was supposed to move on to my other rooms an hour ago!"

Kieras frowned. Ziani was the closest thing to a friend she had found since leaving Kassia. She didn't want to get the girl in trouble or anything, though she really didn't understand how entertaining a guest would be a problem. Perhaps that was one of those human things that she, as a kitsune, just couldn't understand. "Well, if your boss gives you problems, you can go ahead and tell him that it was my fault. It was my story that kept you, after all." She paused. "Or at least, I'll accept the blame if you can remember to use my name instead of 'mistress' all the time."

She saw Ziani out the door, locking it behind the girl before returning to her bed. She considered switching back to her fox form for a more restful night, but decided she was much too tired.

Besides, she thought. *Someone might come in before I wake up. I don't want anyone in this town to know I'm a kitsune.*

Mathis and Torkki had to wait much longer than they anticipated, but used the time well. Torkki was in the middle of explaining the fine details of his defensive plans: He intended to build a gatehouse, four towers, and a wall of wood as quickly as possible – taking no longer than a few weeks – and then gradually make those walls and buildings permanent as stone and brick material became available. How much of that could be done before the expected attack was still uncertain. Torkki had argued extensively with his engineer about deadlines for certain projects, but some form of defensive structure would be achieved quickly. At least some of it would be made permanent before the attack, though how much was still uncertain. Torkki had just started his explanation of the proposed pits and entrenched earthworks when the person they had been waiting for emerged.

The innkeeper, waiting at the foot of the steps in the inn's reception area, called out to Ziani. He was carrying a beeswax candle that had burned down farther than anyone had expected to need it to that night. That would probably cost Mathis and Torkki another few pennyweights of copper to replace, but at least the innkeeper was being co-operative. "Ziani, these gentlemen would like to discuss some matters with you about our latest guest."

"Yes, sir, right away," Ziani replied submissively. She undoubtedly suspected she was in trouble for being late returning from her rounds, and Mathis knew she would have been on any other night, but she had nothing to fear on that front tonight. Any worries she might have had, though, vanished the moment she saw who had asked for her. "Torkki!" she cried out breathlessly.

Mathis eyed the girl running towards his brother so anxiously with a look of both amusement and, he had to admit, perhaps a little underlying envy. Ziani was quite an attractive young woman, and he had noticed her following his brother around ever since they were both young children. She was always admiring him from a distance, but was too nervous to speak with him. She had regarded his brother with a great degree of hero-worship, but had never acted quite as ridiculously as the pack of girls who had hounded Torkki for his hand in marriage in the years leading up to his departure for Norre. In the intervening years, it seemed her crush was still there. Torkki – as always – was completely oblivious.

All the cute ones go for Torkki, he sighed mentally. It was not the first time he'd had that thought, and it probably wouldn't be the last. Not that he particularly wanted to be hounded quite like his brother was, but having one or two girls look his way might have been nice.

"Er, Ziani, wasn't it?" Torkki said uncertainly.

Mathis winced, expecting the girl to be devastated that he needed to ask, but she took it pretty well.

"You remembered," she laughed. "So, you had some questions about Kieras?"

"Yes," Torkki said. "You were in her room for an awfully long time. Did the two of you talk?"

Ziani frowned, looking a little put out. "Well, of course. Did you think I was in her room fluffing her pillows for two hours straight?"

"Well, no," Torkki replied, taken aback. "That's not what I meant. I... well, what we wanted to know was what you two were talking about."

Ziani smiled secretly. "Oh, that's for us to know and you to never, ever find out."

Torkki shot a flustered look at Mathis. Clearly, that was not an answer he had expected.

"We're not looking for any deep, dark secrets," Mathis said, amused about his older brother's faltering uncertainty. Veteran soldier he may be, but he was still clueless when it came to women. "We are, however, somewhat... concerned about Kieras."

"What do you mean?" Ziani asked.

"We think she's a spy," Torkki answered bluntly, cutting off Mathis.

There was a long pause, during which Ziani's face dropped with greater and greater horror. "I... I don't believe it! She can't be a spy. She just *can't!* She's too nice of a girl to possibly be a spy!"

Mathis glared at his brother for a moment. One thing Torkki had never learned when they were growing up was tact. Then again, neither did he, really – if he had, maybe he wouldn't have been put on Kuralt's blacklist. "Actually, he's over-stating it. We are pretty certain she's lying to us, since the story she told when I found her doesn't hold water. Her accent shows she comes from the northern regions, which is where the enemies Torkki is here to protect us from are located, so there's real concern that she might be a spy... but there's a few things that don't quite agree with that, as well. If you could tell us what the two of you were talking about, that might go a long ways towards clearing things up either way."

Ziani calmed down, but still looked distressed. "Oh... well, I knew she had lied to you."

"You did?" the brothers chorused. Torkki followed it up with, "Did she say why?"

Ziani nodded. "Yes, but... I can't tell you the reason."

"Why not?" Torkki asked.

Ziani hesitated. "I... uh, I promised her I wouldn't?"

The disbelief on Torkki's face would have been comical if the situation hadn't been so potentially serious. "Do you think she's bespelled?" he asked Mathis.

"No," Mathis sighed. "I'm pretty sure she's not."

"Bespelled?" Ziani repeated, unable to hold back a few giggles. "How in the world would she do that?"

It was Mathis' turn to demonstrate the classic family lack of tact. "She's a kitsune." He nearly bit his tongue when he realized what he had just blurted out.

A large number of emotions played upon Ziani's face to that one – regret, fear, concern, and curiosity being the most identifiable ones. "I don't believe that one, either. She's... well, she's much too human."

"Kitsune *are* human," Mathis pointed out, which seemed to surprise Torkki. "Or at least the nogitsune and myobu varieties are. The huli jeng, kumiho, and lesser varieties might not be, but Kieras is clearly a nogitsune. Her hair gives that away – a kitsune cannot change their hair color for very long."

"How do you know all that?" Torkki asked, astonished. "I don't even know that, and I've worked with kitsune before!"

"I know a lot of things you don't, brother," Mathis taunted. When Torkki gave him a mock glare, he got serious. "Mother told me about some things about kitsune before she died. You had just joined the militia, and I had to wait a couple years before I was old enough to join myself. We would always finish the chores together before your weekly training sessions, which left me moping around the house, bored. Mother filled some of the time with stories from her youth, including some about her own meetings with a family of white-furred kitsune from Eskesa. I didn't remember much about those stories until a year ago, when Jaffray opened a print shop."

"Ekholm has a printing press, now?" Torkki interrupted, and then shook his head. "I'll never understand my home town. Huge trade industry. Resources aplenty. Large industries in brick making, pottery, candle making, honey harvesting, farming, fishing, granite mining, marble mining, textiles, tanners, vintners, brewers, masons, apothecaries, pearl divers, millers, butchers, jewelers, glaziers, bankers, boat builders, carpenters, and now even a printing press. Yet we've had only one blacksmith worthy of the name for the past thirty years, and we pay a ridiculous amount of tribute for protection from a nearby country instead of building up our own defenses."

"It's rare, outside of a major city, for there to be more than one master blacksmith in town. There's a reason Kuralt was able to use his influence to remain Archon," Mathis reminded him. "Any other business of any importance has so many redundant sellers or craftsmen that if one of them decides to stop making their goods for you, there will be other places to shop at. He's got the only significant monopoly in Ekholm, and he and Chiarot have been the only blacksmiths serving the towns of Arbeloa, Kinch, and Sugden as well. Thanks to you that's going to change, but back to Jaffray – he opened a print shop about a year ago, and was buying or borrowing any books anyone would let him have. I was out of arrows, and needed more money than I had in hand in order to buy a few dozen arrowheads from Chiarot. He needed help from anyone literate who could help him transfer those hand-written manuscripts to print, so I offered my services for a few weeks. One of the books he had was a treatise on kitsune. I was reminded of mother's stories and learned more beside while reading it."

"But that doesn't tell me how you know that Kieras is a kitsune," Ziani snapped, reminding the brothers about what they were supposed to be doing. "Why do you think she isn't just a girl?"

"Well, there are several small pieces of evidence," Torkki said. "An affinity for lingonberry wine. Then there's her unnaturally red hair, a sense of smell which is clearly better than the average human..."

Ziani blushed, glancing at Mathis. "And I said... oh!" Suddenly she started laughing. "Oh, that's hilarious."

"It is?" Torkki said.

Mathis, just as baffled as his brother, decided to try and get them back on track. "And those aren't the only reasons we believe she's a kitsune. However, whether she is one or not, the fact remains that she was lying to us, and that it seems rather suspicious timing for her to be here. If she is a spy, we need to know for our own sakes. If she isn't a spy, we need to confirm that for her sake, because we'll probably have to imprison her as a precaution otherwise."

Ziani hesitated. "Well... I suppose if it's for her own good...."

With some hesitation, the chambermaid recounted the story Kieras had told her. As she spoke, Torkki started to get a hint of recognition in his eyes. When she was done, he said, "You know, I think I know something about this."

"You've heard about a Kassian girl running away from an arranged marriage?" Ziani asked, surprised.

"Well, no, not that part of it," Torkki replied. "But it strikes me as very plausible. One of the founding fathers of the Kassian Empire was a nogitsune kitsune named Lahti. He has worked as the personal bodyguard of the royal family of Kassia for almost a century, now, thanks to a promise he made to its founding king. If I correctly recall what the Norre Hegemony's spymaster told me, he should be free of that promise in another few years. Arranging for his daughter to marry the prince in order to force Lahti to continue in their service is quite plausible, I would think. Lahti is known to have had several children. Most of them have moved away from Kassia decades ago, but I believe his youngest – a daughter – is thought to still live with him. Or was still living with him, if Kieras is indeed that daughter."

"So... does that mean you believe she isn't a spy?" Ziani asked.

"It gives her a plausible story," Torkki said. "But that isn't enough to prove it. I need a few more assurances before I'm willing to let her go free."

Mathis grinned slightly. "I have an idea...."

Kieras' nose was about to drive her crazy. They were once again in Hesketh's tavern, which apparently also served as the headquarters for both the local militia – currently drilling on the village green outside – and whatever project it was that Torkki was working on. He was in intense discussion with someone in the corner. What was making her nose go off, though, had nothing to do with any of this. It was the large pile of baked goods which had just been delivered to the tavern that was drawing all of her attention.

Much of it was just rounds of bread that Hesketh would use throughout the day in his service as soup bowls, but there were some sweet treats in there, as well, which would serve as breakfast for both the militia and Torkki's people. There were even some things in there for her, she had been told.

She smelled lingonberries. Very good, ripe ones which had been cooked into some of the breads. Her mouth was starting to water, and if her ability to transform into a human had been any less perfect she would have reverted to her fox form the moment the baker came in with the goods.

She tried to distract herself by listening in to the other conversations, but she didn't understand enough to really follow them.

"I'm about to call in another engineer for a second opinion," Torkki was saying. "Look here, Dubnyk. I've been looking into the things you've been telling me, and quite frankly your time estimates seem incredibly far off what they should be."

"Are you a master engineer of castle-works with forty years experience?" the aforementioned Dubnyk questioned. "What gives you the idea you can even suggest that my estimates are off?"

Torkki sighed. "In the Republic of Vincour is the famous Wall of Limnell. That wall is over seventy miles long, ten feet wide, and fifteen feet high. There is a fortress embedded into the wall every mile of its length. That wall took fourteen years to build... and just six years to complete the principle work. You are suggesting that it will take twenty years to build a wall roughly one tenth that length, three feet shorter in height, and less than half the width, with just four small archer's towers and a gatehouse. Can you explain the disparity?"

"That wall had two thousand people working on it, all professional soldiers in the peak of their athletic condition," Dubnyk said, lecturing as if to a child. "We only have a hundred soldiers, at most, and they aren't even here, yet."

"We also have the cooperation of the entirety of Ekholm, which has hundreds of craftsmen in masonry, brick-making, carpentry, and other forms of construction," Torkki replied. "And my soldiers should be here tomorrow. More than enough to make up the difference. Any other excuses?"

"Their construction technique is so much more primitive than what you are talking about," Dubnyk continued. "Much of that wall is little more than piles of dirt and turf. You want a stone wall made out of... what was it you said was available locally?"

"Granite... and maybe we can get some marble if we need it. The marble quarry was closed a few months ago due to flooding, but it should be safe to work in now," Torkki replied. "So, basically, you're saying your engineering techniques are so complicated they'll add decades to the construction work?"

"Well—"

"Then perhaps it's time to turn to someone more willing to use a simpler plan," Torkki concluded. "If you can't cut the time, yourself, that is. We have eight to ten months to get this done in, sir. After that, a horde of people with nothing to lose will be trying to assault whatever defenses we've put in place. If those walls are not complete by then, then the engineer in charge of that wall will be left just as vulnerable as all the rest of the people of Ekholm. If you aren't prepared for that, sir, then—"

Dubnyk looked horrified. "I'll see what I can do."

Kieras' stomach rumbled, diverting her attention from the conversation. "When is breakfast going to be served, anyway?"

"When the milkmaid delivers the milk, cream, cheese, and butter we're waiting for," Mathis said. He was sitting at the table by her, and he looked as if he were following his brother's conversation with her, but he'd been glancing over at the stack of breads, as well. "She should be here any minute."

Just then, the door to the tavern opened and a young girl came in. "Milkmaid!" she called. Dubnyk and Torkki's conversation ended in an instant, and Mathis started standing along with the two of them. "It's a larger delivery than usual, so could I get some help getting everything out of the cart?"

"I'll do it," Torkki offered, standing up to follow the girl outside. Kieras noticed this bit of generosity, and added it to her tally of deeds which may be worthy of her service.

Hesketh, who had been out with the militia, training, entered moments after Torkki left. "Did I see the milkmaid arrive?"

"Yes," Mathis said. "Torkki's helping her bring in the delivery, now."

"Breakfast time, then," he said. "Dubnyk, would you lend me a hand?" He and the Norrish engineer picked up two of the five large trays of breakfast items and went outside to feed the militiamen. Hesketh returned a moment later and picked up the other trays, just as Torkki was returning from bringing in a large crate. On his way back out the door, he called over his shoulder, "You guys can all have anything from that last tray, on the house, today. I hope you lot won't forget this bit of largesse on my part."

Kieras wasted no time in securing three of the large lingonberry pastries. Before the others had even finished serving themselves, she had finished the first and was making good headway on the second.

"Good thing these are free, today." Mathis said, watching her eat with a look of mixed amazement and disgust on his face before sitting down at the table across from her. "If you keep going at that rate, I'm not sure we'd be able to feed you."

"That brings up a good point," Torkki said, sitting down at her left. "The terms of my enlistment only pay me in lump sums once a year, and all of my money is with the bankers in Norre at the moment. I am living on a stipend given to me for this assignment. My brother, while a skilled hunter, hardly can provide for you by himself on a permanent basis. We can provide you with lodging for a time, but for food and other necessities you may need to find a job while you're staying here."

"Oh!" Kieras said, startled out of her meal. She hadn't really considered that Mathis and Torkki were paying her way through that town. Mathis had given her a few coins, but not nearly enough for what they were talking about. Her father had provided her with a small purse, too, before sending her out, but all of the coinage was Kassian currency. While that would probably be accepted in a trading town like Ekholm, she was trying not to let anyone know she was from Kassia.

She could use her illusory magic to make that Kassian money appear to be a different type of coinage for a few hours, just like she could with leaves and acorns. With coinage valued at the weight of medal, any of her foreign money should be valued roughly the same amount as any other similar coinage that Norre or Ekholm would have, so she could use it with no problem. She had seen coins from Skorran people before, thankfully, which she could use as the illusory design. "Um, I think I still have some money that my father gave me, if I didn't drop it during the wolf attack," she said, reaching for a pouch on her waist.

It was somewhat unusual wearing real, human clothing instead of illusory clothes. She had started with human clothes the night before after changing into a nightshirt provided by the inn. The clothes she had magically generated when she first encountered Mathis had dissolved by that morning, and she didn't bother to generate a new set since Oberta had managed to deliver one of her completed outfit before she awoke. It was much easier to say that she had thrown out her old, worn clothing than it was to explain why she wasn't using the new clothes she had received.

Her illusory clothing was as good as real, even a few hours after being removed from her skin (though it would fade away in time). Other people could even handle it and not realize that it was an illusion. A big difference, however, was that she would be the only one to know exactly where on her belt her coin purse was tied, as her illusions always made it look about three inches to the right of where it actually was. In the confusion of using real clothing, instead, however, she initially put her hands on her chatelaine – the decorative chain belt-hook on which she kept her scissors, a measuring tape, a knife, a whistle, a few writing tools, a small mirror, a vesta case, a few (now empty) vials of spices, and some pouches – instead of the coin purse. None of the bags on her chatelaine held any money, but her *hoshi no tama* was in one. Taking the opportunity, she held that bag with one hand while her other continued to look for the money. Finally, she found the coins, and as subtly as possible shunted her illusory magic into the purse to change their appearance from Kassian taels to Skorran drachmas. Finally, she spilled the coins out onto the table.

"There you go," she said. "I'll let you take whatever you think is necessary to keep me in food for the next month or so – if I have to wait much longer, and I may leave to find my father on my own."

Torkki picked up a few of the coins, examining them closely. Then he looked meaningfully at Mathis. "Just like we thought – Kassian money."

"What?" Kieras said, startled. "What do you mean Kassian? Those should be Skorran coins!"

Mathis, who had been examining a coin himself, tossed it over to her. "See for yourself."

Kieras frantically examined the coins. *This isn't possible! It just isn't possible! How in the world did my magic fail like that?*

"Kieras?" Torkki said sternly, drawing her attention back to him.

"This Kassian money pretty much proves what we've known all along. You've been lying to us, girl, and we want to know why."

"Oh no!" Kieras cried, reaching for her *hoshi no tama*. Grabbing the bag that was holding it, she tried to change back into a fox and make her escape... but she wasn't changing. Panicked, she overbalanced her chair trying to get away from Torkki. She was saved from hitting the back of her head against the inn's stone floor by Mathis. He had come around the table to stand behind her and was quick to catch her before she could fall.

"I'm afraid that running is not an option," Mathis said, gently but firmly setting both her and her chair upright again. Surprisingly, he let her go instead of holding on to keep her from running. "Not that I'm going to keep you here by force, if you insist on leaving, but you aren't going to want to leave permanently until after we're done with our little chat." With that, he went back to his side of the table, sat down, and continued eating his breakfast pastry.

Kieras couldn't believe he was being so casual, and as she studied him she realized he wasn't. Both brothers were quite tense, ready to act if she tried something, but their actions and words were the very picture of studied casualness.

As Mathis ate, Torkki started picking up her money and counting it, breaking it down into various denominations. Neither one appeared to be paying any attention to her, but she knew better. They didn't seem to be in any hurry to proceed, however. "Okay... um, what do you mean by that? What hold do you think this place has on me?"

"First of all," Mathis began. "It would be impolite to leave in the middle of breakfast." He took another bite of his pastry and grinned. "Eat. Believe it or not, while we don't want you leaving before answering our questions, we don't bear you any ill will. At first we were worried you were a spy for the Knodelians, but now that we know you're from Kassia we just want to know why you were lying."

Kieras blinked. They thought she was a spy? But that meant... "Wait a minute... how did you know I wasn't telling you the truth in the first place? Did... did Ziani say something?" She hoped not. She really liked Ziani, and a betrayal from the younger girl would have been quite upsetting. *Not to mention it should have been nearly impossible,* Kieras thought. *Considering that my magic was binding her to her oath... though there are always circumstances that allow that kind of oath to be broken.*

"Only after we'd already figured out you were lying," Torkki said. "And only to protect you when she did. By the way, would you like anything to drink? Water, milk, tea?"

Kieras shook her head impatiently. "No, thank you."

Mathis finally answered her first question after washing down part of his own breakfast with a swig of milk. "Your story didn't add up," he said. "There were a lot of inconsistencies, but the most obvious is that you speak with a Kassian accent, and there aren't any Kassian traders who would come here by way of the Knapp River."

Kieras' eyes widened. "I didn't even know I had an accent."

"It's not very distinctive, I have to admit," Torkki said.

Mathis' lip twisted amusedly. "Or perhaps my brother isn't very observant. A Kassian accent is distinctive in several ways. Most noticeably, you draw out your s's when it ends a word and have a brief roll of your r's when they are following a vowel. All you need to do is say your name and you give yourself away as a Kassian. If you were from Skorran lands, you would have drawn out your o's and your r's would sound like a mix between r and l."

Torkki glanced at his brother oddly. "When did you pick all this up? We had the same education, as far as I know, and foreign accents weren't covered."

Mathis sighed. "Thanks to local politics, I've had to buy a lot of things from foreign merchants. Kassian, Skorran, Norre, and even Erixonite traders pass through here every day, and none of them have me blacklisted. After a while, you start to recognize their accents."

Torkki frowned. "You need to tell me just who has been following Kuralt's blacklists. I need to have a word with them."

"Well, there's old Oberta across the street. She's nice about it, though, and always apologetic – I think she's just one of those people who are scared about what he can do to her, rather than one of his toadies. Then there is Azevado, the chandler. He's no surprise, though, considering how much he liked bullying our friends when we were all children – I don't think he cares about Kuralt either way, he just wants revenge on me for putting a stop to his foolishness. Then there's...."

Kieras realized that the brothers were essentially ignoring her as they chatted about this blacklist, whatever it was. She could have made a run for it, then, but Mathis was right – it would be impolite to leave in the middle of breakfast. They didn't seem mad at her for lying (though she still couldn't believe they had thought she was a spy) and, to be honest, she was still hungry. With that in mind, she went back to work polishing off her final lingonberry pastry.

It didn't take her long, and afterwards she was left with nothing to do. The brothers were still discussing local politics, which she neither cared about nor understood, yet it felt like she shouldn't be leaving just yet. She hadn't answered any of their questions, after all, and she really wanted to clear the air before moving on.

Still, if they weren't going to pay any attention to her she would like to go out and do something, perhaps just look around town to familiarize herself with the area. Maybe she could quietly change into her fox form and leave without them noticing. She'd come back to talk with them as they asked.

That might prove problematic, however, as her magic, even her transformative magic, had been failing her lately, and she had no idea why. It appeared to be a focus issue, which she had never had problems with before, but it was easy enough to deal with. Probably she could compensate through more direct contact with her *hoshi no tama*, but if her focus problems continued she could be in real trouble.

She found the pouch attached to her chatelaine once again, reached inside, and without looking pulled out the orb. Yet something was still wrong – it was too warm to the touch, and didn't feel like her tama at all... and when she held it tightly, it started crumbling.

"My... my *tama!*" she cried, pulling it out so she could see it. It was in pieces, and had lost all of its jewel-like appearance. She had never seen a broken tama – in fact, had never heard of one breaking unless its owner was dead – but she knew that tama would change forms when they broke.

Mathis blinked at her. "You mean it's survived until now? You must take real good care of that thing."

"Of course it's 'survived until now.' It's my *hoshi no tama!* An essential part of my being a kitsune! It's been with me my entire life! It's—"

"A fake," Mathis said. "I swapped it with a *hikaru dorodango* I made while you were passed out from the smells from the tannery. And yes, even then I knew you were a kitsune... although if I hadn't, that outburst right now would have just given you away."

Torkki shook his head, laughing. "Indeed. If we needed any more proof you weren't a spy, there it was. No spy in their right mind would have just blurted out such crucial information like that."

Mathis reached into a pouch on his belt and pulled out Kieras' real hoshi no tama. "Don't worry, you'll get it back. But I'd like those questions answered first."

Kieras felt her lips press together in cold fury. "You expect to extort information from a kitsune?" Kitsune were bound by their word when it was given as a gift, but they were also bound to deceive anyone who attempted to extort a payment from them. As her father had shown, when a kitsune's tama was taken that no longer applied, but the brothers didn't need to know that.

"Not *reliable* information, no," Mathis said. "But I'm not extorting it. Now that we know you aren't a spy, we'll be giving this back to you whether you answer our questions or not. In fact, here!" He tossed the orb to Kieras, who caught it in mid-air. "We really would like to know your real story, though."

Kieras looked at the orb closely, but she could tell right away that it was indeed the real thing. "Thank you, although I wish you had not taken it from me in the first place."

"Surely you understand why I did, however," Mathis said. "And I figured a kitsune, the masters of illusion, would appreciate my attempt at creating an illusion of my own."

Kieras was rendered speechless at that. It was true – it had taken more than a day before discovering the switch, even though she knew she was having focus problems. And yes, as a kitsune, she respected that ability. Just not when it was directed at *her*.

"It appears as if your magic is useless when your *tama* is missing," Torkki said. "Leaving you somewhat vulnerable."

"Somewhat, yes," Kieras admitted reluctantly. "Although not completely. Solid magical illusions I create before letting go of my *tama* hold their form while in contact with me. Also, my father has trained me extensively in hand-to-hand combat, so I have a great deal I can do even without my magic."

"I've heard stories about kitsune who revert to their fox forms when scared or startled," Torkki said. "For instance, the bark of a dog can change them to a fox. I'm surprised the same doesn't hold true when you lose your *tama*."

"Those stories aren't entirely true," Kieras said. "But there are grains of truth in them. Kitsune and other canine species rarely get along – I think they see through our illusions or something, and we are instinctively fearful of them. When we kitsune are born, we are often – though not always – born as foxes. We struggle, at first, to turn ourselves human, and in some cases it can take centuries before we master that ability, only managing partial or incomplete transformations. If we are scared or startled while only partially transformed, we revert." She paused. "I was especially gifted in the art, and mastered the technique at an extremely young age for a kitsune. I have three older brothers who left my father's household before mastering it, and they were older than I am now. I'm *still* very young for a kitsune."

"How old are you, really?" Mathis asked, sounding slightly amused.

Kieras glared at him. "Now, is that really a question you ask a lady? Humph!"

"You have mentioned your father and your brothers," Torkki said. "When we questioned Ziani, she did mention your father. I hope you hold her no ill will, for she clearly told us as little as she could and only spoke in order to protect you from the accusation that you were a spy. I am certain she left things out, trying to keep her promise to you and to protect you. As we said, we would like to know more about you, to know why you have lied to us. Between what Ziani said and what I know about Kassian politics, I have a few pieces of the story put together already – that you are the daughter of the legendary Lahti, for example – but why don't you explain everything else to us?"

"Maybe we could help," Mathis added. "And at the very least, we would know exactly how important it was to keep your secrets."

And there it was. As Mathis said, it was not extortion, but their partial knowledge of the situation could cause misunderstandings where they revealed more than was safe to her pursuers.

"Very well," Kieras sighed. "For me, it started when I grabbed a chicken off a roasting spit...."

IV. Broken Iron

It had been almost a month since Kieras had entered Ekholm. Torkki, Mathis, Ziani, and Hesketh were still the only ones who knew her real story, so far. Her original yarn about the wolf attack had a few minor details changed so that it wasn't quite so apparent that it was a lie, and other things had been done to help her settle in, however temporarily. She no longer needed to "search for her father," at the very least. In addition to providing her with room and board, the four people in Ekholm that Kieras knew were helping her keep her identity secret – something she definitely appreciated. Of course, no one was told that she was a kitsune.

She wasn't quite sure why she had remained in town, despite their kindness. Ziani was becoming a fast friend despite the difficult position Kieras had put her in when they met, but the chambermaid was often too busy at her inn for them to have much time together. It was clear that Torkki, Mathis, and Hesketh no longer thought she might be a spy, but they also did not seem to trust her. Discussions about the progress of the defenses they were constructing in Ekholm would end abruptly as soon as her presence was noticed, though it was rather hard to hide the completion of several temporary wooden structures.

Of them all, Mathis seemed to be the one least involved in the planning – a fact that was an apparent source of contention between the two brothers. Torkki really wanted Mathis to take more of an interest, but Mathis seemed to feel as if he could be of no help. However, it left the younger brother with enough time to act as her "keeper," for lack of a better word, which the older brother grudgingly accepted as a necessity.

She was still quite annoyed with Mathis for taking her tama, but he was her only regular companion. He had been quite respectful since that incident, and she found it increasingly difficult to hold a grudge. With his help, her first couple of weeks were spent familiarizing herself with the town of Ekholm. She quickly learned to avoid the riverfront areas, where the stink of fish being preserved could knock her out just as quickly as the tannery. The butcher's shop, thankfully, wasn't as bad, nor were the general stores, which sold the fish after it had been preserved.

She also made acquaintances with several of the newly arrived workers from Norre. Dubnyk, the engineer designing the wall, was very hard to get along with, but he had assistants who were younger, almost as skilled as he was, and much more personable. The most notable of these was Donati, who had apparently been made the liaison to the quarries and was grading the quality of the granite and marble that was to be used. Without giving away her background, she had been able to question him about any sightings of myobu kitsune around Norre, and found his information quite useful. Many breeds of kitsune – some even Kieras had never heard of – passed through Norre every day, and they had a whole library dedicated to them. It seemed as if Norre would be an ideal jumping off point in the search for her mother.

Then there were also the new master blacksmiths: Adamek, Radek, and Kordic. Questioning them had been less useful, but still quite interesting. Adamek had seen a vaki before, but not of the veden variety. Radek, the oldest of the trio, had a lot of stories... but only stories, and nothing really useful. Kordic was perhaps the most interesting of the three, but also the least helpful in her quest. He was the only member of the new "immigrants" who did not come from the actual City-State of Norre, but rather one of the other member states of the alliance – the Tornvall Republic. Before moving to Norre (and now to Ekholm), he had been the winner of the Tornvall Republic's strongman contests seven years in a row. Tornvall was a place that valued physical strength more than scholarly knowledge, he had explained, and they would have no records of kitsune or vaki even if some lived nearby. However, winning the strongman contest in Tornvall meant that Kordic should have quite a bit of authority in the city, so if she ever found herself in that area she could use his name and any of the locals would be happy to help her on her quest.

And she might. The city-states of the Norre Hegemony had, according to Mathis, been the location of several kitsune sightings, most starting within the past fifty years – in other words, around the time her mother and their clan left Kassia. The major cities of the Norre Hegemony – Tornvall, Gronvall, Almgren, Myrvold, Winnick, Perna, and Norre itself – as well as smaller towns such as Ekholm – were the perfect place to begin her search for her mother.

The problem was, she wasn't searching. She had yet to leave Ekholm's boundaries since she had arrived, and all she had done was ask a few questions. She was quickly boring of the town, but couldn't bring herself to leave just yet. She couldn't say why, either – it was just... instinct. She listened to her instincts, and they were screaming at her that she wasn't meant to leave just yet.

Apparently, however, she *was* meant to take on a menial job in order to support herself while in Ekholm. After initially teasing Kieras about getting her a job with the chandler (the smell of whose candles would irritate her nose the entire time Kieras was working for him) or in the kennels (the mere thought of being in such close proximity to so many dogs ran shivers down Kieras' spine), Mathis found her work as a serving girl for Hesketh. She had no experience, and Hesketh's tavern had operated well without any such help, but it was something to do and Hesketh didn't seem to mind. She was mostly paid in food and drink, but it wasn't a bad arrangement.

She wasn't exactly thrilled with her lodging, however. Torkki had only paid for her room at Ziani's inn for three days. Since then, she'd been living in a spare room in Mathis' house. The room gave her little space outside of her bed, though she supposed beggars (which she had to admit that, currently, she was) could not be choosers. There was little more privacy than a small curtain, however, which Torkki had no compunction about moving aside without warning if he wanted to talk with her (though Mathis at least had the courtesy to warn her he was coming through). The constant presence of two men and zero privacy made her very self-conscious. She barely ever transformed into her fox form any more. It was too much of a hassle making sure she was safe from curious male eyes before she turned human once again.

Not transforming was helping her, however. Everyone might know she was interested in kitsune, by now, but with no local fox sightings no-one suspected she was one. At least, not yet – she hoped it never came out.

On this day, she was out delivering meals for Hesketh to the workers building the town's new wall. The just arrived Elite Brigade soldiers were temporarily billeted to Ziani's Inn. The inn's staff had been employed to look after the soldiers. Those soldiers had little use for a chambermaid's normal services, however, so Ziani volunteered to help Kieras out. It was not a purely altruistic move. While Kieras knew that Ziani was genuinely her friend, the younger girl made a point of scheduling their meeting times to "coincidentally" be when she was most likely to meet up with Torkki. Their last stop for the deliveries would be in Ekholm's future gatehouse, which was currently just a few temporary wooden walls and a roof built over a more permanent foundation. It was currently serving as the headquarters for both the newly arrived Elite Guard and the engineers designing the wall, which meant Torkki was often present to handle many of his duties.

Ziani and Kieras were chatting amiably as they walked together, talking about a new jeweler who had just opened up a shop near Ziani's inn. Kieras was generally uninterested in the baubles and trinkets most jewelers would make for ladies in Ekholm, but that didn't mean she had no interest in the art at all. Her mother's choker was a beautiful item, of course, but was hardly the only piece of jewelry she owned. Her chatelaine was an especially fine example of a jeweler's craft, as were each of the attachments on it.

"Well, I know it's unusual to have a chatelaine that doesn't include many sewing tools," Kieras was saying. "I've got a pair of scissors and a tape measure, of course, because those are useful even to me, but... while I know how to sew, I've never needed to. Sewing needles, thimbles, and the like just don't seem necessary to me."

"You might want to consider asking the new jeweler to find some, though," Ziani said. "Just for appearance's sake, if no other reason. You do want to fit in, right? It's strange for a girl to be carrying a chatelaine that has no—"

"What is that?" Kieras asked, pointing over at a procession of a few dozen people in strange robes. The man in front of the procession was arguing with a carpenter working on the temporary wooden walls as well as one of the construction foremen overseeing the digging of the foundation for the permanent stone walls.

Ziani looked over and sighed, rolling her eyes. "Oh, that's his 'eminence,' the reigning Archon of Ekholm, Kuralt the Great. Just about everyone calls him Kuralt the Extortionist when he's out of earshot, however."

The shouting picked up enough so that the two girls could hear a few distinct words. Kieras made out an angry shout of "Blacksmiths!" as well as some sort of question about Torkki, to which the foreman pointed to the temporary headquarters building. Suddenly, Kieras had a very strong feeling she needed to be in that building before Kuralt was. Kuralt continued arguing with the foreman, but it was clear that it would only be a matter of time before he stormed the meeting going on inside.

"Ziani... I hate to leave you in the middle of the rounds, but I need to go."

Ziani glanced at her friend, grinned, and nodded. "I feel like seeing Torkki, myself. How about we both head over there? We can just reverse the order of our deliveries and start with headquarters first. Kuralt certainly won't know the difference."

Kieras grinned fiercely. "Nor will he question the presence of a couple serving girls... which will be a pretty big mistake on his part."

Mathis, despite distancing himself from most of his brother's defense plans, found himself at one of the daily war councils, for a change. He felt needed at this one, to his surprise, as they were trying to decide what to do about including archer's slots and platforms in and along the wall, and he could provide his skill as an expert marksman to decide which of the usable designs would provide skilled archers like himself the best view of any attackers while still leaving them at least partially protected.

The wall had undergone significant design changes. Many plans that had already been started were just tossed out by Dubnyk, who was almost panicking from the time crunch. The wooden walls had originally been intended to provide just a temporary defense, but now they would become the structure for things such as archer's platforms and walkways between various sections of the wall, as well as the interiors for the gatehouse and the four planned towers. As temporary constructs, the gatehouses and towers – which had already been half-built by the time the plans were revised – would be retained, but now the plans to integrate them into the final design had been changed. Any 'temporary' wooden structures would be sheathed in stone on the outside, while on the inside the wood would only gradually removed and replaced with more durable materials, such as the clay bricks Ekholm manufactured, in a process that would take many years longer than the Knodelian conflict was expected to last.

When the topic of defenses across the river was brought up, Mathis had suggested an archer's tower be built there as well. The original plans only accounted for some makeshift wooden spikes that were already near completion by the time Dubnyk had arrived. This would give a small selection of people stationed on that side of the bridge time to destroy it, if the enemy chose to attempt that particular outflanking maneuver.

Mathis was told that there weren't enough archers in Ekholm to man both the wall and any proposed archer's tower. It would come down to a choice of one or the other, and sacrificing the bridge's protection (and thereby the bridge itself) seemed to make a lot more sense than failing to provide for the core defense of the town. Mathis' idea tabled (for now – he intended to bring it up again), the council moved on to discussing other things – the protection of supply lines, construction of shelters, and more revisions to the plans for the wall.

There were no doors in any of the new buildings yet, merely curtains hung over doorways to dampen noises both outside and in. People could go in and out of the room without disturbing any of the ongoing discussions. Mathis' attention had momentarily wandered when they stopped talking about his area of expertise, so – without the supplies needed to indulge in his habitual *dorodango* making – his attention wandered around the room, people watching. That was probably why Mathis was the first person to notice when Kieras and Ziani entered the room, carrying food and drink. It surprised him a little to see them – they were early in their lunch delivery – but he still wouldn't have thought anything about it if he hadn't seen Ziani's face. Kieras was pasting a pleasant smile on her face – one which, looking closely, Mathis could tell was fake – but Ziani was clearly agitated and rather spectacularly failing to hide it. The two girls separated, Ziani heading for Torkki and Kieras heading for him.

Kieras bent over to whisper in his ear as she served him some food. "Kuralt has returned and will be here any moment."

Mathis didn't have a chance to ask her why she was telling him this, or even how she knew who Kuralt was, before she had moved on. Most people she just served their lunches to, but there were a few to whom she would whisper something to before moving on. Opposite Kieras, Ziani repeated her actions. Mathis made a note of exactly who the two girls were talking to – himself, Torkki, their uncle Savard, Hesketh, Kordic, Radek, Adamek... in other words, might be expected to challenge Kuralt.

Mathis started to wonder just what he should – or even could – do with that information. Torkki seemed to have some idea – Mathis could see him loosening his blade just slightly, ready to draw his sword in a moment's notice, but not committing himself to doing so. Hesketh started watching the doorways. Savard closed his eyes and took in a deep breath, bracing himself against the rough table he was sitting behind. Mathis, however, had no clue what Kuralt's presence would mean after the recent developments.

Kuralt had, for the past couple of years, been ruthlessly trying to make himself into a dictator and not just an Archon. He'd done so largely through intimidation, but still following the strictest letter of the law despite his complete disregard for customs which supported it. He certainly couldn't have any objection to the wall, not in the face of the Knodelian threat.

There was the possibility that Kuralt might try harassing the newly arrived blacksmiths. As long as they were in town, it wasn't likely Kuralt would retain his position. The election for Archon would take place when the council vote was taken in two weeks, regardless of what plans Kuralt made. If there was anything legal to prevent those blacksmiths from staying in Ekholm for the next year or so, Mathis couldn't think of it, but that was the only avenue Kuralt still had to win the election. What more could Kuralt do, short of sacrificing the support of the Norre Hegemony? That would be suicide, in light of the Knodelian threat.

Mathis was startled when Kuralt stormed through the curtain-covered doorway into the room. Thanks to a piece of ornamentation on his boots snagging the thick boiled wool of those curtains in a rather awkward way, down they came in dramatic fashion. Everyone stopped what they were doing to stare at the newcomer. Ziani was once again behind Torkki, and Kieras was in the corner of the room with the messenger boys.

Not only is his presence neither needed nor wanted, Mathis thought, but *his entrance is completely undignified. Why do we have to put up with this power-hungry, arrogant, would-be petty tyrant?*

"Ah, Archon Kuralt," Savard said, appearing totally unflapped. "How good of you to finally join us. How was your pilgrimage?"

"I found what I was looking for, of course," Kuralt said curtly. "But I did not expect to come back and find all of this going on. Tell me, what has happened to Regent Cizikas?"

"The laws do not require us to respect his orders nor to involve him in these meetings, despite your absence. It was only custom which dictated we do so, and as you pointed out when you were re-elected as Archon, 'Custom is not law,'" Savard said coolly. "So, the council voted to ignore his decisions in your absence, and instead to act as current events demand."

"My full authority was given to Cizikas," Kuralt snapped. "The council—"

"Archon Kuralt," Savard interrupted, sounding as if he were scolding a child. "You would probably be surprised to learn that I agree with you on many issues. You wish to restructure the government in a way that would allow you to appoint regents when you are absent, and to follow more closely the tenets that our forefathers in Eskesa built their nation upon. I wholeheartedly agree the government needs to be restructured. When the council was first established, we relied on tradition to maintain order in a small displaced township of a few hundred people. Ekholm has grown, and hoping that mere tradition can effectively govern several thousands of people is a pipe dream."

"What—" Kuralt began.

"However," Savard continued, now locking his eyes with Kuralt's. "You seem to wish to reform the government not to deal with the issues we have as a growing city-state, but rather to strengthen your own power and to fashion yourself into something of a dictator." He gestured to the three new master blacksmiths. "Thanks to the generosity of the Norre Hegemony, we now have removed the leverage you were holding over the council. The government has already been reformed, as you wanted, but you are not in our plans."

"I don't—"

Savard refused to let Kuralt get a word in. "The old council will meet for one last time in two weeks. During that session, whatever transitional needs between the old government and the new government will be satisfied. After that, your time as Archon will end. When that session is over, Ekholm will transform itself from the last surviving remnant of the fallen City-State of Eskesa into the new Republic of Ekholm, with a codified government that will not be made slave to tradition, nor to those who selectively use tradition to strengthen their own power. A new set of laws has been drafted, a new interim Archon has already been voted into power for the transition, and a new Senate is being appointed. If you respect the new laws and behave yourself properly, you can probably remain a voice in the government and receive a new seat on the Senate. In a few years, you might even be able to regain the title of Archon." He paused. "I wouldn't count on that last bit happening, however."

Kuralt closed his eyes, taking in a deep breath. "How long is this 'interim' Archon in power for?"

"Two years," Savard said. "As will be the length of term for every Archon succeeding him. In the future, Archons may serve several consecutive terms, although they will need the support of at least two thirds of the Senate in order to retain power past the first term. As I said, Archon Kuralt, there are many things I agree with you about – among them, that an Archon really needs more than one year in power in order to get anything of significance done."

"And who," Kuralt said, his eyes still shut, "has been appointed this 'interim Archon?'"

"The departing council had many recommendations," Savard said. "Some wished the past Archon, Abney, returned to power. Others felt, with the advent of war upon us, an experienced military man such as Hesketh was needed for the job. A few people, some of whom were even against you during your last run for the position, felt that you would make a fine candidate, provided your power was limited by the code of laws we had enacted."

"I am a 'fine Archon' without them," Kuralt insisted.

"In the end, however," Savard continued. "The council elected me to serve in the position."

"I see," Kuralt said, finally opening his eyes and locking them on Savard. "Then you are the usurper behind this treason."

Kuralt did not travel around unarmed, but for all practical purposes he might as well have. He wore a sword that was more ceremonial than functional, and even if it had been forged to survive a duel he had no skill with it. Still, even if he rarely did much work since becoming Archon, Kuralt was a mountain of a man, with muscles on top of muscles from working long hours as a blacksmith.

He didn't need a weapon to be a lethal fighting force. Swords proved useless as Kuralt picked Torkki up despite a quickly drawn blade, tossing him into the trio of blacksmiths from Norre and toppling all four of them.

There was still a table between the two Archons, but it proved to be no barrier as Kuralt reached across it and yanked Savard from his chair, pulling him over said table and holding him dangling in the air. Kuralt glared into Savard's eyes, insanity clear in his gaze, but Savard stayed firm and unflinching as he awaited Kuralt's next move. Savard was no fighter, but he was also no coward, as Mathis knew well.

Kuralt growled. "As 'tradition' as well as 'law' states, the penalty for treason is *death!*"

Mathis never found out just how Kuralt intended to exact his declared punishment, as before he had a chance to do any more a large clay decanter flew into the side of his head. The piece of pottery bounced off, merely staggering the large blacksmith, but it did distract him for a moment as he glared over in the direction of the projectile – an ashen-faced Ziani, terrified of what Kuralt might do but already reaching for a tankard to add to her assault.

"Are even the serving girls traitors, now?" Kuralt's voice cracked. "Everyone – all the people in this building, from the Councilmen to the maids delivering the food – are to be executed, even if I must do it myself!"

Just who he thought he was talking to was not clear, but Kuralt seemed to grow even more upset when he realized that Savard had managed to free himself and crawl away in the distraction. He stepped over to the nearest person – Dubnyk, the head of the team of engineers from Norre – and grabbed him in Savard's place. With a sickening crack, Kuralt broke Dubnyk's neck with his bare hands, then tossed him to the ground.

By that point Torkki was back on his feet, his sword recovered and now held at the ready. Standing as he was, he provided protection for Mathis, Savard, and all three blacksmiths, causing Kuralt to hesitate before advancing in that direction. Instead, he turned his attention to the serving girl who had thrown a pot at him. He jumped onto the table Ziani was hiding behind, knocking aside the tankard she tossed his way. He reached down to pick her up, presumably to do to her what he had done to Dubnyk, but that was as far as he got.

A simple backhand sent Kuralt flying from the table, and within seconds Kieras had leapt onto the tabletop with vulpine grace to stand over him, just as he had been standing over Ziani. In one hand she clenched her *hoshi no tama*, the opaque jewel faintly glowing as she filtered her magical energies through it.

"I don't usually like killing things I'm not planning to eat," she snarled, a little bit of her vixen-like nature shining through. Mathis wondered if she knew just how much of it she was revealing in both her actions and her voice. "But I'm willing to make an exception in your case."

Kuralt stared at her in confusion. "I don't even know you." He slowly got back to his feet, looking around the room. "I don't understand. You all voted me in to the office of Archon. You wanted me as your leader. Why do you all now betray me? Is it the influence of you outsiders from Norre? Are *you* trying to usurp my throne?"

"The leaders in Norre don't care who leads Ekholm," Savard said hoarsely, struggling to breathe normally. "The council first voted for you to be Archon because of your promises to make changes, to make us great again. Most of them didn't understand, then, that your idea of 'change' was to turn the role of Archon into that of a petty despot. No-one wanted there to be a 'throne' in Ekholm at all, much less to put you on it. You chose to rule over this country as if you were given free rein to enact laws at your whim, and to punish those who opposed you as if they were criminals or outlaws. By the time the next vote rolled around people knew who you were and what you were doing. They wanted to vote you out, but you used blacklists and bully tactics to keep all but the most courageous councilmen from voting against you. But if you really feel that the way you have been leading us would bring anything more than rebellion and distrust, you are not just the power-hungry idiot I thought you were – you are a sad, deranged man who is living in a world that exists only in his own mind."

Kuralt seemed to digest that for a long moment before nodding slowly. "Yes... yes, I see. I see I was right. It must have been the influence of these outsiders! It must have been! Yes!" He then drew his worthless sword, spinning to face Kieras. "This must be your fault!" he screamed.

His wild but powerful sword swing was casually blocked, however, by her bare hand. Or rather, the fingernails on her hand – which seemed to have grown a couple inches in length, becoming thicker and more claw-like as they grew. Mathis recalled, from his mother's lessons, that the claws or fingernails of a kitsune could be made harder and sharper than a set of steel blades. Kieras' reflexes must have been hardened and sharpened, as well, because Mathis knew of no human who could have moved quickly enough and precisely enough to block that swing.

With the flick of one finger, the ceremonial Sword of the Archon, a blade Kuralt himself had created to represent his office, was torn into two pieces. She reached over and plucked the remains of the sword from Kuralt's hand, and proceeded to shred it like a cat at a scratching post.

"I am stronger, faster, and smarter than you, and I possess magic of a sort you probably have never encountered in your life," Kieras said. "I can create illusions that either cloud men's minds or grant them clarity of thought. I swear, though, that I have not used them on these people to direct them against you. Your insane fear that I am the sole reason these people are rebelling against you are the mere ravings of a lunatic, at best, but even if they were true... what do you think you can do to stop me?"

Kuralt was trapped in her eyes for a long moment before he broke into tears.

"I have to wonder why my two favorite nephews didn't tell me that there was a foreign kitsune in our midst until now," Savard sighed, glancing Kieras up and down thoughtfully. The headquarters had been cleared following Kuralt's rampage, and Kuralt had been taken to the local jail. There were some suggestions he should be transported to Norre, as they couldn't arrange the proper trial in Ekholm until after the Knodelians had been dealt with, but it was decided that discussion would be tabled for later.

Once those more demanding issues were dealt with, the brothers brought Kieras to their uncle to explain her presence. She wasn't entirely comfortable with the examination, and she was still unsure just why she had acted the way she did when Ziani was threatened. True, the girl was her friend, but there had to have been ways for her to protect the human without revealing herself so definitively.

"Well, now that you know her story," Torkki said, "I would hope you would understand why we felt that it was a secret worth keeping."

"I'm not denying that," Savard said. "I just would have expected you to trust me with that secret, since you seem quite willing to trust me with governing our home and country."

"Knowing international politics as well as I do," Torkki said, "I figured that our presumptive head of state might be better off not knowing, should representatives of the Kassian Empire show up asking for information... even if I would normally have trusted the man who is that head of state with such a secret."

Savard rolled his eyes, though a slight smile betrayed his amusement. "Yes, yes, I understand. Well, now that the cat – or rather the fox – is out of the bag, I suppose we need to decide what to do with her."

"Can't we just keep my presence a secret?" Kieras asked hesitantly. "If word reaches Kassia that I'm here, I will have to leave town."

"I'm afraid that's not really practical any longer," Savard said. "We might be able to get the council to keep quiet, but Kuralt knows what you are. Though he'll surely hang for today's events, he may denounce you on the way to the gallows. Not to mention I doubt the messenger boys who were present can be trusted with such a secret, considering how fascinating a story it is."

"Then... perhaps it really is time for me to move on," Kieras said hesitantly. She didn't really want to go. While she knew she needed to start the search for her mother at some point, she was hoping she might be able to pass some time in Ekholm, fulfilling her father's request that she place herself in a human's service for a year.

She had been even further impressed by Torkki's actions and bravery during Kuralt's rampage. True, Torkki had been tossed around like a rag-doll, and his effort weren't enough to save that Norrish engineer – Dubnyk – but he had rolled with the punches, got back on his feet, and moved to defend half the people in the room after his early difficulties.

"Now why would that be?" Savard asked. "Don't get me wrong. If you wish to leave, that is perfectly fine... but there is no reason for you to go now. Considering how you just saved the lives of many important people, including my own, it would be rather impolite of us to make you leave."

"What do you mean?" Kieras said. "If agents of the Kassian Empire arrive, they will almost certainly find out that I'm staying here. I am not ready to return home, so I have to leave."

"They will know that you're here?" Savard said. "How, exactly, would they know that?"

"If you want to say you'll lie to protect me, well, I appreciate the gesture," Kieras scoffed, not thinking for one second it would do any good. "However, the moment they ask around town, and they will, they'll know I've been here."

"Who says I'd lie?" Savard said. "If they come asking if we have been visited by a kitsune, of course I'll tell them that we have."

"What? But—"

"Ekholm has been visited by many kitsune throughout its existence," Savard continued, cutting her off. "They come and go at a whim. However, since most of the kitsune we've seen have been of the rather distinctive myobu variety, I doubt that any of those we have seen are the one they're looking for."

"Which means uncle Savard will tell them the whole truth, and they still won't know anything," Torkki said, grinning.

"Perhaps not the whole truth," Savard said. "And, to be honest, it would be better if you really did 'come and go at a whim,' I suspect. But if you wish to make yourself a home here, we could easily accommodate you."

"I need to look for my mother," Kieras said uncertainly.

"We get a lot of traders and travelers in this town," Savard said. "Some of them might be able to point you in the right direction. And it is not a lie that there are a lot of myobu kitsune in the area who are known to occasionally visit this area, one of whom may know of or even *be* your mother. At the very least, it is good to have a rally point when you're searching for someone, and Ekholm can be that for you. Like I said, it might be a good idea for you to 'go out at a whim' on occasion, but having a place to rest and resupply will make your search much easier. Also, there are certain trade missions we need to send out in the near future. If you were to decide, 'on a whim,' to accompany our ambassadors, you could search through most of the Norre Hegemony with the aid of a number of our townsfolk as guides. Kitsune are plentiful in most of the areas we wish to send these missions."

Kieras noticed that the two brothers seemed a bit surprised at this offer as well. "And just who would these ambassadors be, and why would they want her along?" Torkki asked before she could say anything to either accept or reject it.

"Well, for the first mission, I believe Mathis would be a good choice," Savard laughed. "After all, who better to announce the election of a new Archon than one of the Archon's nephews? As to why we would want her with us... well, a friendly kitsune is always an asset, but trying to tell them what to do will only cause trouble. If she chooses to help us, in whatever way she chooses, that is her prerogative. But certainly she will try nothing to hinder us while we are helping her, now, will she?" This last bit was said as he eyed her carefully.

Kieras laughed. "I think that's a fairly safe thing to promise." Despite her good humor, however, she felt through her magic that she had, in fact, just made a binding promise. While hardly the year-long servitude her father had suggested, she would not be able to intentionally hinder any of their ambassadorial missions. Not that she had planned to, in the first place. She only wished she would be accompanying Torkki and not Mathis.

"But before we launch this diplomatic mission, we have something else to discuss," Savard said, his voice sobering. "Kuralt killed Dubnyk. Now that our wall's engineer is dead, do we have to wait for Norre to replace him?"

"Dubnyk's plans have survived," Torkki said. "And Laing, the engineer making the initial surveys of each town's defenses, will be returning to Ekholm before too long, so he can take over if necessary. It shouldn't be necessary, however – Dubnyk's assistant, Donati, has all of the skills of a master engineer in his own right, he merely lacks experience. He can be trusted to interpret Dubnyk's plans adequately. He may even be more innovative. He will—" Torkki paused, reconsidering his words. He sounded much less certain than Kieras suspected he would like to be as he finished. "*Hopefully*, he will be up to the task."

"He'd better be." Savard frowned. "Dubnyk requested many supplies, and some will need to be imported at a significant expense. Donati had better know how to use them all. Those supplies are why I'm sending you out on these missions, after all."

Mathis frowned. "What am I supposed to be trying to get for us?"

Savard pulled a paper off of his desk. "First off are the products needed to produce mortar. We can get plenty of sand and water from the river and lime from our quarries, but he wanted us to use, quoting from his request, now, 'a mixture of lime and the volcanic ash known as pozzolana, rather than just lime alone, as the binding agent.' We should be able to purchase this volcanic ash from the relatively nearby city of Dahlberg. Unfortunately, Dahlberg is not a member of the Norre Hegemony, so we're probably going to have to make a less-than-favorable deal to get it. We need it pretty quickly, I understand – the trench for our wall's foundation will be complete in two weeks time, at most, and we'll need to start mixing up the mortar once that is done. Torkki, you'd better give him whatever support you can – that won't be an easy first task."

Mathis glanced at Kieras, then took her by the elbow to escort her from the room. "Well, then, I guess I'd better start packing. And if you're joining me, you'd better pack, too."

V. A Fire in the City of Ash

Mathis was a little surprised by the size of the expedition accompanying him to Dahlberg. Torkki's lieutenant, Jobinh, joined them, leading an armed honor-guard of four young but experienced pikemen of the Norre Elite Brigade – Boedker, Eakin, Jarmon, and Prusek. Donati would also be with them to inspect the ash that was being purchased, and there was a parcel of drivers with empty wagons into which the ash they hoped to purchase could be loaded. And Kieras would be accompanying them 'on a whim,' of course.

While it was never explicitly stated, Mathis knew that Kieras' safety – and her conduct – would primarily be his responsibility. For that reason, he had decided it was his duty to inspect her belongings and make sure that she was taking everything she needed. That inspection didn't take very long, however.

"What do you mean, you aren't packing anything?" Mathis asked after taking a deep breath to steady himself.

"Well, nothing except some food and water for the journey," Kieras said. "I don't need anything else."

"Nothing?" Mathis replied dubiously. "Not even, say, a change of clothes?"

"I'm a kitsune," Kieras said, as if that explained everything. "The only clothes I have are the ones you and your brother bought for me, and those aren't exactly good for travel."

Mathis nodded slowly, feeling slightly embarrassed for not having realized that before. "Yes, you create the illusion of clothing when you need it. But... well, we're going to be traveling to some places with... unusual weather conditions. Are you sure you don't want to bring an outfit to wear in the rain, or the snow, or... well, you get the idea."

Kieras laughed. "My illusions are good enough even to provide protection from the weather, as long as I am in otherwise good health. I could even make some for you that you could wear, though without direct contact to my magical powers they would eventually dissolve."

"Then... do you really intend to bring nothing with you but a bag of food and some acorns?" Mathis asked.

"Well, a bag of food and the couple things I wear on me," Kieras replied. "My choker, coin purse, and my chatelaine are certainly not illusions."

"I knew the choker wasn't." Mathis glanced at the piece of jewelry in question. To anyone familiar with kitsune lore, that was one of the clearest pieces of evidence that she was one, although he hadn't seen her use it properly in the entire time he'd known her.

Kieras reached up and felt the choker, glancing over at Mathis in surprise. She started to say something, but seemed to reconsider it. "Well, no, of course not. It was my mother's. I intend to use it to prove my identity when I find her."

Mathis nodded. "But since your illusory powers will be so important, why are you not carrying your *hoshi no tama?*"

"But I am," Kieras said. "It's on my chatelaine."

Mathis glanced at the chatelaine in question attached to her belt, and saw there was, indeed, a small filigreed silver container large enough to carry the *tama* attached to it. "Well, that works, I suppose. Are you ready to be on your way, then?"

Kieras looked around, gesturing at the highly disorganized troop of wagon drivers assembling for the journey. "I'm more ready than they are, at least."

The journey to Dahlberg had not been pleasant for anyone. The dirt pathway connecting the Orrpars Road to the mountain pass it bordered had been inundated with heavy rains, making wagon transport slow and difficult. The need to complete this trade mission as soon as possible made stops for the purpose of bathing or equipment maintenance a luxury they rarely could afford, and when they could stop they lacked the bathwater and supplies needed for either activity. To top things off, the population of Dahlberg were not quite what Kieras was expecting.

"W-what *are* they?" she shrieked, shrinking back when she first spotted a small group of Dahlberg's citizenry working fields outside of the city shortly before they arrived.

Mathis glanced over at her, raising an eyebrow. "You've never seen wulvers before? They're fairly common, though I do admit they usually keep to themselves."

The very notion of a creature like a wulver existing would be a shock to the system of any kitsune, especially one as sheltered as Kieras had been most of her life. Extremely muscular, eight foot tall human-like beings with the heads of wolves would be intimidating to anybody, but for a creature with the instinctive fear of dogs and wolves like her they were downright terrifying. "Seen them?" she said, her voice trembling. "I've never heard of anything like them. And I probably wouldn't have come on this trip if I'd known about this!"

Mathis cocked his head, studying her carefully. "Are you really that scared? How strange. Wulvers have typically gotten along well with kitsune, or so I've read. I know you are supposed to be afraid of dogs and wolves, but wulvers are a different being altogether despite their appearance."

"Tell that to the little part of my brain screaming at me to run away," she grumbled sardonically. "All right, if I'm going to be in their company for a while, I'd like to at least know a little bit about them."

Mathis chuckled briefly. "Well, I only know what the books say, both about wulvers and their relationship to kitsune. They are an ancient race of beings, said to be even stronger than their appearance would have you believe. Despite how dangerous they look, they are an inherently gentle people, but when angered can be just as dangerous as they appear to be. They tend to live either in tight communities or they wander isolated and alone, and tend to shy away from the rest of the world regardless. Their forefathers were simple fishermen, forced to flee their island home when a volcano erupted and destroyed it." He frowned. "For some reason my books did not explain, the survivors resettled around volcanoes once again, whether they went to islands like their original homeland or miles inland here on the continent."

"That might be why I've never heard of them in Kassia, then," Kieras mused. "We have no volcanoes in Kassia."

Mathis shrugged. "They may be in Kassia and you just didn't know about it. They rarely venture far from their homes, so unless they were living in your home castle you would never know they were there. Their cities are very heavily populated for their size, but they rarely have any settlements outside of them. Even these farms we're seeing are unusually far from their city for a wulver community, and we're only an hour's walk from the gates."

Kieras nodded slowly. "All right, but where does their relationship with kitsune fit into the picture?"

"Again, all I can go by is what I've read," Mathis said. "The city-state of Norre was founded shortly after the destruction of the wulver's original homeland, through an alliance of humans, kitsune, and wulvers. Once the surrounding threats had been dealt with, however, the allied races went their separate ways. Wulvers and humans are rarely seen together nowadays, but the same can't be said of wulvers and kitsune. Wulvers and kitsune have often been seen together around the myobu shrines to Inari, those few times a human has found one. They have been known to help in the construction and care of those buildings, from what I've read."

That threw Kieras for a loop. She had not understood it, but she knew how the magical draw to Inari affected her mother's breed. She could feel it, herself, even if she was able to resist it far easier than any full-blooded myobu kitsune ever would. She instinctively knew that it wasn't likely that any myobu would allow anything to care for a shrine dedicated to Inari unless they trusted them implicitly.

"Considering their wolf-like appearance," Kieras said carefully. "I find that quite remarkable."

"As do I, to be honest," Mathis admitted. "But if there is even a drop of truth in what I have read, I would say that shows how highly your people think of them."

"Then I might actually learn something useful in this journey, after all," Kieras said, though she was still uncomfortable with the idea of dealing with these people. "I don't know anything about Inari shrines other than some myobu make them their homes, but an Inari shrines must be near Ekholm, if the number of times my people have been seen is to be believed. Perhaps these wulvers know."

"Those locations are rarely revealed to humans," Mathis said. "I doubt they would trust any creature who would give up those secrets lightly, even to another kitsune. Still, it could be worth the effort to ask. Just remember not to push it too far – I'd rather you not be arrested as a spy while we're here."

Kieras stiffened. "I have promised not to hinder your negotiations. I am a creature of my word."

"I know you have promised, and I believe you will try and hold to that promise," Mathis said. "I also know you are a kitsune. It is not always in your nature to understand human interaction, much less wulver interaction, and before today you had never even heard of wulvers, much less learned to deal with them. Does ensuring that you understand how to do what you have promised count as an offense against your honor as a kitsune?"

Kieras gritted her teeth, but knew he was right. Nevertheless, the implication that she was not trustworthy stung.

"No more so than your lack of action when Kuralt attacked brands you as a coward," she snapped. She knew the attack was unfair of her, but it had been on her mind since the incident. Savard had refused to back down, even when clenched in the fist of a madman. Ziani was but a slip of a girl, but she had the courage to challenge said madman wielding little more than a clay pot. Torkki, ever the professional soldier, was quick to act and quick to recover. Mathis, however, had disappointed. He failed to prepare himself despite being warned and failed to act when the need arose. There was no real cause to call him a coward just from his inaction, but the accusation was just as fitting as his accusation that she might embarrass his people.

Mathis immediately froze, allowing her to continue down alone with the carts and drivers. She only went so far, however, before looking back to see him staring at a patch of ground, shaking his head. Kieras flushed slightly, wondering if she had gone too far in her insult. They had been getting along quite nicely, and he had been a fount of knowledge for her since the day she'd first stepped in Ekholm. Perhaps he wasn't worthy of her service, like she felt Torkki might be, but neither had he earned her scorn. She turned around and went back to him.

"I'm sorry. That was uncalled for, on my part."

"No," Mathis sighed, looking back up at her. "I needed someone to say it to my face. I've been thinking the same thing, going over the incident again and again, and I am left with one inescapable conclusion: When the situation called for me to act, I did nothing." He paused. "I don't think I'm a coward, and I'm still unsure what I should have done in that situation, but I can't trust myself to act courageously when the situation calls for it. Yet more proof that I was never meant to be a soldier as my brother was."

Kieras wasn't about to argue with him on that point, but she recognized just how painful that was for him to admit.

"Just like I should not trust myself to deal with the wulvers as diplomatically as you might want me to," she said, unable to meet his eyes. "I am still sorry. And you are right – I promised not to cause problems on this journey, but it seems, through my ignorance and temper, that I have already caused one."

Mathis smiled sadly, and turned to look her in the eyes. "Not really. You only said what needed to be said." He paused, then started walking quickly in an effort to retake the lead in front of the carts. "So, was there anything else you wanted to know about wulvers?"

Kieras recognized an attempt to change the subject when she saw one, and decided to play along. "Well, maybe," she began in a wry, lilting voice. "Is there anything they're particularly known for other than fishing and unusually poor judgment in choosing their homeland?"

"Not particularly," Mathis said. "At least, nothing about wulvers in general. Dahlberg is known for a few things, however. I've never been here, myself, but we often trade raw goods with them. They import almost no wine of any kind, but they import more beer than Ekholm can produce alone. We even buy from several of the Norre Hegemony's city-states to sell their beer to Dahlberg, at a substantial profit, and even that is barely enough to keep up with their demand. That's about *all* that we manufacture that they seem willing to purchase in any quantity, though. They primarily export gemstones and charcoal in addition to the volcanic ash we're going to try and purchase from them."

"Gemstones?" Kieras mused. "They must be fairly wealthy, then."

"Not in coinage, as far as I know," Mathis said. "Most of our dealings with them involve trading goods for goods, rarely with any exchange of money whatsoever. They do *use* money – I've seen Dahlberg minted coins on occasion – but they don't seem to want our money."

Kieras was about to ask another question when several of the objects of her curiosity emerged from the trees in front of them. "Halt!"

barked the leader.

The wulvers were heavily armed and armored. Kieras was unfamiliar with many of the weapons they wielded. Their leader's impressive array of sheaths held what appeared to be a hand axe, a short sword, a long sword, and something which resembled a short-handled farming sickle with a long chain extending from the handle. His companions likewise carried swords and axes, but also each wore a series of thick wire or thin chains with heavy iron balls at the ends on their belts. At the ready – but not in any threatening stance – they all held a form of polearm that Kieras had never seen before, with a sharp hook at the end instead of a spearpoint or blade. Overall, their appearance and body language communicated two things more clearly than any words: That their challenge to the Ekholm contingent was more formal than hostile, and that they were a force to be reckoned with if they decided to become hostile. Their wolf-like heads, some of which were trembling slightly in growls, made Kieras quite uncomfortable.

Mathis stepped forward, and while he appeared confident in stance and demeanor, his eyes swept around them uncertainly. "Greetings, honored warriors of Dahlberg. My companions and I desire entrance to your city in order to discuss a matter of diplomacy and trade."

The wulver leader surveyed the long wagon train before responding. "Your company seems overlarge for an expedition bearing no obvious goods. I find this peculiar."

Mathis nodded. "I bring a letter authorizing me to bargain on behalf of the Norre Hegemony. I can promise to deliver the trade goods of any Norre Hegemony state in return for what I seek."

"Amazing," the wulver said, lips curling to reveal his teeth in an intimidating snarl. Kieras shrank back, eyes widening, but managed to hold her ground without running away despite all of her instincts demanding she do so. "And what is it you require such bargaining power to purchase from us? Jewels, perhaps? Rubies, diamonds, sapphires? Or some other pretty but worthless bauble you humans seem to place such great value on?"

"All we seek is some of your volcanic ash," Mathis said.

The wulver shook his head as if to clear it, and then glared at Mathis. After a brief pause, he yipped and his tongue started wagging through a wide open mouth. It took a moment for Kieras to realize this was his way of laughing, and to her wonder she found herself relaxing as he did.

"How very interesting," the wulver said finally. His men lowered their polearms as he gave a cordial bow. "I am Captain Mrazek of the Dahlberg Guard. Come. I will guide you into the city."

There wasn't much time for Mathis to glance around at the wonders of Dahlberg before he found himself hurriedly escorted into the Royal Court, accompanied by Mrazek, Kieras, Donati, Jobinh, and his four Norre Elite honor guardsmen. They were 'asked' to leave most of their weapons outside of the doors, but not all of them. As a courtesy, Mathis was allowed – and expected – to retain an honor blade, which caused some problems.

He carried no sword. He couldn't wield one effectively, and so hadn't seen the need, but the requirement to carry an honor blade left him in an awkward position until Jobinh lent his spatha to the cause. It was a rather nondescript weapon for an honor blade, manufactured on a simple design dating back to the heyday of the nameless ancient city upon whose ruins Norre had been built, and was intended for function and not ornamentation. Lacking any alternative, however, Mathis decided it would serve.

"On behalf of my people, I offer you hospitality and greetings," the Dahlberg monarch said, flanked on either side by soldiers armed much like Mrazek had been. His throne had dark, flickering flames burning on either side – an effect Mathis found rather sinister.

Mathis sketched a bow, holding the hilt of his newly acquired honor blade out to the wulver as Mrazek had instructed him. Protocol was something few in Ekholm bothered to study and Mathis was no exception. He had no idea if he was being formal enough, but as Ekholm's representative he was determined to try and behave properly. He had even spent time on the trip memorizing a formal greeting that, in the heat of the moment, he was having trouble remembering.

"T-thank you, King Skygger. We, uh... oh, right! We, the representatives of Ekholm and the Norre Hegemony, graciously accept your hospitality," he recited awkwardly.

"Bah!" the wulver barked. "Titles such as 'king' are a human affectation. I am the Alpha of all Alphas in Dahlberg, which perhaps makes me the equivalent of your 'kings,' but my name is Skygger. Address me as such. Now, I understand from my loyal guardsman that you are interested in purchasing some volcanic ash. It is quite peculiar for an expedition of this size to arrive here seeking little more than a slightly less common variety of dirt. May I ask what it is you need it for?"

Mathis took a deep breath. He had to tell the truth. Wulvers could literally smell it when someone was lying to them, and that could prove disastrous in these negotiations. He had no idea how they would react to Ekholm preparing itself for a war, however, even if that war had nothing to do with Dahlberg or any wulvers.

In the end, he decided on a long, truthful, but incomplete explanation. "Since the fall of Eskesa, Ekholm's government was initially set up to govern a few hundred people belonging to a half-dozen clans. However, it has grown exponentially in recent years, necessitating a change in government. We have now formed ourselves into a proper republic, with a written code of laws, a new Senate, and a new ruling Archon. In an effort to make it clearer to others that we are truly an independent nation and no longer just the last outpost of a dead empire, we are going to build walls around our city. We need this volcanic ash as a component of the mortar we intend to build our walls with."

Skygger cocked his head at Mathis. "Curious. I can tell you are not lying, but your explanation begs many questions. For instance, why is Norre supporting you in this endeavor so fiercely that it will provide the sorts of funds building a wall like this require?"

Mathis sighed. He should have known better than to try and hold anything back. Perhaps Dahlberg might appreciate a warning regarding the threat that the Knodelians posed, but now he was on the spot for not having mentioned it to begin with. Shifting uncomfortably, he chewed his bottom lip as he tried to think of just what to say. He spent so long trying to think of an answer that Jobinh, standing behind him, coughed slightly as a warning.

"I'm sorry. I should have been more direct. Norre fears there will be attacks against some of the more lightly defended cities and towns in this region. Ekholm is one of the most critical settlements to trade throughout Norre's allies here, yet it lacks sufficient defenses to hold off this threat," Mathis explained. "We have some time to begin preparations, fortunately. Norrish engineers are designing and building a defensive wall around Ekholm, but we need more resources to complete it in time." he finally said.

"And Norre will be providing the funds to build this wall, of course," Skygger concluded, tongue wagging in amusement. "You are, of course, talking about the Knodelian threat, correct?"

Well, my first ever diplomatic visit has started just wonderfully, hasn't it? Their king has caught me out in a half-truth, and probably knows more about why we're here than I do, Mathis mused. "Yes, of course."

"We, too, have been concerned about the advancing Knodelian forces," Skygger said. He cocked his head slightly. "Volcanic ash is a plentiful resource here, and not something we have much demand for outside of a few small farming communities. You may have however much you require, and we will spare the Norre Hegemony's coffers by charging them nothing for it. We wish this Knodelian threat ended just as much as you do."

Mathis faintly heard muffled gasps coming from at least two people behind him – Jobinh and Donati, most likely – but he was able to keep himself from the same reaction. It was a deal too good to be true, so he focused on figuring out what the catch was. "You say that this ash is not particularly valuable, and that you wish our success. I cannot believe, however, that you are doing this purely out of fear of the Knodelians. They pose little threat to you, either militarily or economically. You may not desire money from the coffers of the Norre Hegemony as payment, but surely there is something you want that we could provide."

The other wulvers around the room started growling slightly at the challenge to their Alpha's word, but Skygger called them off with the wave of a hand. "You are, of course, correct, and none of my people should be at all offended," he said, gently admonishing his guards. "But what I will ask for in return should be of benefit to both our peoples."

Mathis had heard that phrase used quite often in his life, but no deal he had run across ever truly benefited both sides. Still, there was always a first time... and to accuse Skygger of lying, at this point, might lead to swords being drawn. "Ask, then, and I will let you know if we can agree on the terms."

"Ekholm is located at the junction of the river Knapp and the Orrpars road," Skygger said. "But you have only settled one side of the river so far, leaving plenty of room for Ekholm to grow onto the other side even after you erect walls around the entire city as it stands today."

"For the most part, yes," Mathis said. "Much of the other side of the river is marshland, and prone to floods. We generally restrict the construction of housing there. It is not, however, completely undeveloped. We have grown rice there, from time to time, and there are some small shelters for the convenience of the woodsmen who hunt in the surrounding forests."

Skygger reached up and scratched himself behind the ear. Mathis could not help but be distracted when his left leg started twitching slightly in time with his scratching. "I had not considered the issue of flooding," the Alpha said. "But it would not completely prevent the construction of housing on the other side, would it?"

"Hmm." Mathis gestured behind him. "I'm not sure I understand how it pertains to our discussions, but if it really matters then I am not the best one to answer that question. Perhaps Donati, one of the engineers helping us build our wall, could speak to that."

For the first time, Skygger looked at the other people in his court. Mathis followed the wulver's eyes, and noticed some slight reaction – good or bad, he couldn't tell – when they fell on Kieras. However, they didn't stay on her very long, instead moving to the human who was stepping forward as he had been beckoned.

Donati, being more formally trained in court manners, gave a much more elaborate bow before introducing himself, and held himself there.

"Alpha Skygger," he said, not yet raising his eyes. "I am Donati, an engineer trained by Norre's finest institutions, at your service."

"Rise, Donati," Skygger barked. "As I told your companion, wulvers do not stand on such ceremony."

Donati stood up, shifting uncomfortably as he did. "Alpha Skygger, I have not properly studied the terrain on the other side of the Knapp River, so I cannot speak with any certainty. However, there are cities in the Norre Hegemony which have grown and prospered along other flood plains through the construction of dams, levies, aqueducts, and similar items. A terrain wet enough for rice patties, however, might be somewhat problematic."

"If you had a detailed engineering study about that side of the Knapp River you could be more certain, correct?"

Donati nodded slowly. "Yes, perhaps. If it is recent enough."

"Then one shall be provided for you," Skygger said, making some hand gestures that sent one of the other wulvers running off. "We have a survey of the entire Knapp River made just six years ago. Would that be current enough?"

Mathis turned to Skygger in disbelief. He had read all of the reports on wulvers he could find as the expedition had been arranged, and he knew there had been no sightings of any near Ekholm in over a decade. Any surveyors of the river would undoubtedly have needed to make a stop in Ekholm's ports to present their credentials, which would have shown up on his reports, yet he had seen nothing mentioning any such expedition. "How would you—"

"I believe so, yes," Donati replied, not allowing Mathis to finish.

Skygger stood up and clapped his hands twice for emphasis. "Good! It may take some time to find the material in our archives. As you and your people will be staying for at least a few nights while we gather the ash for your project, why don't I have my people escort you to your rooms? We can resume our discussion in the morning, after your engineer has had enough time to study this survey."

"But—" Mathis began.

"Not now," Jobinh snapped with a harsh whisper in his ear. Mathis hadn't even heard the guardsman approach him, so was startled into obeying him while Skygger left the room. Jobinh continued before their escorts had organized themselves. "I know you aren't familiar with court protocol, but this isn't the time to be asking the Alpha questions. We must regroup and reassess in private."

Mathis glared at the Norrish officer. "Is it really a wise idea to end negotiations before we have any idea what he expects from us?" he whispered back harshly, though still mindful of the assembling escort.

"I've dealt with wulvers before," Jobinh replied, still whispering and now in a much calmer tone. "If I read the Alpha correctly, he saw or heard something he didn't expect, and he's pausing to think it over. My guess is that he's already pulled that survey from the archives, and we'll have it within the hour. No, his hesitation has nothing to do with flood plains or anything of the sort. He had knowledge of a six year old river survey at his fingertips, and clearly had that aspect of the conversation well planned. He'd just have talked circles around any deal until the real issue is resolved."

"We don't have time for long, drawn out negotiations. Building that wall is the keystone of Ekholm's defense," Mathis snapped, still frustrated. "We need the deal to be completed now."

"Skygger is aware of that," Jobinh said. "I'm sure he isn't lying about collecting the materials we need, either. He's probably confident we'll agree to whatever deal he's offering, or he wouldn't bother with that just yet."

"Then what's keeping him from giving us his price?" Mathis asked.

"I'm not sure," Jobinh said as the wulvers finally arranged themselves into escort details. "But I doubt it will be long before we find out."

Kieras wasn't particularly happy about being awoken unexpectedly by a creature with a wolf-like head snarling at her to keep silent. If her transformation had been any less skilled, she would have reverted to a fox before the wulver's very eyes.

She soon found herself escorted, with repeated warnings to stay quiet, to a large chamber several flights of stairs underground, where they unceremoniously left her and closed the door behind her.

The room – well lit by several flaming braziers hanging from the ceiling – appeared to be far different in construction than the surrounding castle. It was built out of polished black marble with white mortar instead of the rest of the castle's more typical grey granite. Aside from a few benches formed from the same black marble, furniture was sparse. Artwork protruded from the walls that Kieras couldn't quite distinguish, but which was nevertheless oddly familiar to her. Three pieces, however, clearly caught her eye. All were of the same subject – a kitsune, mid-transformation into a human – but they were made of different materials: Obsidian, alabaster marble, and red granite.

"Where am I?" she asked uncertainly, the first distinct words she'd managed to say since her rude awakening.

"You should know," a familiar voice said. Kieras spun around to see Skygger standing in the same doorway she had come from, though his more distinctive features were hidden behind a cloak. "You should be able to recognize this place from its description. They would have told about this place before they sent you."

"Before they sent me?" Kieras repeated incredulously. "Before who sent me?"

"The myobu priesthood, of course," Skygger said. "Come, girl, we are allies. I know kitsune are prone to deception, but here it is needless."

Kieras blinked. "Well, I suppose it would be too much to believe I could fool a wulver into thinking I was human and not kitsune, but on this I am not deceiving you. I am not a part of the myobu priesthood. I doubt they'd even let me in, considering I'm not a myobu."

Skygger's tongue wagged in laughter. "The next time you wish to convince someone of that, I suggest you do so without wearing the traditional jewelry of a myobu, enchanted to be worn by no-one else."

Startled, Kieras hand rose to her mother's choker. She had almost forgotten she was wearing it, but apparently it could identify her to someone in the know. Sadly, even she was not in the know.

"I... I am telling the truth," Kieras said bitterly. "My father was a nogitsune, as you would plainly see were I in my other form. I was raised as a human, to some extent, which kitsune priests certainly are not. I simply would never be accepted as a myobu. That does not mean I don't have myobu blood flowing in me, however. My mother was a myobu, and one of high standing, but I am not; this necklace was hers."

Skygger's tongue retracted, and he studied her closely. "I am almost inclined to believe you. A member of the myobu priesthood would not keep the deception up this long if she were truly here to discuss business."

Kieras started trying to turn into her fox form, to prove she was not a myobu, but found she was having troubles. All illusory or transformative kitsune magic required a degree of concentration she was unable to collect thanks to the instinctual fear she felt in the wolf-like presence of the wulvers. She couldn't prove she was telling the truth right away, but it was too late to try deception.

"I am telling you the truth, whether you believe me or not," she said finally. As a kitsune she was naturally deceptive, but when she did tell the truth she was quite frustrated when no one believed her. This made her problem transforming even worse. She closed her eyes and took a deep breath. Then another one. Finally, she felt herself calm enough to make an attempt at it. Once she was fully transformed, she turned and glared defiantly at the Alpha.

Initially, Skygger just cocked his head, glancing her over as if to check for mistakes. That brief moment of calm, however, ended when he bared his fangs, crouching down and drawing a sword on her. "Just what is the meaning of this?" He snarled, gesturing wildly with the naked blade.

"Yip!" Kieras whimpered, stumbling back. In her effort to prove that she was telling the truth, she had neglected to consider that the wulvers just might not be as friendly with the nogitsune kitsune as they were with the myobu. To make matters worse, she was backed into a corner, with the only entrance or exit to the room on the other side of the room, closed and locked.

After a few terrifying moments, however, Skygger relaxed, sheathed his sword, and – hiding his teeth back behind his lips – gave her a wulver smile. "Well," he said, cocking his head curiously, "there's no way you could hold a false nogitsune form through that, so you must be telling the truth. Imagine that – an honest kitsune!"

"We don't always lie," she snapped back, though the harshness in her voice was not entirely because he had frightened her. Unlike her father, she had difficulty with human tongue while in her fox form. Her voice came out clipped, interspersed with throaty, high-pitched growls and yips as she tried to soften syllables or pronounce percussive sounds, respectively, but she managed to make herself understood.

"I wouldn't be dealing with your kind if you did," Skygger replied, settling onto one of the benches. "You're pretty young, aren't you? I don't see many one-tailed kitsune any more. The priesthood tends to keep them sequestered in the kitsune temples, nowadays. Still, your transformation abilities are phenomenal – you held your form even when I was threatening you; a rare feat even amongst the older kitsune I've met."

"Thanks," she muttered. She knew she was being too informal, even though the wulver had demanded that none of them stand on ceremony, but the limitations of her fox-form speech made the brief reply much more palatable to his ears, she was sure. Plus, outside of thanking him for the compliment, she wasn't quite sure what to say.

"So," he said, "now that we've determined you really aren't a member of the myobu priesthood, and you really don't have a message for me, I suppose my next question is why are you here? This region is myobu territory, not nogitsune."

"I am looking for my myobu mother," Kieras began. Over the next half hour, answering many of Skygger's questions along the way, she explained the reasons for her exile from home and the things she needed to accomplish before her return. With the floodgates open, she found herself unusually honest in her answers, and told him things that she had yet to reveal even to her friends in Ekholm.

"So, you must find both your mother and a veden vaki before you can return home," Skygger said when she was done. He looked at her briefly, as if sizing her up, before continuing. "I may be able to help you with both goals."

Kieras' eyes widened. "You know my mother?"

Skygger shook his head. "I cannot be sure. I don't know the names of many of the kitsune I meet from the myobu priesthood. They make it a point to remain anonymous. But I see members of the priesthood frequently, so perhaps I can get them a message and they might know her."

Though slightly disappointed, Kieras was quite pleased to have a possible lead. It might not ultimately turn out to be useful, but it was progress nonetheless. She had to set aside both the disappointment and the hope, however, to focus on the other things Skygger might be able to help her with.

"And... the veden vaki?"

"I cannot tell you where to find one," Skygger said. "But I know someone who can." Kieras looked at him expectantly. "You may have heard that my people prefer to live near volcanoes. That is only partially true. We like to live near the tulen vaki who inhabit those volcanoes."

Kieras was confused slightly. Vaki were very solitary beings, rarely enjoying even the company of other vaki much less any other creatures. Tulen vaki, who were the guardians of fire, were no exception.

"There was a tulen vaki who lived on our former island home," Skygger explained, seeing her confusion. "For us to co-exist, we had to forge an alliance with him. That alliance has proven to hold even as that vaki passed on and we have moved to other lands in which tulen vaki inhabit. Tulen vaki are not powerful healers like the veden vaki, but they do have some talents. Perhaps Dahlberg's tulen vaki will be able to assist you. I will take you to her."

"Thank you," Kieras said. Once again, she felt somewhat disappointed – she doubted a tulen vaki would really be able to help – but she was grateful nonetheless. At least it was worth asking.

"Now, change back to your human self, and we will be on our way," Skygger said, gesturing.

Had it not been for her fur, Skygger would undoubtedly see a full body blush on her. "Um... right now?"

"Your friends in Ekholm will need me to sell them the volcanic ash they need as quickly as possible," Skygger said, cocking his head at her. "So we must get this over with as soon as we can. Why delay?"

"Well," Kieras said, looking doubtfully as the ivory sculpture of her myobu brethren mid-transformation. "I... uh...."

"Is there a problem?" Skygger asked, and then noticed what she was looking at. "Oh, I never answered your question about this room, did I? When my people arrived on this land, it was the home of a kitsune village. We negotiated a treaty with the myobu priesthood that allowed us to settle here, and built our city upon the foundations left behind by those departing kitsune. This room was a part of the village chieftain's house and by treaty is to remain unchanged even as we built our new homeland around it. We hold all our meetings with the myobu priesthood in this room, but beyond that I know nothing of its significance."

Kieras shrunk down into her fur, looking up at Skygger bashfully. "That's not my problem. I... uh... I have a certain problem changing from a fox into a human that I don't have changing from a human into a fox."

"Oh?"

"I... I can't make clothes while I transform. I need a moment to recover from the transformation before I can make them"

There was a long pause before Skygger started a snorting, tongue-wagging, human-sounding belly laugh that echoed throughout the room. "I shall leave you to your transformation then. If you will meet me outside in five minutes?"

Mathis flexed his arm painfully after Jobinh disarmed him for the seventh time. The Norrish soldier must have gotten frustrated after watching him pace across the room impatiently, and had suggested some sword training to kill the time.

"I'm not quite sure how to say this," Jobinh said hesitantly. "But among all the people I've seen who've had enough training with a sword to use one without cutting off their own arms, you are the absolute worst swordsman."

"I am well aware of that, thank you," Mathis said with a sigh. "Why do you think I never followed my brother into the army?"

Jobinh nodded, considering him briefly. "Did you ever try working with a spear, or a pike?"

"Yes. I'm even worse with those," Mathis said. "I'm a crack shot with a bow, and I'm good unarmed, but I simply don't seem to be able to handle any weapon in close quarters combat with any degree of skill. The way that modern armies use archers, I have no desire to take on that role, either."

Jobinh nodded. Archers in the Norrish army rarely, if ever, reached officer status, and had almost no opportunity to show off their skills. He knew just why someone like Mathis would prefer not to join such a unit.

"Keep in mind," Jobinh said. "That the way an archer is used on the walls of a castle is vastly different than the way he is used in the field. Since the bulk of Ekholm's militia will be responsible for defending its new walls, not for marching in the field, there could soon be a role more fitted to your talents."

Mathis was still trying to figure out what to say to that when the door opened and Donati entered the room. The architectural engineer appeared distracted but otherwise pleased.

"Well?" Mathis prompted.

"Hmm? Oh, sorry," Donati said. "Got a lot on my mind. I'm not sure why, but it sounds as if they want us to continue our city walls onto the other side of the river, as well."

"We won't have time for that before the Knodelians arrive," Jobinh reminded him.

"They are well aware of that," Donati replied. "And they don't expect us to have that portion of the wall complete before the expected invasion, or really any time in the next few years. To complete everything they were talking about, we'd have to build levees, fortify the bridge, clear cut several acres of forest, possibly drain some swampland, and more – a project which will take years to complete. I gather they want us to not just fortify the river, but to wall up expansion room within the city walls of Ekholm – enough to more than double our current size."

Mathis frowned. "Setting aside the time and money needed to complete such a project, I'm all for Ekholm's expansion, but why in the world would they want us to do that?"

Donati shrugged. "I have no idea. It never came up, but it's pretty clear those are the engineering challenges they were asking about.

They had plans to handle these issues, though, so this might just be a delaying tactic for the negotiations."

"But why? What is the point of delaying the negotiations?" Mathis asked rhetorically. "Nothing we've heard so far even begins to explain why we can't just make an offer. We mustn't take too long getting these supplies, so they need to stop playing around and offer us a deal for that ash soon."

Boedker, one of Jobinh's soldiers, cleared his throat to draw their attention. "We have a kitsune with us," he pointed out. He and the other soldiers in the expedition had been told of her identity, should a situation involving her arise during the negotiations. "We could always ask her to sneak around a bit and see if she could find something."

"That would not be wise," Mathis replied stiffly. "If she chooses to help us of her own accord, that's one thing, but I don't like the idea of asking her to do anything specific. Kitsune do not like being pressured, and are most apt to betray you if they feel you are insisting on something undeserved."

Jobinh shrugged. "You may be right, but Boedker does have a point. She could be a very useful tool, however little we can trust her. At the very least, we should invite her to these discussions. She may decide to help us without being asked."

Kieras certainly had the ability to help them, but what they were suggesting would be construed as spying. Her skill at transformation was rather impressive for a kitsune of her age, from what he'd read, but she had to be very inexperienced, given what else he knew about her. Indeed, for a kitsune, she seemed unusually lacking in the art of deception, and revealed herself much too regularly for him to be confident in her ability to act as a spy. On the other hand, Jobinh was right – she should, at the very least, be invited to their council.

"Boedker, I agree your idea has merit, but she must approach her carefully, and it must be entirely her decision whatever she decides to do. Fetch her for us, would you?"

"Right away, sir," Boedker replied, snapping to attention. Mathis had only been making a suggestion, not giving an order, but nevertheless he was impressed with how quickly the soldier moved from casual conversation to militarily efficient action. Torkki and Mathis had their contingent of Norrish soldiers well trained.

All of that was forgotten when the soldier returned. "Sir! The Lady

Kieras is not presently in her room, sir."

"She isn't?" Mathis exclaimed and then paused. "Where did she go, then?"

"Maybe she has anticipated us?" Jobinh suggested. "She's a kitsune. They love spying and causing trouble."

"I doubt it." Mathis felt like admonishing Jobinh – in the course of four minutes, he had accused Kieras of lying, suggested she wanted to cause trouble, and dismissed her as a mere tool – but nothing would be accomplished by it. "She has her own agenda here, which I know something of and I don't begrudge her in pursuing it. I just wish she would have let me know what she was doing, first. She won't do anything to intentionally cause us trouble; of that I'm sure. Unintentionally, though...."

Jobinh nodded. "She could ruin the whole deal without even realizing it."

The passageway Kieras followed Skygger down was more old construction, but the floor and walls surrounding it seemed even more ancient than the meeting room. The ceiling started out looking like the castle's foundation, but after a certain point gave way to newly added wooden planks with earth crumbling through on occasion, and further in still became rough-hewn stone. The passageway was oddly warmer than she would have expected, and grew hot as they walked – unpleasantly so, making her wish she'd formed more lightweight clothing after changing back into a human.

It wasn't that long, however, before they finally reached their stopping point – a balcony overhanging a deep pit with glowing cracks on dark, patchy soil.

"Where are we?" she asked.

"Inside the volcano," Skygger answered. "Much of the path we just walked was constructed by our kitsune predecessors to act as a vent in times of eruption. Most of their society dwelt on the other side of the volcano, so in an eruption the lava would – they hoped – bleed out through that tunnel and not over their village. The volcano has not erupted since, however, so we have no idea if this plan will work. It nevertheless provides us the perfect path to travel to visit our host, the tulen vaki."

Kieras' eyes widened. "But that means you built your city right over where the volcano is supposed to erupt! Why—"

"Because, child, I can tell them the exact day that the volcano will erupt, allowing them ample time to move on to a new home," a new voice said. Kieras didn't see it at first, but then a small creature landed an acrobatic jump from nowhere onto the balcony she was standing on. "They have many decades before it will become an issue."

There was not much light, so its features were indistinct, but Kieras could not help but think how much she looked like this little creature. It almost looked like a slim, adult human female of about her build, with long, red hair much like her own but with more of an orange tint. One pretty big difference, though, was that the creature was only as tall as the length of Kieras' arm.

"You're... a haltija of fire?" Kieras said, using the more archaic – and considerably more polite – term for the vaki, which she had drilled herself senseless trying to remember to use. "I think I was expecting something different."

"You were expecting some sort of spectral giant covered in flames who could destroy whole forests just by sneezing, weren't you?" The vaki laughed. "Everyone's always surprised by how small and helpless we look. If you want to find a spectral giant, try the kalman vaki, our cousins who protect the graveyards. But I assure you, while I might not manage it by sneezing, I am powerful enough to destroy whole forests and I am still one of the haltija."

Kieras nodded slowly. "I... see."

"You are here to ask a favor of me, yes?" the tulen vaki said. "You wish help in healing."

"How—"

"I can hear anything in the air spoken near my fires. I heard you and Skygger speaking through the torchlight."

Eyes wide, Kieras nodded slowly. "Does that mean every fire in the world, or—"

"I said my fires," the vaki replied. "My domain only extends as far as the roots of this mountain, upon which the wulvers have built their city. Now, tell me about this man you need healed, and I will tell you whether I can help you. It would be in both our best interests if you were to disregard your kitsune influences and be truthful about it – do not try and recruit my services by lying, for you will merely waste our time if you try." The vaki wagged one of its tiny, flame-lit fingers at

Kieras.

Kieras scratched her head. "Well, I don't really know what was wrong with the man. He was missing an arm, but that had nothing to do with it. According to my father, he had lost that arm many years before I first saw this human. He had no visible wounds, so I doubt he had been stabbed or strangled – but outside of that, I know nothing of his illness. My mother had placed him under a spell to keep him alive, but asleep, shortly after I was born."

The vaki sighed. "I feared as much. With no visible wounds, he is beyond my abilities to heal. Perhaps he was poisoned? Regardless, you must consult with one of my brethren haltija."

Kieras nodded. "I was afraid of that. Thank you for considering my petition, anyway."

The vaki smiled serenely at her. "I may not be able to heal this human for you, but I may still be able to help. I believe I shall, since we look so similar, and since we are both half-breeds."

Kieras cocked her head. "Half-breeds?"

"You are the daughter of a myobu and a nogitsune," the vaki replied. "I am the child of a haltija of fire and what you call a vuoren vaki, or a haltija of mountains. It makes my chosen habitation... appropriate, don't you think?"

Kieras nodded in agreement. "Then I am grateful for the help, from one half-breed to another."

The vaki inclined her head thoughtfully. "I may not be able to heal this human, but I know of one who can, and I know where she lives. A haltija of water."

Kieras wrinkled her brow, intrigued. "How would a haltija of fire come to know a haltija of water? I've never heard that you were that... social."

"I suspect many of us with a dual heritage have traits none would expect," said the vaki teasingly, looking at Kieras' necklace. "In my youth, I had a choice of whether to follow the path of fire, or of earth and mountains. In that time, I met haltija of many paths, for those of mountains and water congregate as do those of fire and air. One I knew well was a haltija of water – a veden vaki, as you call them now. She lives in a fountain near the marina of the human city now known as Norre, though I doubt the humans living there now know about her.

"I am not sure how you will get to it, but she dwells in a lake underneath the fountain's central statue. If you approach her and ask for her help on behalf of the haltija whose former domain was Byvald Mountain, she should agree to provide you with the needed aid. Though she may ask you for a favor in return."

"Again, thank you," Kieras said, gracing the vaki with a curtsey. She wasn't sure if human courtesies were appropriate for one of the haltija, but it seemed appropriate at the time. "Any help at all is appreciated."

"Kitsune child..." The vaki paused, as if sensing something, or perhaps recalling a thought. "I think that it may be important than you realize that you seek out the haltija of water. Perhaps for reasons beyond the fate of your friend."

"Beyond?"

"There is something... moving, for lack of a better word. Forces are emerging, aligning... reviving powers not seen in an age of man. I have sensed hints of the pattern in the fires. For good or ill, I do not know, but the origin is beyond my knowledge. The haltija of water you seek may know more. But be careful around her, for she could aid both sides in the coming conflict if you are unwary."

Kieras stared at the vaki for a moment and then nodded. "I shall see what she has to say. Do you have any other advice?"

"Just one other thought. Unless it proves impossible to complete your quest otherwise, I suggest you remain in the lands defended by the Norre Hegemony until you are ready to return to Kassia. There are all too few friends to the kitsune and other mystical races outside of this region."

Mathis was pacing around the room at a rate that made those watching him tired. Jobinh was one of those watchers, and couldn't help now and again shaking his head at the inexperience – and what he was beginning to believe was incompetence – of the man who was ostensibly in charge of this expedition.

"Sir," he said, "I think it would be best if you calmed down."

Mathis glared at him. "I am calm. I'm merely considering the implications of Kieras' continued absence. We have no idea where she's gone or what she's doing, Skygger has again delayed his meeting with us, and that the guards outside of our door merely laugh at us when we ask why he's so late."

"You already knew Kieras had her own reasons for being on this mission," Jobinh said. "And Skygger is only a few minutes late. The guards are not acting hostile, and have allowed us to retain our weapons since leaving Skygger's presence. There is no cause for alarm."

"The guards were still laughing at us for asking about the meeting," Mathis snapped.

"You could tell?" Boedker said. Jobinh's eyes snapping towards him instantly caused the junior soldier to snap to attention. "I mean, sir, uh...."

"All right, let's review our situation from a tactical perspective, then," Mathis said. "Assume Kieras does something that causes the wulvers to view us as hostile. Would there be any way to rescue her and get ourselves out?"

Jobinh rolled his eyes. Mathis' nerves seemed to be pushing him to the point of irrationality, and he really didn't want to have to put up with this kind of ridiculousness. Still, he figured he should give an answer – at least Mathis might stand still long enough to hear him out while he was speaking. "Well, let's see. There's, what, seven of us here? Maybe we could find another dozen or so of the wagon drivers to help us, but I wouldn't count on it. We're armed at the moment, though if we're summoned to the throne room only you will have any weapons, and you are incompetent with them. The only door to the suite of rooms we occupy may only be opened from inside, so if it came down to a fight we could defend the room. We might be able to climb out a window, run across the courtyard, and if we're lucky their gate will be open and we can escape out of it. Assuming, of course, they don't do the sensible thing and intercept us along the way, or shoot us down with archers, or just close the gate while we're running."

Mathis looked slightly annoyed. "Well—"

Deciding it would be worth the effort to break down any possible silly fantasies Mathis might have had about heroic rescues – if for no other reason than to distract him from his pacing – Jobinh continued. "Not that we would get far. Your average untrained, unskilled wulver is far faster and stronger than what would be considered an elite human warrior. We have no mounts, and the wulvers aren't likely to be stabling any outside of their gates that we could conveniently steal and ride away on, since they don't ride mounts themselves."

"Jobinh—"

But Jobinh was on a roll. "As far as any rescue attempts go, I think I need to remind you of the odds, here. We have five trained soldiers. We are in the castle of the largest wulver city in the known world. There are nearly eighty thousand wulvers present. That means we're outnumbered something like sixteen thousand wulvers to each of our soldiers. Wulvers are far stronger, faster, and tougher than your average humans. A wulver with minimal training should outstrip even an elite human soldier. If we do something to try and rescue that kitsune girl – who could probably do a better job of rescuing herself, mind, if it comes to that – the odds are not exactly in our favor."

"Enough, Jobinh! I knew all of that before I asked the question. I just wanted a professional opinion to make sure there wasn't something I hadn't considered. So, moving on," Mathis said crisply, "let's turn to our diplomatic concerns. Briefly, if you can, tell me how do you think the wulvers might react were they to learn that Kieras is a candidate to be the princess consort of Kassia's heir apparent?"

"They'd see through any lie," Jobinh said, mollified.

"It isn't a lie, though," Mathis replied, shaking his head. "She ran off from the court of the Kassian Empire because they sought to use her as a pawn in a political game by arranging her marriage to one of the Kassian princes."

Jobinh raised an eyebrow. "Well... in that case, they might imprison her and demand that Kassia pay a ransom for her. I doubt she'd appreciate us revealing that to the wulvers, however, considering her situation."

"No, no she would not," Kieras said from their door, a slight edge of her fox-like snarl in her voice despite being in human form. "And she's not exactly happy you've been discussing it with these other humans, either."

Looking vastly relieved, Mathis spun around to see the kitsune girl standing there, an angry frown on her face.

"Kieras!" he cried, running over to pull her into the room and then inspecting her. "Are you all right? Where have you been?"

Kieras seemed rather startled at Mathis' reaction, but quickly recovered enough to answer his question. "I'm fine, why would you think otherwise? The wulvers were somewhat concerned since it was obvious to them that I was a kitsune and had not declared myself. Once we cleared that up, I figured I could talk with them about the state of wulver-kitsune relations."

"But—"

"And, by the way," Kieras continued. "Skygger is ready for you to return to the negotiations, now."

"He is?"

"Yes, he is," Skygger said, emerging from the door that Kieras had just come from. "And he – or rather, I – have heard a great many extraordinary things. Jobinh, your assessment of my wulver's abilities is quite flattering, I must say." Turning to address Kieras, he continued, "Milady, rest assured that none from Kassia will learn your whereabouts from my people."

"Thank you, Skygger," Kieras said, giving the wulver ruler a curtsey.

"Now, I imagine the rest of you wish time to collect yourselves," Skygger continued. "My guards, here, will escort you to my court when you are ready... assuming you decide not to try leaving my castle through the windows and making a run for it, that is."

Jobinh wasn't completely familiar with wulvers' forms of expression, but he was quite certain that Skygger was laughing as he departed.

"Well," Mathis sighed. "That could have gone better."

Kieras needed a moment to herself, so she lied about needing to get something from her room. It was a ruse they all should have seen through, since she didn't *have* anything in her room, but they let her go anyway. Mathis, however, was quick to follow.

"Hey," he said from her doorway, looking in awkwardly.

She turned to glare at him, still upset about him revealing her secrets to so many people. She had intended to tell him everything that she had learned about Skygger, the kitsune, the vaki, and Dahlberg's history, but now he was lucky he had gotten as much from her as he did. The only reason she didn't just toss him out of her room right away was that he seemed so contrite already. She figured he could at least be afforded the opportunity to apologize... but that didn't mean she had to make it easy for him.

"What?" she snapped.

"I... I'm sorry," Mathis said nervously. That much, she had expected – the rest of his apology, however, was a bit more surprising. He bowed deeply, almost kowtowing to her, and looked up self-consciously. "You gave your word that you would not endanger our mission. While I knew you intended to keep your word, I wasn't confident you knew how to avoid causing a stir. And... even if it didn't affect our mission, I feared you could get *yourself* into serious trouble as well. Because I didn't have confidence in you, I may have caused a stir and could have endangered you in the process. I suspect my apology is not enough, but it is all I can offer at the moment. That, and my word that I will not reveal any of your secrets again without your permission, no matter the circumstances."

Kieras, seeing him on his knees begging her forgiveness, felt her cheeks flush in embarrassment. "Oh, get up," she said weakly, pulling at his shoulder to stop him from bowing to her. "I'm sure anyone of Jobinh's background is trustworthy, and I doubt your brother would assign you soldiers who didn't know how to keep their mouths shut when they need to. As far as Skygger is concerned, he already knew about my story because I told him. And so what if you distrusted my abilities or not – I certainly wouldn't have, so why should you?"

Mathis stood up, but still didn't seem able to meet her gaze. He sighed. "Some diplomat I am. I manage to insult both my host and my companions, all in one go."

Kieras snorted. "Well, at least it's a refreshing change from the usual obsequious idiots I'm always encountering among the Kassian diplomats who regularly promise lies even a kitsune would be ashamed of. You did nothing but discuss your fears honestly. I doubt Skygger will change any of his intended demands because of that. As far as the insult to me goes...."

Mathis finally looked at her. "Yes?"

Kieras was still of two minds about Mathis' behavior. He revealed a secret of hers which could cause her serious trouble, and possibly endanger her for the remainder of her search for her mother. On the other hand, he did apologize – so genuinely that she almost felt embarrassed for him at the display – and she believed he only revealed that secret because he was genuinely afraid for her. She could not let him go unpunished, though.

"You're right, I'm afraid," Kieras said. "Your apology isn't enough to make up for the trouble this may have caused me." Mathis' head fell as he once again couldn't seem to meet her eyes. "Some time in the future, when you're least expecting it, I'll pull some sort of humiliating prank on you. That should satisfy my honor as a kitsune, and your apology will do well enough in the meantime."

He glanced back up at her with surprise that slowly turned into laughter. Kieras felt her own lips twitch with amusement as he replied. "I suppose I'll have to live in fear until then. I do ask that you hold off until we're out of Dahlberg – I doubt the negotiations will survive if I embarrass myself any further."

Kieras reached over and patted him on the cheek, shooting him a dangerous smile of her own. "I make no such promise, of course, but I think you might be right about the negotiations, so my earlier promise to not intentionally harm this diplomatic effort should stay me. But there's always the chance I can do something on our way back to Ekholm, so live in fear, my friend. Live in fear."

"All calm, cool, collected, and composed now, I presume?" Skygger said, greeting the contingent of people from Ekholm and Norre as they returned to his throne room. "Good. Then let us resume these negotiations."

"Alpha Skygger," Mathis said. He was uncomfortable using the wulver term for king, but he felt it was important to remain especially courteous. "I feel as if I should give you some sort of explanation. I—"

Skygger raised his hand to cut him off. "You were concerned for one of your people. I respect that in a leader, and so there is no explanation or apology required. If anything, it assures me that Ekholm is in good hands, which will make our negotiations far, far easier."

Mathis could not stop himself from gawking in surprise. A poke from behind – coming from Kieras' direction, he noted – reminded him that he had to say something. "Thank you, Alpha Skygger. I am not sure I deserve the compliment, but I will gladly take it."

"Perhaps, then, we can get down to business," Skygger said. "As I recall, you were asking for sufficient volcanic ash to make the lime for your new wall's mortar – something you were quite short on time to acquire."

"That is correct," Mathis replied. "And we have the coffers both of the city of Ekholm and the entire Norre Hegemony to pay for it."

Skygger scratched at the fur at the base of his neck. "Suppose we were to ask Norre to pay someone else on Dahlberg's behalf, well after the wall has been built. Are you allowed to offer such a payment?"

Jobinh stepped forward. "As Norre's representative to these negotiations, I should speak to that. We will guarantee any reasonable payment made to anyone you name, even if Dahlberg and Ekholm both fall in the coming war."

Skygger appeared to ignore him, keeping his eyes on Mathis. "Very well, then, I believe we can help each other. We will provide as much volcanic ash as you need, as quickly as you can transport it."

"Thank you," Mathis replied, sketching a bow, though he knew that there was more coming. "And what do you ask for in return?"

Skygger turned around to face his throne, hands clasped behind his back. He didn't say anything for such a long time that Mathis started to worry he'd said something wrong, but an almost puppy-like whimper escaping from the wulver monarch told him there was more to it than a simple question.

"Many wulver cities, including Dahlberg, are growing increasingly overpopulated," he said finally. "We have been searching for additional places to settle, but as yet we have too few families of trained colonists, no location, and insufficient resources to start a new city from scratch. We might have the resources, however, to settle them into an *existing* city that has room to expand. When you return to Ekholm with your ash, you will also have thirty families of wulvers looking to settle into new homes with you. They will help you to build your wall, and once the Knodelian threat has been dealt with they will begin helping Ekholm to expand to the other side of the Knapp River. The Norre Hegemony is to help offset the costs until Ekholm doubles it's current size, so as to accommodate our new colony." He paused. "Many of these people are trained to work in our militia, and we will also be sending a few dozen wulver soldiers to help in Ekholm's defense. If we are going to invest our people into your success, we will help protect our investment."

Mathis was a little taken aback. "A moment, Alpha, while we confer," he said, pulling Jobinh with him as he stepped out of earshot. "Am I allowed to agree to that?" he asked in a whisper.

There were several seconds before a flustered Jobinh said anything. "Well, I... I'm not entirely sure. I believe it is within the scope of what Norre has authorized, but you know best about what Ekholm's new Senate or its people would think."

"Then let me ask you not as the representative of Norre, but from your own perspective," Mathis continued quietly. "I understand his need, and it seems a possible solution that would benefit us both. Do you foresee any downside?"

Jobinh frowned uncertainly. "I would normally be suspicious of someone offering to help garrison my walls unasked, but they are wulvers – as a race, they are inherently trustworthy. Given Ekholm's situation I don't think you can afford to refuse any help, much less the sort of support a set of stalwart wulver soldiers could provide. Beyond that... there is so little we know about how wulvers act. It is very rare that a single wulver will make a home in a human settlement. Thirty families and several dozen soldiers of wulvers moving into a human settlement? Completely unheard of. "

Mathis took a deep breath and then nodded. Stepping forward towards the throne, he bowed formally. "Alpha Skygger, we accept the settlers unconditionally. We accept the soldiers as well, but the Senate must confirm their right to remain beyond the immediate crisis."

Skygger inclined his head in acknowledgment, still showing a touch of amusement, at least to Mathis' eyes. "A careful answer. Good. I believe you'll find our people a worthy addition to your city."

As Mathis reported everything that happened in Dahlberg to his uncle and his brother, Kieras found her attention drifting. At first, she amused herself making plans for the prank she intended to play on Mathis. She still wasn't quite sure what she was going to do. It would have to be big enough that he would never even think about revealing her secrets again, yet tame enough that it wouldn't get him seriously injured or killed. It was the second part of that which was causing her problems.

That only kept her busy for a little while, however. As much fun as planning pranks was, the dull room they were in – which was a hurriedly constructed wooden structure with crude tables, a few stools for sitting, and little other furniture of any kind – was not particularly inspiring. Searching for ideas, she turned her attention to the other people in the room. Kieras, Mathis, Jobinh, and Mrazek – the former captain in the Dahlberg Royal Guard who was to temporarily lead the wulvers in Ekholm – represented the expedition in this meeting. Torkki, Savard, and Hesketh were receiving the report. That was it – there were no scribes, no servants with food or beverage, no assistants, no other members of the Senate. Outside of the wulver, none of them would be useful in pulling any of the pranks she came up with, and she didn't know wulvers well enough to involve their kind, yet. It was somewhat disconcerting. There was an old saying that "the only kitsune who can't pull a really good prank is a dead kitsune," and she was having a lot of trouble coming up with a prank – good or otherwise.

In the end, all she had left to do was to fiddle with the attachments for her chatelaine. She started out playing with her mirror attachment, but as the room was lit only by a few torches it was so dark that she couldn't annoy people by reflecting light in their eyes. She moved to her vesta case attachment, where she was now fully stocked with a fresh batch of matches. She didn't know how well they worked, though, so she experimented with them. She was wearing a mix of human and illusory clothing that day, and she was interested how easily these matches would light when struck against these different surfaces.

Her attention was drawn back to the report when she heard her name mentioned.

"...Kieras' secret, I'm afraid," Mathis was saying. "Thankfully, Skygger has promised not to reveal it to anyone."

"Unfortunate," Savard replied. "What about the soldiers who were with you?"

"I talked with them about it, sir," Jobinh answered for Mathis. "Soldiers like to gossip, but our unit also understands the need for secrecy far better than most. If I tell them the subject is off limits, they won't speak of it."

"We'll have to hope they don't," Savard said. He smiled over at Kieras. "We're taking a great chance on you, young lady – Ekholm certainly does not wish to provoke a war with Kassia, should they learn we are sheltering you. Already we have turned away one party from Kassia looking for word on your whereabouts, so we are now committed. Our safety now is linked with your secret."

Kieras' eyes widened. She had not really thought of the possibility that Kassia would retaliate against Ekholm should they find her hiding there. She had too many friends in both countries to enjoy the thought she might be risking war between them. "I understand."

Savard held her eyes for a moment, then nodded. "Good." He turned back to Mathis. "Well, we now have all the lime we'll need – and then some. I can't say I'm too upset at having so many wulvers to help with the construction and defense of the town, either. Good job, all of you."

Mathis' bit his lip uncertainly waving off the complement with an unsteady hand. "But, Uncle Savard, I did a terrible job. I nearly insulted Skygger several times and I let my concern for Kieras' inexperience – and her safety – interfere with my judgment. In the process we exposed her secret. I... I don't think I'm cut out for this sort of diplomatic work."

"You got the job done," Savard said. "Yes, you had a few bumps along the way, but you did what was important. Now, go rest up. We're going to need you as an ambassador again, soon. The rest of you, too – we're done here. Jobinh, stay for a moment, would you?"

Looking somewhat dazed, Mathis left for his home without a word. Mrazek started on his way to the tent city which had been set up initially for the Norrish soldiers and now also the newly arrived wulvers.

Kieras wasn't quite sure where to go, herself. She had yet to find a permanent place to live while in Ekholm, and considered finding Ziani to ask if she could stay with the other young woman rather than follow Mathis to the second bedroom in his small home. However, Ziani was still working, and it would be several hours until they could meet.

Instead, she decided to head to a tavern and see if she could find some more of that wonderful lingonberry wine Ekholm was home to. She reached to find her purse and see if she could afford it, but her hand encountered nothing.

Oops, she thought to herself. *I must have dropped it when I was fiddling with my chatelaine.*

She didn't want to disturb the meeting in progress, but she couldn't wait to retrieve her purse. With that in mind, she found a convenient stand of bushes she could duck into and transformed into her fox form, using the few human pieces of clothes she had worn to help conceal her chatelaine.

It was easy to return to the meeting room unnoticed – there was no actual door covering the doorway, just a curtain with enough of a gap at the bottom that a fox kit could slip under it undisturbed. She quickly found her purse sitting on the floor over where Jobinh, Savard, and Torkki were in conference. Moving as quietly as she could, she bounded over and picked the purse up in her mouth. It was only then she started to take in what Jobinh was saying.

"...in a panic when Kieras turned out to not be in her room. He was utterly incompetent." Jobinh shook his head. "I really don't know what you're thinking, sending him out for those negotiations. He's worthless as an ambassador."

"If his report is accurate – and I suspect it is – then you're exaggerating. And even if not, then what would you have us do with him?" Savard asked. "He's my nephew. He needs to be involved in the war effort in some way. He's worthless as a soldier, and he hasn't the skills to administer the construction workers as they build the wall."

Kieras had intended to just run in and out, but this caught her attention. Mathis may not have been the most proficient of envoys, but he had not done so poor a job that he deserved Jobinh's venomous ire. She found herself disliking this man intensely, and decided she would stay and see what else he said.

"Mathis lacks confidence," Torkki said. "My brother is no swordsman, but he has considerable talent with a bow and arrow and a great mind for tactics. He can be a great asset in the coming battle, if he can find his niche."

Had she not been in her fox form trying to remain undiscovered, Kieras might have cheered – Torkki was standing up for his brother, once again affirming her belief that Torkki was a worthy candidate for her year of service.

"I sense a 'but' coming here," Jobinh prompted.

Torkki sighed. "But his better skills are not appropriate for any of the jobs we have around town at the moment. He broods over how his incompetent swordsmanship sabotaged his childhood dream of following in my footsteps. He has much to offer, but he needs to feel involved so that we can start rebuilding his confidence."

"As a figurehead – and a member of Archon's family – he is ideal for diplomatic circles," Savard continued. "And his negotiating talent should improve with time. It's not that poor – the year he spent serving our family on the Ekholm Council proved that quite well, despite the conflict with Kuralt. He merely lacks experience with courtly etiquette. Most of the missions we're sending him on are to backwater places – small villages which produce certain goods we'll need in abundance during a siege and are incapable of producing behind the walls of Ekholm – so he shouldn't have to deal with many shrewd diplomats or unfamiliar courtly functions from here on out. He should be fine."

"Now, what about the wulvers themselves?" Torkki asked.

Kieras slipped away at that point, not wanting nor caring to hear any more. When she thought about it, there wasn't really anything too harsh being said – it was a simple evaluation of Mathis' abilities in certain areas based on the expedition to Dahlberg. What bothered her the most was how Mathis' own family was talking about him behind his back after praising him to his face. It was uncomfortable to listen to their evaluation. Even Torkki seemed to be suggesting that this – and any future diplomatic assignments – were being given to Mathis merely to patronize him. Torkki slipped a notch in her book for that.

It finally came to her why this upset her so much. Mathis was being treated as an "inconvenience" by his own family, shunted off to backwater towns in the guise of a diplomat so as to keep him out of the way. It was a tactic she had seen used far too often in the court of Kassia, and not one she approved of. Rarely did the "inconvenient" family member deserve it, and often they were made to feel quite lonely during their exile.

Mathis was not really being sent into exile. Unlike the families of those "inconvenient" people, Torkki and Savard seemed to be thinking of Mathis' interest as well as their own. Nevertheless, it would undoubtedly bring about some of the same loneliness.

She had made a great deal of progress in the search to end her own exile, and her next step would be to head to Norre to seek the veden vaki, but she believed she could afford a slight delay. She would ensure that she was with Mathis on his 'diplomatic missions,' to keep him company and to be a friend. He would need friends, and with the way Jobinh was talking behind his back it didn't sound like he could count on one from his 'escorts.'

After Mathis' temporary estrangement from his family ended, things could go back to normal. With the wall complete and the Knodelian threat ended, Mathis would likely be able to resume his old life as a hunter, and she could take the next step in her own mission by heading to Norre.

And maybe, somewhere between the exile and resuming her mission, she could hit him with that prank she'd promised.

VI. The Kitsune Stratagem

Prince Czerniak rarely enjoyed his tutoring sessions, no matter who that tutor was. Gedig made a fine advisor to his father – perhaps the only one Czerniak respected – but he was no exception to that statement. In fact, he was perhaps the dullest lecturer that the prince had ever encountered.

"...largest industry was moa farming, before the Erixonite invasion turned those farms into a battlefield. And... and you aren't listening to me at all, are you, my Prince?"

Czerniak blinked. His inattention usually wasn't caught. "I... well, I... no, I'm afraid not, Gedig."

The Royal Majordomo laughed. He was not the usual Royal tutor; that role was typically taken by a number of different people. By law, the Royal Doctor would teach him nutrition, the Royal Historian would teach him history, the Royal Barrister would teach him how the laws of Kassia worked, and Lahti would teach him armed and unarmed combat, tactics, and strategy. Plans had been laid out to replace Lahti in this role in the future with the Chief of the Royal Guardsman, but in the meantime Czerniak would be his last Royal student. Unfortunately, Lahti's office was the only one of those that wasn't vacant.

Gedig did his best in their absence. He was no student of medicine, but he had lived through much of Kassia's history and he helped in the creation of more laws than most barristers were familiar with. He had no gift for teaching, however... and he knew it.

"My apologies, my Prince. I know this is of little interest to you, but the history of our Kingdom is important. King Kazdri knew this when he founded our kingdom – it is why he crafted laws that all cities and towns in his kingdom should record any significant events in the local chronicles. His insistence was so great that these laws were emulated by the likes of Norre, Eskesa, and the Vincour Republic."

"And is that why I need to know about former moa farms in what is now Erixonite territory?" Czerniak asked.

Gedig laughed. "Perhaps some of these details that fascinate me aren't necessary for you to learn, but there is much that history can teach you. I was hoping to use this history lesson to teach you economics, as well – I would rather you learn that from me, and not, ahem, from your Royal Treasurer. It will be important when you become king."

Czerniak shrugged. "Lord Kobach isn't all bad. He's the one who put the idea of arranging my marriage to Kieras in father's ear. And I'm not likely to be named king any time soon – father is still young and healthy."

Gedig frowned. "My Prince... you might not want to get your hopes up about that marriage."

"What do you mean?" Czerniak asked. "I know it's been delayed, but father has already arranged it."

"Kobach has... well, no. You need to draw your own conclusions about that. But you must talk it over with Lahti," Gedig said. "I am sure that Kieras cares for you. Nevertheless, your marriage would not be a love match. With a kitsune as the bride...."

Czerniak winced. When Lahti's mate departed nearly two decades before he was born, so did the last of the myobu clan that once inhabited the region. Because of this, Czerniak had only known two kitsune in his life – Kieras and her father. However, there had been many people in his youth – and still were a few, here and there, such as Gedig himself – who remembered those myobu and were quite willing to tell tales. Unlike most other breeds of kitsune, Myobu did not get into relationships of that nature with normal humans, but they were quick to intervene if they felt a human relationship needed it. The stories of what those "interventions" entailed were frightening.

"It may not be a love match, but I'd treat her well," Czerniak said. "She is a wonderful woman, kitsune or no. I would do my utmost to make our marriage a happy one."

"Things may happen beyond your control," Gedig said, stressing the word 'control.' Czerniak could tell the old tutor was trying to tell him something, but for the life of him he couldn't figure out what despite these hints. The marriage not being a love match aside, there didn't seem to be any real explanation for all these warnings. "Again, if you find yourself alone with Lahti, you might want to talk about it with him. Just don't ask when there are a lot of people around – this kind of conversation could be embarrassing for the both of you."

"I guess I have no other choice," Czerniak said. "Next training session, I'll ask. Now, about those moa farms...."

In his role as the protector of all of Kassia's Royal Family, it was rather difficult to avoid King Heshka, but Lahti had managed to do so for much of the past month without neglecting any of his duties.

Kitsune magic proved invaluable in this endeavor, allowing him to disguise himself as an extra armoire or making curtains appear just a touch longer to disguise his feet. There was even one occasion where Heshka was coming down a hallway towards him. Lahti had turned a corner, transformed himself into a fox, and used his superior agility to leap up to the supporting beams over the corridor. He hadn't paid enough attention to his third tail, however, which dangled down and neatly knocked the crown right off the King's head. A quick sprint across the rafters and out a nearby window kept Lahti from being seen while the king pursued his crown, rolling down the hallway without him.

There was a regular fall meeting between the King and all of his guardsman that even Lahti could not avoid, however – it was the meeting to decide the King's upcoming itinerary. He was obligated to sit close to the head of the table, in the seat nearest the King, in fact. He just hoped the meeting was well attended by other guardsmen and he could get away quickly – he was not looking forward to more questions about Kieras' whereabouts.

So far, things had worked out. There were increasing rumors that more guards would be pulled from the castle to reinforce one of the front lines in Kassia's many ongoing wars, and that encouraged every guardsman who was allowed to attend the meeting anxious to show up and prove just how indispensable they were to the castle's defenses.

King Heshka had sat through the whole meeting in a stony silence as each guardsman made their case, for once not fidgeting in his ridiculous ceremonial armor and misfit crown. Lahti had to hold back a wince several times as most of the guardsmen only proved that they were great warriors who would benefit the forces on the front lines, neglecting to (or unable to) make claim of those abilities that would distinguish a good guardsman from a good front-line soldier: An instinct to identify the out-of-place, an ear for subterfuge, and a healthy bit of paranoia. He needed to start doing a better job of screening these guardsmen for intelligence and cunning.

Neither Lahti nor Heshka ever spoke a word throughout the meeting. It was being run by a scribe – one of Gedig's assistants – who knew the King's travel schedule better than either of them did. That the King was expected to inspect so many of his outlying holdings always gave Lahti fits – it was impossible to make all of the preparations for the King's safety that he needed to. That was why Kassia had lost a dozen kings in the past forty years. Kazdri had made the same number of trips each year, but it was peacetime and Lahti actually trusted his king to obey his orders in those days. Having someone reliable as king made all the difference.

When the meeting was over, the scribe rushed out to elaborate on his notes of the meeting and to faithfully record its decisions; decisions which would most likely be disregarded once the King actually started his tour of the Kingdom, in Lahti's experience. The rest of the guardsmen started filing out the door to resume their duties, and Lahti hoped to lose himself in them, but it was not to be.

Heshka rose and paced over to a point between between Lahti and the door, halting his escape. "Ah, would my Honorable Kitsune attend me for a moment?"

Lahti tensed, and it took all of the kitsune guile he possessed to not visibly wince at the 'request.' If the King was actually asking for him, this would not end well. It would have been better for both of them if he had made it out of the room, Lahti was sure.

"Of course, your majesty," he said anyway.

With Lahti present, no guardsmen were needed to accompany the King, but the two who would regularly act as his escort stayed by the door nonetheless. One of them wasn't someone Lahti had vetted, but rather was a guardsman brought in by Lord Devane to replace one of the many who had already been drawn off by the war effort. Those guardsmen weren't exactly trustworthy, in Lahti's opinion, but it wasn't within his authority to eject the man from the room.

Heshka noticed the guardsmen as well, though what he thought of them was anybody's guess. The King seemed to like everyone when he was happy, and dislike everyone when he was in a disagreeable mood. It was hard to assess just which mood he was in at the time. He did, however, shift uncomfortably in his armor and crown much more often than normal.

What a shame that the scions of Kazdri's line have descended into this, Lahti lamented.

"Any word from your daughter?" Heshka grunted. A disagreeable mood it was.

"Not yet, your majesty. My apologies." Lahti disguised his sigh with an apologetic half-bow.

Heshka, surprisingly, didn't continue that line of questioning. "Not a surprise. You kitsune sure know how to hide when you want to."

"I am not sure she is trying to hide, your majesty. She—"

"Yes, yes, I know." The King waved a hand dismissively. "That's not what I wanted to talk with you about. It has to do with my travel plans. You were planning to accompany me, yes?"

It was an odd question. Lahti hadn't accompanied one of the Kings of Kassia out on these trips since Kazdri's death, instead preferring to arrange for his safety and security from the castle. The systems he put in place worked as long as the King followed his instructions – it was only when they ignored them that danger presented itself.

On the other hand, this might have been another 'request' made under the influence of his rival advisors. Having Lahti out of the castle might be important to any number of plots and subterfuges that the likes of Kobach and Devane might be planning.

"Well, your majesty, I—"

Heshka pivoted to face Lahti square on, a determined look on his face. "Well, don't. I know how to take care of myself, and I'll be accompanied by our best guardsmen." Heshka took this moment to nod at the two people at the door. "Or do you not trust your subordinates?"

Alarms went off in Lahti's head. Those words had preceded more than one king's assassination over the years. "Your majesty, it has been many years since I toured the kingdom, myself. I was hoping to get a firsthand view of forty years of changes I have only heard about."

Heshka's eyes widened in a mild panic. That puzzled Lahti – what did the king have to panic about? Even if he were engaging the most elicit or horrific acts, Lahti was bound by his pledge to protect him. There should be no concern about his presence for anything the King planned on.

"No, my Honorable Kitsune," Heshka said, recovering his composure in an instant. "You must wait here for word on your daughter. And even if she does not return in that time, I must ask you to step up my son's training – his swordplay is lacking, from what my Lord Devane tells me." There was a brief pause, and Lahti almost answered the King before he continued. "I am aware of no plot against me that would strike at me in the countryside."

Now, that was an unusual way of putting it. No plot that would strike him in the countryside? Did that mean he was expecting some plot to strike, but not in the countryside? Was he worried for his son?

Lahti had never thought of Heshka as the most parental of men, but somehow he felt the King was trying to send him a message that he could not say aloud: "Protect my son."

Or perhaps what the King was saying was more "Unmask the conspiracy that is in my very home."

Or perhaps he wasn't trying to tell him anything at all beyond what his words actually said. Lahti would never have accused the King of delivering subtle messages, before.

"If that is what you desire, your majesty, than I will do my best to see it done."

Czerniak had gone to his lessons with Lahti fully intending to follow Gedig's suggestions, but the moment he stepped into the room all thought of that left his mind. Lahti was pacing furiously, and looked to be talking to himself, but no words that Czerniak could distinguish were forthcoming.

It was a picture of undisguised indecision, and on a kitsune of Lahti's reputation undisguised *anything* was something to marvel at. Given that he was also responsible for Czerniak's training and safety, it might also be something to have nightmares over.

"Um... father?" he said, testing out the appellation. With Lahti in such a state, the question Gedig insisted upon would have to wait.

How he reacted to that name, however, might give him a hint.

Except there wasn't any reaction. Lahti continued pacing and muttering, not even noticing his presence. Shrugging, Czerniak walked over to the rack of wooden practice swords and selected one to start limbering up with. He'd realize that his Prince was there at some point, and if Czerniak wasn't ready for training when he did, there would be consequences. Czerniak shook his head, focused, and began his basic footwork practice, gliding across the room with the sword in hand, using the position of his feet to balance the position of the sword.

Yet when he had completed his warm-up, there was no change. Not wanting to waste his practice time, Czerniak started running himself through each of his solo exercises. It wasn't until part-way through the third set that he had any indication Lahti was aware of his presence.

"You should be saying something."

Czerniak froze, startled. "What?"

"Don't stop!" Lahti snapped, almost jumping towards him. "Get back into your sets! In a fight, you need to both focus on one target while simultaneously being aware of everything going on around you. That starts with making yourself able to do two things at once, both with intensity. Concentrate on making sure you complete your exercises as close to perfect as you are physically able, but I also want you to speak to me as you do. And think about what you're saying – I don't want complete gibberish. Now! Move!"

With a frown, Czerniak began his sets again, advancing from the corner of the practice ring to the target in a winding series of parries and swings. "But Lord Devane said you should never speak on the battlefield."

Lahti stepped back into Czerniak's view, grabbing a shield. "Lord Devane is correct. Or rather, there are two styles of mental preparation for combat out there, and for his style he's correct. If you had Lord Devane's skills and mentality, you would never want to let yourself be goaded into speaking, because then your focus is broken and you are vulnerable to attack. In fact, you're better off not listening, either, since you don't want to allow your enemy to taunt or intimidate you into error."

Lahti stepped in front of him again, and Czerniak eased his stance a little. "You aren't that type of fighter, though – you are more like me, and my daughter, and King Kazdri, and even your father. On the battlefield you will be the man giving orders, as the heir to the throne of Kassia, but you need to be able to do that while also engaged in battle. So... learn to converse while you fight. When you are not in command, you can still use that ability to taunt your opponent – more people can be goaded by a taunt than will admit it."

"Um..." Czerniak hesitated, trying to think of a reply, and suddenly he felt a sharp rap across his knees that forced him to change his stance. He didn't see how Lahti managed the strike without him seeing it, standing in front of him like he was, but it was an instructional tap.

"Don't let your performance slip as you think!" Lahti commanded. "Separate your thoughts. One part of you always needs to focus on the fight, even as the other is concentrating about what orders to give or what taunt to use. Now, start your set again, but taunt me as you progress through the exercise."

The perfect thing to say came to Czerniak as he returned to his first stance. He took his first couple of moves before saying anything. "Yes, father." He tried to keep his thoughts separate, as instructed, and observe Lahti's reaction with one part of his mind while he performed the set with another. He was successful, more or less, in separating his thoughts, but he still could glean nothing from the kitsune's reaction. Upping the ante he added, "Has my future wife mastered this technique?"

"Before you were born," Lahti replied without missing a beat. "Harder! I want to feel it when that sword hits my shield."

Czerniak dropped the matter of Kieras, then, deciding he wasn't going to get anywhere probing Lahti for insights on his daughter. He was able to complete the set without having to start over, but his ability to speak at the same time was very hit and miss. This would take some getting used to.

Coming to the final ready stance that signaled the end of the exercise, he didn't let himself relax. "Again?" he asked.

"Eventually," Lahti said, nodding. "But set yourself at ease for now. We need to talk."

"Yes, father?" Czerniak said again, hoping one last time to get some kind of reaction.

Lahti shook his head, but Czerniak wasn't sure if that was in response to what he'd said or something else. "Your father is about to start his annual tour of the kingdom. I was thinking of leaving with him."

Czerniak's eyes widened. "But you haven't done that—"

"Since Kazdri's day, I know," Lahti said, nodding. "And, truth be told, I'm not doing it this time, either. Do you want to know why I'm not?"

It sounded like an innocent enough question, but Czerniak knew from experience that they rarely were.

"I'm not sure I do."

Lahti looked at him for a long moment, then gave a nod as if deciding something. "Lord Devane has criticized your swordfighting abilities. He expressed these to the King, who in turn has ordered me to accelerate your training. So... since your lack of training is the reason I'm stuck here in town, do you have any guesses what I'm going to be doing instead of accompanying him across the countryside?"

Okay, perhaps now really wasn't a good time to have a heart-to-heart about marrying Lahti's daughter. Still, giving the obvious answer might just get him into more trouble than giving a clever one.

"Sneaking out and following him anyway?"

Lahti snorted back a laugh. "Not a bad idea, but I don't think I'll do that this time. No, I'm going to be taking over your training for the next few months – *all* of your training. I'll let Gedig know that he needs to concentrate on the law and economics, because I'm going to be taking over your history lessons. We will discuss tactics. Strategy. Government. I will also step up your hand-to-hand combat, and I will start introducing you to weapons other than sword and spear."

"Why?"

"I do not like the system of one King ruling over an entire country," Lahti said. "But it is better than allowing a corrupt system to take over that country... as long as the King himself isn't weak or corrupt. Since Kazdri was usurped, the line of kings in Kassia has been either weak or corrupt. I'm not going to tell you which I think your father is, but he is no exception. In you, however, I intend to forge the sort of ruler that Kassia can be proud of again. Your father's enemies will not plot against him, because they will know that his son will make their plans even worse. That is how I will protect him while he is away... so, I ask you, are you ready for my training? Or should I just sneak out and follow the king, leaving you to your own devices?"

Czerniak's eyes widened. There was something unsaid in that...

or maybe it wasn't so much unsaid as obscured. He knew Lahti well enough to read those unsaid cues, however, so... was someone plotting against his father?

He would have to think about that later, much as he would the matter of his future marriage to Kieras. In the meantime, Lahti was waiting for an answer.

"I'm not exactly looking to take the job any time soon," Czerniak said. "But sure, I'll let you teach me how to be king. It's about time someone other than Gedig cared about that."

Just as the King had regular meetings he was required to attend, so did the members of the conspiracy to replace him. The principle leaders of the meeting were Lords Kobach and Devane, but there were many others who had joined in. Some were friends of Kobach or Devane, while others did not trust King Heshka. Many were just looking for any opportunity to increase their own power. Devane respected that, but detested their banality and lack of individual cunning. Still, he needed them.

They had to be careful to avoid prying ears, which is why the meeting was being held in a cramped scullery. It was still too soon to displace Heshka, so they had to ensure that their meetings could not be observed by the King's Honorable Kitsune. Lahti almost certainly knew something was going on, but Devane was comfortable that he didn't know anything he could act on. His ignorance of the details was critical to their success. Fortunately, most of the conspirators were familiar enough with the castle to know what rooms Lahti could eavesdrop unobserved, and which he couldn't.

Yes, the kitchen staff undoubtedly wondered why so many high-ranking nobles were taking up their room they couldn't wash the breakfast dishes, and undoubtedly news of this meeting would get to Lahti, but it wasn't the meeting they had to keep secret. It was what was said during it. That need for secrecy made the choice of such a pedestrian room only common sense.

Or so these nobles kept telling themselves whenever one of them knocked over and shattered yet another stack of ceramic plates.

"This is our first meeting since the start of your 'Kitsune Stratagem,' Devane," one of the lesser nobles in the conspiracy said. "We still don't know the details of your plan. I must say, I don't think many of us would be standing in this room right now if we weren't expecting you to explain them."

Devane hesitated. It wasn't exactly his plan to begin with – it was Kobach's. Devane's original plan was simply to assassinate the King and the Prince, and name himself King in their place. The line of Kazdri once had many branches, but by attrition over the past forty years had been whittled down to just those two – when they died, another family line would take their place, and why wouldn't the person who killed them be able to found that line?

Kobach, however, had pointed out that a direct assault on the throne might result in rebellion. Devane was a war hawk – it was partly why Kassia was involved in so many conflicts right now – but even he dreaded a civil war. There was no territory or strategic advantage to be gained in a civil war, and there was no telling who was friend or who was enemy. Kobach had a plan to avoid one, though, and Devane wasn't so foolish to turn him down.

He just didn't quite understand the plan, himself.

"The whole plan is to use Lahti's kitsune cunning against him," Devane said, explaining it to the other lords as Kobach had explained it to him. "He inevitably knows about us, but he cannot act without proof. Our plan is to use his partial knowledge of our plan to do our work for us. The Kitsune Stratagem is to manipulate him into manipulating the last of Kazdri's heirs into surrendering control of Kassia to us. Assassinating the King will not be important when we are done; Heshka may still be alive, and still hold that title. He will still be a symbol of power. But that is all – a symbol. We will hold the real authority over the kingdom."

"Yes, but how?" the lord demanded.

There were too many people in this conspiracy, Devane decided, but they needed numbers... for the moment. Once the King was out of the way, they would be able to whittle down their 'allies' until it was just he and Kobach.

"Lord... um..."

He was saved from having to remember the lord's name when Kobach stepped forward. "Please, friend Devane, allow me to explain. Milords, the plan is well under way. We have convinced the King to arrange Prince Czerniak in marriage with Lahti's daughter, which is the first step of our plan."

"But won't that extend Lahti's service? Kitsune are loyal to their families, even families by marriage."

"Yes, but it won't matter," Kobach said. "In the end, Lahti can be as loyal and protective of the King as he wants. The King won't have any power, so Lahti can keep him alive for as long as he likes."

"Yes, we understand that," the lord said, almost knocking over another set of crockery in his frustrated gestures. "But we don't know what it is you are going to do to take power from the King. I'm not comfortable changing Kassia into a republic, either – I do not want to give up my own power just to remove some from the King."

"No, we are not creating a republic," Kobach said. "We are the Lords of this land – we will not give that up. No, we will re-establish the feudal system that we once enjoyed before the Erixonite invasion, and each of us will be able to use our hereditary titles not to merely collect taxes over and run the defense of the King's territory, but rather we will be as kings of our own lands."

That was news to Devane. He didn't think it made much sense for Kobach, who had no lands of his own, to advocate a government that would strip him of what power he currently had, but that didn't mean his plans were any less effective. He believed in this plan, and he would push it.

"Is that not what we all want?" he asked. "Yes, we will still all be a part of Kassia, united in the defense of our lands, but we will actually have some incentive for defending them other than just the glory of the King. We will be protecting our own lands. And that is why I feel this plan works so well – we return to our glorious past, as friends and allies but rulers in our own right."

"Yes, and that is why I signed on," the lord replied. "But *how?* How is it that you are going to go from an arranged marriage for the Prince into a total abdication of all of the King's powers? You have yet to explain that."

Kobach grimaced, but threw on a smile before answering. "The thing to remember is that Kieras is a kitsune, herself. But she is a young one – we can use that to manipulate her far easier than we could an experienced kitsune like Lahti. So... we marry her off to Czerniak, tying their affairs together. Once they are linked legally and emotionally, we start manipulating her."

"And what good would that do? She isn't royalty, she's just marrying into it! She will have no authority, no matter how much you manipulate her."

"Ah, but the Prince is a lovesick fool," Kobach said. "He *is* royalty, and whatever we can manipulate her into doing, she can manipulate him into doing. It won't take much to get them both embroiled in a scandal that will require they abdicate power, or better yet even go into exile. And that is when we'll act – with the Prince as hostage, we can force Heshka to allow us to pass a law that will strip him of his own power. Lahti will be inadvertently helping us with his effort to protect his daughter. In return, we'll concede that the line of Kazdri may retain the royal title, and we will absolve the Prince of any wrongdoing, but it will hardly matter when they're so powerless."

The other lords shifted about uncomfortably. Devane wasn't sure why – it wasn't like this was any worse than murdering the King or whatever else they might have thought they were doing when they signed on to this plan – but they were. He would have to reassure them.

"Kitsune are bound by their promises," he pointed out. "That's the only reason Lahti is still around, after all. I've had my guardsmen pretend friendship with Kieras, and they tell me she is a little too free with her promises for a kitsune. It is an easy weakness to exploit."

There was a loud crash as one of the lords knocked over yet another stack of crockery. The kitchen staff could be heard muttering outside of the door – even if it was relatively safe for the kitchen staff to know about these meetings, it wasn't a good idea to encourage them to actually listen in.

"I am not sure I fully understand," the lord said. "But it seems the time we have for this meeting is coming to an end. We will discuss this later."

As most of the lords filed out of the scullery, Devane waited to discuss things with Kobach. When the last lord left the room, however, there was still someone with his co-conspirator who he didn't recognize. He wasn't another lord, that was for certain.

"Don't worry," Kobach said, smiling slightly as he approached Devane. "We are free to talk, here. Allow me to introduce you to my new aide-de-camp, Yulaev. He's been in my employ for several years, but I recently learned just how useful he would be to our plans."

"Yeah, our plans," Devane said. "That story you told the other lords – that isn't actually our plan, is it? The kitsune girl really is that naive, but I don't see her manipulating her husband into exile on our say-so."

"No, of course not," Kobach agreed. "But I think a few of our 'friends' might be a little squeamish about the real plan."

"Which is?"

"Simple enough. Kitsune are treacherous creatures – everyone knows this. So, our Prince gets his 'happy' marriage... and then his bride murders him brutally. Or rather, someone murders him brutally, and an investigation 'proves' it was a kitsune who did it. Well, that sets the King against Lahti, who will order the execution of the woman who murdered his son. That will set Lahti against the King, who will not be happy about his daughter being executed. It won't take much to kill the King and once again make it seem like a kitsune – Lahti, in this case – murdered him. And that, my dear Lord Devane, is how you kill off the royal family and usurp power without causing the public to rise up against you."

Devane frowned. That was a different plan than he ever remembered Kobach hinting at, before, but it made more sense than the over-the-top manipulation of manipulators that had been told to the other lords. It had flaws, though. "But the girl has run off, so what do we do now?"

"We could not have planned that better," Kobach laughed. "We will need to retrieve her, of course, but her departure shows she is against this marriage, at least as far as the public sees, which gives a motive behind her murder. We still don't have all of our people in place – we need enough men in the guard to ensure the 'investigation' finds Kieras responsible for Czerniak's murder. I can only see a few weaknesses to this plan."

"Which are?" Devane asked.

"Well, first off, you need to make sure that King Heshka lives until the marriage takes place. He will soon go on tour until winter, which will make him vulnerable. You need to protect him like Lahti does until he returns."

"That should not be an issue," Devane said. It wasn't – yes, several kings of Kassia had been murdered on such tours, but usually those murders were instigated by the King's own children usurping the loyalty of the guardsmen protecting them. That was not likely to happen, considering Czerniak's lack of ambition for the throne, and it was Devane who would control their loyalty.

Kobach nodded. "Good. The second is... there are three people who, by their singular action or working together, could prevent our success – the King, Prince Czerniak, and Gedig. The King could negate the marriage, the Prince could flee the castle before his marriage... and Gedig is possibly the most dangerous of them. If there was concern that the investigation might blame Lahti, it's possible the King would assign Gedig to investigate personally... and Gedig would be able to tell. That would set both the King and Lahti against us, which would be disastrous. We need to know how these people will act if there is evidence of a conspiracy – who will seek aid from whom and the like."

"We can do that," Devane said. "By mid-winter, I'll have enough people in place that we can risk early discovery – if they start to act against us, it may take civil war to complete the coup, but we should have enough people in the castle to manage it by then."

"If that's what we can manage. We will test them in mid-winter, then, and see how they react." He turned to Yulaev. Devane wasn't sure, yet, what role Kobach had in mind for the servant, but Kobach seemed almost deferential to him. "In the meantime, we must continue the search for Kieras. Since we are not yet ready to act, there is no rush to find her, but she must be found."

"I will put out a reward for any information on her whereabouts," Yulaev said with an exaggerated bow. "But I doubt we need to act. She will come to us."

"Are you sure?" Kobach asked. Devane was a little surprised at the uncertainty in his voice. "None of Lahti's other children have ever returned, whatever reason was given for their departure."

"Not entirely true, but you wouldn't know about that," Yulaev said. "His children return now and then, bringing him news, but they are always hidden by kitsune illusions. I know how to look through those illusions, so they will no longer be able to enter this city without my knowledge. She will be no different."

"But it could still be years before Kieras returns," Devane said. "We can't wait that long!"

"It won't be long," Yulaev replied. "Her father did not send her out as punishment, as he claimed – that you probably know – but he did send her out on a mission. I happen to know where that mission should take her. I give it one, two years at most for her to return... and then I... I mean we will act."

VII. A Pinch of Salt

Kieras had accompanied Mathis on each of his seven diplomatic missions since their return from Dahlberg, and so far had yet to regret her decision. She hadn't been doing much for her own quests, but she was enjoying Mathis' company. His talent at negotiation had improved, at the very least, and she was finding him a good and loyal friend.

She was learning a great deal about the world outside of Kassia, as well. Nothing relevant to her quest beyond a few odd kitsune sightings, but she did learn of things she hadn't even known to be curious about prior to these missions.

For example, there were the buildings. As Kassia had evolved from small town to city, every house, building, keep, set of stables, warehouse, store, or any other kind of building had been torn down and rebuilt in flagstone, conforming to the appearance of the castle itself. This left it fairly uniform. In Kassia, Kieras knew of only one type of building – those built of the cut grey stone, with houses and stores built in long rows separated by streets.

Ekholm was only a little different than the city she had left. Most of the buildings were built of brick, which usually looked similar to the stonework she was familiar with except for the color (red or yellow as opposed to grey). Dahlberg's buildings were more like the cut-stone structures found in Kassia, save for those paths cut directly into the volcanic rock by the ancient kitsune.

Traveling with Mathis, however, allowed her to see whole new types of architecture. In the small town of Sorkham, where to ward off scurvy they negotiated the purchase of a large supply of fruits for preservation, most of the houses in the town were built out of a material known as cob – a clay-like substance constructed in layered walls almost two feet thick. The houses were generally small, but they were warm on cool nights and cool on warm days. Additionally, there was often a small parcel of land between each home – another first for Kieras. While they were in Sorkham, a forest fire threatened its plentiful orchards, but the cob houses were quite safe, as cob was impervious to fire and had few wooden structural supports for the fire to undermine. Or so Mathis had explained as the fire approached.

While looking for the silk thread needed for sutures – a vital commodity in the aftermath of any battle – they had visited the town of Pogge. Even smaller than Sorkham, the entire population lived in one of just eight longhouses built of woven bamboo and thatched roofs. There were no walls inside these longhouses, and consequently no privacy – everyone lived together, slept together, ate together, and worked together. The people of Pogge would rarely leave their home longhouse unless it was to move to one of the neighboring longhouses after marriage. There appeared to be no sense of propriety, either. Nudity was commonplace, married couples were either observed passively or ignored as they had sex, and even activities reserved for the privy – which, thankfully, were generally done outside and not in the longhouse – were done in full view of everyone. Kieras found herself constantly blushing during her entire time in Pogge. Mathis was gracious enough to help her protect her own privacy, when necessary.

They were currently visiting the salt-panning town of Arsene, another tributary village in the Norre Hegemony. Arsene should have been supplying Ekholm with the salt they so vitally needed to preserve their foods for the expected siege, but the unexpected delay of a major shipment had required diplomatic intervention.

Many of the buildings in Arsene were built of brick or flagstone, which Kieras was familiar with, but not all. Their inn was one of many buildings built using wattle and daub, something she had never seen before. Mathis, though, knew the technique quite well. Wattles, made of thin split branches woven together, were slotted into a timber frame.

Next, the daub – clay or lime mixed with crushed stone and reinforced by horse hair or straw – was applied on top of the wattle. Finally, the whole thing was painted to help protect it from the weather – a step the barracks builders in Ekholm had completely skipped, much to their later chagrin.

Mathis had told her the story of how, when he was very young, he had worked alongside his brother and several other members of Ekholm's militia to build a "proper barracks" at the insistence of the militia's then-captain, Fornier. No one had ever built a building using wattle and daub techniques in Ekholm, and Fornier was the only person involved in the construction who had seen what such a building was supposed to look like.

They relied on books and drawings during the build. Why Fournier insisted on building his barracks out of a material that none of them had ever used before, Mathis never found out, but their chief architects and foremen tried their best to accommodate him. The timber frame went up perfectly. From then on, however, it was one disaster after another.

The book they were using to figure out the technique suggested that "thin" branches, split in half, be used to make the wattles. They thought this meant a branch the size of the switches that mothers used to color the backsides of their children for time immemorial. Splitting branches this thin often resulted in them breaking, and then weaving enough of them together to form just one single panel of wattle took longer than it should have taken to complete the entire building. What none of them knew until later was that the book meant branches of one or two inches thickness.

That was only the first of many errors. Several of the wattle panels they produced wound up not fitting where they were supposed to. As amateurishly as they had been assembled, they were prone to even more breakage as they were slotted in. When the wattle was finally completed, it took quite several failed attempts before they were able to perfect their daubing material. They found that applying the daub was considerably more difficult than the books had made it seem. Their technique was sloppy, and they were so slow that the material would dry and harden in the mixing barrels after less than half the daub had been used.

But finally the barracks were completed, and Fornier moved his offices and their training indoors. Unfortunately, they had neglected what proved to be a vital step – they hadn't painted the outside of the building. Without paint, wind, rain, and the occasional snowfall aged the structure prematurely. A leak in the roof after a particularly nasty ice storm had Fornier abandon the building "temporarily" as they waited for friendlier weather to repair it. When he returned in the spring, however, rain and melted ice had seeped into the building repeatedly, pooling in many areas and breeding mildew and mold throughout the barracks. Kieras found tears dripping down her face with laughter as Mathis described the stench of cleaning all of that mildew and mold out of the building.

Mathis promised to show Kieras that building once they had returned from Arsene. It was just ruin, now, as all efforts to repair it proved futile. That would have to wait until their mission was complete, however.

He had only had time to tell her that story because the Arsenians were delaying them. They claimed a lack of adequate containers to safely transport the salt. This was a serious concern – salt was literally worth its weight in gold, and Arsene was already selling it for far less than it was worth because of their affiliation with Norre. Any containers which might leak would be extremely costly, both for Norre (which would have to pay to replace the lost salt) and Arsene (which was already losing money on every speck of salt it sold to Norre).

The salt-panning town was also building up its own defenses against the Knodelian threat. These were far less complex than Ekholm's, but then they had more defensive structures in place to begin with. While trying to supply the entire region with desperately needed salt, they were also constructing several trenches and wooden walls. They already had several stone towers which could serve as both barracks and archers' towers, but between the costs of building those walls and equipping soldiers they needed the money from that salt to pay for it all. Norre was providing some assistance, of course, but Norre's coffers weren't limitless, and wealthier towns such as Arsene generally were asked to help offset the costs of their own defense.

"I realize that the Arsenians aren't making things easy for us," Mathis said to his ambassadorial train, breaking Kieras from her thoughts. They were assembled in the inn's great room, which doubled as both a tavern and – thanks to the sizable brick fireplace – a kitchen in the evenings. "I'm not convinced they are in as desperate of a situation regarding salt containers as they claim, but proving that is going to be difficult. It will be even harder, however, if you people go around upsetting the townsfolk."

"And you had best not antagonize the Arsenian leaders, yourself, Mathis," Jobinh warned, sounding like he was scolding a child.

Kieras frowned. Mathis had grown as a leader and as a diplomat over these past few months, which she was quite pleased to see. Jobinh, however, still treated Mathis like he was an idiot. In deference to Mathis' efforts to keep the peace, Kieras held back her wrath, but if the man started neglecting their duties or insulting Mathis in front of the foreign delegations he was meeting, she wouldn't restrain herself.

Mathis merely rolled his eyes at the implied insult. One area where Kieras thought he still needed improvement was in his patience – he had too much of it when dealing with Jobinh, ostensibly because "preparing for the coming battle was more important than complaining about an otherwise good soldier from an allied power with an attitude problem." She would have torn the Norrish soldier to shreds (perhaps just figuratively, but she was quite capable of doing it literally) by now. Perhaps Mathis' patience in this matter was another one of those human traits that kitsune such as herself would never understand.

"Of course – none of us should," Mathis said – proving once again, to Kieras' eyes, that he was a far better diplomat than Jobinh gave him credit for. "To that end I suggest that we all stay in or near the inn as much as we can bear it from now on. When you do have to go out, if you are not involved in the official negotiations, try not to call attention to yourselves. There's plenty of the local civilian garb available in our provision chests for all of you, including gear for our soldiers."

"I'm supposed to meet with the town's chronicler, today," Kieras said. "Should I 'wear' a disguise when I go?"

Mathis chewed his lip. "I doubt there's anyone in Arsene who can see through your illusions, so I doubt it would cause any distress should you use one. This town is small enough, though, that you might still be recognized as a stranger, and you could very well be the only redhead in Arsene right now. Our relations with the Arsenians aren't so bad that we really have to disguise ourselves – the concern is more in drawing their attention. It's your call, of course, but I don't think all-out disguises are needed, just yet, as long as you treat the locals with respect and don't call attention to yourself."

Kieras considered what Mathis said. Nodding slightly, and with a bit of a smirk on her face, she grabbed her *hoshi no tama* and concentrated her magic through it. In an instant, her clothes adjusted themselves to appear more Arsenian, but she didn't change her own appearance any further than that. "How's that?"

Mathis was speechless for a second, then gave a bit of a swallow and nodded. "Whenever you do that, I worry you'll... ah, never mind. It should be easy for you to fit in dressed like that."

Kieras frowned, wondering what Mathis had left unsaid, but she didn't have enough time to work it out of him right then. Her appointment with the chronicler was early in the day, and she was hoping to stop at the town's bakery and purchase a pasty for breakfast before the meeting. "Well, I have to get going. We're all meeting back at the inn for dinner tonight, right?"

"That is the plan," Mathis said.

"I'll see you then." Giving him her best smile, Kieras headed out the door. It was mid-morning, but there weren't many people out and about. She was able to make her way to the bakery pretty quickly.

"What do you mean there aren't any chicken pasties?" she heard from outside the door of the bakery. Her face fell in disappointment – she loved this bakery's chicken pasties – but she still needed breakfast. "I've been coming to this bakery every time I come to this town, and I've never known it to be out of chicken pasties!"

"Sorry, sir," came the familiar voice of the baker. "We didn't get our chickens delivered until it was too late for this morning's batch. We'll have some baked up by lunchtime if you want to come back."

"I'll be back, then," the speaker said. Kieras was nearly knocked over as a man wearing the clothes of a Norrish trader stormed out of the bakery. He glanced at her in surprise, almost said something, then shook his head and walked off without a word.

"Well, that was rather rude," Kieras muttered as she stepped into the bakery. There was something about the stranger's features that was calling her attention, but then the baker spoke to her, making her lose her train of thought. The baker had quickly become a good friend during her stay in Arsene, and she would much rather talk with him than worry about rude strangers.

"Oh, I know," the baker agreed, chuckling slightly. "Every time he comes to town, he wants our chicken pasties. If we don't have them – which, despite what he says, happens more often than we'd like – he goes around town causing trouble. If we do, he's actually a rather pleasant person." He frowned. "We do have some awfully strange occurrences whenever he's in town."

Kieras would have asked for more information on that, but she was in a hurry. "You're out of chicken – which is what I wanted for breakfast, too – so what *do* you have right now?"

"Well, there's plenty of bread, of course. We also have these stewed beef pasties, but they're pretty heavy for breakfast – we usually sell them to our local workers to take with them for lunch. We have some cheese filled pasties, but they're starting to go a little stale. You deserve something better. There are a number of fruit-filled pasties, which many people prefer for breakfast: Plum, cherry, apple, pear...."

As the baker droned on about pasty fillings, Kieras tuned her out to focus on the bakery's scents. When not in her fox form, her nose wasn't nearly as good, but it was still far better than your average human. The scents in this particular bakery were delightful. She tried to identify each smell, hoping to find the one which appealed to her the most for breakfast that morning. She definitely could identify the pervasive odor of bread as well as other strong, fresh odors such as the beef stew and several of the fruits that the owner was listing.

Underneath those, however, there was another smell. It was faint, but fresh nevertheless, and vaguely familiar. Kieras wasn't quite sure why it caught her attention so much, since after a moment of study she could tell that it wasn't food at all, but nevertheless it was something appealing to her. She tried to search her memory for just why it seemed so important. It was on the tip of her mental tongue...

Suddenly, she remembered. It took all of her self-control not to announce it to the world, but once she made the guess she was absolutely certain she was correct.

"My goodness, girl," the baker said, attracting her attention. "I've never seen your face light up like that before. You must really like almond butter to get that kind of reaction."

"Hmm? Oh, yes," Kieras said, trying to cover for her inattention. In fact, she had never had almond butter, but didn't particularly like almonds in the least.

"Well, give me a minute, and I'll warm one up for you. You've been such a good customer while you've been here, you can have this one for free."

"Thank you," Kieras said, feigning enthusiasm. She was actually very touched by the baker's generosity, even if she didn't really want the almond butter pasty, but her mind was elsewhere. One name kept running through her head, filling her thoughts with both hope and more questions.

It can't be him, *can it?*

The so-called "negotiations" had broken for lunch, and Mathis was feeling rather frustrated. It was becoming increasingly clear that there were no real issues with transporting the salt and the Arsenian town council was simply pushing him for a bribe. He really wanted to drink away his troubles in the tavern, but he would have to go back to the negotiating table in a couple of hours. Still, maybe he could find some nice wine to go with his lunch and take the edge off.

As he was trying to decide whether to buy a bird roasted at one of the smaller taverns in town or to return to his inn for their regular stew, Kieras appeared out of nowhere. It took him a moment to recognize her in the Arsenian clothing, but that wasn't the only reason he was so surprised to see her.

"Why are you here?" he asked. "I thought your meeting was going to take all day."

"The chronicles weren't as useful as I thought." Kieras had a smile on her face, but it looked pasted on. "So I figured I'd stop by and get you to join me for lunch."

Mathis scratched the back of his head. "Well, I was hoping to stop by at one of the local drinking holes, but I suppose if you want to come with me—"

"No," Kieras snapped. "You need to come with me. To the bakery. Now."

That wasn't subtle at all, which had Mathis worried. "What's wrong?"

Kieras glanced around frantically, and then seemed to sniff the air. Apparently satisfied, she drew close to him and whispered in his ear.

"There's another kitsune in town. He's going to be at the bakery for lunch. I need you with me when I meet him."

Mathis raised an eyebrow. "Wha—"

"Shh! Just do what I say. Trust me!"

"Well, okay." He cautiously followed her to the bakery as she pulled on his arm. She seemed rather anxious – well out of proportion for the possibility of meeting another kitsune – but Mathis accepted it at first. Then, a suspicion rose in him. "This isn't part of your prank, is it?"

"What?" she replied incredulously, staring at him. "What are you... oh, that. No. I swear to you this has nothing to do with any prank I have planned or am planning."

That surprised Mathis – if she felt this was serious enough to make an oath, that meant it was genuinely important. "Well, then, if that's the case, we'd better hurry, hadn't we?"

She gave him a grateful smile before leading him at a fast walk – almost a run – towards the bakery. He'd heard of this bakery from her before – she had talked extensively about their delicious chicken pasties – but had never gone in, himself. He hoped they found whatever or whoever it was she was so anxious about, because she seemed only a knife's edge away from falling into absolute panic.

There were two people visible when they stepped inside the bakery. One was obviously the baker, himself – nothing remarkable, there. The other was dressed as a Norrish trader wearing a buckskin coat, perfect for traveling through the elements, with finer, more comfortable clothing underneath. He also had on a hat that did an excellent job of hiding his hair from view.

Kieras stepped towards the trader, ignoring all sense of propriety and startling the baker. She took a deep sniff before nodding. "It's him!"

"What is going on?" the baker asked, confused.

Mathis watched as the trader took a sniff, himself, and then widened his eyes comically. "Are you—" the trader started to ask.

That little sniff revealed the trader as a kitsune, as well – a myobu, if the tiny bit of hair he could see under the hat was any indication. Mathis didn't want either kitsune to reveal themselves unnecessarily, so he decided to interrupt. "Maybe we could step outside to have this conversation, where we won't disturb this wonderful baker whose food I gather *both* of you enjoy?"

"Yes... yes, of course," the trader stuttered. He turned and bowed to the baker. "My apologies, good sir, but I knew this lady many years ago and didn't recognize her until just now. We'll be back for those chicken pasties soon enough."

The baker gave a confused smile back. "Of course, sir. Always happy to have your business."

Mathis took Kieras by the elbow, guiding her out of the bakery. The other kitsune followed obediently, to Mathis' slight surprise. He led the pair in silence back to their inn, then up the stairs to his room.

"All right," he said once the door was securely closed. "Who are you and what is going on?"

The trader's eyes widened. "Kieras didn't tell you?"

"Just that you were another kitsune," Mathis said, looking uncertainly at the young woman. "Nothing more than that."

Kieras gave a weak, apologetic smile. "I didn't have time to explain any more than that. I needed to be sure we made it to the bakery in time."

"Then allow me to introduce myself," the other kitsune said, pulling off his hat and bowing. The hat had concealed rather long silvery-white locks of hair, though perhaps not as completely as the kitsune wished. Mathis wasn't going to say anything about being able to see through his illusions, however, until he knew that ability wouldn't be used against him. Now that Mathis had a good look at him, the man seemed to bear a striking resemblance to Kieras. "My name is Daneyko, son of the Lahti and Tianhyu... and Kieras' older brother."

"Who I haven't seen since I was six!" Kieras said. "I wasn't sure it was you, considering the last time I caught your scent was over forty years ago. That's partly why I didn't tell him anything more – I wasn't sure you were who I thought you were."

Mathis gawked at her briefly. He had a hard time remembering that the young woman who seemed to be about his age – maybe a shade younger – was actually more than twenty years his elder. He then shook himself, recovering his senses.

"Forgive me for not introducing myself earlier," Mathis said. "I was a little surprised. My name is Mathis of Ekholm, a friend of your sister's."

Mathis noticed a slight flash in Daneyko's eyes as he mentioned Ekholm, but it was hard to tell for sure. "Well, Mathis, it is good to meet you. And now that the introductions are out of the way, I would like to know just why my sister is traveling with you. Or what she's doing in these lands at all, for that matter."

Kieras spoke before Mathis could say anything. "Father sent me on a quest. The people of Ekholm, and Mathis in particular, are helping me on that quest. Mathis is my host while I live in Ekholm."

"Ekholm, huh?" Daneyko muttered, seemingly unhappy about something. "Well, in your case, that's probably all right. So, what is this about a quest?"

Kieras gave a hesitant smile. "You don't happen to know where mother is, do you?"

Daneyko claimed to have not seen their mother since leaving Kassia, but thought the myobu priesthood might know where she was. As Skygger had also agreed to try, Daneyko said he would contact the priesthood to see if they could locate her.

Kieras told him of the other parts of her quest, explaining just how far she had progressed in her searches. She did notice that Daneyko seemed uncomfortable every time she mentioned Ekholm. She resolved to find out why.

"Have you had some dealings with Ekholm?" she asked. "I have been there for several months, now, and I have found it a very pleasant place to live. I also know that other kitsune are supposed to visit there, regularly, though I admit I haven't seen any in my time there. But you seem... uncomfortable, every time I mention it."

Daneyko glanced apologetically at Mathis. "Sorry. It isn't my problem with Ekholm at all... it's just that the myobu priesthood has forbidden any myobu from entering any of the former towns or cities of Eskesa until certain conditions are met. I don't know why – you would have to ask one of the priesthood, and while I may work for them I am not a member. I'm still too young to join."

"Too young?" Mathis asked.

"You have to be at least a two-tailed kitsune," Daneyko said, looking embarrassed. "Usually, we kitsune grow a new tail every hundred years, but that doesn't start until we're two hundred years old. I won't grow a second tail for another century, at least."

"What is the myobu priesthood, anyway?" Mathis asked. "And why would they be able to forbid other kitsune from entering Ekholm?"

Daneyko grimaced. "How much do you trust this human, sis?"

Kieras considered the question carefully. She liked Mathis as a friend, but there was a big difference between liking a person and trusting them. He had revealed her secrets to others at least once, so far. However, looking at it honestly, he only revealed those secrets to people he felt he could trust, and only because he thought he needed to do so in order to protect her. He would do everything in his power to protect her. She also believed his promise to never reveal any of her secrets again.

"He is prone to making mistakes sometimes," she finally said. "But then, so are we all. I trust him to help protect me to the best of his ability." She paused, trying to figure out how to phrase the rest of her thoughts on Mathis. "I also trust him to keep his word when given, and to keep my secrets, but only so far as those two things do not interfere with his ability to keep me safe."

Daneyko raised a curious eyebrow, and Mathis himself seemed a bit surprised, though he said nothing to interfere with the siblings' discussion.

"I suppose that's good enough," Daneyko said. He turned to face Mathis. "Since you've been dealing with my sister this long, you probably know enough of kitsune nature to not believe much of what I say. I will make this oath: I am not going to lie to you about what the myobu priesthood is. I may, of course, leave out some vital details, but I will tell no lies."

Mathis gave a wry grin. "A half truth can be worse than a lie, as I'm sure you know. Still, to a man who knows nothing, even half-truths count as education."

Daneyko laughed. "Careful with this one, sis – he is no fool."

"I already *know* that," Kieras groaned in disgust. "He saw through my illusions pretty much from the moment I first met him, and then pulled one of his own against me by swapping my *hoshi no tama* with a nice ball of mud until I admitted what I was. He was nice enough to give it back to me without making any demands, though."

"Really?" Daneyko replied, surprised, studying her anew. "As I recall, your illusions were pretty good, sis – better than mine, even though you were young even in human years when I left. A 'prodigy of transformation,' as mother put it. How did he see through your illusions?"

Mathis flushed. "Her, uh, nose gave her away."

"I fainted passing by a tannery," Kieras said with a snort.

Daneyko grinned. "I'm going to have to get the whole story out of you later, sis. Now, about the myobu priesthood..."

"Yes?" Mathis prompted.

Daneyko's face went blank, and he started speaking rhythmically. "The Priesthood of the Myobu Kitsune was forged two millennia ago to protect the legacy of Inari. They direct and maintain his Shrines and forever continue the effort to search for Inari's Heirs." He paused, his face softening. In a more natural tone of voice, he continued, "None of which really means anything. In human terms, they provide guidance and governance to the myobu kitsune." He gave a bit of a grin. "No myobu is actually required to obey the priesthood's orders, of course – not even other members of the priesthood. However, they do have to follow certain general restrictions, such as the order forbidding any myobu from entering the former cities of Eskesa."

Mathis frowned. "Kieras is partly myobu. What could this 'myobu priesthood' do to her if they decide to enforce this restriction?"

"Nothing," Daneyko said confidently. "Because of her red fur, she is not recognized as a myobu. That cuts both ways – she is not granted the privileges of the myobu, but she is not subject to their laws."

"You're white furred, I believe," Mathis said, glancing at his hair. "What would they do to you if you went to Ekholm?"

Daneyko blinked. "I'm not sure I can. These restrictions are not 'rules,' as you humans have them. I believe the priesthood uses kitsune magic to prevent myobu kitsune from being *able* to enter Ekholm, though it may only be a restraint against members of the priesthood, themselves. Even if their magic does not bind me because of my nogitsune blood, however, making the attempt to violate their mandates is grounds for a half-blood such as me to be exiled from the priesthood. I would lose my status among the other kitsune, and I would likely be permanently exiled from the Inari Shrines."

That seemed to satisfy Mathis, but something confused Kieras. "Wait a moment. I can wear mother's jewelry, which is magically restricted to only be worn by myobu. Yet I am not magically restrained from entering Ekholm, as you claim other myobu are."

"You can wear mother's jewelry?" he said, surprised. When she pointed to her choker, he frowned. "I can't explain it. I guess that's a question you'll have to ask mother when you find her."

There was a knock on the door. "Mathis, are you in there?" Jobinh called from the other side.

Mathis groaned, realizing the time. "I'd rather stay and talk, but duty calls. You are welcome to join us for dinner, tonight, Daneyko – I'm sure your sister would enjoy your company, and I'm still quite curious as to why you are here."

"I'll be there," Daneyko said. "I haven't seen Kieras in decades – you can bet we'll still have things to talk about, tonight."

Jobinh's muffled voice came through the door again. "I hear voices. Mathis, is that you?"

"Yeah, it's me," Mathis called back reluctantly.

"The town council is about the reconvene," Jobinh replied. "We need to get to the town hall right away."

"I'll be right there," Mathis said, running for the door. He paused before leaving and sighed. "For a moment, I almost forgot I still had this mess to deal with."

Once the door finished closing behind Mathis, Daneyko turned to his sister. "Well, now. We still have quite a bit to catch up on. Let's start with that story about you letting this Mathis character steal your *tama....*"

Mathis sat in the inn's great room, rubbing his forehead to try and abate his growing headache while the inn's staff set up their kitchen. The meeting with the town council was thankfully over. It had ended prematurely when storms erupted over Arsene, and the roof of their meeting room started leaking like a sieve. He was quite grateful for the rain. The meeting had consisted of little more than the councilmen making him listen, for several hours, as they described various things they had "studied" to load the salt on the wagons. Somehow, cloth bags which had sufficed for transporting salt for hundreds of years were too easy to tear, barrels which could hold water, beer, and wine were leaking salt, and anything else they tried they either could not replicate in sufficient quantity (without the addition of some money, it was hinted) or simply did not work.

"How does a village become the largest salt exporter in its region if they cannot export *salt?*" he muttered disgustedly.

Jobinh sighed impatiently. "Of course they can export salt, they're simply holding out—"

"I know that," Mathis snapped. Seeing Jobinh come to attention at the interruption, he sighed. With a wave of his hand, he said, "Sorry.

I'm just getting frustrated." He paused. "I might be plotting to burn this village down to the ground, but I *probably* won't go through with it."

Giving a reluctant smile, Jobinh said, "Well, I suppose that's okay, as long as you keep those plots to yourself and don't discuss them in hearing distance of the town's leaders."

"You know, we can't afford to give these people a bribe," Mathis said, trying to bring the conversation to safer territory. "Ekholm doesn't have the money for it, and you know better than I that Norre has already paid these people as much as they're going to pay them."

"Yet we need to do something," Jobinh said. "We have to have that salt."

"Yes, but *what?*" Mathis said. "Have you ever been in a situation like this, before?"

Jobinh frowned. "It is your job to figure this mess out, not mine."

Mathis was rather startled at the hostility, but tried not to let it show. He knew that Jobinh had been rather uncomfortable in his presence ever since the Dahlberg mission, but it had never manifested itself in this way.

"I know it is, but it seemed appropriate to ask for your opinion as one of the key members of our diplomatic mission. I'll come up with a plan soon enough, with or without your advice. Perhaps Kieras' brother will be able to help spark some ideas."

"Kieras has a brother?" Jobinh said, startled. "Since when?"

"You didn't know?" Mathis replied, feigning surprise. "You usually know all of my comings and goings, whether I tell you of them or not."

"This one escaped me," Jobinh replied dryly. "Now, what about Kieras' brother?"

"Kieras was at that bakery she's been talking about – the one with the chicken pasties?"

"I know about it."

"It turns out she's not the only kitsune infatuated with that particular delicacy," Mathis said wryly. "Her brother happens to be in town, and she was going into the bakery just as he was coming out."

Jobinh's eyes narrowed. "Why is he here?"

"I'm not sure," Mathis replied. "I was going to find out, but I was called away to that pointless meeting with the town council before I could. He doesn't appear hostile, however."

"He's a kitsune. They are known to be quite treacherous."

"That's more than a bit harsh," Mathis said irritably. "I do know what you are referring to, of course. I've actually become something of an expert on kitsune since meeting Kieras. Even so, I'm pretty confident he is not our enemy."

"Not knowingly, perhaps," Jobinh admitted grudgingly. "But suppose he is behind this Arsenian desire to blackmail additional funds from Norre, without knowing it is us he is actually targeting?"

Mathis rolled his eyes. It was a possibility, but it wasn't the most likely scenario. "I suppose that could be. I'll keep an eye on him, of course. We'll just have to see if he's a friend or an enemy, won't we?"

As Kieras finished a (heavily exaggerated) story about getting drunk on lingonberry wine, her brother laughed into his beer. "Dinner" had been going on for several hours, now, with many introductions and a lot of good food, good drinking, and terrible singing. It was nice and warm in the inn considering how heavy and cold the rains were getting outside, and no one wanted to leave for their own rooms or homes. Finally, though, when the rowdiest patrons had either passed out or retreated to their rooms in the inn, both siblings found some space for themselves to continue telling each other tales from their past.

"This Ziani girl you've been conspiring with sounds hilarious," Daneyko said. "I hope I get a chance to meet her some day."

Kieras' face fell slightly. "Well, that's unlikely, since you can never come to Ekholm. In fact, I probably won't be able to see much of you, even though I know where you spend most of your time, now. I'll be staying in Ekholm for a while, at least."

Daneyko raised a curious eyebrow at her. "Yes, so you say. Tell me, my dear sister, just what is going on between you and this Mathis fellow?"

"What do you mean?" Kieras asked, taking a sip of her wine.

"You seem quite certain that this man will protect you at all costs," Daneyko said. "And, from your stories, you seem willing to listen to his orders quite readily. Even if he couches those orders as suggestions, you seem unusually compliant for a kitsune."

"What are you suggesting?" Kieras wondered if she should be offended, but was a little too wine-fogged to figure it out.

"Well, father did suggest you find a deserving, trustworthy human to serve as a guardian for a year...." Daneyko sounded as if he really wanted to suggest something else.

"A... with *Mathis?*" Kieras sputtered incredulously.

Daneyko shrugged. "Well, if you trust and respect him as much as you claim to, why not? He seems like a nice enough human, and his little trick with your *tama* makes me think he could teach you a thing or two about deception – a skill father seems to have left you lacking in."

"Father wanted me to fit in with humans more than he wanted me to learn kitsune traditions. He raised *you* much the same way, as I recall."

"He did." Daneyko shifted a little uncomfortably. "I'm just saying I like this Mathis, and I think you could do a lot worse."

Kieras frowned. Mathis might not be that bad of a choice, but there were others she had met who were more deserving. "I haven't even considered him. Actually, it's his brother – Torkki – to whom I'm more interested in swearing allegiance."

"The soldier, right?" When Daneyko got a nod in return, he shrugged. "I suppose that's reasonable. Still, it sounds like his brother can take care of himself without your help. If Ekholm is going to war, your Mathis may need help to survive."

Kieras grimaced. "I think Mathis will be okay on his own. He's an excellent archer, and if he can outsmart a kitsune he can probably think on his feet pretty well, too. Torkki is more deserving, I believe."

"Is someone talking about me?" the subject of their conversation said jovially. Kieras spun around to see Mathis approaching them lazily, drink in hand. He probably hadn't been able to listen in on them, but she narrowed her eyes in suspicion. He gave her a slight smile. "I was all the way across the room when I heard my name cried out in indignation. Did I do something wrong?"

Daneyko laughed. "No, not at all. Come, sit down, join us – we were just talking about her adventures since entering Ekholm. Tell me, did my sister really help this Ziani girl try to spy on you and your brother in the baths?"

Mathis laughed, taking a seat at their table. "They were both rather drunk at the time, but yes. She was using her 'illusory magic' to make Ziani appear to be a mirror. What she probably doesn't remember was that it might have worked, except it was the most garishly extravagant mirror to ever appear in Ekholm. It was about the size of a large horse, and it had little foxes 'carved' all around the frame. Not to mention she passed out after transforming Ziani into that mirror, so she was still asleep on the floor when Torkki and I got there. Ziani was terrified she'd be a mirror forever, forgetting she could escape the illusion merely by walking out of the corner. I don't think they ever got that drunk again."

Kieras blushed. "I think I'm more embarrassed about that illusion than I am about falling asleep in the bathhouse, to be honest. That thing was hideous."

Daneyko laughed harder. "I asked Kieras if she'd ever managed to catch you in the bath, since then, which prompted the outraged squawk you heard that got you over here."

"Ah," Mathis said, his eyes narrowing. "You're lying, of course, but I'll assume it's because you're protecting the propriety of your sister rather than any more nefarious reason."

Daneyko slowly raised an eyebrow. "Either you're kitsune yourself, or you're unusually perceptive."

Mathis grabbed an apple off the table and inspected it. "No need for unusual perception, here." He took a bite of the apple. "I just know that Kieras wouldn't get embarrassed by that question. She's more than just a bit brazen recounting her adventures with Ziani, so I seriously doubt she'd be too surprised by the suggestion they tried again."

Kieras giggled drunkenly. "We have. Ziani caught Torkki a few times, but we never caught you."

"That's because you two aren't exactly subtle about it." He washed down his apple with a swig of some dark beverage she was unfamiliar with. "I generally see you two coming a mile away and avoid the bath when there's a chance you're on the prowl. I don't always remember to let Torkki know I've spotted you, though. He might notice, himself, but I think he likes showing off to you girls."

At that, all three of them chorused in laughter. They fell into a comfortable discussion of all of their pasts – each of them getting ribbed and managing a ribbing, themselves. Kieras made a point of sobering herself up while pretending to still be drunk, while Mathis finished his apple and Daneyko, as far as Kieras could tell, just enjoyed the conversation.

Mathis reached for another apple, but they were all gone. "That was a good apple. I'm going to get some more. Either of you want anything?"

"I could use another beer," Daneyko said.

"I'd love some more chicken," Kieras said brightly, feigning drunken enthusiasm and licking her lips.

"Sure thing." He reached into his purse, then frowned. "I don't have enough, though. Could I borrow a couple copper coins? I'll pay you back in the morning, once I've had a chance to access the mission's coffers."

Daneyko pulled out some change. "Have mine."

Mathis took the coins and frowned. He checked it over, and finally popped it into his mouth and bit down. "No, thanks," he finally said, returning the money. "I'd rather not pay for our dinner with an acorn."

Daneyko blinked. "I've never had anyone see through that one, before. I'm afraid I don't have anything suitable, then."

Kieras sighed, reaching into her own purse and finding a half dozen copper Ekholmer taels. "Papa would be disappointed in you, Daneyko," she slurred drunkenly, handing the taels to Mathis. "You do regular business in this town. Use too much illusory money, and the humans will stop doing business with you. You should know that."

As Mathis stepped away, Daneyko shot back a rebuttal. "I saw you using illusory money, yourself, though. You gave the owner of that other tavern some Arsenian sols, which I know you don't have in your purse."

"That was different," Kieras said. "I changed real money – Ekholmer taels – into those sols. By weight, taels are slightly more valuable than sols, so I actually overpaid."

Daneyko raised an eyebrow. "Why would you do that?"

"I gave a promise that I would not cause trouble for Ekholm's diplomatic missions when I joined them to search for our mother." Promises were sacred to Kieras, as they were to all kitsune. "Right now, Ekholm is not held in high regard in Arsene, and I didn't want to cause a commotion by paying with Ekholmer currency. Here they already know that Mathis and I are from Ekholm, so they wouldn't care if we used taels, but at that other tavern it could inspire some anger from the managers."

"And when your coins turn into taels a few hours later?" Daneyko asked.

Kieras shrugged. "Not a big deal. They know that there are

Ekholmers in town, and Ekholmer currency *does* get circulated around here. A lot of Arsene's trade traffic goes through Ekholm, after all. It'll get sorted into their regular stock of cash, and they won't think anything of it. It's just that, if I used only taels to pay for our meal, that would probably identify me as an Ekholmer pretty quickly."

"Or at least as someone who does business with Ekholmers," Mathis said, taking a seat next to them. He handed Kieras her chicken and Daneyko his beer. "This inn is taking a bit of flack for hosting us. That's partly why I'm not a regular customer of that bakery you two like – I don't want to cause the baker any problems."

Daneyko leaned in. "What's the source of these... problems? Aren't you just buying salt from them?"

"Mostly, they feel that Norre is unfairly doing a lot more to protect us than them," Mathis replied. "Which, truthfully, is a fair criticism. Norre is fully funding the construction of our defensive wall and providing a group of elite soldiers to man it. They're providing Arsene with a much larger contingent of soldiers and engineering assistance for the construction of their own walls, but they are not getting any additional coin, and are in fact losing a great deal of their regular profits trying to keep this entire region of the alliance supplied with salt."

Daneyko frowned. "Sounds like their argument should be with Norre, and not with you guys."

"I agree, of course," Mathis said, "but try telling them that."

"Why don't you tell me the whole problem," Daneyko said, "and then let's see if we can't solve it together...."

Finished recounting all of the antics of Arsene's town council, Mathis glanced at his audience. Kieras looked more drunk than ever, but he knew better. She hadn't touched a sip of wine since he'd sat at their table, and she was eating enough to offset some of the alcohol that had been in her system earlier. That was okay – he didn't have to spoil all of her illusions, as long as she wasn't harming anyone.

Daneyko, on the other hand, looked disturbingly all too interested in Mathis' tale. He still wondered if the older kitsune sibling had ulterior motives behind his meeting with Kieras. Mathis had told Daneyko nothing that he couldn't have figured out, himself, with just a few well-placed questions to Arsenian commoners, but he still bore watching.

"So... they claim they can't transport your salt," Daneyko said.

"Not quite," Mathis said. "We're in charge of the transportation, and have been from the beginning. What they claim is that the salt cannot be *packaged* in such a way that they can load it onto our carts. It's an absurd lie, of course, but one they'll cling to until we come up with a bribe for them large enough to replace the profits they're losing on this discounted salt sale. Which we can't afford – despite all of the coin Norre is granting us, we don't have *that* much money."

Daneyko scratched his beard. He hadn't had one when they first met, but seemed to grow one whenever he wanted to scratch it. It was an unusual kitsune illusion, to say the least. Mathis wondered if he were really bare-faced, and just grew the illusory beard because of his beard-scratching affectation, or if he were really bearded and had to drop the illusion of being bare-faced in order to scratch the odd itch. Realizing his thoughts were drifting down the road of illusory beards, Mathis started to wonder if he was getting a little drunk, himself. He had been sipping some wine with his apples, after all.

"I might have an idea, but that Jobinh guy that sis told me about probably won't like it," Daneyko said.

Mathis frowned. He didn't like the idea of operating behind the back of the people assigned to protect him, but then again he wasn't exactly thrilled with Jobinh as an advisor, either. "It's my job to get this salt for my home's very survival, so I'm willing to try anything. Give me your idea and I'll see if I can make it work."

Daneyko grinned. "Good. Now, if the Arsenians are claiming the problem is that they can't move their salt from their storehouses to your carts, and you know they are lying in order to get paid more, the obvious solution is to make them, in fact, move the salt to prove it can be moved."

Mathis nodded slowly. "Yes, of course. But how would we do that?"

"Well," Daneyko drawled. "We could manufacture some kind of disaster where the Arsenians would have no choice but to evacuate one of their storehouses or lose all the salt inside."

"That makes sense.... Wait, what?" Mathis said, his slightly sluggish mind finally catching up with Daneyko's suggestion. "What kind of 'disaster' are you suggesting? Arsene is an ally and one of Ekholm's major trading partners. I certainly don't want to start a war with them, nor am I willing to endanger them if I can help it. They're being threatened by the same enemies we are."

"That shouldn't be a problem, as long as we do everything right," Daneyko said, smirking. He gestured outside when thunder rumbled in through the door. "We'll have them blaming it on the storm. Here's my plan...."

Kieras wasn't sure about this plan. She knew that, while she had sobered up a great deal, she was still not fully recovered from her drinking binge earlier that day. Mathis looked like he was a bit tipsy, too, and she had to wonder if he would have agreed to this plan had it not been for the drink. The only one of them who didn't appear to be affected by their earlier alcoholic consumption was Daneyko, who had come up with the plan.

"Brother," she said. "I sure hope you aren't going to get me or my hosts into trouble with this one."

Daneyko smiled at her. "You are my little sister. I wouldn't get you into trouble. Trust me."

"Me? No. But you might get Mathis in trouble."

"Which brings up a point," Mathis interjected. "Daneyko, I've thought this plan of yours over, and I agreed that it might work. I'm willing to try it, but only if you give me a promise."

"Are you trying to extract a promise from me?" Daneyko asked, giving a slightly different, more dangerous smile his direction.

"I know the dangers of trying to do that from a kitsune," Mathis said. "But in this case, it's more dangerous to go in without one, considering the circumstances. This is your plan, and you waited until I was noticeably drunk before suggesting it."

"Well, you figured that one out, too," Daneyko said. "Yes, I wanted you at least a little drunk before suggesting this plan, but not because I wanted to act against you. I honestly believe this is the best plan to accomplish both of our goals, and I'm merely worried you might allow human ethics to interfere in attempting a common sense solution."

"You still seem to want me to do this a little too much for comfort," Mathis said. "I won't demand any specific promise. I would merely like some reassurance in the form of a promise before we get started."

Daneyko gave Mathis a searching look, but for what reason Kieras wasn't sure. "Very well. I promise that I do not intend to harm you or

Ekholm with this plan."

"Not good enough," Mathis shook his head.

"And why not?" Daneyko asked, snarling angrily. "Is my promise not good enough for you?"

"If your promise covered even half of my concerns," Mathis replied coolly, "it would be."

"And what concerns of yours have I left out?"

"My concerns include Arsene, as well. While the town council is being unreasonable, and the townsfolk themselves are a bit upset with us, Arsene is our ally and friend. I don't want to do anything which would make them vulnerable to the Knodelian threat."

Daneyko rolled his eyes. "Fine. I—"

"That's not all!" Mathis interrupted. "While you and your sister appear to get along, I have no proof that you wouldn't come up with a plan intended to harm her. For all I know, someone in the myobu priesthood might have ordered you to make it difficult, if not impossible, to complete her quest. That would not be acceptable."

A grin slowly spread over Daneyko's face. "Now *that* is what I was hoping to hear. As you know, demanding a promise from a kitsune can be dangerous, but those we deem worthy we do reward. Your concern for my sister makes you a worthy one. I promise that this plan, and anything I might do or not do involving it, will only help you, and is not intended to harm you, Kieras, or Ekholm in any way, including your diplomatic mission and my sister's quests. As far as Arsene goes... what I intend for it is not something its allies would be concerned about."

Mathis eyed him for a moment before he gave a satisfied nod. "Good enough. Let's get this started."

Focusing into her *hoshi no tama*, Kieras created two oilskin coats, one of which she gave to Mathis. "This should last for a few hours even without me helping to maintain it," she explained as she and Daneyko donned their own illusory oil coats. "It should keep you dry long enough for this."

With that, they stepped out into the rain. The storm was fierce enough that there were no people out on the roads. In the distance thunder rumbled ominously. The heavy storms were the key to their plan, but it was still unpleasant to be out in. Nevertheless, they pushed forward, staying as concealed as they could. It was fairly simple to remain unseen thanks to the empty streets and their dark oil coats, as they pushed on toward one of the salt storehouses near a tavern on the other side of town from their inn. Mathis had suggested it because it was made of wattle and daub – which, given his experience, he knew would be far better for their plans than the other warehouses in the area built of brick or stone. Daneyko agreed because it was close to a well-occupied tavern yet far enough away from their own inns that they would not be suspected if sabotage was discovered. Kieras didn't particularly care what building they picked.

"All right," Daneyko said once they were in place. "I can create the illusion of thunder or of lightning, but not both at once. Which do you want to do, Kieras?"

"I've never learned how to make illusions of sound," Kieras admitted, feeling rather embarrassed. "So I guess I can only do the lightning."

"Father didn't teach you?" Daneyko asked.

"Father was busy trying to keep a bunch of spoiled royals alive in spite of just about everyone in the city plotting against them, including the other spoiled royals," Kieras spat. "He did his best, but he was overwhelmed. I was lucky to get the lessons I did out of him."

Daneyko nodded, pulling a torch out from behind his coat. "Did he ever get around to teaching you foxfire? A proper, hot, burning foxfire, that is?"

"Of course." Kieras snorted, grabbing her *tama* and concentrating. "Father was always concerned with our ability to defend ourselves, so even before he trained me in the use of any illusion he made sure I knew how to use our greatest weapon. Foxfire!"

A small ball of blue flame – a little smaller than she intended, but effective nonetheless – flew from her tama and onto the oil-coated rag wrapped around the torch, igniting it.

"I'm not sure I'd call that a 'proper' foxfire, but it'll do." Daneyko handed the torch to Mathis. "You need to work on control, sis."

"Yeah, yeah, I know. I can make it larger than that, you know... um, sometimes."

Daneyko grinned. "You'll get there – kitsune magic grows as you age, and redoubles with each tail you grow. Most kitsune your age have none at all, and can barely put any heat in that flame, which makes many humans believe it's just another illusion. It seems to run strong on both sides of our family, though. Your foxfire is good enough for our purposes, so it's time to create the illusion of a lightning strike. Looks like this'll go easier than I thought. You're right about this wattle and daub stuff, Mathis – the warehouse should go up like tinder despite the rain."

Like many of the inn's guests that night, Jobinh had fallen asleep in front of the great room's fire instead of returning to his room. The inn's staff encouraged it for a number of reasons – the chief of which was to save money on the coals needed for individual foot warmers on such a cold, wet night – and Jobinh had been quite amenable. The inn was probably rather happy that said decision had resulted in an impromptu party, where a great deal of money was spent on food, beer, and wine.

However, the patrons who agreed to sleep in the great room, Jobinh included, were not nearly as happy when their sleep was interrupted in the middle of the night by the front door of the inn slamming open and several panicked townsfolk bursting in, shouting incoherently.

Jobinh, unaccustomed to being awoken so dramatically when not in the field, took a moment to collect himself. The commotion didn't abate itself in that moment, however, so he decided someone needed to take charge, and that someone was him.

"All right," he snapped, startling the babbling crowd into silence. He pointed to a random person from the crowd. "You! Explain what happened."

"The salt store house near old man Niskala's tavern was struck by lightning and is on fire!" the man cried. "We have to hurry. The fire needs to be put out, and the salt will need to be moved out before the storms wash it away!"

Jobinh frowned. "I thought you were having problems moving salt out of your warehouses."

The villager looked at him like he was crazy. "What are you talking about? Oh, never mind – this is an emergency! We need fire brigades and people to move the salt, now!"

"Right," Jobinh said. "Boedker! Eakin! Prusek! Jarmon! Each of you organize a detail from these civilians. Help them put out the fire and move the salt to wherever they direct you. Mathis!" He frowned, looking around. "Has anyone seen Mathis?"

"He was at the table with your girl and that trader from Norre," the innkeeper, who had also arrived on the scene, said. "If they aren't still there, they must be in their rooms."

Jobinh rolled his eyes. "I'll go up and get them. Mathis needs to know about this."

He muttered to himself about the frustration of working for a pretend ambassador who only got the job through nepotism as he made his way through the crowd his soldiers were organizing. His men were very good at their jobs – by the time he made it to the stairs, four teams of workers had been organized and were charging out to deal with the fire.

As he approached the door belonging to Mathis, he thought he heard feminine giggling. *Great,* Jobinh thought. *He's 'entertaining' a girl. Irresponsible behavior for a diplomat, and I have to interrupt him in the middle of it. Embarrassing for the both of us. He'll probably be angry about that, too, even though we discussed months ago about how he couldn't get too close to the local girls. I hate this job.*

"...better for you if it's off when the illusion dispels," he heard Kieras saying.

Oh, it's just the kitsune girl, Jobinh thought. *Still, what are they doing together in his room? Well, considering what I know of kitsune vixens, I suppose I might not be that off about Mathis 'entertaining' a girl.*

"...make one of those when we get back to Ekholm," Mathis' muffled reply echoed through the door. "Maybe old lady Oberta could make me a real one just like it."

"Maybe," Kieras replied. "I was so glad to hear her apology to you when Kuralt was ousted. She treated me so well—"

Glad to hear he wasn't interrupting a lover's tryst, Jobinh gave the door an urgent knock. "Mathis, I have some important news."

There was some scrambling and hushed whispers. Jobinh caught a third voice he didn't recognize say "dispel," and then a little more scrambling.

Finally, Mathis called back, "Come in!"

Jobinh opened the door and stepped inside. He found that the voice he hadn't recognized belonged to Daneyko. The male kitsune had a bit of a knowing smirk on his face, while both Mathis and Kieras were grinning like naughty schoolchildren who had just gotten away with something. He wasn't sure what to make of it all.

"Sir." Jobinh stood at attention and addressed Mathis formally.

Daneyko was a foreigner, so being overly casual with Mathis around him was not advisable... whatever he thought of their ostensible 'Ambassador.' "A group of villagers just arrived with important news. They say that one of their primary salt storehouses has been struck by lightning and caught fire."

"Really? You don't say?" Mathis replied, not sounding surprised at all. If anything, in fact, he seemed amused, which was a rather inappropriate reaction in Jobinh's opinion.

"Yes, sir," Jobinh replied, nonplussed. "I have dispatched my men to lead the firefighting efforts. Also, they will be helping the villagers move the salt to a different building."

"Really?" Mathis said, still sounding more amused than anything else. "I suppose this proves that this village *can* actually move its panned salt out of their warehouse when it needs to, doesn't it? I guess the council was lying to me."

"I... well, yes, sir," Jobinh replied. Yes, he'd had the same thought, but he wasn't so crass as to express it publicly, and it wasn't something he was certain about. His earlier concern that the village might not be able to remove that salt from the burning warehouse had been an honest one.

Mathis nodded slowly, suddenly taking on an almost apologetic look. "Well, your efforts are appreciated. See if you can find out the value of the building. While Ekholm cannot provide Arsene with anything close to the payment they were requesting, we should be able to help them replace this lost warehouse as a courtesy from one ally to another."

"Yes, sir." Jobinh started to say something else, but then noticed three roughly equal-sized puddles of water on the floor. "Is your roof leaking, sir?"

"What? No." Mathis looked somewhat surprised.

A strange thought came across Jobinh. "Sir... have you three been outside?"

"Of course not," Mathis said. There was a little tension around his lips, and he seemed to be trembling with restraining laughter. "If we had been outside in this weather without some oilskin coats, which I don't have, we'd be soaked to the bone, now, wouldn't we?" Kieras let out a not-very-ladylike snort behind him. "But you can check all of our clothes and you'll see they're all as dry as they can be."

Jobinh couldn't argue with Mathis, however, despite his and Kieras' odd behavior. "Yes, of course, sir." He still had the feeling he was missing something, but he couldn't quite figure out what. "Any additional orders, sir?"

"Just keep me informed," Mathis said, sobering up slightly. "If that fire goes beyond that one warehouse, let me know. We'll then see if we can do anything more to help contain it. There's not much else we can do at the moment, though, except let the Arsenians deal with it. The Arsenians might resent it if it appears we think they cannot handle their own problems."

"Yes, sir." Jobinh stared at the puddles again, trying to puzzle things out. "Well, good night, sir. I'm going to go inspect the scene."

The laughter that erupted behind Jobinh after he left Mathis' room just convinced him even more that he had missed something. He wished he had a clue as to what it was. It was most annoying.

Daneyko had completed his business – which, he'd told them, was simply a legitimate trading mission between one particular band of kitsune and the town of Arsene. Mathis had successfully forced the town council to admit that yes, they could, in fact, make transportation arrangements after all. It was time for Daneyko and his sister to part ways.

Daneyko had so wanted to see the town council's reaction now that their woefully ridiculous lies were proven false that he'd transformed himself into a brooch that Mathis wore. It had taken all his self-control to avoid breaking his illusion with laughter at the extremely bitter way the councilmen were forced to thank Mathis for funding the repairs to their damaged storehouse, even though that small amount of money was a mere pittance compared to the size of the purse they were hoping to extort from Ekholm. The only down side to the whole meeting for Daneyko was that Mathis was too polite to call them all liars to their face, noting instead how the villagers' "remarkable effort in the face of a near certain disaster" had shown the way to solve the problem of loading Ekholm's wagons.

It hadn't taken long for Mathis' expedition to finish loading its wagon train full of salt after that meeting, and now they were all standing together at the crossroads outside of Arsene. Mathis, Kieras, and their company would head down the path towards the Orrpars road, while Daneyko would split off with his own large bag full of salt toward a nearby kitsune holding. It wasn't a tearful goodbye, but then kitsune were very good at hiding their feelings. It was, however, very cold. The storm which they had taken advantage of to create their so-called "natural disaster" might not have been freezing, but there was certainly freezing weather coming in behind it. Their breaths could be seen in the air.

"Don't be a stranger," Mathis said, breaking him from his reverie. "I understand that you can't go into Ekholm, but nothing says that you can't send messages to us. The farming village of Arbeloa, just up the road from Ekholm, did not exist in Eskesa's day and so should not be included in your priesthood's edict. They have a messenger service that can reach us in mere hours. If you ever want to visit with your sister, feel free to head there and let us know you are in town. Though if the Knodelians have launched their assault, you might have to wait – we've agreed to shelter the Arbeloans for the duration of the Knodelian conflict."

"I'll keep that in mind," Daneyko said. "Now that I know she's in the area, I'll be looking forward to visiting her regularly." He turned to say his goodbyes to Kieras, but was surprised when she enveloped him in a hug before he could.

"Goodbye, brother," she said. "I've missed you."

"Bye, little sister," he whispered back softly, genuinely touched. "Don't get into any trouble you can't get easily out of."

"All right, you've all said your goodbyes," Jobinh snapped, walking up to the trio. "We need to get going if we want to reach our encampment by nightfall."

All three glared at him with eyes like steel. Jobinh stood his ground, though he briefly flashed a terrified expression before covering it up. Daneyko doubted Kieras would have noticed, and Mathis, whose skills of perception were almost as good as an adult kitsune's, might not even have seen it. He barely caught it, himself, and he had better eyes than either of them, but he was privately amused at the stuffy soldier's fear.

With a slight smirk, Mathis moved toward Jobinh. "Well then, let's get going. Unless, of course, you want some more practice trying to order around a pair of kitsune and the head of your own delegation."

Jobinh grimaced but said nothing, striding back to his men who were studiously attempting to avoid any hint of amusement.

Kieras gave Daneyko one final squeeze before releasing her hug and following Mathis and Jobinh down the path to the Orrpars Road, which would in turn lead them to Ekholm. He watched them go until they were out of sight, and then took his own path away from Arsene.

About four hours out, Daneyko sat down to take a rest. He started to break out some of his provisions before an intruder made herself known by tapping him on the shoulder with a stick.

"Very funny, mother, but I've known you were following me for the last hour," Daneyko said, not even bothering to look.

An older, but still quite beautiful, silver-haired woman stepped out of the shadow of the tree he was leaning against. "Well, I did train my boy to be perceptive. I guess that you really *have* outgrown all my old tricks."

"Only the ones you've been using on me since I was a four-year-old kit." Daneyko laughed and gestured for her to sit by him. "Come – we'll share lunch today. And warmth – winter is hitting fast, this year. I managed to get a nice supply of those chicken pasties I like right before I left."

"I'm happy that I'll finally get a chance to taste these things you always come home raving about," Tianhyu said, taking a seat next to her son. "How was Kieras?"

"Alpha Skygger told you the truth – she is searching for you under father's orders. She doesn't appear too anxious about it, though – she seems to be treating these 'diplomatic missions' she's going on to be some sort of holiday, keeping up only the slightest pretense of a search for you. Other than that, she seems to be doing well. She's with good, smart people she can trust. Well, most of them, anyway – I don't quite know what to make of the Norrish representative, a man named Jobinh, but I don't like him. Skygger was right, though – this Mathis guy is quite protective of her. He's also quite smart. He saw through several of my deceptions right away. I even got him drunk, once, but still he was able to read me when I tried to trick him. He'd have made a good kitsune."

"Good," Tianhyu said. "I'm glad to hear my daughter is in good hands."

"Why didn't you want her to know that you were nearby?" Daneyko asked suddenly. "Skygger told you about the urgency of her mission.

Father—"

"Can wait," Tianhyu said. "The myobu priesthood is keeping an eye on my mate's situation. While it's hardly pleasant for him, it's not likely to get much worse without a trigger... like my return. He will be fine until we are ready."

"But—"

"Kieras has her own roles to fulfill." Tianhyu sighed. "If she knew I was here, she would have left Ekholm to come to me. We need someone in that city, and neither you nor I can enter it, yet."

"What happened in Ekholm, mother?" Daneyko asked. "Why are you banished from that city?"

"It isn't so much the city itself, as who is in it. While the last few refugees from Eskesa remain living in Ekholm, we cannot go near any town they inhabit, but once the last survivor – an old man named Fornier – dies, we can enter it again. I had friends in Ekholm, once. Many of them have passed on, but I believe this Mathis you've mentioned may have been the son of one of them. I had certain... suspicions about her, and the traits which made me suspicious seem to have passed on to him. I want Kieras close enough to this boy to see if I'm right."

"But why? What happened in Eskesa that made the Priesthood impose this edict?"

Tianhyu sighed sadly. "It was all pure folly. Eskesa was a great ally to the kitsune in years past. A fool of a drunken Archon, discovering his son in a lover's tryst with a kitsune, tricked and insulted the myobu. I won't explain how – it would reveal secrets that are not mine to give – but in the end we swore to leave Eskesa's holdings while any of that city's residents still lived. As I said, it was pure folly. We were a vital part of Eskesa's defense. With us gone they were easy prey for the Erixonites.

"The myobu priesthood still considers Ekholm an ally, but we can do nothing as this Knodelian threat approaches. Kieras, despite having myobu blood in her veins, can help them. I have been ordered to wait until the Knodelian threat is extinguished before I can make contact." Tianhyu sighed. "I so wish to see my daughter, but as you well know duty is a powerful thing for a myobu, and duty forbids it."

Daneyko nodded. "So we have to wait for a while, then. But when the Knodelians are gone, I can go to Arbeloa and send her a message letting her know you're here, right?"

"What would be the fun in that?" Tianhyu laughed. "No need to send her any messages – we know where she'll be going once her 'vacation' is over, after all."

VIII. Huli Jeng

In the months since sending his youngest daughter out into the world on her own, Lahti had grown increasingly uncomfortable with the state of affairs in the royal city of Kassia. King Heshka was unthinkingly ceding more and more of his power to Lords Devane and Kobach. Gedig, the only sensible member of the court, was essentially removed from it, his role losing more and more significance until all he could do was act as Prince Czerniak's tutor.

It was very strange. Lord Devane, in his role as commander-in-chief of the armies, was still incompetently stretching their armies far beyond what was reasonable. Lord Kobach, in his role as treasurer, was still breaking the backs of their people in order to fill the royal coffers ever higher. Despite that, nothing they were doing, from what Lahti could see, would have pulled the king away from his other advisors. Something else was at work, but he had yet to identify what.

Lahti didn't have much say with Heshka, either. He had been left with little more to do than put his energies into training Czerniak. While Gedig taught the young Prince's academics, Lahti worked on his swordsmanship.

"Watch your guard, your highness," Lahti said, tapping the flat of his longsword against Czerniak's undefended kidneys. "Relying on your armor to defend your flanks could be lethal, even if you are using plate armor... which we are not."

"Sorry, father," Czerniak said.

Lahti couldn't hide his wince. Ever since Czerniak learned of the betrothal, he had treated the kitsune as if he were his own parent. Again, Lahti had to remind him, "I'm not your father yet, Czerniak."

"Sorry, father," Czerniak said again tonelessly.

That caught Lahti's attention. Czerniak's mind clearly wasn't on his sword drills, and apparently he wasn't listening to what Lahti was saying, either.

"What is it?" Lahti snapped, rapping Czerniak's knuckles with the back of his blade. "Your head's been in the clouds all day."

"Oh, sorry," Czerniak said, though at least he seemed to be paying attention that time.

"You've said 'sorry' three times, now," Lahti said. "Which is three more times than a prince like yourself should ever apologize, and I still don't know what's wrong."

Czerniak did not look up to meet Lahti's eyes. "Kieras knew about the arranged marriage before she left, didn't she? She doesn't want to marry me, does she?"

Lahti's eyes widened. He had fallen into the practice of relaxing his guard in Czerniak's presence, somewhat, but he didn't think he'd said anything which might hint of his daughter's real reasons for leaving. In fact, they hadn't talked about his daughter at all in months.

"What brought this on?"

Czerniak glared at him. "Just answer the question."

Lahti rolled his eyes. "Remember what I am. Do you really want to insist on an answer like that, and if so would you actually trust my answer?"

"Well, then, how am I supposed to get any honesty about this matter?" Czerniak shot back, his frustration apparent. "I need to know."

Of all the surviving members of the Royal Family since the fall of King Kazdri, Lahti liked Czerniak the most. He was too tentative in his dealings with other members of the Kassian Royal Court to rule effectively, but he was personable, and seemed to have a good head on his shoulders. Unlike his father, it would be harder to lead him blindly astray. However, he would suffer fools – and worse – far too much, and to his detriment. He could be groomed to become a somewhat competent king provided he had good, honest advisors. Unfortunately, with the likes of Devane and Kobach dominating the Kassian Royal Court, that hope seemed doomed to failure.

Still, Lahti had to admit the young man deserved an answer, even if he couldn't be told the complete answer. Telling him part of the story might be enough.

"I can tell you a few things which I swear are the truth," Lahti said. "First off, my daughter left for reasons far beyond any fear of an arranged marriage. However, while I am not entirely sure of my daughter's feeling in all matters, I believe she only thought of you as a friend. I doubt she would wish to marry you if she had a choice, but she would not hate you for your father arranging this marriage."

Czerniak slowly nodded. "I suppose that is a good thing. Lahti, I believe there is a plot against my father centered around my marriage to your daughter."

Alarm bells immediately went up in Lahti's head – not because of the possibility of a plot, since he already knew there was one in motion, but because Czerniak had learned of it seemingly by himself.

He sniffed the air and opened his ears, trying to sense if anyone was around them. Convinced that it was safe, he said, "We're alone for the moment, but who knows how long that will last. Tell me what you have heard, and you had best do so quickly."

"I'm not sure if what I heard will make sense by itself," Czerniak said. "A lot of it has to do with a number of disturbing rumors I've heard regarding Lord Kobach and his aides – the programs he's been trying to set up for the treatment of the old or the infirm, for example, appear to be little more than death camps. More than that, while he's supposed to only be the royal treasurer, he seems to be dabbling in things that have nothing to do with money. I have seen him reading through intelligence reports, and I overheard one of his aides discussing troop movements with some of the Royal Guardsmen. Something doesn't smell right about him."

"I quite agree," Lahti said. "But what does this have to do with my daughter?"

Czerniak took a deep breath. "Several things. Those intelligence reports I caught Kobach reading? One was on the inquiries our soldiers had made with Kassia's neighbors regarding Kieras' whereabouts."

"Do they know where she is?" Lahti asked, a brief moment of fear that his enemies knew her whereabouts better than he did striking him.

"Not specifically," Czerniak said. "Not from those reports, anyway. They seem to feel that she is somewhere inside the Norre Hegemony or its surrounding territories, but nothing more definite than that." He paused. "They're also searching for her mother, who they believe may be in the same area."

Lahti's blood turned to ice upon hearing that. He had not seen his mate, Tianhyu, in decades. Their feigned estrangement let her escape the city in such a way that there were no suspicions about her disappearance, and so far that had been enough to protect her. That protection appeared to be waning. "That... is not good. Any insight as to why?"

"Nothing I have heard." Czerniak shook his head. "But that isn't all. I was trying to get an appointment with the royal treasurer on behalf of my father. I started looking for him by heading to his office, where two of his aides were talking between them. Something about how they hoped that Kieras would return soon, because the 'plan,' whatever it is, kept getting more complex the longer it took to get me married to her. If my marriage to Kieras is going to be used to endanger my family or the kingdom, then I don't want to marry her after all."

Lahti took a deep breath. Outside of the hunt for his mate, nothing Czerniak was saying was new to him. However, Kobach was being unusually incautious in allowing someone like Czerniak to discover this much. That could mean a number of things: Kobach could be far enough along in his plans that he was growing overconfident, or he could be hoping to provoke Czerniak into doing something rash, or it could be a trap. Regardless, he had to protect both Czerniak and Heshka – from themselves, if necessary.

"Don't tell anyone else about this," Lahti said. "If Kobach learns that you told me, we may both be in more danger than I can protect us from. If anyone approaches you about planning your wedding to Kieras, go along with it and tell me the details later. Or if you need to speak with me, tell me you want to talk with me about the wedding plans and I'll arrange to meet you somewhere that we cannot be overheard. Do you understand?"

Czerniak nodded. "Yes, I do. Secrecy is of the utmost importance to my safety. But what about my father's safety? He is the king, after all – his life is more important than mine."

"By my near century-old oath, both of your lives are equally important," Lahti snapped. "Don't worry – I'll be thinking of ways to protect him as well. There is only one of me, though, and there are two of you. The less time I have to worry about you, the more time I can spend worrying about your father. Understand?"

Czerniak grimaced. "I understand. But you keep him safe, understood?"

"Like I said, I have an oath promising that already. Now, it's time you made your way down to Gedig's etiquette class. You're late enough as it is. I'll keep your father safe."

A comical look of surprise erupted on Czerniak's previously stern face. "I'm late? Crap! He said he'd make me work in the kitchens like a commoner if I was late again!" With that, Czerniak ducked out the door, moving almost as fast as Lahti could run, himself.

Lahti sighed, letting his face show the concern he actually felt as he talked to himself. "I'll keep your father safe, Prince Czerniak, I just have to figure out what's going on, first."

King Heshka II wasn't as clueless as most of those around him believed. He knew he looked ridiculous in his royal accoutrements. They could not replace or re-size the crown that had adorned the King of Kassia's head for almost a century, even if it didn't fit. And the ceremonial armor that had belonged to his father was just as unalterable, even though it was worthless. He also knew he had advisors who were taking advantage of him and his temper.

Which was largely why he was allowing them to think he was so naive. He was not in a position to confront them face to face, and if they knew what he really thought of him they would have simply killed him and forgotten any concerns about maintaining 'legitimacy' in their coup. To many of the guards and other lords were more loyal to Devane and Kobach than they were to the throne. Heshka was beginning to believe that one aide of Kobach's – Yulaev, he thought the man's name was – was also involved somehow... in fact, he may have been more dangerous than either of the lords. But Heshka could use his reputation to maneuver them all in various ways – for example, he'd allowed them to steer Gedig, the only advisor he trusted, away from him, but in the process had positioned Gedig to be the central advisor for his son.

He did a very good job of playing the fool – good enough, he believed, to fool even a natural master of deception like Lahti. Allowing his enemies to think they were tricking him yet again, he agreed to arrange his son in marriage to Lahti's daughter. However, he also found a way to let Lahti know of the plans far enough in advance to get Kieras out of the way, thus frustrating Kobach's plans.

Unfortunately, that was the limit of his ability to challenge his supposed "advisors." He was just barely more than a figurehead – a king in title only – and it would not be long before that "barely more than" would no longer be true. He might, however, be able to save his son from the same fate and his friends from being caught in the crossfire by estranging himself from them.

Which made it quite uncomfortable for him when one of those intentionally estranged friends somehow managed to pull him into an empty room for a conversation.

"I bring you urgent news, Your Majesty!"

Heshka groaned. "Gedig... why did you *do* this?"

"This is important, Your Majesty," Gedig insisted. "Your advisors are conspiring against you!"

"It's too dangerous to meet here," Heshka said. "In fact, it's too dangerous to meet, period."

Gedig frowned. "But... Your Majesty...."

Heshka sighed. "Please, don't be stubborn. Leave, now! There's still a chance they don't know you've spoken with me!"

Gedig cocked his head. "Your Majesty? What are you talking about?"

"Don't ask questions!" Heshka replied. "If it concerns my security, you must contact Lahti, and have him make sure you are alone. Talking to me is too risky!"

"Your Majesty, your safety is far more important than any risk to me," Gedig insisted.

Heshka's head fell into his hands. He rubbed his temples, hoping to stem the headache he knew was coming. "I can tell you aren't going to leave. Fine. But be quick about it – if they don't know we're meeting already, they will soon."

"I don't know all the details," Gedig said. "But I overheard a discussion between two of Lord Devane's men and one of Lord Kobach's. Lord Devane is planning to embroil us in more wars, pulling loyalist forces from the castle until his own forces far outnumber those who remain."

Heshka waited for more, but nothing more was said. "That's... it?"

"Isn't that enough?" Gedig asked, not understanding just how underwhelmed his king was. "The general of your armies is trying to pull the soldiers who would support you in a coup out of the castle. That seems pretty serious to me, Your Majesty."

"Oh, you poor fool," Heshka lamented under his breath, dropping his head into his hands. Gedig was a good man, and an unmatched dispenser of wisdom... but he was also fairly lacking in common sense. Heshka had known of Lord Devane's efforts for more than a year, and this "news" wasn't news at all. "Well, you've told me. I appreciate your loyalty, but you should not have come directly to me. If you hear of anything else like this in the future, go to Lahti, and *only* to Lahti. He will know if it is safe to talk. Follow his instructions, even if they are to not contact me. It is his goal to protect me and my son's lives. Whatever his plans may be for this situation, I trust they will be in my best interest. Now, go, and don't let yourself be seen! My safety depends on my supposed ignorance."

Without giving him a chance to reply, Heshka left the room as quickly as dignity would allow, desperately hoping to go unnoticed. It wasn't long before one of his servants spotted him walking around the castle "unescorted," and guards were called in to surround him "for his protection."

He could only hope Gedig managed to escape unseen, because he could not.

"Well?" Kobach asked.

"We have one maybe, and one definite," Yulaev said. "The others either failed to discover anything, or didn't approach anyone." Kobach's newest spymaster and assassin, Yulaev had proven himself to be far better than his predecessors. He was an expert at setting up traps and had managed to kill well over a hundred men undiscovered. His disguises were so effective that Kobach sometimes wondered if he was a kitsune, but if so Lahti had never said anything about it and Yulaev had never admitted it.

"Give me the full report," Kobach said.

"Gedig took the bait, as we expected. Went running to the king first thing, not even paying any attention to anyone who might see him. He managed to separate King Heshka from his escort and get him into a room alone. We don't know how much he told the king, but it's not like we let any of these people know anything too surprising. It was pretty clear that Gedig intended to tell the king everything he heard, however."

Kobach nodded with a grimace. Gedig was an institution in the Kassian Royal Court, and despite his age, an opponent to be respected rather than ignored. Kobach bore him no malice, but this bit of news meant that he could pose a serious problem. "I understand. Go on."

"It is also possible that Czerniak has told Lahti some things, but we have no proof. There are regular periods of time when Czerniak is alone with both Gedig and Lahti, when we cannot observe them without drawing more suspicion than we are willing to deal with. Czerniak seemed to be disturbed by some of the things he heard, and was walking around in a state for several days prior to one of his tutoring sessions with Lahti. Lahti, however, does not appear to have taken any action since then, so it is possible that Czerniak simply focused his distress into his training."

"Even if he did," Kobach said, "Czerniak is the only one we 'tested' who we cannot do anything about, thanks to his importance to our future plans. We fully expected Lahti to learn these things with or without our telling him. The key will be to contain his efforts to protecting Czerniak, and not the whole kingdom."

"Lahti is not perfect," Yulaev said, a gleam in his eye. "He will not learn *everything*."

"Well, I certainly hope not," Kobach said. "That is why I've hired you, after all."

Yulaev glared at him dangerously. "Are you doubting my abilities?"

The very question terrified Kobach. Challenging Yulaev was a very foolish thing to do, even unintentionally. People who did wound up dead, and usually in very painful ways. "No, of course not! I think you are his equal. And as I hold a very healthy respect for Lahti's abilities, I also hold a very healthy respect to those I regard as his equals."

Yulaev's glare turned into a smile, but that smile still made Kobach's spine crawl. If anything, he felt like he was in more danger than ever. "Well... I shall have to really challenge Lahti, one of these days, to see if I should think that a compliment or an insult."

Kobach swallowed nervously, unsettled by that grin. "We need to decide what to do in the meantime."

"As you said," Yulaev began, finally breaking eye contact with his employer. "Your plans demand that we leave Czerniak alone. Gedig, however... well, there's really only one thing we can do about him, isn't there?"

Transcribing any notable events into the Kassian Chronicles, as established by laws set forth even before their founder, King Kazdri, had established the throne, was a job that had fallen to Gedig many years before. This now was a part of his daily routine. It was getting more and more difficult as his eyes were starting to fail him, but he was too proud of the responsibility to find another scribe to take his place.

After inscribing all three of the day's births, the nine deaths, a supposed haunting discovered in the cemetery, and a few notes on repairs to one of the castle's outlying buildings damaged in a storm, Gedig was done for the day.

However, as always, Gedig didn't leave when he was finished. He found the chronicles absolutely fascinating. As was his custom, he went to the older chronicles to review another few month's worth of recorded history.

He had spent ten years reading through history from the beginning, when Kassia was just a small town on the northern border of another kingdom, just to get to Kazdri's coronation. It took several more years to the end of King Kazdri's reign.

"Hmm, that's interesting," he mused to himself. "Kazdri's body disappeared after he was poisoned. In the chaos following his assassination, it was stolen from the crypt before it could be prepared for his final internment, and hasn't been seen since. If that is true, then who is buried under his Memorial Gravestone?"

"An interesting question. Any hope of finding an answer will have to fall on your replacement's head, I'm afraid."

Gedig spun around. His eyesight was not yet so bad that he couldn't see others in the same room, but there didn't seem to be anyone present. "Who's there?"

An odd shadow reflected in the flicker of some candlelight was enough warning for him to move. He had once been a soldier, and while well out of shape he still had excellent reflexes. Ducking and rolling out of the way, he spun around to see an amorphous fox-like shape slowly resolving itself into a human figure. *A kitsune!* Gedig thought.

"Impressive," the human figure said. He was carrying a knotted rope of the kind often used by assassins to choke out their target. "You're the first to escape my initial attack. At your age that is even more of a surprise. I was told you were an enemy to be respected, but until now I wasn't sure if I should believe the talk."

"You aren't Lahti," Gedig said, trying to gauge this unexpected enemy. He surveyed the man, recognizing him as one of Lord Kobach's many aides, but couldn't recall his name. It was Yul-something, but the name was unimportant – he was an assassin, and that was all that mattered at the moment.

Or perhaps not quite all. Gedig noticed something else; the kitsune's hair was brown, which meant he wasn't a myobu or a nogitsune. The thought that Kobach was dealing with some other breed of kitsune chilled Gedig more than his own danger. Not all of those breeds were hostile, but none of them were even as trustworthy as a nogitsune. This one... if Gedig was right, this was worse than just a hostile kitsune. Just how foolish was that man to even talk with one of these creatures? "You aren't one of the human-friendly kitsune, either, are you?"

"Oh, I don't know," the figure said, a dark smile on his face. "I hate human civilization, true, but there are some individual humans I consider myself a friend to. Generally because they are such useful tools, and they also pay so well...."

"You're Kobach's servant?" Gedig asked, trying to buy time. The answer was pretty obvious, but if he could get the man talking then maybe he could find a way to escape and get some help.

The kitsune didn't take that very well. With a fierce fox-like snarl, he snapped, "Servant? Hah! Kobach is *my* pawn, not the other way around." He paused, pulling back his temper. "He did order me to kill you, and I plan to do so. I suppose that means I'm taking his orders. Of course, I'm the one who convinced him to give me these orders."

Gedig knew he had no chance in a hand-to-hand fight with a kitsune – not unless he held the kitsune's *hoshi no tama*. He couldn't tell where, on this kitsune, the tama was being kept, so acquiring it during the fight seemed unlikely. He didn't stand much of a chance trying to escape from a kitsune intent on killing him, either, but he probably had a better chance running than not.

"Get back here!" the kitsune snarled as Gedig took off. "Foxfire!"

A blast of heat struck Gedig's back, scorching through his clothes and penetrating into his body. Sharp, stabbing pains went throughout his chest as he found it hard to breathe. Then that pain went away... but it became impossible to even draw a breath. His lungs weren't working properly, he could tell, but he had to keep running.

He knew where he needed to go, but it would be hard getting there. His vision was greying and his heart seized up, but the scariest sensation was the complete numbness on his back and in his lungs, It was an agonizing three minute sprint, made purely on willpower, but he finally found the room in which Lahti was most likely to be found. He didn't see anyone else there at first, but within a moment a nearby fox transformed into the redheaded form of the Lahti he knew.

"Gedig!" Lahti cried. "What happened to you?"

Gedig tried to speak, but found himself unable to speak. He could only be thankful that there was no more pain, and he was feeling remarkably light-headed. He turned, hoping desperately that Lahti could read his lips.

"Huli jeng..." he mouthed, before his vision faded out for good.

Since the fall of King Kazdri, Lahti rarely approached the Royal Court while it was in session unless summoned. The last three times he had appeared without being requested, it was to announce the death of the king. King Heshka was clearly still alive, as he was sitting on the throne, so Lahti's unannounced entrance caused quite the stir. It was hard to see what was happening outside of the court itself, but enough guards could be heard moving around outside of the room that the crash of their armor could be heard almost non-stop.

"Well," Heshka said, not quite concealing his anxiety by feigning disgust at Lahti's presence. "What brings this 'Honorable Kitsune' into Our presence today?"

Lahti's face showed undisguised hatred. It was perhaps the most severe expression Heshka had ever seen on the kitsune, which only increased his anxiety. Tears were reflected in his eyes, as well, and more honest tears had never dotted his face. Even the kitsune magic which usually covered up an ancient scar across his lips was failing as it peeked through his illusions. He was horrifically distraught and disturbed, to the point that most of his kitsune affectations were simply abandoned. The last time Lahti was so rattled that his scar had shown itself was said to be the assassination of King Kazdri, an event which was rumored to have – among other things – caused the infamous estrangement with his wife, Tianhyu. Suffice it to say, this was something big, and Heshka started to wonder if posing as his usual antagonistic self was a wise move this time.

Lahti's fierce eyes darted to those in the room, and the entrances. Even this angry, his concern for the king showed through. "Ten minutes ago, the Royal Tutor and Chronicler, Gedig, died. He was murdered. His assassin may still be in the castle."

"Gedig!" Czerniak, in attendance that day, cried out.

Amid the shocked gasps – both real and feigned – Heshka could not help but wince. *Damn*, he thought. *I guess we were discovered, after all. I am so sorry, my old friend.*

"He was struck in the back with an intense ball of flame," Lahti explained harshly. "The fireball burned through his clothes, burned the skin underneath black, and cooked his lungs so horribly that I could smell them roasting when he tried to talk."

Heshka's eyes widened, and his control slipped. "What could have done something like that?" he demanded.

"Gedig must have known he was already dead, but he still ran as fast as he could to seek me out, desperate to give me a warning. He could only say two words to me before he died," Lahti continued. "Huli jeng. A breed of kitsune that – unlike the nogitsune or myobu – were never human in their creation, though have often assumed human form. They are pure agents of chaos, despising humans and human civilization. While all kitsune possess the magic of foxfire, the huli jeng are the most lethal with it, and it was this power that was used to kill poor Gedig. These huli jeng are known to take the worst habits of the kitsune race and amplify them – they will use treachery and deceit not to amuse or to teach, as myobu and nogitsune do, but to ruin relationships, to devastate lives, and to demolish nations. A huli jeng would never have approached a human city without the aid of a human ally... and given how things have been around here lately, I'm guessing his ally is one of you. Whatever idiot decided to ally themselves with a huli jeng should know that they *will* betray you in the end. When they do, don't come running to me, for I shall not help you!"

Heshka took a deep breath. "And those of us who did not employ this huli jeng, how are We to defend Ourselves?"

Lahti cocked his head, fiery eyes staring at the king. "For Your Majesty, I suggest you keep yourself surrounded by guards. Make sure there are always at least four, and that none of those guards have brown hair. No kitsune can change their hair color for very long, so he would give himself away before he could act."

Heshka nodded slowly. "You are the captain of Our Royal Guard. We would like your advice for which of Our guards to include in an expanded detail."

Lahti's fists clenched, but he nodded. "I'll go over it with you shortly. However, I must also ensure Prince Czerniak's safety, so my time here is limited. Once I set up the initial rotation, I shall appoint a lieutenant who will be in charge of arranging your guard when I cannot."

That caught Heshka by surprise. The defense of the king should be his first priority, in word if not in deed, but he was publicly admitting that it was not the king, but the king's son, that was his first priority – a rare mistake on Lahti's part. Heshka studied him closely, and for the first time in his life, with Lahti's face no longer obscured by the illusions of his kitsune magic, Heshka could read the man through his eyes. Lahti was panicked, desperate, and stretched too thin, the depth of the lines on his face showing that he had been for a long time, probably since the fall of King Kazdri. If that stress wasn't relieved soon, it would cause him to make even more mistakes. Heshka wasn't in a position to provide much help to his loyal kitsune retainer, but he could help cover up that first mistake

"As We have instructed you before, We fully understand that Our son is your top concern. We would like to know what you will be doing to protect him, however."

Lahti glanced around, glaring in a certain direction. Heshka was pretty sure he was glaring at Lord Kobach, but it was hard to tell for certain without looking that way himself, which would not be wise if he wanted to maintain his pretense of naiveté regarding the royal treasurer.

"Your Majesty," Lahti began, refocusing on the king. "I cannot explain everything here. The huli jeng – or his allies – could be anywhere. However, I intend to increase His Highness' sword training threefold, and to take over for Gedig as his tutor. In Gedig's honor, I intend to ensure that Prince Czerniak learns all of his academics. In this crisis, however, I must concentrate on being sure he can protect himself." There was a brief pause. "I promise you that I will protect Prince Czerniak until I feel him ready to assume responsibility for his own safety... however long that takes."

Heshka's self-control was severely tested as he tried not to react to that. Lahti was effectively extending the promise of service he made to King Kazdri for an unspecified period of time, but then tied it to the survival of his son. That was a huge commitment. One that he hoped, for all their sakes, did not come back to haunt them.

IX. Honor of the Vixen

The original builders of the Orrpars Road were lost to history, but they certainly knew how to build roads to last. While some parts of it had been altered – either because of intentional sabotage during war or a change of style – most of the road had endured for over two thousand years without requiring significant repairs.

Almost ruler-straight between each of its ancient crossroads, it was uniformly thirty feet wide for the entire length of its original construction. It was formed from blocks of hard volcanic stone bound together with cement mortar in a slight dome (allowing water to drain off to the sides), laying on top of successive layers of very fine leveling cement, thick concrete, large stone rubble, and hard-packed earth. These ancient roads had survived rain, ice, and flood undamaged despite centuries of neglect, and were still the most widely used roads in the world.

Those ancient builders made more than just roads, however. Every twenty miles, four buildings were built: A stable for the changing of horses, a low-class inn with small rooms for poorer travelers, a higher-class inn with larger rooms for wealthier travelers, and a small guardhouse. Every hundred miles, this group of buildings was also joined by a fifth, which Norre's scholars believed were postal service buildings of some sort. Villages, townships, even whole cities had grown up around some of these clusters of buildings. Most, however, had been abandoned, and had long since fallen into disrepair.

The Norre Hegemony had decided to try and restore some of these outposts, intending to use them as a backbone for a new postal system. Twelve of these groups of buildings had been fully restored and seven more were in the process of being renovated. Captain Djobukly of the Norrish Regulars, 27th Brigade, commanded the guardhouse in once such outpost, located near the northernmost border of Norre Alliance territory.

At the age of thirty, Djobukly had been through greater adversity than many veterans of the service with decades more experience. His career had started before he was supposed to be old enough to join the army, as soldiering was all he had ever wanted to do, but it had been a hard eighteen years of military life.

Djobukly's mother had been an auxiliary to the army, a "camp follower" some would say insultingly, working as a seamstress to help make the many uniforms, packs, tents, flags, banners, and so forth required by any regular military. She had taken her ten-year-old son with her to a supposedly well-protected army camp several miles behind the lines of a battle between the Norre Hegemony and a group of Erixonites. The camp was not nearly as safe as advertised, however, and was attacked shortly after they had arrived. Djobukly had been forced to wield a dagger in defense of his mother, killing two of the attackers but receiving several nasty wounds in the process.

Having decided he had a talent for soldiering from that adventure, Djobukly joined the military as soon as he could. The army required that its boys be at least fourteen years old before accepting them into service, but the Norrish Navy employed children as young as twelve. On his twelfth birthday, Djobukly walked to the docks in Norre and signed up for the first warship he saw.

That ship was sent on a two-year tour of duty throughout the Sointu Sea, working to protect the trade routes between Norre and the many nations in the Skorran lands. During that particular voyage his ship distinguished itself in battle, fighting a major pirate fleet and running the gauntlet between two warring Skorran factions' crossfire. His tour ended with a battle against a beast of legend – a kraken of unprecedented size. Djobukly discovered from the start that he was prone to violent seasickness, which made him miserable throughout the voyage. At the end of his voyage, he found himself in the pilot boat, helping to pull his ship alongside the dock, when he was thrown overboard in the early moments of an attack by a wani – a rare, poisonous, sea-going lizard that looked like a cross between a shark and a crocodile. Bitten by the creature in the ensuing battle, he spent a whole year recovering his health from the wani poisoning, during which time his ship returned to sea. Last he'd heard, it was lost in a hurricane.

Having served the terms of his original naval enlistment, and tired of seasickness, he left the navy. Still enamored with the military, however, Djobukly entered the army at the age of fifteen. In what was a remarkable coincidence, the army unit he signed up with was desperate for young men of about his age.

A nobleman from the Kingdom of Gronvall, a member state of the Norre Hegemony, wanted an honor guard assembled for his daughter composed entirely of boys his daughter's age. So, with no time for training, he was assigned to this detail and sent with the nobleman's daughter on a diplomatic expedition to the Republic of Vincour.

Disaster after disaster befell the expedition. The sole experienced soldier, their captain, had been killed when they were hit by a bandit raid. Disease and wild animal attacks cut their numbers down by well more than half before they even reached Vincour. With his time in the navy, he was named the most experienced of the surviving honor guardsmen, and consequently found himself promoted (through attrition) to captain of the expedition.

Like most of the young men in the honor guard, Djobukly found their charge a rather attractive sight and was quite devoted to her. He saved her from four assassination attempts while in Vincour, enduring both stabbings and poisoning in her service. He then had to lead the expedition back, which he did by sea in spite of his problems with seasickness. They were attacked by pirates, and fought them off, but both ships were sunk in the action. Only three people – Djobukly himself, the girl, and one other young man – survived the battle, but were left adrift in an open boat. Sick from his earlier brushes with poison, burnt from the sun, and starving because he sacrificed much of his share of their meager rations to give the girl more to eat, he almost didn't make it back to Gronvall. He once again spent a year recovering from his wounds. The girl married the other survivor of the expedition while he was laid up in the care of the army's chief surgeon.

For the next fourteen years, Djobukly found himself on the front lines for just about every raid or major battle involving the Norre Hegemony. He had survived over a dozen stabbings, four wild animal attacks, and three potentially lethal poisonings. He had developed a reputation for being something of a bad luck charm wherever he was stationed. The longest period of peace in his life since foiling the attack on his mother (outside of those times he was laid up by severe illness or injury) was in his current command. He'd been there just under a year, and the worst problem they had was a lack of the supplies needed to complete the restoration work in a timely manner.

When the Norre Hegemony put together Djobukly's company, they staffed it exclusively with volunteers. His reputation left only the least superstitious of soldiers willing to work for him, which left him somewhat undermanned. The civilian detail sent along to do the restoration work helped fill out his company in non-combat roles, but they weren't expected to fight in the case of a battle... not that he had been sent out in anticipation of a battle.

There were some advantages to being understaffed. The restored guardhouse wasn't exactly the largest barracks in the world. As rebuilt, it had housing for about two dozen soldiers, and storage space for four times that much armor and equipment. A typical company was a hundred men strong. Hot-bunking four people to a bed was never pleasant, especially since – until the other buildings were restored, at least – there were only the most rudimentary of laundry facilities. Djobukly had a bit less than fifty people under his command, and with only two people to a bunk they were at least able to keep the bed sheets clean.

Regardless of the size of his company, that many men – accompanied by just as many civilian construction workers and restoration specialists – were susceptible to bouts of cabin fever, as anyone was. Djobukly's soldiers and the civilians had all been stuck inside the restored buildings (the guardhouse and the high-class inn, respectively) for nearly three months, now, as snows buried the surrounding lands. It was finally starting to thaw out, however, and for the last week he had been able to take his soldiers out to the road and drill them (working them hard both to keep them busy and to keep them warm), while the civilians were clearing the last of the snow out of the remaining ruins they intended to restore.

"Captain," the civilian foreman, Yeo, called. "Could I speak with you?"

"Certainly," Djobukly said, walking over to the foreman. Yeo had been standing at the edge of the road as Djobukly ran his men through their drills, and only interrupted him when he was about to give his men a break. "How can I help you?"

"My people and I have finally finished digging the remaining snow and slush out from the building we've been working on. We've found that a temporary beam we placed shortly before winter's snows stopped work has fallen. We need to replace that temporary beam to prevent further deterioration, and since the last one proved insufficient we were hoping to make it a larger beam than before. We'd need extra manpower to lift it, though, and I was hoping I could borrow your soldiers to help."

"That should be possible," Djobukly said slowly. "How many do you need, and how soon?"

"All of them," Yeo said. "And as soon as you can spare them. We can't do anything else until this is accomplished."

Djobukly frowned. "I can't spare them all, but what I can spare you may have right away."

Yeo raised an eyebrow. "Why can't you spare them all? It seems as if they're just doing busy-work."

"Well, they are," Djobukly admitted. "But that busy work is hiding our true purpose out here. About eight months ago, Norre sent new orders to my unit: An entire nation has uprooted itself and is expected to come marching down this road with plans for an invasion. They hadn't yet left their homes when that word came, and that many people takes a great deal of time to move – especially as much of it will be through hostile territory – but with winter ending it could happen any day. Tens, maybe even hundreds of thousands of soldiers are expected to reach this border soon – and that's not even counting the civilian population. There is no way for us to fight them off alone – fifty men against an entire nation of people is not good odds. While this is a fine guardhouse it isn't the most defensible of fortifications, so if we see them we are to evacuate your men and send the alarm to all of the nearby villages. While I may be drilling my men to stave off boredom, I'm doing so on the road in order to keep a lookout. If I were to stop these drills and give them an assignment helping you in your work, I would still need a detail out here watching the road at all times."

Yeo rolled his eyes. "Captain Djobukly, if this threat is as dire as you suggest, why would Norre not have evacuated us much earlier than this?"

"We plan to," Djobukly said. "The Norre Alliance is sending a fresh detachment of soldiers to relieve us – soldiers who will be specialists in surveillance and border patrols. Once they get here, you will be asked to secure what you can and accompany my men as we escort you to a safer position until the threat is over. We were hoping to have you out of here before winter set in, but the snows came early this year and our relief was delayed because of the weather."

"If you're going to make us abandon this place," Yeo snapped, now visibly angry, "why are we bothering to restore it?"

"Well, we aren't planning to *abandon* it. This is the border to the Norre Hegemony, after all, and we intend to secure it. We plan to build this place up, increasing the garrison until this becomes a well-defended border crossing. We also hope to build up a civilian presence to support the garrison, which may result in this site becoming a city, in time. Once the Knodelians have been dealt with, we're hoping you will return to complete the work you've started."

"But the work we're doing—"

"We're reasonably sure they won't loot this place or damage any of your work," Djobukly said reassuringly. "It's too unimportant for them to bother. We want you to continue working and get as much done as possible until you leave."

Yeo clenched his fists. "If this is their goal, why bother restoring these ancient buildings to begin with? Why not raze them to the ground and start over, building something a lot more useful for defending the border from?"

Djobukly sighed, shrugging sympathetically. "Politics and money. A proposal to build fortifications along likely border crossings was disallowed by the government because it was too expensive. There was, however, this program already in place to restore these little outposts for the postal service. So, in order to circumvent the politics involved in getting new border fortification proposals through the government, someone high up in the army office came up with the idea of using this program to achieve the same effect. They can't use it to protect every route into Norre, but our higher-ups will take what they can get." He paused. "At this stage, we can do little more than provide early warnings when an enemy is sighted, but it is hoped that eventually this outpost can become the outermost of Norre's defenses."

Yeo looked dumbfounded. With a bitter laugh, he said, "What a mess. At any rate, if we're going to be temporarily abandoning this place soon, it's more important than ever to get that beam put up to prevent further damage. You can look down this road for miles and not see any armies marching on it. The snows end later the further north you go, so the Knodelians are probably still stuck in the winter weather. Surely you can afford to allow me the use of your men for just a few hours while we get this beam set up, right?"

Djobukly chewed his lip. Yeo had a point. The snows hadn't fully melted yet, and there was still snow and ice on parts of the road. It would be even worse up north, where the Knodelians were coming from.

"I suppose that we could spare a few hours." Djobukly agreed with Yeo only very reluctantly, and he had a bad feeling about it.

Torkki, accompanied by Donati and several of his assistants, escorted Master Engineer Laing for his inspection of the entire length of the newly built "Fangs of Ekholm," as the wall had become known. Working through rain, snow, wind, and every other imaginable form of harsh winter weather, the wall was more or less complete. Laing was there to check on the workmanship of a project he only reluctantly approved eight months before.

The nickname for the wall came from its towers. They could not produce enough granite or limestone to sheath their wood structure to defend against fire in time, so Ekholm's engineers used another stone instead: Ivory-white marble. Looking at the wall from outside of the city, each tower looked like a white fang rising from the ground.

Inside, however, it still looked like a haphazard wall of mismatched wood. Each tower, platform, and walkway had been hastily constructed out of whatever lumber was available at the start of the project, and was reinforced as work on other parts of the wall progressed – more to help in the construction than with any thought of making them permanent. Now, this framework was integral to the wall's defense, since every archer or war machine needed to use those platforms as a base.

Laing stroked his beard, studying the seams in the mortar of the wall's capstones. "Hmm...."

"Is that a good 'hmm' or a bad 'hmm?'" Donati asked nervously. He had told Torkki that this was his first major project in the employ of the Hegemony, and he was hoping for a good review which might lead to more jobs for him.

"This mortar is acceptably strong," Laing said. "But it was applied a little sloppier than I would like. If this wasn't such a rush job, I might suggest you chisel off these capstones and re-set them."

"I hadn't had a chance to inspect this part of the wall, myself," Donati said, wringing his hands together behind his back. "How bad is it?"

"It'll hold, but let's hope it doesn't get hit by catapult," Laing said. "How long would it take to replace, if you had to?"

"We don't have any granite of this size mined," Donati said. "So we would have to re-use this piece. It would take a week or two to chisel it out and chip away the existing mortar. After that, though, we could replace it in a few hours."

"You might want to do that, then," Laing suggested. "As bad as the winter has been, we may still have months before the Knodelians arrive. You've at least got a reasonably solid stone wall, already. Most of the cities and towns I've been working with could barely manage crude wooden barricades, if that. Has anything else been done, or is this wall the extent of your new defenses?"

"It's the cornerstone," Torkki said. "There is more, however. Not that I actually authorized anything else, but our new allies insisted—"

Laing cocked his head. "New allies?"

"Wulvers from Dahlberg," Torkki said. "They're settling some of their people here – and helping defend Ekholm – as a part of the deal for some of the material we needed to build the wall. When they saw the state of our defenses, they also provided us with some of the war machines you see on these platforms."

"They're experiencing a crisis of overpopulation," Donati continued. Torkki nodded for him to go on – Donati, after all, was the only one present who had been in Dahlberg. "The wulvers wanted to settle some of their people here, in Ekholm, in exchange for the volcanic ash we needed and some military support. Their people were invaluable in the construction of this wall... or were up until about a week ago."

"What happened then?" Laing asked.

"Their leader in this town, Mrazek, approached me some time ago,"

Donati said, looking rather embarrassed. "He... requested—"

"After getting you drunk," Torkki pointed out, amused. Laing's lip quivered as the anecdote continued.

"After getting me drunk," Donati acknowledged, shooting a nasty look Torkki's way. "He convinced me to design a 'siege tower' that would be large enough for wulvers to use. I came up with a functional design, despite my... lack of sobriety. He took that design, and that was the last I saw of it... for about two months."

"Wulvers are tireless workers," Torkki said. "When they weren't helping us build the wall, they were constructing kits for these siege towers... with a few minor modifications."

"Modifications?" Laing prompted.

"The 'siege' component of the siege towers was removed," Donati said. "They eliminated the wheels that would make them mobile, the bridge design that I had incorporated between the tower and the wall it was intended to besiege, and reinforced the wooden shielding."

"A week ago, construction was fairly complete on the wall," Torkki said. "There were some last-minute touches needed – like laying the capstones here and elsewhere – but we had more than enough workers to do that, so the wulvers left us humans to complete the wall. Meanwhile, without our knowledge, they went across the river and assembled two of these siege tower kits, making, instead, temporary archer's towers to protect the bridge with."

"Really?" Laing sounded intrigued. "I would like to see them, if you don't mind."

"Sure," Torkki said, gesturing towards the stairs down to ground level. "This way."

Donati sighed. "Just remember, I was drunk at the time, and they've changed my plans considerably. I take no responsibility for the state of those two towers."

Laing cocked an eyebrow. "Of course. Is there something wrong with them?"

Torkki chuckled. "Well, you'll just have to see. Let's just say the wulvers weren't quite as clever as they thought they were being."

Unbelievably, it took six hours to get the supporting beam up and solidly in place at Djobukly's outpost. The engineers, while otherwise well equipped for their job, had no tools which could measure a piece of lumber of that size. The best they could do was guess, and so they overestimated its length rather than underestimated it. Also, thanks to the condition of the building, they could not afford to construct a pulley system or something similar to aid them in lifting the beam, so it had to be lifted up entirely by hand. Six hours where almost a hundred men would pick up the beam, holding it in place until the engineers got a better idea of how much to cut it, then setting it down (gently, so as to not damage either the beam or the surviving floor it was resting on) while the engineers would trim it down and try again. It took four tries before the beam was small enough it could be lodged into place. Then they had to keep holding it up until support beams could be put in place.

"I'm not looking forward to taking this thing down when you get ready for the permanent beam to be put up." Djobukly's arms were tired, and his men looked exhausted.

"We probably won't need you or your men for that," Yeo said. "We have a few other options. We could leave it up there permanently, which I'm thinking we might do considering how hard it was to get it into place. Or we could cut it apart and take it down in smaller, more manageable pieces. Or—"

"Captain Djobukly, sir!" one of his soldiers called from the door to the outside, his voice wavering. "You, uh, better come take a look at this."

"What is it?" Djobukly said, walking over. "Is something... wrong.... Oh."

If Djobukly were to line up all his men across the road in marching formation, they would be ten men abreast and five men deep. Some ways down the road, there was an army ten men abreast and countless men deep, trudging through the snow. They were probably several miles away, but on a road that straight and a day that clear they were easily visible.

"Th-that's them, isn't it?" Yeo asked. "That's the invading army you were telling me about, right?"

There was a long pause. Hidden somewhere among the civilian workers, Djobukly heard a voice he recognized as belonging to one of his soldiers say, "He really is cursed!"

With a sigh, Djobukly stepped back into the inn. "Well, it's hard to tell at this distance – they're still quite a ways off – but as far as I know there really isn't anyone else expected down this road with that many people. So probably, yes."

"What are we going to do?" Yeo asked, voice trembling.

Truth be told, there wasn't much Djobukly could do. They were undermanned, under-equipped, and poorly positioned. Even if they weren't all three of those things, there was no way a tiny, unfinished, understaffed outpost built essentially to protect postal routes could hold a full-scale army off for any length of time. They did, however, have certain obligations which needed to be met, even in the face of an overwhelming enemy force.

"We need to alert as many local towns and cities as possible," Djobukly said. "The Norre Hegemony has spent eight months setting up defenses against this threat, but without some advanced warning all that work might go to waste."

"Okay." Yeo wrung his hands. "Alert the towns. Good plan. Um, but how are you going to do that?"

"The stables have enough horses for every one of my soldiers to have a mount," Djobukly said calmly. "Once the postal building was completed, we were supposed to be able to ride to the defense of any postmen should they be attacked by bandits, and while the Norrish government rarely gave us all the supplies we needed, they made sure to equip us with the horses and fodder to do that part of the job. These horses were bred for speed more than combat ability, and should easily be able to stay out of the reach of the bulk of the Knodelian forces."

"How soon are you going to be able to leave?" Yeo asked.

"I'm not leaving, and neither are my men," Djobukly said, resigned. "You are, and as soon as possible."

"What?" Yeo cried incredulously. "By ourselves?"

Without protest, Djobukly's soldiers immediately started escorting Yeo's people to the stables, explaining in low tones the idiosyncrasies of their individual horses. This had been something Djobukly was prepared for, even if he'd hoped it never would come down to it.

"As soldiers of Norre, we have two responsibilities here," he explained to the startled engineer, gesturing towards his men. "The first is warning the rest of the Hegemony about this threat. The second is protecting our civilian charges – that is, you. I'm fairly certain you can see how this plan takes both of those responsibilities into account."

"But what about you and your men?" Yeo asked.

"That's partly why I want you to start walking with me to the stables *right now*, rather than waiting until I'm done with this explanation. If you please?"

"Oh, of course."

"Now, about my men and I," Djobukly continued, guiding Yeo a little further down the road toward the stables. "We have an evacuation to carry out. Norre's spies don't believe that the Knodelians would have any interest in a tiny little unfinished outpost like this one, but that doesn't mean we can just leave it alone for them to take it as it is. It may be a mere drop in the bucket for an army that size, but we nevertheless cannot allow them to have the arms and stores we've been keeping here. They will need to be destroyed or buried to keep them out of Knodelian hands. Once you civilians have escaped and we've completed that, we will be able to leave ourselves... if we have any time to do so. Which means you need to leave. Now!"

"But we can't leave you alone like that!" Yeo insisted. "We may not be trained to fight, but at least we can help you destroy those supplies. It will give your men a better chance of survival, and—"

They entered the stables. "But then who would inform the Hegemony that the Knodelians are here? That is extremely important and it will be your job. Each civilian is being given a town or city to send your warning to as they are helped onto the horses. You need to head all the way down to the small town of Arbeloa and get further instructions. Arbeloa is undefended, but it maintains a messenger service which can send warnings to several other townships."

"Arbeloa," Yeo replied as Djobukly helped him onto a horse. "Got it."

"Now, ride!" Djobukly cried, slapping Yeo's horse on the rump to get it going. It wasn't the first horse to leave, but it also wasn't the last, and it took several more minutes before all of the civilians were gone. All in all it had been a quick evacuation, considering.

"They're away, sir," one of the soldiers said, approaching him. "What now?"

Djobukly sighed. "Well, I told Yeo that we would be destroying the supplies to prevent their capture. We might as well do that while we wait for the Knodelians to arrive."

"Sir?"

"The Norre Hegemony has had eight months to prepare a defense against the Knodelians," Djobukly said. "But the Knodelians are early. What defenses have been completed might hold, but they need the advance warning that those civilians will be delivering. We need to hold here only long enough for the civilians to get fully away."

The soldier swallowed. "But... there are fifty of us. We're outnumbered a thousand to one, at least. What can we do?"

Djobukly grinned darkly. "They're marching down the road ten men abreast. That's all that can walk side by side on this road. We will match that... at least for a little while. Eight hours, perhaps." He paused. "Eight hours to make eight months of work succeed, and to save the eight million people of the Hegemony. Worth dying for, don't you think?"

The soldier shot him a wry smile and squared his shoulders in return. "Yes, sir. I believe it is."

If it weren't for the constant presence of Ziani and Mathis, Kieras was sure she would have gone crazy that winter. The trip back from Arsene was plagued by sleet, rain, ice, and snow. Things only got worse as the season went on, proving to be one of the harshest winters in Ekholm's history. Traveling anywhere out of town would have been too dangerous to even attempt, thanks to the weather, but almost everyone in the town was too busy constructing the wall to look after a lonely young kitsune vixen.

Ziani tried her best to find ways to keep Kieras entertained. More than ever, the two girls tried to catch Torkki and Mathis in the bathhouse (Ziani because of her crush, and Kieras because she now felt challenged as a kitsune after Mathis' admission that he always discovered their plans ahead of time). Eventually, it got too cold to even try that, but not before they caught Torkki several times. To Kieras' annoyance, Mathis continued to avoid them quite successfully. Even after that weekly adventure ended, Ziani continued to involve Kieras in the odd prank or bit of light mischief.

Mathis, however, helped her fulfill her sense of purpose during those long winter months. Ziani had ensured that her job of delivering food from Hesketh's tavern to the workers on the wall was retained, but it wasn't the sort of thing Kieras liked doing every day. Mathis had recognized this and found her a job that challenged her, made her feel useful, kept her busy, and even gave her a chance to practice her kitsune trickery.

While Torkki's Elite Brigade was working as labor on the wall most days, they also needed to keep in shape as soldiers. Torkki had come up with the idea of having his men run an obstacle course designed to train their combat skills. He also wanted the course to be changed periodically, to keep his men on their toes. However, it had to be the sort of obstacle course which could be constructed and changed with little labor, thanks to the demands of the wall project.

Mathis had recommended Kieras for the job. Using her illusions in subtle ways for the design and her kitsune-enhanced strength for the actual build, she was able to construct the obstacle course and keep it challenging without requiring that any laborers be taken away from the wall.

Winter was ending, however. The need to use the soldiers as laborers was almost done, and they were going through regular, more organized drills instead. She was needed less and less in the town, which left her thinking, once again, about the search for her mother. As there were no plans to send Mathis – or anyone else – on another diplomatic trip until after the Knodelian threat had been met, her quest might require leaving Ekholm and going on her own... but she had some unresolved things to take care of first.

To start with, she had made two oaths regarding Mathis. The first was complete: She had succeeded in ensuring he had at least one friend on each of his diplomatic missions so far, helping him to deal with Jobinh, and it didn't seem likely he would be sent on many more for a while. However, she still had to pull at least one prank on him – she had sworn she would, and as a kitsune she was required to fulfill that oath.

There were many problems with pulling a prank on Mathis. To begin with, she no longer was so upset with him as to actually *want* to embarrass him like she'd originally intended. He was her friend, and while pranks between kitsune friends were common, they were rarely *too* embarrassing.

That was easily solvable. She could merely arrange for his prank to be something which was either only mildly embarrassing for him, or for which there would be few, if any, witnesses other than herself. But that proved to be more of a challenge than she thought – he was exceptionally good at seeing through her deceptions, so finding a way to get him alone for such a prank was almost impossible.

It wasn't just the need to prank Mathis that was keeping her in Ekholm, however. She also felt obliged to help them with the Knodelian threat. While no real challenge for another kitsune, she could be considered a great warrior compared to the average human. Ekholm would need all the warriors it could find to fight off the Knodelians. As much as they had helped her, she felt the need to help them.

Finally, there was the whole matter of the third part of the quest her father had sent her on. She still felt that Torkki was an ideal person to pledge her year of service to, and wanted to get that out of the way before resuming her journey. There was a problem with that idea, however.

"I still don't think he'd be the right guy for you," Ziani said. The time to pledge her oath was approaching, and Kieras had chosen to discuss the matter with her closest confidant during dinner. For some reason Kieras didn't understand, however, the human girl was opposed to Torkki being the recipient of her boon, but she had yet to figure out why. "He doesn't need your help in anything he does. He wouldn't ask for it, that's certain. In fact, he might view you pledging your service to him as a burden more than as a blessing."

"No kitsune would willingly give their service to someone who *asked* for it," Kieras said. "It goes against our nature. No, Torkki is clearly the noblest human here, and therefore is the worthiest of my service."

Ziani's eyes tightened. "Listen, Kieras, you *are* my friend, right?"

"Why would you even doubt that?" Ziani was the closest human friend she had, even including the people back home in Kassia, and in fact she liked the human girl a great deal more than she did several of her own family members. "Of course I am your friend! I swear it."

"You would not betray me while in Torkki's service?" Ziani asked insistently.

That confused the kitsune girl. "Betray you? I'm not sure what you mean. I'm choosing Torkki because he is deserving; he would never betray Ekholm, so why would you think I would—"

"No, I don't care about any loyalties you might feel to Ekholm." There was a seemingly panicked frustration in Ziani's voice. "Would you ever betray *me*?"

Kieras shook her head in confusion. "Ziani, I honestly have no idea what you are talking about. What are you so afraid of? I certainly would never tell him any of your secrets, if that's what you're afraid of."

Ziani stared at her, gaping slightly, before shaking herself and sighing. "You know, sometimes I forget that as a kitsune you don't always understand what it's like to be human... and then something like this comes along."

That troubled Kieras. Her father wanted her to take on this part of the quest for precisely this reason – so as to avoid hurting her human companions because of simple misunderstandings. Maybe, if Ziani was willing to help her through it, she could weather this storm without endangering their friendship. "What do you mean? What am I not getting?"

Ziani took a deep breath. "In the entire time we've known each other, it has been pretty clear that I am in love with Torkki, has it not?"

"*Very* clear," Kieras agreed. "Which is why I don't understand why you are so unhappy that I want to protect him and his interests for a year. While I know my people have the deserved reputation for being tricksters, we are also fiercely loyal to those we deem worthy."

For some reason, that last line had Ziani visibly clenching her fists. "And could that fierce sense of loyalty also inspire you to *bed* those people?"

Suddenly, it all made sense to Kieras. "Oh! Is that all?"

"Is that *all?*" Ziani replied incredulously. "Isn't that enough?"

Kieras shook her head. "Ziani, how much do you know about the different types of kitsune?"

Ziani blinked. "Uh... the white and red furred kitsune are generally friendly with humans, and the brown and grey furred ones generally are not? And you never know with those rare black furred ones. I don't remember those childhood tales all that well."

That inspired a bout of laughter to erupt from Kieras. She couldn't help herself – she hadn't heard anything so funny in a very long time. "Oh... oh, dear! No wonder you were so concerned!"

Ziani pinched the bridge of her nose. "Okay, now *I'm* the one who's missing something, here...."

Kieras took a deep breath, knowing this would take a bit of an explanation. "I was born the daughter of a myobu kitsune and a nogitsune kitsune – the 'white' and 'red' furred kitsune, as you called them. Each breed of kitsune has its own code of ethics, which is largely ingrained into their instincts at birth, and that code involves things like when it is appropriate to 'bed' a human."

"And that code of ethics forbids you from stealing your best human friend's love interest, right?" Ziani asked hopefully.

Kieras chuckled. "I'm afraid it's not that simple, but you have nothing to worry about from me in this case. There are four major breeds of kitsune, and a number of minor ones like those 'black furred' kitsune you mentioned. The oldest of these are the myobu, created by the great sorcerer Inari from his own youngest daughter, forged with his magic in order to save her life. It gave her powers, and so other humans desired he turn them into kitsune as well. He was not the only one to create kitsune, however. Inari's older daughter, however, felt some of the safeguards he had placed into the myobu make-up were too strict, rebelling from him and forming the nogitsune. They shared many traits with the myobu, but differed in some others... such as hair color. Still later, copycat wizards created other breeds, including those known today as the huli jeng and the kumiho, the other two major breeds.

"Each breed of kitsune inherently treats relationships with normal humans differently: The myobu, my mother's breed, are the most forthright in such matters; they will never mate with a human who has a committed relationship with another human, and the human must be made aware that the person interested in them is a kitsune and must make the choice to enter into a relationship entirely of their own free will."

"Torkki is aware you are a kitsune," Ziani pointed out, troubled. "And we aren't exactly in a committed relationship."

Kieras shrugged. "Seems like you are. At least from your end, which is good enough for me."

Ziani let out a sigh of relief. "Oh, good. Then, as long as I'm interested in Torkki, you won't do anything with him yourself, would you?"

"No, but not only because of that," Kieras said. "I'm a nogitsune, too, after all – more nogitsune than myobu, if my fur is any indication. As a nogitsune, I'm not bound by that restriction."

Ziani's eyes widened. "Then—"

"It all comes down to the nature of each breed, really," Kieras said. "I really don't know it all that well, myself, but right before I left my father insisted I learn a few things. The myobu look upon themselves as guardians and protectors, but beyond that they are somewhat isolated by both custom and design. They rarely permit relations of any kind outside of their own race, indeed their own breed, which makes my birth something of an oddity. They look to protect Inari's legacy, first and foremost, so there simply is nothing to gain and much to lose by tricking humans into relationships. The nogitsune have a touch of a protective streak in them, as well, but are much more social. The best description I can give you is that we're a bunch of meddling do-gooders, with our own ways of deciding what 'do-gooding' means, which isn't always what most humans would think of as proper. We also believe the ends almost always justify the means."

"Okay," Ziani replied uncertainly.

"It really matters in all of our relationships," Kieras continued. "Nogitsune will sometimes use human relationships against those we feel are... dangerous. Sometimes this entails forcing apart a bad relationship by entering into one with them ourselves, or disguising ourselves as their lover and pretending to be that lover in order to further a plot against them. But we would never do such a thing against people who are worthy of respect. I know we kitsune have a reputation for promiscuity and interfering in good relationships, too, but most of that comes from the deeds of the other major breeds. The kumiho are especially nasty – never get in bed with a man whose breath smells of carrion, because they're probably a kumiho in disguise. Kumiho are cannibals and carrion eaters, and any relation they may want with you won't go well."

"I'm confused. What does this have to do with Torkki?" Ziani asked desperately.

Kieras smiled at her friend. "He is worthy of respect, of course, so neither my myobu nor my nogitsune natures would allow me to trick him in that way. You are also worthy of respect, so I would never betray you this way."

"Well, that's a relief." Ziani let out a deep breath. "But I still don't think he's the right person for this plan of yours, and not just because I'm worried you'll fall for his good looks."

"Why, then?" Kieras asked.

"Simply because he wouldn't like it, and neither would you," Ziani said. "Torkki is a soldier. He has been an army man his whole life. He is also a leader and he expects people under his command to be committed to self-discipline, to never complain, and to do what he tells them to without question. You would, in effect, be placing yourself under his command, but since you are a kitsune he could never trust you to respond to his orders with army discipline, and he would never be happy having to couch his orders so as to not offend your kitsune sensibilities. You would be upset because of how much you would have to restrict your behavior. No fun and games, no peeking on him in the bath, no pranks, nothing."

Kieras sighed. She knew that was likely, but she still felt Torkki was most deserving of her service. "Who else should I pick, then?"

"Honestly, I think you'd be well off with Mathis." A secretive smile slipped onto Ziani's face. "You and he seem to have become great friends. He understands kitsune better than any other human I know of, and he would be willing to let you live the life you want."

"He might be a good friend," Kieras said, "but I can't just swear my service to him because he's a good friend. He has to earn it, and I'm not sure Mathis has it in him to do that."

Ziani opened her mouth a couple of times as if she wanted to say something, but then just shook her head. "I think it will be a big mistake to swear your service to Torkki. But it's a mistake you haven't made, yet. I hope you change your mind before it's too late."

Head cocked at a forty-five degree angle, Laing couldn't believe his eyes. "How is it still standing?" He, Donati, and Torkki had crossed the bridge to see the wulver's towers, and he was stunned at what he saw.

"Near as I can tell, the swamp mud is holding it up," Donati said. "I'm worried it will fall if anyone tries to go in it, though. The wulvers were hoping to find a way to salvage it and slip a working foundation underneath it, which is the only reason we haven't torn it down, yet."

"The other tower looks more-or-less upright," Laing said, glancing at it. "Did you already fix that one?"

"The other tower was fortunate enough to hit what we believe to be fairly level solid ground as it was sinking," Donati said. "Whatever it's settled in, however, can act as enough of a foundation that we can safely man it, if necessary, though I wouldn't trust it long-term."

"We'd better get to manning it while we have it, then," Mathis said, approaching the group from the bridge. He had a grim expression on his face.

"What do you mean?" Torkki asked.

"The Knodelians are coming," Mathis said. "Word just arrived. The Arbeloans are at the gates to take refuge, as we had offered earlier, and they've brought with them an architect name Yeo. He claims to have just escaped from an outpost he was helping to construct on the Norrish border. The Knodelians are coming right down the Orrpars road, snow or no snow."

Torkki's lips pursed. "How far out are they?"

"Yeo wasn't sure. He rode the first horse he was given to death, spent another day hiking to a nearby village, and then rode another horse at a more sedate pace for another day before he arrived in Arbeloa yesterday. I suspect they're not much more than a week or two's march away, at most."

"I'd better get back into town and start billeting the Arbeloans," Torkki said darkly. "Then we'll have to man the wall we spent all this effort building and get ourselves on a proper war footing. We've spent eight months getting ready for this moment; let's hope it was enough."

Kieras was walking down the road aimlessly, still a little rattled from her conversation with Ziani, when the wulver captain, Mrazek, approached her from out of nowhere. His appearance was so sudden that she would have been startled back into her fox form had she been any less skilled in her human transformation.

"Milady," Mrazek said, nodding slightly at her. "Archon Savard has sent myself and my companions out to assemble the women, children, and civilians on the city green no later than dusk, tonight. We now have word that the Knodelians are less than a week away, and final preparations for the non-combatants must be made."

Kieras frowned. "Very well; I suppose you should be about it then."

Mrazek paused uncertainly. "Does that mean you will be there?"

Kieras shook her head. "Of course not. You said non-combatants. I'm neither a child nor a human woman. I'm a kitsune with decades of combat training under the Kassian royal family's Captain of the Guard. I doubt Torkki himself could match me one on one."

Mrazek gave a huff that she had come to know as a wulver sigh. "Milady, I was not told to do anything more than deliver a message. I am not the person who you should argue that with."

"Then who is?" Kieras insisted. "The principle reason I've stayed in

Ekholm this long was to help with this coming battle. I'm not going to be tossed aside now that it's here!"

"Torkki is in charge of assigning the soldiers to their stations, both his own elite forces and the members of the Ekholm militia." Mrazek hesitated, considering her earlier words. "But challenging him to single combat on the eve of invasion would be a poor use of both your talents. And most likely anything less would do you little good, milady. He has spent a great deal of time preparing his men as well as the local militia to defend the walls and man the machines of war that they need to operate. He will not want to put someone unfamiliar with his plans into the action – he would not even let his own brother have a spot on the wall, even though Mathis is a very skilled shot with a bow."

"Mathis won't be allowed to fight?" Kieras was a bit surprised at that. Then again, she knew Mathis' confidence for battle was shot, so perhaps it wasn't just Torkki's decision. "Did he even want to?"

"I was there, milady," Mrazek replied. "Mathis was begging both his uncle and his brother for a spot in defense of his home, but they refused. He argued with them for some time before I stepped forward and offered him a spot in the tower my wulvers will be manning on the other side of the river. Torkki and Savard have no say over how that tower is defended."

Kieras knew what tower he was talking about, of course. The leaning tower was a great joke among the villagers, and its more upright mate was considered something of a death trap should anyone try attacking its walls. "And Mathis agreed?"

"Not without reservations," Mrazek admitted. "But he and I are of like mind: Losing the bridge is too great a risk to leave it unguarded. Nor would he sit idly by while Ekholm is attacked, Torkki or no."

Kieras sighed. It sounded like Mathis had made a serious effort to get Torkki to include him in the fight, and that failed. Mathis was Torkki's brother – what chance did she have to get him to give *her* a spot? Still, she didn't want to be stuck hiding with Ziani and the other civilians when the battle broke out.

"I don't suppose your tower has room for an overlooked kitsune who seeks to join in the fight, does it?" she asked hesitantly.

Mrazek stared at her for a long time. It made her nervous, but she knew she had to endure it or there was no way she was going to be involved in the coming battle, however small the role. Finally, however, he gave her a huff and broke the stare.

"Very well. Report to the tower tomorrow morning, where we'll go over individual assignments. In the meantime, help me get the civilians assembled in the village green."

"Right away!" Kieras snapped crisply, saluting in a close imitation of Mrazek's wulvers. She'd passed whatever test he had given her. Now to run and tell Ziani the news... and, perhaps, to pass along the message about the assembly. She'd agreed to help collect the civilians, after all.

As the leader of Ekholm's defenses Torkki could not afford himself the luxury of taking a watch as lookout on the gates, but he could have done the job well. Over the past several days, refugees from various small, undefended villages had trickled into Ekholm, and it was his uncle's job to find billets for them all while still finding shelter for Ekholm's own civilians. Another job Torkki felt he could manage, but he had been reminded several times (usually by Hesketh) that these were not his duties any more. Torkki's job, for the moment, was simply to maintain a calm and collected appearance and to set an example for his men. This left him with little to do, and he would much rather keep a lookout watch or figure out the billeting requirements for countless civilians and refugees than simply sit calmly and wait for news.

To keep himself busy over the past three days he had already checked the edge of his sword blade seven times, oiled it twelve times, and polished the leather in his armor and sword sheath four times.

Just to find something to do, Torkki had decided to bring in Yeo, the refugee from the border outpost, for an interview. Unfortunately, the architect was late.

A knock on his door stopped his fingers from drumming on the table that served as his desk and had him yanking his feet off said table. "Finally," he said under his breath. Aloud, he called, "Come in!"

Jobinh entered through the door. As the wall was completed offices and barracks were also constructed, but Torkki was still the only one with his own solid door. He needed it – if it weren't for his ability to let loose behind closed doors every now and then, he would have gone stir crazy long before the week was over.

"Sir," Jobinh said, "we have a sighting reported from the lookout on the wall."

Torkki stiffened. "The Knodelians?"

"No, sir," Jobinh replied.

"Oh. More refugees, then?" Torkki said, relaxing.

"Not unless there's a group of refugees out there that wear Norrish armor," Jobinh replied. "Are we expecting reinforcements, sir?"

Torkki slowly stood. "No... we are not," he said uncertainly. "Let's go see who they are, shall we?"

As Torkki left his office following his lieutenant, a small man he didn't recognize was about to enter it. "Ah, are you Torkki? I believe I was told to come here."

"Yeo, I presume?" Torkki asked. Receiving an affirmative nod in response, he continued, "You're late. I still would like to talk with you, however. Walk with me ."

"Of course, of course. Sorry for being so late – I got lost." Yeo fell in behind Torkki and Jobinh as they made their way out of the barracks, down the road, and up the wooden steps to the observation platform by the gate. "Could I ask why I was summoned?"

"I have some questions about the Knodelian force you saw," Torkki said. "But we don't have time for that, at the moment."

They arrived at the lookout platform, and Torkki stepped ahead. One of his scouts turned and saluted him. "Sir, an unidentified Norrish force is approaching."

"I know that – I wouldn't be here if I didn't. Anything new to report?" Torkki asked peevishly, looking over the wall.

"Nothing you can't see for yourself," the scout replied, carefully not taking any offense to Torkki's temper. "Looks like a small force escorting a large wagon train. It wouldn't be all that notable, except we weren't expecting anything, especially of this size."

"Could they be more refugees?" Yeo asked, peering over the wall himself. "They're coming from the same direction I would have if I hadn't gone to Arbeloa first."

"They're soldiers, not civilian refugees," Torkki said. "They might even have already seen some fighting. It's a bit hard to see at this distance, but that armor they're wearing has seen better days."

"You can tell that from here?" Yeo asked, squinting. "I can barely see anything of those men."

"My family has always had exceptional eyes," Torkki replied. "It's why my brother is so good with a bow."

"Is that the only reason?" Jobinh asked. Torkki wasn't pleased with his lieutenant's attitude towards his brother, but he was a fine officer in all other aspects and did his job despite any biases he might have had. Pointing out a few of Mathis' good parts might soften Jobinh's bitter tongue a bit.

"Not entirely," Torkki replied. "He's almost supernaturally strong, allowing him to use bows with a draw weight one of our wulver companions might even struggle with. He has one bow that proves it. It's a daikyu-style longbow, which few of even the most experienced archers in the Norrish army could handle. He claims a personal record of hitting a target that was seven hundred feet away with the thing, and I believe it. He doesn't use it very often, but it's made of laminated wood and has the heaviest draw I've ever heard of – it's almost as strong as a ballista, if you can believe it. While I never saw that record-length shot, I've seen him hit a two inch wide bullseye from three hundred yards away, and the target was made of plate armored steel with a bale of straw and a granite block behind it. The arrow passed through the target, as well as the straw hay, and wound up embedded into a stone wall some twenty yards further downfield. Couldn't do that with a normal bow."

Jobinh looked vaguely disturbed. "How could anyone wield such a weapon, and so precisely?"

"You would have to ask Mathis that," Torkki said. Peering at the arriving army, he frowned. "That suit of armor... I haven't seen it before, but I've heard stories...."

"What do you mean?" Yeo asked. "Stories about armor? What kind of stories?"

"Officers in the Norrish Army of captain's rank or better are provided an allowance to purchase their own custom made armor," he explained. "In order to find an armor type that will fit anyone, Norre has had to rely on designs which only provide partial protection. There really is no other way to equip an army the size that the Norre Hegemony requires unless you insist that your soldiers pay for their own armor, but it can afford to subsidize its higher ranked officers. Over time, with some inside knowledge, you can sometimes figure out who some of these officers are by their armor."

"I noticed that the captain of my outpost's garrison wore a different set of armor than his soldiers, but I didn't think anything of it," Yeo said. "So, you think you know who is in command of this approaching army?"

"Well, I can't identify *all* of our officers by sight, but I recognize this one from stories I've heard," Torkki replied. "Most Norrish officers will mark their armor in some way for every campaign in which they see real action. There are different ways this is done – with stripes of ribbon in unobtrusive places, gemstones mounted into shoulder pieces, or even notches carved into those parts of the armor that are more decorative than functional. There is one officer, however, who has seen action so many times that none of those methods seemed adequate. Instead, he had a crest embedded into his chest piece that was made out of copper. That copper crest is fashioned into the Old Norrish rune for 'endless,' because, it is said, he fears he will be in the front of battle for the rest of his life."

Yeo's eyes widened. "You mean Captain Djobukly?"

Torkki looked at Yeo, mildly curious. "You know him?"

"He was captain of the garrison at the outpost I was restoring," Yeo said. "He sent me – and the other civilians – out on the soldiers' horses. They stayed behind to destroy supplies before attempting a retreat. I'm glad to hear he made it out okay."

"Ah." Torkki grimaced, catching Jobinh's eye. Jobinh nodded. As Torkki started glancing for certain telltale signs from the approaching army, his lieutenant made his way back down the ladder to alert the men in the barracks.

Yeo frowned. "What's wrong?"

"Djobukly may have told you he would be following you once he was done 'destroying supplies' or whatever, but your survival would be his first priority," Torkki said. "To that end, he would have organized a delaying action. Fifty men cannot stop as massive an army as we've been told the Knodelians possess, but even one man can slow down an army for a little while as long as the enemy is forced into a tight enough passageway... if they're willing to die in the effort." He grimaced. "Considering that, I find it highly unlikely that this approaching army is actually Djobukly's command. I believe that our long-awaited battle is finally about to begin."

Mathis scrambled to grab his equipment, making absolutely certain he had the right weight of replacement bowstrings, the proper arrowheads for his arrows, and a pair of spare bows just in case. He even grabbed the so-called "shaving knife" that his brother had given him as a spare dagger in an emergency. Thinking of his brother, he grumbled mentally about the assignment he had been given. He had long ago accepted the idea that he was not suited for duty as a regular soldier, so being placed somewhere that might be considered "out of the way" made some sense, but it still annoyed him.

He had spent much of his youth preparing to go into the army alongside his brother. He had also been a part of the militia for several years, now, and was widely regarded as the best shot with a bow in the history of Ekholm. This battle was the defense of a wall, where the skill of the archers manning that wall would be paramount to Ekholm's success. If there was any time that Mathis' skills would lend themselves to a proper military role, it was now... and here he was, being directed to the defense of a poorly-built out of the way tower that Torkki hadn't even intended in his original strategic preparations.

Given his assignment, Mathis didn't feel like he had to run. The Knodelians weren't even in position to begin their principle attack yet, and any assault on the tower would take a while for them to set up. As soon as he was sure he had all of his equipment, a few emergency provisions, and a bedroll (in the likely eventuality that they needed to sleep at their stations), he was out the door and making his way to the bridge.

He was very nearly trampled by a certain kitsune vixen heading the same direction at a full-out sprint.

"Oof!" he said, catching her and dropping to one knee to stop the both of them from tumbling to the ground. "Where are you headed off to so fast?"

"The same place you're headed." Kieras seemed surprised to have been caught – most people, she would have toppled in such a collision. "I took an opportunity offered by Mrazek to be a part of the tower's melee force. He wanted a few people who he could send out in a sortie, if necessary, and was glad to have me. Most of the wulvers he brought with him will be too busy acting as archers."

Mathis frowned, but gestured for her to follow him anyway. They shouldn't be late for the call to muster, so he decided to ask his questions as they walked. "You don't have any weapons with you, and they won't be able to provide you with any. How—"

Kieras grinned, flexing her fingers. Her fingernails extended a couple of inches, and changed shape and texture to look like knives. "I'm never far from a weapon." Retracting her claws, she continued, "I've been learning how to fight as a kitsune under my father since I was just a kit barely able to hold my human form. Between my claws and my foxfire, I can be a rather formidable enemy. Of course, I can also fight with more... traditional human techniques, as well." Clenching her fist, a reasonably effective-looking facsimile of a sword faded into existence.

"And armor?" Mathis asked. "If you're going to be a part of a sortie, you're going to need some protection."

Kieras frowned, and soon adorned herself with illusory greaves and a molded illusory breastplate with the appearance of hardened leather. "I'm not as good as my father – and probably wouldn't even come close to catching him if I had a hundred years to practice – but he taught me everything I should need to know for this fight. Assuming we fight at all, that is."

Mathis snorted. "Oh, we'll be involved in the fight. Although perhaps not today, since they shouldn't have known anything about the wall we've been building and will need time to plan. They'll probe the wall for weaknesses, first, and it won't be long before they discover we didn't wall up the other side of the bridge. Then we'll be in the thick of it."

"Your brother, the veteran elite soldier, seems to disagree."

"My brother, the veteran elite soldier, has probably never either defended or assaulted a fortified position like this, before," Mathis said tersely. "The Norrish Elite were constructed to intercept enemy armies on the move and vanquish them. They're very, very good at that, but they lack experience in other aspects of warfare. Their understanding of how to conduct or defend against a siege is merely academic, at best. My brother has never been on either side of this kind of battle."

"While you, on the other hand, you have been involved in countless sieges, correct?" Kieras replied sarcastically.

Mathis laughed. "Well, no. But over the years I've studied the tactics of siege warfare at least as much as he has. Perhaps more so."

"Then what makes you so sure you are right and your brother is wrong?"

"Well, to start with, there really isn't much disagreement between us," Mathis said. "He agrees that they'll probe the wall for weaknesses and will see our nearly undefended bridge as a vulnerability. The one question on which we don't see eye to eye, however, is whether the enemy will try to exploit that vulnerability."

"Well, why wouldn't they?" Kieras asked.

"Our army is very limited in size. If they assault the bridge, we'll be forced to destroy it, but until it's destroyed we must spare some of our men to defend it. There's also the logistical problem of getting an army of sufficient force across the water to make the assault, only to return them once the bridge has inevitably been destroyed. By not assaulting the bridge, they will not have to split their armies and our wall defenses will be weaker."

Kieras nodded. "Makes sense. So, why do you disagree with him?"

"Everything we know about the Knodelians suggests they aren't intending to make this a prolonged siege," Mathis said. "They can't afford the time to starve us out. That gives them two options – they can try to scale the walls, which is nearly suicidal and would take a great deal of time as they built ladders, battering rams, siege towers, and the like. Or, they can try to rush the bridge and take it before we have a chance to destroy it, still leaving the first plan as an option should that fail. Which would you choose?"

Kieras gave an unladylike snort. "Well, when you put it that way, there's really only one choice."

"They'll want to cross the river in secret," Mathis observed. "They'll set up an initial assault on the wall while there's still daylight, but once night falls they'll find some way to get some people across the river. By dawn tomorrow, you and I should find ourselves in action. Maybe even earlier."

"That long?" Kieras said flippantly as they started crossing the bridge. "I should have brought lunch."

Mathis snorted in amusement and checked his supplies. He separated the dried meats from the dried fruits and nuts and handed the jerky over, complete with a knife sharp enough to cut it. "Here. Hopefully, the quartermaster will remember to send us some food over the next few days, but just in case..."

Kieras took the dried meats, glancing at him peculiarly. "Um... thank you. Good luck in the coming battle."

Mathis's lips tightened. "Let's hope this battle doesn't come down to luck... but if it does, good luck to you, as well."

"Sir," the lieutenant in charge of Ekholm's militia archers (a hunter by trade, much like Mathis, but not nearly as skilled) called to Torkki. "When do we open fire?"

"Not until I give the word," Torkki replied. "I may believe this is the Knodelian army in disguise, but as long as there is the slightest chance these really are Captain Djobukly's forces I don't want anyone to fire on them."

Jobinh approached from another part of the wall. "It's a rather brilliant subterfuge on the Knodelians' part, if we're right. I never would have suspected a small division of our soldiers escorting a bunch of refugees of being anything but that. We were quite fortunate to figure out these aren't the people they appear to be." He paused, then nodded to Torkki. "We've had just enough time to prepare the liquid fire device the wulvers sent us. The wind seems like it will be quiet enough to use it by the time battle is joined. I'm told the device will only be able to protect the gate itself, and that we only have enough supplies to keep the stream going for a few seconds, but it should startle them something fierce."

"What would we need to make more?" Torkki asked.

Jobinh shrugged. "Honestly, sir, I don't know. It's remarkable stuff. It will burn on water and will produce a fearsome noise when set aflame. The only thing I know of that will stop it from burning, other than time, is to douse it with tons of sand. They can spread it with a siphon, so it can cover a large tract of land. But as for what it's made of, I couldn't even begin to tell you. About the only things I do know is that it needs to be pre-heated before it's put through the siphon, but not ignited until after it leaves the siphon. I tried to watch the wulvers make it, and only caught three ingredients – something that smells like old piss, naphtha oil, and some sort of resin. Beyond that, your guesses are as good as mine."

The man in front of the incoming army, dressed in Djobukly's armor, stepped forward from the bulk of the forces and called up to the wall. "The Knodelians are approaching," the soldier called. "I seek refuge for my men and the civilians we are escorting!"

Torkki glanced to the observation platform on his right. He had positioned Yeo in one of the more protected stations on the wall for just that moment. A head shaking negatively was all the confirmation he needed. This was it, then – the battle was about to begin.

"If there were any of our allies' civilians seeking refuge," Torkki said, risking exposure over the lip of the wall to address the imposter, "we would be glad to take them in. I see none here. I see only Knodelians trying to pretend they're something they are not." He gave a slight smile. "In the future, should you seek to use a soldier's armor to impersonate him, might I suggest you try one less famous?"

Torkki could make out the imposter's mouth opening and closing a few times while making incoherent sounds. Finally, the imposter said, "Well, I suppose there's no point in waiting, then. Atta—"

With a gesture, Torkki signaled his archers to open fire. Before the imposter had finished his call to attack, he was down with four arrows in his throat. That had no effect on the Knodelian assault, however. Within moments, the wagons of the wagon train had dropped their sides, revealing hundreds, possibly even thousands of hidden soldiers.

Ladders and battering rams were the simplest and most dangerous to use of all siege weapons, and they also were the easiest to transport and the most readily hidden. Within moments, teams of Knodelian soldiers were charging the walls carrying ladders, and a battering ram carried by forty men was running for the gates.

Ekholm's well prepared archers, Norre Elite and militia-trained alike, felled the ladder teams easily enough, and did so quickly as they had been instructed prior to the battle. The battering ram was another matter. It could have been handled with far fewer men than were carrying it, but with more than double what they needed the Knodelians were able to adopt an ancient tactic for protecting their soldiers – half of their men held shields to the side with one hand, carrying the ram with the other. The other half of their men also carried the ram with one hand each, using their free hands to hold shields overhead. Arrows would not penetrate, and they were moving too quickly for catapults to accurately target them. The gate had been rushed to completion, and might not hold against a prolonged assault.

With the archers taking out the ladder teams and the catapults concentrating on more distant targets, Torkki wondered if the battering ram team had thought they had escaped notice up until they were about ten yards from the gate, but that is as far as they got. With a roar of thunder and a blast of heat that even Torkki felt from behind the wall, the wulvers' siphon machine started spraying liquid fire straight at the battering ram. The effect was immediate – the ram was on fire, and most of the soldiers carrying it were running and screaming in pain and terror as they were covered in a flaming substance they could not extinguish that burned through their very armor. Deciding not to waste the opportunity, the soldiers manning the liquid fire engine targeted several other nearby ladder teams and clusters of Knodelians, causing a great deal of panic and damage until it ran out of fuel.

The element of surprise completely ruined, and their siege tools destroyed or rendered worthless, the Knodelians started to retreat, but found another surprise that had been laid out for them: The catapults had not been targeting Knodelian soldiers or equipment, but rather had been laying caltrops behind them, forcing a retreat off of their original path and into covered oil pits (remnants of the original plans for Ekholm's fortifications that had been re-purposed for this moment). Pits which were promptly set aflame by archers with flaming arrows.

In the end, it was a rout. It was not, however, decisive: Despite the initial confusion and the destruction of many of their war machines, the bulk of the Knodelian soldiers survived. So did many of their wagons, which undoubtedly carried additional surprises that could be unleashed at any time.

"Well, we won the initial skirmish," Torkki said with a grim smile.

"That went better than I could have hoped," Jobinh said. "Yet you still seem concerned. What's wrong?"

"Nothing, I suppose. But this isn't over. They'll be back, and they'll be better prepared now that they know what we can do. And we've used up the liquid fire, so next time we won't be as well prepared ourselves." He sighed. "If we had more soldiers, I'd send out a sortie to harass them further, but with so few men...."

"We could have used the wulvers who are now uselessly stationed on the other side of the bridge," Jobinh said bitterly. "Then you would have been able to send out your sortie. Launching a counter-attack at this point might be enough to have them abandon the assault on Ekholm entirely, chasing the Knodelians away forever."

"Manning that tower makes sense, if you believe, as my brother does, that their next move will be to attack the bridge. I think that he's mistaken, and our best move would have been to have the wulvers on hand as you suggest, but that was their decision and not mine."

Torkki sighed. "The wulvers have their own leaders, and they agree with my brother. Whichever of us is right, that tower may turn out to be decisive in this battle... one way or another."

Ziani took a breath of nice, fresh air – one of the most pleasant sensations she had experienced in the last several hours. She, like most of the civilians in Ekholm, had been relocated to one of several shelters to wait out the ongoing battle. Her particular shelter was an old smokehouse for fish with a moderately reinforced roof and walls. The odors inside likely would have knocked her kitsune friend unconscious before she stepped through the doors.

She and the other civilians had just been told that they would not have to stay indoors for the evening, but they did have to stay close to the shelter and could not return home. The shelters were distant enough that they were out of the range of enemy arrows, and so far catapults and similar siege weaponry had not been seen among their enemy's arsenal. If such heavy weapons appeared, the "fortified" shelters would provide a modicum of protection. The shelters were also useful for keeping the civilian populace together near their best escape route. If something happened and the enemy actually was able to enter the town, any surviving soldiers would fight a delaying action as Ziani and her companions in the shelter escaped aboard the fishing fleet moored nearby.

While they were allowed outside for air at night, they were still crammed into the building to sleep and only allowed out in small batches. It was difficult for their guards to keep track of them all, otherwise. Ziani wasn't going to miss her chance to get out of the stink of fish, so even though her shift outside wasn't until well after her bedtime, she took the opportunity when it was presented.

Her breath was just barely visible in the night air, and a moonless sky didn't add much light to illuminate the world around her. She didn't care, but she was starting to get a little bored with nothing to do and nothing to see.

Until there *was* something to see. A small reddish-orange light emerged from one of the towers, descending slowly. It was followed by two or three others, and then seemingly hundreds arced through the air, speeding into the horizon down-river.

"What the—"

"Ma'am?" Boedker, their bunker's guard, began. "Is there something wrong?"

Boedker had been a part of Mathis' security detail during his ambassadorial expeditions; upon the conclusion of the latest of those, he and the other members of that detail – save for Jobinh – had been assigned as guards for the civilian bunkers. Since they had not been around to be given roles in the defense of the wall, Torkki asked that they assist in the case that an evacuation was required. When she found out about their assignment, Kieras had been sure to ask him to look after several of the friends she had made around Ekholm, and Ziani was on the top of the list of those friends. Ziani, upon learning of the connection, was quick to wheedle any inside information she could from him.

"What is going on over there?" she asked incredulously, pointing.

Boedker grimaced. "Well, we weren't able to wall up the river side, so we were prepared for them to try and outflank the walls by coming around the river. My guess is we're trying to sink a fleet of boats."

"Are we in any danger?" she asked, startled.

"Not at the moment," Boedker replied, though he kept a careful eye on the water. "With those fire arrows and a few ballista installed at the top of the towers to guard the waters, we can easily sink a large fleet of boats trying to come into town before they even get within their own arrow shot range. The Knodelians know that, of course, so they're probably just trying to cross the river downstream, and we're warning them off."

"They're crossing the river? Does that mean they're planning to try and take the bridge?"

Boedker nodded slowly. "It looks like Mathis was right after all."

"Archers, string your bows!" the call from Mrazek came, echoing up to Mathis' station from a floor below.

Mathis took a deep breath. When dawn came, it was clear he had been right. While the entire Knodelian army had not crossed the river, a large enough raiding party to give them serious trouble had. Torkki had done his part the previous day. It was finally time to see if he was up to the challenge as well.

He considered using his standard longbow, but then changed his mind. This was a real battle, not practice nor simple hunting. It called for his best weapon. He instead reached for the one-of-a-kind laminated daikyu-style longbow he had build for himself, one which would out-perform even the greatbows the wulvers were armed with.

As he pulled out the bowstring, one of his fellow archers, a wulver named Teslak, approached him. "That's a mighty bow for a human. Need any help with it?"

Mathis snorted, and then with one quick motion strung it without any noticeable strain at all. "Does that answer your question?"

Teslak let out a loud bark of laughter. "I suppose it does, yes. Laminated yew and ironwood, with a linen string... a hundred strands thick?"

"A hundred twenty." Mathis checked the wax coating on the string. "Double the average longbow string. Even so, it breaks too often for comfort, which is why I also have a greatbow and a longbow already strung, as well."

"Interesting," Teslak said. "As powerful a bow as that seems to be, I imagine it's hard to be accurate with it, especially for a human."

"Most humans, maybe," Mathis said, "but I've never had a problem with it."

"I find that hard to believe."

Mathis glanced out the window, seeing that the Knodelian advance was about half a mile away and approaching slowly. Normally, that would be out of range even for him, but they were on a platform. "See that man there, with the large purple plume in his cap?"

The wulver narrowed his eyes, looking in the same direction. "An officer of some kind, I suppose." A low-toned thrumming twang echoed to his right. Teslak glanced over to see the arrow string still vibrating on Mathis' bow. Glancing back at the Knodelian army, he was just in time to catch the feather-bearing soldier fall. Then he turned and stared at Mathis, his jaw hanging loose in surprise. "How..."

"Well, I—"

"Hey!" Mrazek snapped, interrupting their conversation as his head poked out the top of the ladder behind them. "Cease fire! Save your arrows. You'll fire when I give the order, and not a second sooner, got it?"

"Yes, sir!" Mathis said along with Teslak and the other wulver archers.

Mrazek started back down the ladder with a seemingly satisfied woof. Before he completely vanished, however, he had one last word to say. "By the way... good shot!"

Torkki frowned. He had taken advantage of what he feared might be the last opportunity in this battle for a good night's sleep, but as he heard the morning briefing he was beginning to regret it... or at least to regret not giving clearer instructions about waking him should the Knodelians make any move. Mathis had been right – the enemy was clearly preparing an assault on the bridge, and there was no longer time to destroy the bridge nor, despite what the wulvers believed, was there enough manpower to adequately defend it.

"We need to send them reinforcements," he finally said.

"Sir!" Jobinh called, running up to him. "The Knodelians have renewed their assault on the walls! Still mostly ladder teams, but they're using shields to better protect themselves against our arrows. Without the liquid fire, it will be difficult to repel them before they get to the wall."

Torkki chewed his lower lip in thought. "How many ladders?"

"As least a couple dozen," Jobinh replied. "Not too many, but we'll be hard-pressed to stop them from reaching the wall this time. Once those ladders are up and secured, we'll need every man we've got to repel the attack."

"It just gets better and better." Torkki sighed. "You're on your own, little brother – I hope you can handle it."

The battle for the bridge had been going on for half an hour, but so far Kieras had simply been left sitting with about two dozen wulvers in a dark ground-floor room, waiting for her call to action. With nothing else to do, she munched briefly on the jerky that Mathis had given her.

She was startled when Mrazek jumped down among them, swallowing her bite of food unexpectedly and nearly choking on it. She was already on edge with all the dog-like wulvers around her, not to mention the battle itself, and that certainly didn't help her nerves any.

"All right," Mrazek said. "Our archers are doing well, but they can't hold the Knodelians back forever. We can't afford to allow them even one foot on that bridge, and they're starting to get close, so it's time for us to meet them on the ground."

"Are there enough of us to actually do anything?" Kieras asked.

"Of course!" Mrazek barked. "This isn't the bulk of the Knodelian army. They have no war machines and few archers. It's mostly foot soldiers in light armor, save for a few of the officers – a couple hundred human men, at most. Our archers have successfully scattered them into small groups, though even one of those small groups could pose a serious problem if they reach the bridge. In addition to our wulver strength, we've still got the archers in the tower to support us. Half of you – those on this side of the room – will hang back behind our barricades to stop anyone who gets through. As for the rest of you, as disorganized as they've become I think a sortie is in order."

Kieras looked around, and the other wulvers seemed as full of confidence as their captain, so she took some reassurance in that. She was in the half fighting in the sortie, so she had little time to steel herself.

"Very well," she said, forming an illusory blade. She was holding her tama in one hand, so she couldn't manage a shield to go with it, but she was ready for the battle if necessary. "Let's be off then."

She quickly found herself leading the charge. The battlefield was somewhat swampy, which had helped to slow the Knodelians but which made it difficult for Kieras and the wulvers to move in, as well. The 'barricade' that they had to cross in order to begin their counter-attack was not an effective wall, but rather simply a number of pikes planted to kill horses and slow charges. This, unfortunately, worked both ways, as it was difficult for the wulvers to get through as well. Kieras, being much smaller than the wulvers, was able to pass through the barricade fairly easily, and being a relative lightweight was not sinking into the mud as much. She rapidly separated from the others, soon finding herself fighting alone. Well, not precisely alone.

Thanks to her foxfire techniques, she was able to keep the enemy soldiers from closing in around her. Foxfire, as she had been trained to use it, was more of a defensive weapon against charging enemies than an offensive one, and she had to close in to attack. She was trying to engage no more than one or two people at a time so she didn't get overwhelmed, but on occasion she was too slow at finishing off an enemy to prevent another from coming in at her flank. Somehow, though, whenever one of those flanking attackers got too close, an arrow from the direction of the tower struck them down. Someone – and Kieras had a pretty good idea who – was looking out for her.

Perhaps she was separated from her fellow soldiers, but those arrows told her she wasn't alone.

Mathis frowned. Keeping Kieras out of trouble required a lot of rapid, highly accurate shooting. He was more than capable of it, but he had just run out of arrows for his best bow, and the greatbow arrows he borrowed from Teslak were horribly out of trim, by his standards. He still had some arrows for his longbow, but only a single small quiver full, and they wouldn't work with his laminated bow.

With a sigh, he turned to Teslak. "I'm heading down to the battlefield," he said, stringing his longbow and exchanging it for the bow he'd been using. "I need to get more arrows."

The arrow Teslak was firing went wide at that pronouncement. "You're what? Alone? Are you crazy?"

"I should be safe enough," Mathis said, checking to make sure he had his knife with him. "This wasn't an organized charge on their part – I'd guess that they were mostly just trying to rush in and take out whoever was responsible for burning the bridge, and only then worry about bringing in a more organized force. If they could have come straight down the road, it would have been fine, but we've been able to pick off anyone who even tries that approach. They didn't really account for the terrain off the road, and that's tripping them up. To be honest, I hadn't, either, but it's worked out well for us. The marshlands have forced the Knodelians to separate into small, slow-moving groups; perfect for an archer to pick them off one at a time, and also making it easy enough for me to head out there and recover some arrows without attracting too much attention. I'll be careful."

"What's wrong with my arrows?" Teslak asked.

"They aren't notched right, nor trimmed right, for my bow," Mathis replied. "I tried firing off a few, but I can't get them accurate enough."

"I could loan you my spare greatbow," Teslak said.

"As well as half your arrows?" Mathis chuckled. "Don't be ridiculous! You would run out before the hour's up, and then we'll be back in the same position. Keep your bow, keep your arrows, and keep up your work. That will help us the most."

Kieras was starting to get worried. The enemy soldiers had fallen apart into even smaller groups of varying sizes, but the arrow fire that had been her protection had ceased. The tower was still untouched, but for some reason Mathis – who she was sure had been the one looking out for her – wasn't firing any more. Had there been archers she hadn't seen among the Knodelians, firing back and potentially wounding him?

It was also getting increasingly difficult to go on the attack without his assistance. If she were better skilled with her foxfire she could use it for more than just knocking enemies back with relatively minor burns, but it was too late to wish she'd trained that better. If she still had someone watching her back, she could continue to use her foxfire to spread the enemy out even further and attack them one or two at a time without having to worry overmuch about someone coming at her from behind. Now she seemed to really be on her own, however, and she was being forced more and more onto the defensive.

Moving toward the tower in the hope of regaining support from the archers, Kieras fought her way through a few groups of footsoldiers (marked by their common leather armor), with the occasional better-equipped officers presenting more of a challenge. The type of armor made little difference to her – foxfire was just as effective no matter of what type it was, and her illusory sword could cut through any type of armor far easier than a real sword might – but usually the officers were older and more experienced, and thus better fighters. Now, however, she faced a group with not one, but five officers – one of whom was paying special attention to her *tama*.

"I had heard these were kitsune lands," the leading officer, marked by a feather plume in his helmet, said. He was holding his sword out as a guard, but was carefully watching her for weaknesses in her own defense. "I had hoped to meet them, but I must say I'm surprised to see one fighting for a human cause."

"You know about kitsune, yet you still want to fight me?" Kieras asked, shaking her head in mocking disbelief. "What foolish bravado."

The officer shrugged, grinning darkly. "If I didn't know your kind's weaknesses as well as I know its strengths, it might be... but, well, I think you might find us something of a challenge."

"I doubt it," Kieras scoffed, though she wasn't quite as confident as her banter suggested. A human student of kitsune – like Mathis or old King Kazdri – stood a pretty good chance of beating her in a fight. This man claimed to be just such a student, and he had the advantage of numbers as well.

"We shall see, then, no?" the Knodelian said. "Parros, Verot... surround her!"

Two of the officers, each with a pair of footsoldiers in front of them, ran to outflank her. Without pausing to think, Kieras sent her foxfire at them in six quick blasts, expecting to knock them away as usual. Save for one of the footsoldiers, however, they pushed through with no more than a stumble or two. She had known she wasn't taking the time to make the foxfire attacks strong enough to kill, but it must have been weaker than she thought if they could run right through them. Either her control had failed her, or somehow the Knodelian officers had realized she was not using her full strength and had compensated for it.

A split second of hesitation cost her. She spun around to deal with the soldiers her foxfire had failed to handle, but one of the Knodelians had enough time to throw a dagger. The knife clipped the back of her wrist and knocked her sword out of her hand, but at least she wasn't injured.

She was never defenseless, even without her sword. Her claws were mighty weapons – maybe not sharp enough to cut through steel plate, but the leather armor of the footsoldiers was easy enough for her to tear through. Two swipes of her left hand, and the two footsoldiers protecting the officer named Parros were dead. She thrust her other hand, holding her tama, directly in his face.

"Foxfire!" she cried, this time putting her maximum power behind it. Parros was sent flying back, and while Kieras had no time to confirm it she was fairly certain from the smell that he was dead.

Knowing that the other flanking soldiers would be approaching her from behind, Kieras spun around with a lethal kick that broke one attacker's neck. On the follow-through, her fist thrust forward to kill the last of the footsoldiers, her claws stabbing through his armor and into his chest.

That last move was a mistake, however. Her left hand was stuck, claws impaled inside the dead body, and her right was holding her *hoshi no tama*. Thrown off balance by the deadweight dragging on her left hand, she staggered to her knees as Verot's longsword swung down at her. In a desperate, last-second attempt to avoid being beheaded, she was forced to drop her tama and use the claws on her other hand to block the sword strike. Her claws wouldn't remain sharper and stronger than steel for very long, but they lasted long enough for that single swipe of her hand. The longsword shattered, and with a kick she was able to finally pull her arm out of the dead footsoldier, but by then her claws had softened and her strength had waned to more human levels. Her illusory clothes and armor would remain intact for a while – her ability to construct solid illusions was most skilled with clothing, including armor, so even without her *tama* it would last for hours more than the weapons she had created, before dissolving into dirt and leaf components – but outside of that she was almost defenseless.

She needed her *tama* back, and fast, but she was startled to see it wasn't where she had dropped it. Her tama was missing, and without it she wouldn't be able to defend herself from these people. She looked around her in alarm.

"Not quite the way I had it planned, but it works," said a voice from behind her. Kieras slowly turned to face the man who had identified himself as the kitsune expert. She noticed the nasty ear-to-ear grin on his face as he showed her *tama* in his hand. "I've always wanted a kitsune of my very own to study. With this, I think I might be able to manage it... but why ever did you keep this thing in your hand? It's hardly safe, there!"

Deciding to play along and buy herself some time to think, she said, "Well, I'd keep it in my mouth, but I'd *really* hate to accidentally swallow it."

"If you say so," the officer said doubtfully. "We're not supposed to take prisoners on this little expedition, but as long as I've still got this little gem I might be willing to make an exception in your case. I am so fascinated by kitsune... especially when they are as pleasing on the eyes as you."

Kieras felt somewhat nauseous at the implication. This Knodelian officer may have genuinely been interested in kitsune, but the looks he was giving her showed he had a lot more on his mind than just studying her.

Her resolve to avoid capture solidified, and whether she lacked her powers or not she was still a kitsune. That meant she was supposed to be a master of deception, so she needed to let him believe she might agree to surrender until she either was ready to strike or would otherwise be captured.

And she could strike. Her father had drilled her on how to fight even when she was disarmed and powerless, and she wasn't completely defenseless. In addition to her illusory armor, she remembered that she was wearing a small, steel knife Mathis had given her as a utensil prior to the battle. At the time, she had thought it a pointless gesture on his part – after all, she could have made her own, if she felt she needed something – but now it was all that she had.

But she would likely only get one chance to attack with it, and she needed to use that chance to get back her *tama*. Which meant at least pretending to entertain the idea of surrender.

"What are your terms?" she asked cautiously, trying to keep her eye on everyone at once. They were re-forming into a unit – the captain in the middle, with Verot, two other officers, and the last two surviving footsoldiers at his side. It was frustrating when trying to assess her chances, because six to one odds would be reasonable for her to handle if she had her *tama* with her.

"My terms?" the officer said, laughing. "Vixen, you are hardly in a position to talk terms."

"Of course I am. There is nothing stopping me from leaving, and considering how heavy your armor is I doubt you could catch me if I ran."

"And leave behind your *tama?*" the officer replied incredulously. "I think not."

"I'm quite content to live without it if certain conditions aren't met," Kieras lied. "But I'd much rather have it, which is the only reason I'm even considering surrender." She paused, trying to think of a question to delay the man with. She smiled slightly when she thought of it. "Let's start with your name. Who am I negotiating with?"

The officer shrugged. "You're probably bluffing, but this might be amusing. My name is Roeder. Since your people seem to have known about our attack well in advance, it seems likely you know much more about us than we thought; my name should mean something to you."

"Never heard of you," Kieras said flippantly. It was true – she had never been to many of the tactical strategy meetings, and none in which the names of their enemy's generals had ever come up – but she wanted him to think she was just being insulting. It would work to her advantage if she could anger him enough to fight rashly, but she couldn't afford to make him so angry he struck her down before she was ready to launch her attack. "My name, however, is Kieras."

Roeder gave a low whistle. "Well, well. You may not have heard of me, vixen – though I doubt that very much – but I certainly have heard of you. A certain Kassian prince would probably pay a very large ransom for the return of his kitsune-bred fiancé."

Kieras flushed, but kept the bulk of her frustration at the slip-up internal so that she could turn it to her advantage. "I guess that makes it all the more important that you catch me, and that I not run away, correct? That just gives me even more to bargain with."

"Really?" Roeder smirked. "Seems to me it helps my cause more, since it's pretty clear you don't want me to spread the word that you're here. If I cannot catch you, I'll simply let the Kassians know where you are, and *they* will, instead. I think you'd rather I catch you, though. Certain elements inside of the Kassian government would not be pleased at your return, and I can at least provide you with *some* protection against them when you are sent home."

As they were talking, Kieras cautiously moved towards them while they were also subtly moving toward her. She was trying to position herself so that, when she attacked, she would have the fewest number of people to engage at one time as possible; they had been trying to position themselves so that they could outflank her and cut off her route to escape. However, she had made several mistakes, and Kieras got more and more angry at herself for her slip-up. Still, she was in the best position she could possibly get into without allowing them their goal. It was far from ideal, but it was the best she could do.

"I'd rather not go back at all, thank you very much." Narrowing her eyes, she saw that there would be had just one chance, and she couldn't afford to make any more mistakes. "So it looks like I'll need my tama back."

That statement was as close as she came to a battlecry before launching herself at Roeder. She probably couldn't kill him – not while he was wearing that armor and she was wielding nothing more than a secondhand knife – but if she struck the appropriate joint in his armor she could probably force him to release her *tama*. If she could get that back, she would regain the advantage instantly.

With her kitsune abilities diminished due to her missing *tama*, her speed and reflexes weren't as fast as she was used to, but they were sufficient. With great precision, her knife stuck into the seam where Roeder's shoulder plate, breastplate, and the armor of his upper arm. It was a perfectly placed strike.

Unfortunately, while it hit the right target, Kieras had miscalculated the amount of strength she would need to drive the knife through the chain mail links and the padding worn beneath his armor plate.

Her own *tama* was used to crack her on the head, sending her tumbling to the ground. She started to try and get up – she should be able to run away at least – but found herself unable to do so. She was conscious, but she must have been more seriously injured than she realized. Her ears rang – she couldn't hear the sounds of the battle or what the people around her were saying, it was so loud – and her eyes couldn't focus on anything. Every move sent waves of nausea coursing through her, and she was incredibly dizzy. She also found herself bleeding from her head. She could heal it all in mere moments if she had her *tama*, but it was starting to look like she wouldn't be getting that back.

The most she could do was roll over and stare up at the man who had struck her. He was saying something, and the ringing in her ears was just dwindling enough for her to be able to hear him.

"...don't really want to do any favors for the Kassians, anyway. I still think it's a shame, but clearly you are too much of a danger." Roeder paused, though Kieras couldn't really see why. "I'll keep this *tama* as a trophy. Captain Verot, Captain Foligno – with me. Lieutenant Quinlan... I do not wish to see the destruction of this creature, but destroyed she must be. Give me a few minutes to get far enough away that I will not hear her screams, then kill her and rejoin me with your men."

"Yes, sir," one of the officers replied. "It's a shame we don't have time for more... interesting diversions with her, however."

Roeder looked disgusted. "Just get it done. I'd better see you soon!"

He left Kieras' range of vision, and Quinlan's smirking face took its place, though it was falling out of focus. "Don't worry, chief – I'll catch up to you."

Kieras must have blacked out briefly, because he had drawn his sword without her noticing it, and was standing right over her while his two footsoldiers held her in place. "W-wait," she said weakly, though she what she would say if he did.

"Sorry, girly – I wish I had the time." Quinlan drew his arm back, clearly intent on beheading her in dramatic fashion instead of just stabbing her cleanly through the heart. "We could have had so much fun...."

Kieras swallowed, closed her eyes, and surrendered to the darkness.

Well, this has been both frustrating and useless, Mathis thought. He'd visited eight sites where he had targeted enemies, finding several dozen arrows for his special bow, but not a single one was still usable, though nine arrowheads and seventeen shafts were intact. Once he returned to the tower, he could assemble some from the parts he'd collected. He hadn't found nearly enough to justify his trip out, yet. To make matters worse, he was down to his last three longbow arrows, most of his supply having been needed to defend himself as he scoured the battlefield.

He was also demonstrably reminded of just why the people of Ekholm had never made a serious attempt to settle this side of the river. Marshes were not the best place to go for a stroll even if there wasn't a major battle going on at the time, and he was fairly certain he would have to burn his boots and trousers when this was all over thanks to the caked-on stinking mud.

At least there were a few mounds of relatively solid ground, resting like small islands even amidst the worst sections of the marshland. Most of the actual fighting appeared to be taking place on such islands, which made it easy to avoid the larger conflicts. Unfortunately, if he really wanted to retrieve enough arrows to make this trip worth it (which, it seemed, would require retrieving his wulver counterparts' greatbow arrows in addition to what was left of his own), he would have to scavenge from the remains of those battles-within-the-battle.

Mathis knew of four such islands near him, and so glanced around to see if any were unoccupied. On the first two he checked, small bands of wulvers were easily manhandling more than triple their number of Knodelian soldiers – a good sign for their success – but not a situation he wanted to walk into while hunting for arrows. A group of Knodelians was also on the third, and he almost passed it by as well before something caught his attention.

Is that Kieras? he asked himself, barely remembering his need to keep quiet and hidden. It certainly looked like the kitsune vixen was standing there, with no allies nearby, surrounded by what looked to be half a dozen Knodelians. They weren't fighting, but talking... and, unless Mathis was mistaken (which he seriously doubted), one of the Knodelians was holding her tama.

"This can't end well," he muttered to himself, forgetting his need to keep quiet. He watched Kieras and the soldiers maneuvering around each other for a moment, and after a second realized her plan... and why it wouldn't work. "Damn!"

Mathis had been able to loan Kieras his old worn-out hunting knife, earlier, because he had a good knife, now, given to him by his brother. He mostly just used it to shave, now, but it had been made for military work. That knife and a longbow with three arrows to accompany it were all he had to work with. He didn't care about that – Kieras needed help, and he would give it to her.

It was slow moving through the marsh, but he set himself a determined pace. That pace quickened when he saw Kieras go down from a blow on the head, and grew faster still as the Knodelians broke into two groups, one of which busily preparing to execute the dazed girl. His eyes focused sharply on the man preparing his sword for the final blow, and thousands of thoughts filled his head too quickly to make sense of them.

Mathis should not have been able to reach her in time – he'd known that from the moment he saw her go down – but he still ran to protect her, putting his whole force of will into the effort. Mathis could not recall crossing the distance, but somehow found himself arriving the instant that the Knodelian officer was pulling back his arm to add flourish to the beheading blow. With no plan in his head or thought about what he might be doing, Mathis reached out and grabbed the sword arm of the executioner.

There was a common misconception that archers were weaker than your average trained swordsman. The idea was that soldiers had lots of heavy armor and weaponry they had to wear whenever training or on duty, and so had to build up a lot of bulk and muscles, while archers sacrificed that strength for light armor, speed, and dexterity.

That archers used lighter armor (or even no armor, as in Mathis' case) was correct, and the idea that light armor gave them more speed and dexterity was also true. But archers – at least, dedicated archers like Mathis – would also spend hours every day practicing their trade, just like swordsmen would spend hours training with their swords. The average sword weighed just four to six pounds, and even heavy plate armor wasn't excessively heavy – not if the soldier wanted to be able to move about on the battlefield on his own two feet.

Every time an archer shot an arrow, however, he had to pull the equivalent of sixty, eighty, even a hundred pounds of weight just to pull back the bowstring, with the same amount of strength pushing the bow forward to keep it in place. Mathis' special bow required almost one hundred sixty pounds to pull back, and he would have to draw it thousands of times in a row to complete a three hour practice. He had far, far more pulling strength than the average swordsman.

That difference allowed Mathis to pull the officer back with one arm while thrusting forward with the other, driving the blade of his dagger right through the officer's plate armor, chainmail, and ribs straight into his heart.

"Lieutenant Quinlan!" one of the foot soldiers exclaimed, releasing Kieras to draw his weapon. Mathis let the man fall, pulling out his longbow and sending arrows between the eyes of both footsoldiers before they could even begin to advance.

He knelt down by Kieras, pulling her head into his lap to inspect it. "Are you okay?" he asked worriedly, pulling out a spare shirt and starting to tear it into bandages.

"D-don't bother with that," Kieras said weakly. "If you can g-get my *tama* back, I'll be f-fine. If not...."

Mathis frowned, and then looked over to see the other batch of officers now well away from them. He gently eased Kieras off his lap. Only one of his expended arrows could be recovered from the two dead footsoldiers – well, he might be able to recover both, but not if he wanted to catch up with that group. Since there were three Knodelian officers in the group with Kieras' *tama*, and he had just two arrows, he was at something of a disadvantage... but the late Quinlan's sword was right there, sticking slightly in the soft ground and looking quite ready for battle, provided it had a hand to wield it. "I'll get it back for you, then."

He grabbed the sword and started running, not waiting for a reply. He felt he had almost no chance against three skilled swordsmen, as the officers he was chasing were certain to be, but he didn't have a choice. If he didn't recover that tama, Kieras would die.

Fortunately, they weren't moving very fast. All three of the Knodelians were officers in heavy plate armor – more suited for a cavalry charge along the plains than storming across a marsh on foot.

"Halt!" Mathis cried as he got near. Mathis knew he was the only bait that could be provided to keep them close.

As the three soldiers stopped to look at their challenger, their leader – who Mathis' keen eyes revealed to be the holder of Kieras' *tama* – turned, giving an exasperated sigh. "Oh, what now?"

Mathis' bow was out and an arrow was on its string before another word was spoken. "Release the girl's *tama*, and I'll let you leave peacefully."

"And if not?"

the Knodelian replied dryly. "Your longbow wouldn't pierce my armor if you were standing right next to me. And you only seem to have a single arrow. Are you planning to skewer all three of us with a single shot?"

"I've more arrows than just one," Mathis bluffed, though in truth two arrows was, indeed, more than one. "And you'd be surprised what kind of damage I'm capable of, even with a simple longbow."

"It isn't worth my time to argue," the captain replied dismissively. "Verot, Dufva – kill him!"

"Yes, Captain Roeder!" they replied.

In a sense, Mathis' plan had succeeded – the Knodelians had stopped running. However, he also had three veteran soldiers he had to fight off on his own. Mathis was quick to send his first arrow into the one closest to him – the man that the Knodelian captain had named Dufva, who fell quickly when the arrow slipped through the opening in his helmet to strike him right between the eyes. Mathis needed another split second to make the tactical decision for his last remaining arrow.

He had one shot. There was a near man, Verot, and a far man, Roeder. The far man was undoubtedly the more experienced soldier, and therefore the bigger threat in single combat, but Verot was close enough to get to Mathis right after the shot, before he even had a chance to draw his sword. Roeder was also a more difficult target, and in fact couldn't be seen behind the nearer Verot. Then again, the captain also held Kieras' *tama*. If Mathis could get that *tama*, he could fall back to Kieras and they could make their escape.

Since when do I care for the easy shot? Mathis mused to himself, drawing the arrow back until his longbow creaked a warning that it was about to break. He still couldn't see a kill shot, but he did have one thing he could try.

The arrow flew straight and true, barely missing the outstretched arm of Verot as he shielded his captain with his body. It flew another ten feet before embedding itself in the only armor joint it could possibly have reached from that angle – a small juncture between the forearm and the wrist, slipping inside and breaking through the thin layer of chainmail until it struck bone.

Hardly a lethal blow, but it did its job. Roeder's hand flinched backwards, sending the tama flying away to land somewhere in the much of the marshlands. Mathis didn't have time to track its descent, however – he was too busy ducking under the vicious swing of Verot's sword.

Mathis slipped behind the towering officer, delivering a powerful kick to the back of Verot's knee and breaking his bow to jam it into the armor joint as he passed. It wouldn't hurt the man much, but it did knock him to his knees, and his plate armor was so unwieldy in the muck that he would probably not be able to return to his feet for a few moments – long enough for Mathis to draw his own plundered sword and properly engage Roeder.

Mathis found himself momentarily surprised to face a man wielding not a sword, but a dagger. His arrow had disabled the man's sword hand, and in that armor it was much too awkward to draw a sword with his other hand, but Mathis hadn't even considered that possibility when he'd taken his shot.

Against an injured man, Mathis should have had the advantage. Unfortunately, as he took a tentative swing with his sword, he found himself still outmatched by a veteran warrior. With a flick of his wrist, the Knodelian officer had disarmed him.

They stared across at each other, dumbfounded for the moment. "You know... I wasn't really expecting that to work," Roeder said. "You killed Lieutenant Quinlan and all his men, accosted me, killed Dufva, shot the tama from my hand, and disabled Lieutenant Verot in just one second... but that was the worst swordsmanship I've ever seen."

Mathis sighed, shrugging, as he adopted an unarmed defensive stance. "Well, there was a reason I went into the militia instead of the regular army."

The captain snorted incredulously and attacked in response, swinging his dagger at Mathis' throat. With surprisingly fluid grace, Mathis grabbed the attacking wrist, ducked under the arm, and spun around, using the captain's arm to throw him to the ground.

"Well, that was more like I was expecting from you," the captain groaned, rolling back to his feet. He had lost his dagger in the fall, and his sword had fallen off his belt, but he was able to stand fairly quickly.

"Captain Roeder!" Verot called. The knee joint in his armor was broken, and he could not rise, but his sword arm was free. He tossed his sword, hilt-first, to the captain's good hand, and started working on his armor joint again.

Roeder seemed to be having trouble using a sword in his off hand, but even his most awkward move was better than what Mathis could have done with the same weapon. Mathis was unarmed and out of tricks. His only option was to run, but he couldn't afford to turn without exposing himself to a slash or a stab. Mathis dodged swing after swing, receiving at least three superficial slash wounds on his forearms despite his best efforts. It wasn't long before he stumbled on an unexpectedly soft patch of marshland and fell backwards.

Roeder stood over him with a frown. "Remarkable," he said... before a ball of white-hot fire obscured him from sight.

Kieras stirred back into consciousness to find her head in Mathis' lap. "...you okay?" he was asking. She saw him pulling out some bandages to treat her.

"D-don't bother with that," she replied, starting off weakly but finding her voice more as she spoke. "If you can g-get my *tama* back, I'll be f-fine. If not...."

He frowned down at her, but took her advice and put away the bandages. Kieras felt him ease out from under her, and watched as he plucked an intact arrow from a dead body and picked up an abandoned sword. *But didn't he say he couldn't use a sword?*

"I'll get it back for you, then," Mathis said, a determined glint in his eye.

Kieras glanced at him, trying to focus. He had just two arrows – including the one he'd just recovered – and the sword. Roeder and his officers were wearing armor that, if her experience meant anything, could probably stop Mathis' arrows. He couldn't manage it himself, and she knew it.

"But..." she started to say, then realized he had already run further away than her weakened voice could carry. He would never succeed on his own, so attempting to rescue her tama was pointless. They needed to find reinforcements first, such as one of the packs of wulvers scattered across the battlefield... but she no longer had a chance to tell him that.

She saw a knife sticking in the back of one of the dead foot-soldiers – she suspected it had belonged to Mathis – and rolled over to retrieve it. The motion caused the world to spin in her eyes, but she endured the dizziness and pulled herself to her feet.

Mathis can't survive this one on his own, she thought. *I must go help him.*

She felt giddy, giggling at the absurdity of it all, but managed to stagger off in the right direction anyway. She wasn't able to travel very fast, but her vision – as blurry as it was – kept track of Mathis the whole way. She saw as he confronted Roeder, Verot, and the other officer. Even she was astonished at Mathis' mastery of the arrow as it struck the small opening in the first officer's helmet. Her attention on the fight was lost, however, as she saw his second arrow hit Roeder, sending her *tama* flying off into the marsh.

Kieras immediately changed course and picked up speed. Mathis had once been able to hide her *tama* without her even noticing it was missing, which to a kitsune was a disgraceful thing to happen, but she took the incident as a lesson. Kitsune were tied to their *tama*, so she should be able to sense it independently without relying on her normal senses. It was a particular discipline she had never bothered trying to master while she lived with her father, but she remembered his lessons nonetheless. She had spent much of the winter months learning how to find it, periodically entrusting Ziani and Mathis with her *tama* in order to help her train.

And now, even with her vision blurred with pain, blood pounding in her ears so loud it was deafening, and her sense of smell masked by the marsh's odor, she knew right where to go. Moving quickly made her feel like vomiting, but that didn't matter – once she had her *tama* she would be healed. Disregarding her nausea, her blindness, and her deafness, she started running as fast as her weakened legs could carry her. When she knew she was in the right spot, she stopped, plunged her hand blindly into the marshy waters, and pulled up her *tama*.

Kitsune healing was not instantaneous, but it was remarkably fast. Enhanced healing was, in fact, the very reason Inari had created the kitsune in the first place, according to the legend, and like many kitsune traits it had only strengthened across the generations. Sometimes it would require spending time in one form or the other to recover, but for relatively minor injuries nothing more than concentrating on their *tama* could fix the worst of it. In mere seconds, her vision cleared and her ears no longer pounded... but she did lose the contents of her stomach thanks to that last mad dash.

She was not fully healed – she could still feel the broken bone in her skull mending itself – but what she saw struck her cold.

Mathis truly was worthless with a sword. He had dropped his somewhere on the battlefield, and now Captain Roeder was in position to execute him much as Quinlan had been standing over her to execute her.

Her voice was gone for the moment, thanks to her incomplete healing and the rawness in her throat after vomiting, but she didn't need it. Projecting your voice when using kitsune magic was only a focus technique – all she really had to do, though, was think the word.

Foxfire....

Kieras was astonished at how intense her fireball became. It blazed white-hot, though green flames that must have been caused by the marsh gas flickered along the edges, and it burned more intensely than any foxfire blast she'd ever attempted.

At first, she was afraid she had accidentally hit Mathis along with her target, but after it had passed leaving Roeder's body indistinguishable from the surrounding ash, she saw him slowly climb to his feet.

Mathis took a few tentative steps in her direction, wiping the muck off his hands. He was bleeding from several cuts along his arms, and appeared to have been dazed by her foxfire attack, but otherwise appeared unharmed. "You feeling better?" he asked, grinning.

"I'll be fine," Kieras said, finding her voice again. She looked around. It appeared as if the soldier named Verot had fled, though not before removing his damaged grieves and leaving them behind. She knew his knowledge of her name could cause problems down the road, but they would have to worry about him later. "You won't be, though, unless you let me bandage those cuts up."

Mathis glanced down at his arms, and seemed a bit surprised at what he saw. "Not as bad as I feared, actually," he said, reaching into his pocket to once again find his bandages. "Here. Thanks for helping."

"I should be the one thanking you," Kieras muttered, wrapping the rags around his cuts. "That was crazy, going after the three of them alone like that."

"What option was there?" Mathis asked. "If we'd gone for help, it would have been too late."

Kieras closed her eyes. He was probably right. She would be dead right now if he hadn't risked his life to save her. That was something she would have to think about, too, when she had the time to think about things like Verot's escape and the implications of Mathis' bravery. In the middle of a battlefield probably wasn't the right time, however.

"We had better make our way back to the tower to rest and recover." She glanced in the tower's direction. "And it looks like there are a few enemies between us and there."

"My bow's broken and I'm out of arrows," Mathis said. "And you might have healed some, but I doubt you've recovered enough for that kind of fight alone. We might want to find some of the wulvers to help us make our way back."

Kieras grinned. "Actually, I've got a better idea." She picked up some leaves from the ground and concentrated hard, designing in her mind, until they changed into a fully formed illusory bow and set of arrows. "You can use these. I've set them up so they can last for a few hours, as long as you stay close to me, but don't get too far away – they're feeding on my magic, and won't even last a minute without me close by. The arrows will only be effective for about fifty yards before they dissolve, I'm afraid, but they should work."

"There are only a dozen of them," Mathis said, examining the arrows. "They seem to be pretty well made, and should fly true, but they're hardly enough to clear the way. Especially since I can't risk aiming for something which might be too far away."

"I'll make more if we need them, but I doubt we will. Why don't you try hitting someone in that group over there?"

Mathis looked in the direction she pointed doubtfully. There was a cluster of several Knodelians, all footsoldiers, about thirty yards to their right. It would probably be better to avoid them, but an impatient look from Kieras convinced him to take the shot anyway. He let the arrow go, and it started sailing towards the group of Knodelians. "There are a lot of people in that group. I'll use up this dozen arrows before we've finished clearing—" He was interrupted when the arrow struck its target and exploded into a brilliant fireball, not quite as intense as the one which had saved him from Roeder but much larger. It took out not just the man he hit but also several people around the target. Mathis turned to Kieras and stared, mouth agape.

Kieras laughed. She had avoided warning him so she could see precisely that hilarious look of disbelief on his face, but now he needed an explanation. "Well, most of our illusions are created with the same power that we use for our foxfire. I just set it up so that your arrows would turn into foxfire blasts when they strike. What do you think?"

Mathis didn't answer in words, but instead started firing off his arrows as quickly as possible. It wasn't long before their path was cleared between them and the tower, and if Kieras didn't miss her guess it looked as if the Knodelians were on the run as well.

The Knodelians had not been completely defeated by Kieras' special arrows. Mathis didn't want her to strain herself trying to make more, however – she was healing nicely, but he suspected all the kitsune magic she was using would start slowing that healing in time. He also could use some medical attention... and maybe a drink to kill the pain from his wounds. They were now standing at the base of the tower, and as much as it might aid their allies in battle Mathis knew they weren't in any shape to attempt another sortie. It was time to go inside and rely on the wulvers to finish driving off the assault.

Upon reaching the tower – and the chorus of congratulatory howls from their wulver allies – Kieras pulled Mathis aside. She had the most serious expression on her face that he'd ever seen on her.

"Mathis," she said softly. Most of the wulvers had to return to duty after the initial celebration, though promises of more festivities to come once there was a break in the battle were heavily implied. "I need to thank you more fully than words can convey. You risked your life to save mine, and succeeded where I doubt most men would have been able."

Mathis flushed. He didn't want her to feel indebted to him, though he enjoyed the praise. His embarrassing bit of swordplay, though, made him feel he didn't deserve it. "Well, you saved my life, too, if you'll recall. I think that makes us even."

Kieras shook her head vehemently. Her dwindling Kassian accent returned and redoubled as her words became more formal. "No, it doesn't. You've done nothing but help me since I arrived in Ekholm, and I have never thanked you properly for any of it. This latest act merely grants me the realization that I can show you that gratitude." She took a deep breath. "Mathis of Ekholm, you risked your life to save mine. You almost lost it because you lack skill enough with the sword, but that does not negate what you did for me. So, for the next year, I swear fealty to you as your guardian and protector, with all of my ability as a kitsune. I shall become the sword you are otherwise unable to wield."

As wide as his eyes got while she was taking her oath, Mathis was surprised they didn't fall out of his head. He knew her father had asked her to make such a vow of service, but never once did he believe he would be the one she chose for it. He was not a paragon, like his brother, who deserved such an honor. He was just a lowly hunter who happened to have a locally important family.

"But... why me? I wasn't asking for this! I was just looking out for a friend. I—"

"And that is why you are worthy," Kieras said, grinning. "Too late for you to argue about it. The oath's made. You now have a kitsune guardian in your service for the next year."

"But what about your search for your mother? Your need to find a vaki to resurrect King Kazdri? You have quite a lot of things you still need to do that being tied to me will hinder."

Kieras sobered. "Yes, I do." She looked up at him fiercely. "But I cannot abandon Ekholm in its time of need, either. You are at war, now, and I will spend the next year serving as your guardian to help you win it."

X. The Arbitors of Norre

"What do you *mean*, 'the war is over'?" Kieras exclaimed. "It just began a week ago. Wars don't end in a week! Especially not wars you spend months and months preparing for!"

"Well, that's sort of why we spent 'months and months' preparing for it." Torkki's lips twitched in amusement. "To end it quickly."

Mathis wasn't quite sure what to make of the reaction his new "kitsune guardian" was having to what was, to most people, very good news, but tried to placate her anyway. "I have to admit, it ended faster than I thought it would, myself." Then he glared at his brother. "Though I might have suspected it could end this quickly if I had known there was a large contingent of the Norrish Army preparing to execute a counterstrike the moment the Knodelian attack commenced."

Torkki shrugged. "Operational security, Mathis. I didn't even know it was going to happen like that. Even if I'd known, I wouldn't necessarily have expected it to work – plans never work like they're supposed to, they just went wrong in our favor, for once."

When the news came to Ekholm that Norre's armies had successfully defeated of the bulk of the Knodelian forces, Savard, in his role as the new Archon, had called the meeting of his military advisors. This included Mathis, Torkki, Kieras, Hesketh, Mrazek, and Jobinh. There had been some resentment that even Savard and Torkki had not been kept in the loop regarding the counter-operation against Knodel, but most of them understood the importance of the secrecy. Kieras seemed to be the only one upset about their victory, however.

"Young lady," Savard said. He tried giving her a calming smile, but Mathis wasn't sure that would work. "Why are you so angry about this?"

Kieras sputtered for a moment, but then took a deep breath and settled down. "I'm not angry," she said through gritted teeth. Then she glanced over at Mathis. "I just made a certain promise to someone assuming the war would last a lot longer than it did, and now I'm stuck with the consequences. Which is... annoying. But I'm not angry."

Mathis had yet to tell his family members about having gained her allegiance as a "kitsune guardian," but Torkki seemed to know all about it. At least, Mathis thought so – his brother was grinning like he did, anyway.

"And just why does this annoy you so much?" Torkki asked, the smirk still on his face. "Does the war being over make it harder to keep your promise?"

Kieras glanced over at Mathis and sighed. "No, it actually makes it easier. But it would be a better tale to say that I was sidetracked from my quest by an oath to protect a man at war than it is to say I was sidetracked by an oath to protect an ordinary hunter from... from horned rabbits and fire-breathing chickens."

Mathis wondered if he should be offended by the implication that he needed protection from the very animals he hunted, but decided instead that he was more worried about whether she would take her frustration out on him in the form of making the still undelivered prank demanded by her oath in Dahlberg that much more vicious. Besides, he would also be annoyed (but relieved) if he had vowed to protect someone from all dangers, and those dangers turned out to be nothing more severe than the odd al-mi'raj or basan attack.

Savard frowned. "What is this all about?"

"Kieras made an oath to become Mathis' guardian kitsune," Torkki said, laughter on the verge of breaking out in his voice.

"How did you know about that?" Mathis asked. "I hadn't told anyone, yet."

"Ziani told me," Torkki replied, a wistful gleam in his eye. "We've been, uh, chatting with each other quite a bit since the Knodelians lifted their siege."

Kieras started to say something, drawing the attention of most in the room, but hesitated. "Oh...."

Savard grinned at her. "Is there something else we should know?"

"I suppose I'll hold my tongue on Torkki and Ziani's secrets, even if it seems Torkki has no qualms about revealing things Ziani has been told or has told others in confidence." She glared at Torkki, who recoiled slightly. "But I suppose you all would have learned of my oath, anyway, and I have no desire to hurt one of my closest friends for something that isn't her fault. I do have another concern, however...."

"Go on," Savard prompted. Mathis and Torkki both looked on interestedly.

"As you know, I was briefly captured during the battle with the Knodelians... before Mathis rescued me." Kieras smiled at him hesitantly in thanks. She probably hoped to convey that she wasn't blaming him for her predicament.

Mathis didn't believe it for a second. She undoubtedly was planning many ways to make whatever practical joke she was planning that much more embarrassing for him.

Jobinh snorted. "Rather foolish of the both of you to put yourselves into harm's way like that, if you ask me."

Torkki frowned at his lieutenant. "And yet it was their effort, more than any other, which finally drove the Knodelians from the bridge, saving all our lives and winning the day for us. Perhaps not as foolish as you believe, Jobinh."

Kieras continued as if she hadn't heard them. "During that time, one of their officers identified me, and even suggested that I was worth ransom money to the Kassian Empire."

Mathis frowned. "I didn't know about that."

"No, that was before you got there. Most of the people who were with him when he made that determination were killed, but one got away – a Lieutenant Verot, if I recall correctly. As long as the Norre Hegemony and the Knodelians were at war, this wasn't a serious problem. Verot would have been too busy to contact Kassia, and they would want to stay out of the conflict even if they heard I was here. If the war had ended after my service to Mathis, like I expected, I would have been able to move on and Kassia would learn nothing until far too late to do anything about it. But since the war is over, if Verot has truly escaped...."

"He could inform Kassia, who would send an expedition to Ekholm that we couldn't put off simply by claiming ignorance," Savard finished for her. "And you are now stuck in Ekholm because of your oath to Mathis. Interesting...."

"Interesting?" Jobinh exclaimed. "Is that all you have to say? This could lead to war between Kassia and Ekholm, and I'm not sure Norre would do anything about it. This would go beyond our tributary accord, as your refusal to hand over Kieras – a citizen of the Kassian Empire – would be an act of war."

"This is true," Savard said. "The solution is pretty simple, however."

"What, to exile both Mathis and the kitsune?" Jobinh asked dryly.

That suggestion wasn't fondly received by the rest of the gathering.

"They turned the tide of that battle more or less singlehandedly," Hesketh said. "And you want to exile them for it?"

"All of Ekholm, including many of my kind, owe our freedom and possibly our lives to their actions," Mrazek growled. "Had it not been for their combined efforts, we might still be under siege. Or worse."

"And I would like to point out one of the two people you are suggesting we send into exile, Jobinh, is the brother of your Captain," Torkki said.

"Settle down, people," Savard said, gesturing for their attention. "While the terminology Jobinh used was... unfortunate, he is effectively correct. For many reasons – not just this particular threat – it would be advisable for my nephew and his guardian kitsune to leave town for a while."

"Leave town?" Mathis' eyes widened. "Where would we go? We've done nothing wrong, here – at least I haven't!"

Kieras glanced at him sadly, and Mathis quickly shut his mouth before he said anything more accusatory. He came dangerously close to blaming her for their potential exile, which wasn't what he wanted to do at all.

"No, you haven't," Savard agreed. "But Ekholm has done something very right, and because of that we have a job which I now believe the pair of you would be quite suited for. The added benefit of getting you out of town long enough for this to blow over is simply a bonus to a mission I was already preparing for you. This will just force us to speed things up a bit."

Mathis frowned. "What do you want me to do, then?"

Savard took a deep breath. "Well, I'm not sure what our resident Norrish contingent will think of this, but this battle and our recent change in government has convinced me that Ekholm has grown too large to rely entirely on outside powers for defense. We needed not just the force of arms and experience that Norre brought us, but also a platoon of wulvers and several war machines from Dahlberg, supplies from half the region, and our own workers and militia – not to mention a rather well trained young kitsune – to defend this city. Along the way, we provided protection for the citizens of Arbeloa and a dozen other settlements that were uprooted by the Knodelian threat. We, as a state – for if we've become responsible for the protection of our neighboring towns, we are no longer just the forgotten outpost of a dead country – must be better equipped for future wars. The next time an enemy comes, we probably won't have almost a year's warning to prepare ourselves. So, I wish to send a diplomatic mission to Norre, for the purposes of ending our tributary status and requesting admittance as a full member of the Norre Hegemony."

Reaction was mixed around the room, with Jobinh and Torkki both looking rather uncomfortable at the suggestion. Kieras was, predictably, the least affected, still being something of an outsider. Mathis detected a slight change in her demeanor, though, and wondered just what was said that caught her interest. Asking would do no good – she was a kitsune, after all – but he'd keep an eye on her and see if he could figure it out.

"I'm not sure how well that would go over in Norre, uncle," Torkki said hesitantly. "I don't think they'll be happy about losing our tribute. Especially not after they just put out all of this funding for our defense."

Savard nodded. "It isn't my intention for Norre to suffer from this, and we are not ready to cut our tributary ties anyway. We merely hope to gradually reduce our tribute as we assume more control over our own defenses, allowing Norre to offset the loss through trade and taxes. The truth is that even with Norre's assistance, we were heavily undermanned in this recent battle. We need a standing army of perhaps a thousand men to truly secure this place against a more determined enemy. Something that will take years to train, if not generations."

"And just what would Norre get from admitting Ekholm to the Hegemony?" Jobinh asked haughtily. "We Norrish people have just shown you loyalty, yet it sounds you intend to reward us with treason."

"Hold your tongue, Jobinh, unless you want to be ejected from this council!" Torkki warned. He looked somewhat uncomfortable with what was being discussed, himself, but that didn't stop him from admonishing his lieutenant when he'd crossed the line.

"Treason?" Savard repeated, rolling the word over his tongue like a bitter fruit. "Even at its worst interpretation, nothing I have suggested amounts to treason. But you are right in one sense – if we want to become a full member of the Hegemony, we should return that loyalty in kind." He smiled and turned to his wulver representative. "Which is where you and your people come in, Mrazek. As well as Mathis, and possibly even our kitsune friend, here. All of you will be quite useful."

"Us?" Mrazek growled. "We did not come to this town to be *used*. We came here to provide a home to our people. What, exactly, are you planning?"

"Many great armies have a small unit of specialists, called into play when no regularly structured force can handle the job. The Erixonite Immortals, for example, or the Ninja of the Vincour Republic, or the surviving Janissary companies in the Skorran lands. Norre has no such force."

"Well, there are the Iron-Body Men of Tornvall," Torkki said. "And my own company of the Norre Elite falls into that role all too often."

Savard nodded. "Powerful units, to be sure. As with your own Elite Brigades, however, the Iron-Body Men are more of an infantry force who are sometimes tasked with irregular duties. While we in Ekholm might not have enough regular soldiers to even man our own walls, we do seem to possess a fair number of 'irregulars' who would fit the mold far better. Mathis has a remarkable talent for archery – though he needs to find a close-range weapon which suits him. If he were to be a part of this… irregular unit, that would hardly need to be a traditional weapon. The wulvers have phenomenal strength, speed, and abilities, and nowhere else in the world do they fight alongside men – wulver infantry would be just as 'irregular' in the Norrish armies as Mathis' archery. Kieras – if she would be willing to enlist for at least as long as she remains tethered to Mathis – has many great talents as a kitsune that could be quite useful, as the recent battle has shown."

Torkki hesitated. "All true… but even so, it's an awfully small unit you're talking about. I'm not sure Norre would find that adequate compensation."

"I expect it to grow as time goes on." Savard spoke so casually that Mathis knew his uncle was hiding something, but he let it pass unchallenged. "Also, once our regular forces grow large enough, we should be able to assist in the defense of local towns like Arsene and Sorkham, and not just provide shelter to our smaller neighbors. Because of our reliance on Norre for defense, soldiers had to be pulled from the other side of the Hegemony in order to protect towns and cities across this region. The Ekholm Irregulars would not be the only thing they would gain from accepting us as full members."

"How are you going to organize this unit?" Mrazek asked. "I'm not sure I like the idea of using my people to form the backbone of your military."

"I'm not intending to use *all* of your people like this," Savard explained. "Just the career soldiers, not the others who fought with us during the battle as militia members. That's... what, about two dozen wulvers?"

Mrazek's ears twitched before he answered. "Roughly, yes."

Savard nodded. "Good. Mathis will be their captain, and I'll leave it up to him for—"

"What?" Mrazek barked in protest. Mathis sort of felt like doing the same, but seeing Savard's expression decided to let the conversation play out, first. "These are my people! I—"

"Your job is to lead your people in *Ekholm*," Savard replied calmly. He was clearly not intimidated by the angry wulver, but rather had what seemed to be an amused twinkle in his eye. "My intent is to create a military force with quick strike capabilities which would largely operate outside of Ekholm. When that unit has to leave Ekholm, who would lead all of your people here? You cannot be in two places at once."

"Well... no, I suppose I can't," Mrazek said.

"Besides," Hesketh said. "I'm going to need your help, friend Mrazek. I'm just an old militia commander. I can train people well enough to act as part of a rarely-used militia intended to fight not much more than the odd collection of highwaymen. If I'm expected to turn a bunch of farmers, fishermen, and the like from part-time militiamen into a full-time standing army, I would appreciate the help of someone of your experience."

Mrazek's ears flicked again before turning to Mathis. "Very well then. It seems as if several of my people will be in your care. They will be your responsibility. I expect you to keep them as safe as reasonably possible."

Mathis smiled nervously. He had always wanted to be a soldier growing up, just like his brother, but as he matured he came to believe he didn't have the talent for it. He still didn't think he had the talent for it, but now it seemed he would have the responsibilities of being not just a soldier, but an officer. It was a bit much to take in. "I'll do my best, of course."

Torkki coughed. "Uncle Savard... I know it's probably not my place to say anything, here, but... Mathis isn't ready for this. He out-guessed me as to the Knodelian strategy, which shows me that he *could* be, but he doesn't have the experience. Are you sure this is wise?"

"He'll have time to learn on the job." Savard eyed Mathis shrewdly. "And... Mathis, you seem to have developed a talent for being where you need to be. The tower, for example. Or your rescue of Kieras. I expect you to make your name by continuing that."

Mathis returned the look, feeling his uncle was leaving something unsaid. "Of course, uncle. But—"

Savard didn't give him a chance to put any of the questions running in his head into words, turning again to Torkki. "You will accompany him, teaching him how to lead troops, how to coordinate strategy with other captains, and the other things that an officer even in an irregular unit needs to know. Mathis, Kieras, and the Ekholm Irregulars will be heading to the city of Norre, carrying with them my letter of intent."

"I can't leave!" Torkki cried. "You'll need my men here. The Knodelians were defeated, but there are still a few survivors who have gone rogue and formed troops of bandits. Wall or not, they could cause Ekholm great damage if it were left undefended."

Mathis found it extremely curious that his brother was so adamant about not leaving, but their uncle didn't seem to notice.

"Hesketh and Mrazek will take command of the Norrish forces," Savard said. "You can take a few of your fellow officers – and maybe a camp follower or two – to help. You'll need at least one civilian to help you cook your meals. I know Mathis can't cook, and I don't even want to think about what the wulvers do for camp food." Mrazek almost protested at that, but decided to hold his tongue.

The suggestion seemed to calm Torkki, however. "Very well. But I don't want to stay away from my men for too long."

Savard shrugged. "I'll leave that up to you. You can come right back the second Mathis' feet cross the city of Norre's threshold, if you wish. Mathis, however, will still have more to do once the diplomatic job is finished."

Mathis froze at that. He was being given command of a small but still effective military unit and being sent off to Norre on yet another diplomatic mission. Not that scary of a prospect – he'd been through enough of those that he was starting to learn how to handle it without too many nerves showing – but that wouldn't be the end of it. It seemed logical that there was still an unsaid part of this mission, and that worried him.

"What do you want me to do?" he asked simply.

"Nothing much," Savard replied. "The Knodelians attacked us because of the Kassian threat. Despite our success, the way things are going I would not be surprised if other powers started duplicating their action, so it seems the best response would be to stabilize Kassia and return a less expansionist king to their throne. Fortunately, we already have a plan to do just that: The Ekholm Irregulars are directed and required to provide whatever support the Lady Kieras requires in completing her quest." He paused. "I'd like both of you to be able to return some day, you know, but that's not going to happen until you solve the Kassian problem."

Kieras scurried about the room she had, until recently, shared with Ziani, trying to identify the things she was being asked to pack for the journey to Norre. She had insisted that she didn't need anything that wasn't already on her person during the conference, but that only led to Mathis insisting on keeping an eye on her to make sure she didn't "forget" anything.

"So," he said, startling her out of her reverie. "Which secret do you want to tell me to distract me from figuring out the other secret: Why you are so interested in heading to Norre, or the secret you and Ziani are sharing about my brother?"

Kieras blinked, turning to look at him. "What?"

Mathis chuckled. "You really think I care that much about what you're packing for our journey? It could be all leaves and rocks, for all I care, although you'll probably want to keep several human changes of clothing for after we arrive in town. Norre is an ancient city, with some buildings dating back to the heyday of magic. I'm told there are some places in it where ancient magical charms are still strong enough to dispel kitsune illusions."

Kieras had not been aware of that, and was suddenly quite thankful that Ziani had ensured that she collect a complete human wardrobe during her stay in Ekholm. She probably should make sure she had some other human equipment, too, just for emergencies.

"I hadn't really thought about it," Kieras said.

"Let's start with why you were so interested in going to Norre."

Kieras paused. "Well... I'm just happy I'll be able to continue the search for my mother and the vaki." She had sworn loyalty and fealty to Mathis as his guardian, and had made additional oaths when formally joining the newly established Ekholm Irregulars, but that didn't mean she was obligated to always be completely honest. Half-truths were still quite acceptable.

Mathis tended to see through them, anyway. "If that were true, you would have been just as interested when it became apparent we were about to be 'exiled,' as Jobinh put it. It was only when Uncle Savard mentioned Norre, specifically, that you became so intrigued. Why?"

Mathis no longer needed a promise to extract her honest answers, if he used her vows correctly, but she still enjoyed playing the game while he let her. She decided to go for a distraction over half-truths or outright lies, this time. "Didn't you say you wanted to know your brother's secret, too?"

Mathis chuckled. "Relax, Kieras – I'm not trying to push you on this. I just want to know what to expect. You know something is going to happen when we get to Norre, and I just want to know what it is so I can prepare for it."

Kieras winced. He was right. If she kept playing the game, she could get them both in trouble. She should tell him something, at least. "When we were in Dahlberg, I got a clue about the location of something which is vital to my quest. As you can probably figure out from that, it's in the city of Norre." She bit her lip, thinking about the haltija of fire's comments. "I don't believe this errand will pose any danger to me or to your mission."

Mathis looked like he wanted to ask her more, but then shrugged. "I guess that's good enough for now – I won't push you any further. Good luck on your packing."

He started to head out the door, but Kieras didn't want him to leave just yet for some reason she couldn't explain. "What, you aren't going to try and challenge me further? You aren't even going to, say, try and get an explanation about Ziani's secret?"

Mathis paused at the door and glanced over at her, a twinkle in his eye. "You mean the one about her 'secret' marriage to my brother? That secret?"

Kieras felt her jaw drop. "How... how did you—"

Mathis laughed. "If you want a marriage to be legal in this city, even a 'secret' marriage, you have to register it with the town clerk, and the clerk writes it down in the town's chronicles. I've gotten into the habit of making sure I check the chronicles every other week since I used to miss out on so many things when I went away on my hunting trips. I've known for a few days, now – ever since we got back from the tower."

Kieras frowned. "Then... why did you ask me about it in the first place?"

Mathis paused indecisively, but then stepped back into the room. "I really hope you don't take offense to this, but... Kieras, for a kitsune, you're absolutely terrible at keeping secrets."

Unprepared for the insult, Kieras flinched. "Wha—"

"I asked you about Ziani's secret," Mathis continued, not letting her finish, "because I knew you had it. I wasn't certain I was right about you having a secret in Norre. I was watching your face to see how you would react. If your reaction to my question about Norre was stronger than the one to my question about Ziani's secret, I would know you were hiding something of even greater importance. It was, so I did."

Kieras found herself both angry and embarrassed at the explanation. "If you can read through my deceptions so easily, why tell me how you know?"

Mathis grinned wryly. "You've vowed to be my guardian kitsune. I trust you in that capacity. I know that even though you're a kitsune, with your vows you won't lie to me when it matters. But you *are* a kitsune, and the ability to lie well is an important survival skill for your people. I'd rather you be equipped to survive and be able to lie to me about the unimportant things, than to be able to see when you're telling me little white lies and have you die because you haven't mastered one of the basic skills of your kind."

In an instant, Kieras' anger vanished. "I... I see. Thank you for trying to help me, Mathis." She paused, and then grinned at him playfully. "I apologize in advance if I use your lessons in deception to make that prank I owe you that much worse."

The journey to Norre itself was relatively uneventful. Jobinh raised some puzzled questions when Ziani attached herself to the expedition as a camp follower to mend and clean the laundry, to help cook, and to warm the bed of a certain Ekholm-born Norrish Captain. He was stunned to learn that Torkki had actually married the girl, and didn't seem happy to hear that, but so far had yet to voice anything against her.

Mathis had needed the help of his friend Teslak, a fellow archer from the tower battle turned new lieutenant of the Ekholm Irregulars, to get the wulvers properly organized into a formal human honor guard. It seemed the formations humans employed were very different from how wulver soldiers "marched." Beyond those early growing pains, however, little of note had happened during the expedition.

Norre was like nowhere Mathis had ever been. It was, at least in terms of size, the largest city he had ever been to, even after his ambassadorial work for Ekholm. There were a large numbers of parks, fountains, reflecting pools, statues, open-air markets, gardens, and other architectural features mixed in with all of the buildings. Many of these were civic buildings, stores, warehouses, workshops, and more, interspersed with the housing for tens of thousands of people. In contrast, while Dahlberg had been a far more heavily populated city, it was also far more densely packed – full of housing and little else, with most commercial activity taking place well outside its walls.

Norre's architecture also stood out. Founded upon the ruins of a long abandoned ancient city, Norre's structures combined the enigmatic elegance of their original design with newly cleaned and repaired surfaces of ancient marble and alabaster. Twelve marble-faced hexagonal towers – the primary reason for reclaiming the city – outlined the borders, providing a strong defense. Constructed more durably than any current method allowed, they had been restored to the best of Norre's ability. White stone walls and gatehouses now connected each tower as well.

The new walls of Ekholm, with their white towers connecting each section of dark stone fortification, had been nicknamed the "Fangs of Ekholm." It had been a bit of a play on the nickname of Norre's walls, "The Teeth of the Knapp." Mathis, seeing the city in person for the first time, recognized how apt the comparison was.

A platoon of five humans (or rather, four humans and one kitsune) and two dozen wulvers drew the stares of many Norrish people. Even in one of the most cosmopolitan cities of the known world, that many wulvers away from their home in one place drew attention, but the only person in the entire troop who seemed uncomfortable with it was their Norrish-born companion, Jobinh. If anything, Mathis, Kieras, Ziani, and the wulvers were far too fascinated by the city itself to pay much attention, while Torkki and his remaining honor guard (who were all from other cities in the Hegemony) seemed used to it.

"Jobinh," Torkki called. He was the last one through the city's gates, but was now rushing up to catch the leaders. "Please familiarize these men and women with the important sites in the city, and then escort them to the diplomatic quarters by evening for dinner. I'll report to command."

"Yes, sir!" Jobinh snapped. His voice was very disciplined, but his face showed he was anything but enthusiastic about the assignment.

Once Torkki had pulled away, Kieras glanced over at Ziani and winked. Mathis caught the signal and was wondering just what they were up to, but then she turned and gave him a wink, too. At that point, he knew that all he could do was stand back and enjoy the scene they were about to make.

"Well, let's start right here," Jobinh began, sounding like he was delivering a practiced spiel. "This is the Guardsman's Green. Unlike smaller townships and cities, which have just one green that serves as a marketplace, meeting place, and a point to muster soldiers for military drills, Norre has many. This one is where the city's guardsmen muster for duty in the mornings and evenings, and where they drill. We have several greens for this purpose in Norre, each in a different location, which has tactical significance for—"

"Excuse me, Lieutenant Jobinh?" Ziani called, a slight trill in her voice. Marriage to Torkki obviously agreed with her, but the humor in her voice seemed uncalled for. Some prank she and Kieras had planned was about to begin, and all Mathis could do was hope it wasn't directed at him. "Who is that?"

Mathis and Jobinh both followed her pointing finger to see a seemingly unremarkable marble statue sitting on a pedestal.

Jobinh hesitated, glancing at the statue himself for a moment as if searching his memory. "I believe that is a statue of Labre, one of Norre's thirty-nine founders. Each of the founders also became the head of one of the clans which makes up most of the city of Norre's citizens today."

"Oooh," Ziani replied, drawing the word out in a sing-song fashion. "What were the names of the other thirty-nine founders?"

Jobinh took a moment before he answered that question. "Well... I'm not sure if I can recite them all from memory, but there was the Labre clan, of course... and I once traced my family back to the Pyatt clan. Let's see, I remember several of their names: Hryciuk, Marson, Dupere, Kryskow, Mohns, Lesuk, Belhumeur... um... Lalonde... look, does it really matter who they all were? Norre hasn't been using a clan system in several centuries, and the names aren't very important any more. Some even called them the founders of futility, because they were all long-gone before Norre really took off. The clans have been all but forgotten for a very long time."

Mathis found that odd. Norre was reputed to emphasize education – even more than Ekholm, which was surprisingly literate for such a minor city – so why would its soldiers not even know the names of its founders?

"How long ago did these thirty-nine clans settle here?" Mathis asked.

"I think it was about seven or eight centuries ago. My memory's a little fuzzy on the subject, and history never was one of my strong suits." Jobinh was looking a little frustrated. "Well, we've walked past the green, now, and here we are in the traders market. We have several open-air markets in town, and each specializes in its own field. This one is where imports arriving from the Orrpars Road get exchanged with local tourist-oriented goods. I—"

"Oh! Can we go shopping?" Kieras exclaimed. Mathis knew right away this was part of whatever joke the girls were planning, since she – unlike Ziani – was hardly ever interested in stores selling anything other than food or wine.

"Not right now," Jobinh replied, his voice cracking wearily. "We have a number of places to get to, and we won't have time to stop at them all if we spend too much time lingering around the markets. Perhaps another day. Moving on—"

"That's pretty. What's that a statue of?" Ziani called, this time pointing to a decorative bronze art piece that looked like a tree emerging from a marble pedestal.

Jobinh frowned, but looked where his captain's lover (and not-so-secret secret wife) was pointing. "I'm not really sure. No one is – it is part of the ruins that Norre was built upon. It does seem to have some magical components to it, since it has been standing there for thousands of years and has never tarnished." He paused, glancing at Kieras. "It has been known to dispel kitsune illusions in the past, however."

Kieras frowned, and then patted down some of her own clothing. "I'd better remember to avoid it until I can put on some human clothes, then," she muttered under her breath. Mathis just barely heard her, chuckling at the thought. He'd cautioned her about things like that in Norre – if she failed to heed his warnings, that was her problem.

"Now, leaving this particular market, we'll take the path which will lead us down to the marina," Jobinh continued. "We'll pass through many sites along the way, as well as several stores I'm sure you will beg us to enter but we won't have time to see."

Mathis let his mind wander as Jobinh continued to lead them through the city, and the girls kept harassing him with inane questions about this statue or that building or whether they could visit the tailor they were passing or the baker or so on. Clearly, the prank they were pulling was merely to annoy Jobinh, so it was safe to turn his attention elsewhere.

He was genuinely impressed with the city – even with the little tidbits of history Jobinh tossed in about this piece of artwork that had been restored from the old city, or that statue to a founder whose name Jobinh sometimes had to go look up himself. There was a definite feeling of being somewhere old and powerful, yet full of life and wonderment. Supposedly, the other major cities of the Hegemony, while not all as impressive as Norre, were roughly equal in size and strength to the old capital. Some may have even been built upon similar ruins.

Ekholm did have a few things going for it that it shared with Norre. There were only two places where an ancient road and the river Knapp met; one of them was Ekholm, and Norre was the other. It was often said that Ekholm had the potential to grow into a substantial city because of this river crossing, with many comparisons to what the bridge across the mouth of the Knapp had done for Norre. Seeing all this, however, Mathis really was starting to wonder just how Norre could possibly see anything of value in their relationship with Ekholm. It really made him wonder why they had bothered accepting Ekholm as a tributary in the first place, since as all the wealth of his home town would be nothing more than a pittance to a city like Norre.

A sudden pinch drew him from his reverie, and he turned to see Kieras glaring at him. Noticing that Ziani was also looking at him expectantly, he came to realize that the girls were expecting him to play along in their little game with Jobinh. He supposed he could manage that.

They had arrived at the marina, so glancing around he saw a great many ships loading and unloading cargo. A particular ship – clearly a military one – caught his eye.

With honest curiosity he couldn't help but ask, "Is that really a turtle ship?"

Jobinh turned around, glancing at the dome-covered warship himself. "Oh, yes. The wulvers aren't the only ones who've developed a weapon capable of spitting liquid fire. Several nations are now employing similar weapons in naval combat. To combat the threat Norre has built six turtle ships. The others are probably in their usual port at Tornvall, but every now and then one will dock around here."

Mathis stared in wonder at the vessel. He'd heard of turtle ships, but always believed the descriptions he'd received were exaggerated. To forge enough hexagonal iron bucklers that could be linked together to cover a dome over an entire warship seemed far too costly to ever be seriously considered. He had always believed that the rumors that the turtle ships were "covered in iron, with spikes to prevent boarding" was a corruption of "covered in iron spikes, to prevent boarding." Evidently he was wrong, for there were indeed iron plates covering the turtle ship from almost any attack.

"How much money was spent to build something like that?" he asked in wonderment.

"I didn't pay for it, so I'm not sure," Jobinh said dryly. "It cost a great deal, however. It would take at least as much money as it would cost to build a normal warship plus the cost of supplying several hundred soldiers with iron bucklers. There are a lot of people in the Hegemony who would say building even one of them was a waste of our resources, but Norre can afford it."

Mathis shook his head. "Would even all of the money Ekholm has paid in tribute for the past several decades put together pay for it? Norre must be far wealthier than I had imagined."

"I suspect it wouldn't." Jobinh sighed. "The costs of defending Norre's tributaries are greater than the money it receives in tribute. That's why Norre no longer accepts new tributaries unless they are of strategic importance to the Hegemony."

"Hey, what's that?" Kieras suddenly chirped. Initially, Mathis was annoyed. He was interested in following that line of questioning with Jobinh, and being interrupted for a childish game of pranks was not something he appreciated. As he looked over at her, however, something in her eyes told him this particular part of her game with Jobinh was not actually a game. It was more serious to her than that.

He and Jobinh both turned to see what she was pointing at. A great fountain was erupting in the middle of a stone-bordered circular pool. There were several bronze figurines decorating it as the water shimmered and rainbowed around the pool.

"Another restored piece of the old city," Jobinh replied. "The Everflowing Fountain. It also seems to have some magical properties – not only was it still running when Norre was founded despite a thousand years of neglect, but the pool and the bronze never need cleaning. The water is always fresh and very, very cold – like ice, almost – even on the hottest of days. That fountain continues flowing perpetually, without a single speck of ice visible in its waters even when the entire River Knapp has frozen over. But I know of no other special properties it may have."

Kieras nodded slowly. Mathis, with his new goal of coaching her into becoming a better kitsune, realized he would have to have another talk with her, later – he could tell right away that she had been interested in that fountain probably since before they came to Norre.

"Oh, and what's that?" Ziani asked, pointing to yet another unusual statue near the marina to resume their game.

He could talk to Kieras about it, later, however, and maybe find out just what it was she was hoping to find out about that fountain. The game of pestering Jobinh with questions was still at hand, and Mathis decided he should maybe play along, after all.

Kieras had to hide her laugh when Jobinh tried to report on their tour to Torkki that evening. Between Mathis, Ziani, and herself, they had been able to keep him talking the entire time, and the lieutenant had completely lost his voice. Torkki didn't look quite as amused, but he didn't seem inclined to complain, either. Instead, he just rolled his eyes and directed them to enter one of the houses in the Ambassadorial District.

Ekholm, like many other tributaries to the Norre Hegemony, had no permanent embassy of their own. They were, however, granted a large suite in the Kryskow House, one of the Ambassadorial residences, for the duration of their stay. It was large enough for Mathis, Kieras, and all of the wulvers to reside in, much to everyone's surprise. Ekholm had not used it in years, but Norre's government routinely paid to have it cleaned and maintained. There was even a kitchen staff, although that was supposed to serve any of several consuls and ambassadors staying in Kryskow House.

As with all things, there was a reason Norre was so generous to its visitors. It would be some time before the Ekholm contingent could even begin the process of negotiations, like they had intended. Indeed, were they to appeal directly to the Norrish Senate directly, they might have to endure an entire year waiting before their petitions were heard. Instead, they were seeking an audience with the Norre Hegemony Parliamentary Council. The Parliament could approve of their inclusion into the alliance as a full member as a temporary measure, subject to later confirmation by the Norre City Senate in the course of its normal schedule. Even the Parliament, however, was booked long in advance, and they had been warned it would be at least a week before they could be heard.

Waiting did not mean standing idle, however. Savard had located a number of likely individuals in Norre for Mathis to contact for support in their proposal, leaving instructions for each one in a separate envelope. Torkki had also made arrangements for Mathis to meet with a member of the Norrish Elite's quartermaster's corps.

Kieras intended to be present at that last one. Just as Mathis seemed to want to help her learn to survive as a kitsune, she wanted to teach him how to take care of himself when her year of service as his kitsune guardian was over. For decades she had been trained in the use of many different weapons by her father. Surely she would be able to help him in finding and training with a suitable weapon.

She hoped that he wouldn't need her during the other meetings Savard had arranged, however. She wanted to explore the fountains she had seen, hoping to find a way inside them to meet with the veden vaki that the haltija of Dahlberg told her of. If she could manage that, then all she would need to do would be to find her mother, and she could complete the quest her father gave her – Mathis in tow or not.

For the moment, however, she was quite content to enjoy her dinner with Mathis, Torkki, Ziani, and the rest of the Ekholm contingent... even if Jobinh was a part of it. The lieutenant clearly didn't approve of his captain's "secret" marriage, given all the looks of disapproval he kept shooting at his commanding officer whenever the former chambermaid flirted with her new husband. Still, even that added to the amusement of the occasion, as Ziani ramped up the flirting when she noticed Jobinh's reaction.

"You know," Mathis said between courses, his tone setting a far more serious mood than Kieras was feeling, "I'd always heard that Norre was wealthy, but I was shocked at just how much coin is thrown around in this city. I saw one of those turtle ships, today. They must have spent enough money to buy all of Ekholm just to pay for one of those, and they have six! It makes the job of trying to get them to accept our tiny little home as their equal... daunting, at best."

Astonishingly, even after all of his protests of the decision to end their tributary status, it was Jobinh who voiced support of Ekholm. His voice still dry and harsh from the day's tour, he said, "Daunting? Certainly! But it's possible. The leaders of the Norre Hegemony have long considered Ekholm a strategically important city. Norre owes much of its wealth to being at one of the three main crossings of the Knapp River meet. With the potential Ekholm has to exploit the same economic opportunities – or perhaps even greater opportunities, given its nearby granite and marble mines – Norre was far from the first power to covet it. Norre actually started working to defend the town from Erixonites and Skorrans even before the treaty of tribute. However small Ekholm is at the moment, the expectation has always been that it would grow to become Norre's equal in time. You might find the reaction to be more 'what took you so long?' than it is a comparison of your relative wealth."

"Even I find the notion that Ekholm could ever be the equal of Norre hard to believe," Torkki said. "And, for years, I've been dealing with Norrish generals who've been telling me the same thing whenever they learned where I was from. Jobinh is correct – that is the mindset of many of the politicians here. Norre may be the wealthiest city in the world, but they have great hope for Ekholm's future."

Mathis shook his head. "And keeping up that impression will be my job." He glanced at his brother. "You've been doing a good job of giving me a crash course at leading an army. I don't suppose you could do the same in court manners? I may have come a long way as an ambassador since I started with the trip to Dahlberg, but the places I've been to haven't exactly been hotbeds of formal protocols."

"Must you all worry about that, now?" Kieras sighed. "This may well be our final chance to enjoy ourselves before the actual business of this journey begins. Let's not concern ourselves with court behavior, politics, the relative economies of a large city like Norre versus a tiny one like Ekholm, and so forth. Let's just enjoy each other's company."

"Well said, sis," came a voice from the doorway. "Today is a day for you to have fun. Tomorrow is when the real work begins."

Kieras' eyes widened as she gazed at the door. "Daneyko! I... where did you come from?"

Now dressed in formal attire, the white-haired kitsune stepped out of the shadows and sketched a cursory bow of introduction. "I've been here for a while, now. I had to sneak in – the Embassy guards might not have let me through, considering I didn't have a formal invitation – but if Mathis had read his orders from home, he should have guessed that I would be coming."

"They're all still sealed," Mathis replied from behind her, sounding a bit wary. "I was going to read them this evening."

"Ah, then you don't know," Daneyko replied, grinning. "Good! Makes this much more fun."

"Makes what much more fun?" Jobinh snapped angrily, voice cracking but far stronger than it had been. "Why have you interrupted our dinner, kitsune? Your kind are always trouble!"

"Always?" Daneyko shot back, his voice amused. "Including those who are invited to your dinner table?"

"Yes," Jobinh replied, shooting a glare over at Kieras that she refused to acknowledge. "Even those who *pretend* to come in friendship."

"Well, that's just mean," Daneyko said, feigning hurt. "I hope that's not the prevailing feeling in Norre, considering the agreements the myobu priesthood have signed with them."

"Agreements?" Mathis replied before Jobinh could interrupt again. "What agreements?"

"Well, your letters from home will tell you more than I could." Daneyko smiled over at Jobinh. "I suppose saying that the myobu priesthood has offered Ekholm its support in their intent to join the Norre Hegemony would be a good enough summary, however. I'm here, now, because I'm supposed to escort you – and my younger sister, whose presence is formally requested and required – to see the priesthood's representative on the Norrish Council, tomorrow."

There was a long pause before Jobinh asked, "When did the kitsune get a seat on the Council?"

"We're not exactly a traditional voting member," Daneyko replied, grinning. "But we've been a part of the Hegemony since its founding...."

Mathis did not recognize the significance of the imposing building Daneyko guided them to that morning. The lone wulver to accompany them that morning, Teslak, also was clearly ignorant as to its importance. He was fairly certain Kieras and Ziani were as well, though Ziani seemed to have had something of a clue – she certainly seemed startled by some of the symbols engraved on the walls. Those symbols were familiar, but Mathis couldn't place them, himself.

Torkki clearly did know, and appeared somewhat amused, but did nothing to inform his brother or the others where it was they were going. He was nodding to himself as if some long-held suspicion had been confirmed, but he wasn't saying anything.

Jobinh, however, was far from amused. "Are you telling me that the Arbiter's Office – the office wholly responsible for settling disputes between Hegemony members – is run by kitsune?"

"And has been since the Hegemony was formed, yes," Daneyko replied, grinning. "Of course, not many people have seen the actual Treaty of Norre, and most of those that have only read the portions of the treaty which are not obscured by kitsune illusions. The Prime Hegemon of Norre knows, of course, as do certain members of the Norrish Senate. It would be rather difficult for agents of the myobu priesthood to operate in Norre as extensively as they do without some formal government recognition." He paused. "And before you ask, I promise you I am not lying about any of that. In fact, I have yet to tell you a lie since you've entered Norre. When we signed the Treaty of Norre, we bound ourselves into a pact of honesty, requiring us to tell the truth in all but a few circumstances."

Mathis saw a hole in that right away. "And I suppose you won't explain what those circumstances are, right?"

Daneyko laughed. "Of course not! We have to be able to have some fun, don't we? But you don't need to worry too much about it, as I'm sure you already know."

Mathis nodded slowly. He had finally read the documents Savard had sent with him, and was startled at what they contained. Shortly after Mathis' first meeting with Daneyko in the town of Arsene, Savard was summoned to the town of Arbeloa. Mathis remembered Savard's brief departure. He had been surprised that he was not included on the journey as he was officially Ekholm's Ambassador at the time, but because it was only a day trip, he assumed that his uncle had gone to the meeting by himself as a curiosity.

What he had not learned until opening his sealed orders was that Savard had spent that day hammering out a secret treaty between Ekholm and the myobu priesthood. That treaty likewise had certain elements compelling members of the priesthood to speak honestly in certain clearly defined circumstances. He believed, based on the treaty, that the kitsune would tell him no lies – at least not while either of them were operating in any sort of official capacity – but there was plenty of room for half-truths.

"I believe you will honor any and all treaties, even if it means having to tell the truth," Mathis replied. "But forgive me if I still wonder whether you've told me everything I need to know or not."

Daneyko smirked. "I told my sister you would be a good person to serve as a guardian, and I stand by that, but she's going to be absolutely miserable when she realizes she won't be able to get anything by you. Won't you, sis?"

"It'll certainly be a challenge," Kieras replied, laughing slightly. "But just think – after a year of trying to pull the wool over his eyes, I'll probably be able to out-doubletalk our parents, even!"

"Your father, perhaps," a new feminine voice interrupted, standing at the doorway to the Arbiter's Offices. "But it would be quite a feat, indeed, if this young human were able to teach you how to outwit me!"

Mathis looked over at the newcomer, and was immediately struck but how much she and Kieras looked alike. If it weren't for the astonishingly white hair and the few creases and folds in her face that indicated the onset of middle age, he'd think they were twins.

"Mother!" Kieras gasped.

While the building was called the Arbiter's Office, the main room more resembled a mid-sized banquet hall than any official government suite that Kieras had seen. Perhaps it was just the occasion, but as they sat around the oval table filled with various fruits, pastries, and beverages (including a number of decanters full of lingonberry wine imported from Ekholm – a taste she and her mother shared, it seemed) it was clear that it was being used as a banquet hall instead of as an office, as well. Tianhyu, Kieras' mother, made sure that her daughter, Daneyko, and Mathis were all seated no more than one or two seats away from her own slightly more elegant seat, but other than that their companions were allowed to sit wherever they wanted.

"Please, eat," Tianhyu said, gesturing to the food on the table. "If I know my son, he probably dragged you out here before you could have breakfast."

"You do say reunions are best had over food," Daneyko quipped. "I think this counts, don't you, mother?"

Kieras noticed Mathis serving his own plate, but holding off on eating anything while he watched their companions. She wasn't sure whether she should be offended that he didn't trust her mother not to poison their food, or if she should follow his example. In fact, she wasn't really sure what she was thinking about anything – she was still in shock.

When given the task of finding her mother all those months ago, Kieras had envisioned herself having to go on a great quest, visiting every nation in the world both known and yet to be discovered, crawling through the ruins of ancient civilizations, encountering creatures she never knew existed and more as she hunted down her mother. She had been investigating the towns and cities surrounding Ekholm since she first escaped Kassia, but had never expected to find anything more than a clue about the direction her mother may have gone.

Here she was, however, found before she had really started looking. It was... somewhat anticlimactic.

"Mother, what are you *doing* here?" she asked, finally, when the strain got to be too much.

"Eating breakfast, dear," Tianhyu replied, smiling slightly. "Why aren't you?"

"Probably because I'm not," Mathis said. "I've been waiting to see if you've done anything to the food as a prank."

Tianhyu laughed. "Daneyko told me about you. My daughter chose well in allying herself to your cause. If you can anticipate kitsune tricks like that, you'll go far. I assure you, though, you have nothing to worry about... as long as you avoid the pickled fruits."

Ziani, sitting across from them with a pickled plum on her fork, glanced over at the kitsune vixen. "Um... and what's wrong with the pickled fruit?"

"Nothing much," Tianhyu assured them, laughing. "I would not poison my allies, after all. You might find a few of them too hot to handle, however, as hot peppers were pickled in the same juice as some of them... as that young Elite has just discovered."

Everyone's attention went to Jobinh, whose eyes were watering as he guzzled his entire goblet full of wine in an effort to stop the burning. Kieras could have warned him against that – wine would merely spread the heat, not contain it – but she decided to let him figure it out for himself.

"This is why," Jobinh gasped, "I hate dealing with kitsune."

Tianhyu's eyes narrowed, but other than that she said nothing in response. Turning her attention to Mathis, she changed topics. "So... I knew, from everything my son told me, that you would eventually become the one to earn my daughter's services. He never explained exactly how the two of you met, however."

Mathis proceeded to tell the tale Kieras had heard many times – and had lived through once – of his discovery of her in the woods, taking her back to Ekholm, learning she was a kitsune, stealing her tama, and extracting her loyalty. When he was finished, however, Tianhyu merely chuckled.

"You know, boy, I knew both your uncle and your mother before Eskesa fell."

"They must have been very young," Mathis replied.

"Mother was just twelve when that happened," Torkki added. "Uncle Savard was only six."

Tianhyu nodded. "I used to think your mother had some kitsune blood in her. She had the ability to tell kitsune from common fox or human at just a glance, without any further evidence that I could see. If it weren't for the fact that the blood of a kitsune only empowers normal humans for a single generation, I would be convinced that was still the case with you."

Mathis' eyes widened. "What do you mean?"

"Ignoring the physical traits I've been told about – not even my eyes are as good as yours, for instance – you seem to have the ability to see through almost any kitsune deception. Furthermore, you can tell a lie or a half-truth better than my own children, since it seems no one has caught something about your story, yet." She paused. "I may no longer be able to enter Ekholm, but I remember it well enough to know you must have gone out of your way to enter town through the tanner's district. Tell me, why did you suspect my daughter of being a kitsune at first sight, as you clearly did?"

Kieras blinked. She had never thought about it, but now that she was as familiar with Ekholm as she was, she knew her mother was right. There was no reason for him to have taken her anywhere near the tanner's. Just why had Mathis taken her that way, anyway?

"I had hides I needed to drop off for sale," Mathis replied. "I'm a hunter. That's how I make my living, at least until recently."

"And it couldn't wait until you found somewhere safe for the poor, lost girl you found in the woods?" Tianhyu replied, shaking her head. "You are a smart boy, but if you expect me to believe that you aren't as smart as I thought."

Mathis looked like he was about to protest, but then shot a guilty look in Kieras' direction. "Well... it was worth a shot."

"The truth, now – how did you find out my daughter was a kitsune?" Tianhyu insisted.

Mathis opened and closed his mouth a few times, then sighed. "Well... before she approached me, she was a fox. She changed into being a human, and I saw her transformation out of the corner of my eye."

Kieras stiffened. Her brother let out a snort of repressed laughter.

"Well, now, why is that such a big secret?" Tianhyu asked. "That's how most kitsune are discovered, after all."

"Sis is a genius at transformation," Daneyko explained, watching her and Mathis both. "But she's very shy about it because she still has one significant flaw in her technique – she cannot form clothes when changing from fox to human."

Tianhyu blinked, and then started laughing. "Oh, my!"

Kieras felt her cheeks burning. "Well... well..."

"I really didn't get a very good look," Mathis insisted. "It's just... I didn't want to embarrass her any more than I already had to by mentioning it."

Kieras wasn't quite sure what to say to that, but knew she needed to say something. "I suppose you realize that the severity of the practical joke I owe you just doubled?"

Mathis sighed, a relieved smile on his face. "If that's all the punishment I get for this, I'll be thrilled."

"There would be a great deal more," Kieras said, letting some of her more fox-like mannerisms come out in a growl, "if I hadn't just sworn to act as your guardian."

"Now, daughter, it is hardly this young man's fault if you transformed where he could see you," Tianhyu said. "It's not as if he was trying to peak on you."

Ziani's giggle had Kieras blushing once more, the memory of the girls' multiple attempts to catch the boys in the bathhouse coming to her. And, chances were, Daneyko had told her mother all about that also. "Well... um...."

"Now that those pleasantries are over," Tianhyu continued, ignoring her daughter's embarrassment, "what are your plans while you're in town?"

"Uncle Savard suggested I meet with several of the potentially friendly representatives to the Norrish Parliament." Mathis smiled wryly. "Which I suppose I am doing now."

"Well, of course you have our support," Tianhyu said, waving him off. "The myobu priesthood can handle gathering all of the council votes you'll need. It's not like it'll be hard to convince anyone. Norre *wants* its tributaries to grow strong enough to become full members, after all, and I'm pretty sure we myobu have better connections than you could hope for. I'm just as sure that neither you, nor my daughter, came out here planning to spend your *entire* time in diplomatic meeting after diplomatic meeting."

Kieras giggled. "Poor Mathis would go crazy if he did that. For an ambassador, he's not exactly comfortable with state protocol and formal political discussions."

Mathis sighed. "No, I am not. And while I should not trust you to handle all of the private negotiations for me, I know my own limits. I'll be grateful for any help you can provide."

Torkki frowned. "Mathis, you've come a long way from that first mission to Dahlberg. You—"

"I'm fine with small town councils," Mathis interrupted. "But Norre itself? I'm so far removed from anything I've ever experienced before, I have no idea what I should be doing."

"It's settled, then," Tianhyu replied, a cheerful lilt in her voice. Kieras didn't like how it sounded – she loved her mother, but they were both kitsune; they were not to be trusted. "We'll handle the bulk of your private negotiations, and you take care of your other errands. That should be fun!"

"Mother," Kieras warned. "If you sabotage Ekholm's chances of entering the Hegemony—"

Tianhyu smiled down at her daughter. "Dear child, there is absolutely nothing you could threaten me with that I couldn't handle. But I am glad to see you are taking your guardianship of your human seriously."

"I..."

"You can rest easy," Tianhyu continued, not letting her daughter say anything more. "I swear we have Ekholm's best intentions in mind. The myobu priesthood has a special interest in the survivors of Eskesa, and we will do our best to guide them and protect them... even if we cannot enter their lands." She paused, studying her daughter. "Although perhaps we are not as restricted from entering their lands as I thought. I was not aware you were able to wear the heirlooms I left behind in Kassia. They should only allow a myobu kitsune to wear them, and would enforce the edicts of the priesthood on you. If the magic in them considers you a myobu, so should the magic restricting our entry to Ekholm."

Kieras frowned, not understanding her mother at first, but then remembered her choker. Her hands went up to touch it. "You mean this?"

"Yes, that. I didn't see it at first, but now that I have I must ask – daughter, where is your *tama?*"

"My *tama?*" Kieras repeated, surprised. Her hands reached into the silver thimble holder on her chatelaine and pulled out the aforementioned gemstone. "Right here, why?"

"Why are you keeping it there?" Tianhyu asked. "You don't need to hide it, you know. This is a kitsune-friendly city."

"Well, I like having my hands free," Kieras replied. "And I hate carrying it in my mouth – I'm too worried I'll accidentally swallow it."

Tianhyu frowned. "That doesn't answer my question. Why... wait. Do you not know?"

"Know what?" Kieras asked, confused.

"You know, all this time I've thought she was just trying to hide the fact she was a kitsune," Mathis said. He sounded somewhat amused. "But I believe you're right."

"Then you know what I'm talking about, right?" Tianhyu said, laughing.

"It was described in mother's journals," Mathis replied, grinning. "I did think it was a bit of a coincidence, but as far as I knew it was a common item for kitsune."

"Well, the myobu priesthood crafted it, and many of us carry similar items," Tianhyu replied, shaking her head. "I know my daughter is only half myobu, and her red fur prevents her from full-ranked status with the priesthood, but myobu magic does not share the same biases as our leaders. That trinket she wears tells me that much more reliably than a bunch of bigoted grey-tails like the myobu elders have become. Perhaps the last human born in Eskesa has died?"

"Not old man Fornier," Mathis answered back. "He's the last survivor. But he—"

"Excuse me," Kieras interrupted. "Evidently, I've missed something important about this choker of yours, Mother. Could someone *please* explain to me what that something is before you try to solve another mystery?"

Mathis sighed, and took her *tama* in his hand. It said a lot about Kieras' trust in the man that she didn't instinctively attack him for doing so – something her mother clearly noticed, given how her eyes softened and her lips twitched in a repressed smile. Holding out the *tama*, he fastened it onto the choker around her neck. She could not see how, since it was right under her chin. When he moved away, she felt a surge in her magic as the *tama* seemed to connect with her in a way it never had before.

"There you go," he said, grinning slightly. "Maybe now you won't be dropping it in the middle of battle, forcing me to rescue you again."

Kieras was too astonished to reply. Her mother, however, continued the conversation as if nothing had happened.

"So, you still haven't said what you plan to be doing in town while we're busy handling your negotiations," she said.

"Well," Torkki said. "I intend to take him to the quartermaster's corps. I have a connection there who I am sure will be able to help my brother with a small problem of his: Mathis is the best bowman I've ever heard of, and I'm not just saying that because he's my brother. However, he's never found a weapon he can use effectively in hand-to-hand combat. In Ekholm's militia, we tried for years to teach him how to use a sword or a spear, but he's just not capable of handling either one. It's like they're trying to fly out of his hands or something."

Tianhyu rubbed her nose thoughtfully. "That reminds me of one of the stories I read about in The Tales of Inari. At one time he was as great a warrior as he was a mage, but his enemies cursed him so that he would be unable to hold a sword. They would fly out of his hand if he ever tried to pick one up."

"I can *hold* a sword just fine." Mathis sighed. "And after many years of practice, I can use one without risking my own life, but I'm no good with them. I'm the captain of a new military unit, but with a blade I'm little better than a raw cadet. I simply cannot make it move where I know it needs to go, like someone is jogging my elbow whenever I swing."

Kieras, remembering what she had seen of his sword work in the battle to rescue her, shot him a dubious glance. She doubted even a raw recruit could be disarmed so easily. Torkki's expression made her feel he shared her assessment on his brother's fitness with a blade, but Tianhyu just shrugged.

"Swords are not the only weapon out there, you know," the older kitsune vixen pointed out. "When Inari's kitsune children heard of his plight, they gifted him with claws of his own so he could fight as they could."

Mathis frowned. "I'm not sure I'd want claws," he said. "They might interfere with my archery."

"We no longer know how they were created, anyway," Tianhyu said dismissively. "And even if we did, you probably couldn't use them. Inari was a powerful mage and could spare the energy, but there hasn't been a proper human mage in hundreds of years and none of any note for two thousand. A normal human would never be able to sustain it."

"Then why bother bringing it up?" Jobinh had apparently recovered from his experience with the overly spicy pickled fruit. "A weapon he can't use won't do him any good. With what I've seen of his sword skills, I'm not sure there *is* a close-combat weapon he can use well, but talking about mythical weapon he couldn't use even if it really existed won't help anyone."

"Inari's Claws may be lost," Tianhyu said patiently. "But the point is that swords are not the only weapon out there. Mathis now has the service of a guardian kitsune. That can be a far more powerful weapon than any sword."

Mathis frowned, and to Kieras' surprise rebuked her mother. "It's entirely possible there are better weapons for me than the sword or pike. That's what we're going to the quartermaster for. But I only have the 'service of a guardian kitsune' for another year, at most, so I should probably spend that time getting myself ready to do without her." He paused. "That, and I don't want to think of Kieras as a weapon. She is my friend. Guardian kitsune or not, she will never be a mere weapon to me. And I'm surprised you'd even suggest that's all she was."

Kieras blushed slightly. Certainly, she never thought for one second that he might see her just as a weapon, but she was startled at how passionate he was in refuting the suggestion she might be one. While kitsune were often adored by children, true friendships between adult humans and kitsune were rare and difficult. It was hard on a friendship to never be able to trust that your friend will tell you the truth. Her father only had a half-dozen real human friends in his entire century of time living in Kassia – several friendly acquaintances, but few true, lasting friendships. Kieras was fortunate enough, she believed, to have found two during her first few days in Ekholm – Ziani (who was as much of a prankster at heart as any kitsune) and Mathis.

Tianhyu noticed her reaction and opened her mouth to say something – which undoubtedly would have been quite embarrassing for Kieras – but Jobinh interrupted before she could.

"Oh, come on! You seriously want to make *friends* with a kitsune? That's the biggest laugh I've ever heard, though as chummy as you were with the beasty I should have expected it. I never thought you were made for command, from the Dahlberg incident onward. Archon Savard and Captain Torkki may have come around to believing in you after your successes in Arsene, Sorkham, and Pogge, but I stuck to my guns... and if you really think you can be friends with a kitsune, that just goes to show me your judgment is so off you could *never* be fit for command!"

Torkki looked over at his lieutenant with narrow eyes. "Jobinh, are you drunk?"

"Of course not!" Jobinh insisted, though his slumped posture seemed to refute those words. "I've only had a single glass of wine!"

Kieras wasn't so sure about that. He certainly seemed to be flying off the handle, and if she hadn't missed her guess he'd just started slurring a few words. But she had to admit she hadn't seen him drink anything more than a goblet full of wine. That shouldn't have been enough to make a hard-drinking soldier like Jobinh so intoxicated. Still, she could tell she wasn't alone in her suspicions. Mathis' eyes were narrowed as he looked at something on Jobinh's plate.

She checked her mother to see what she thought, and was somewhat surprised to see a smug smile on her face. "Tell me, young man," Tianhyu said, her voice almost purring. "Just why is it so ridiculous for my daughter and this young man to be friends?"

"You arrogant foxes," Jobinh spat. "You think just because you can look human, you can actually *be* human."

Tianhyu laughed. "But we *are* human, young man. Inari would not turn his daughter into something inhuman just to heal her. Magic has made us something more, but we are only that which we were made from. We can assume any shape, but there is a reason we only stay in human or fox forms for any length of time."

"Then why are kitsune children born as foxes?" Jobinh said.

Tianhyu paused, cocking her head, before hesitantly explaining. "We're actually born in whatever form our mothers are in when they give birth. It's just that we typically give birth as foxes because, well, it's a lot less painful. My first child was born as a human... although that was sort of by accident."

Jobinh looked flabbergasted for the moment, but quickly recovered.

"Human-looking at birth or not, it isn't your shape that matters. Kitsune are deceivers—"

"Who are bound by our word more strongly than any normal human," Tianhyu said. "We do not lie in everything we say, but the magic used to create us insists we play the part of the trickster for magic itself is wild and unpredictable. It makes it hard for us to deal with human friendships, knowing that we will be driven to lie to them, and yet we take pride in being able to fool both ally and enemy, friend and family. The friendships we do make are usually stronger than the bonds between normal human friendships. But the magic that forces us to lie and deceive also binds us to our promises so tightly that breaking a vow can injure or even kill us. Humans may not lie by nature, but you cannot tell me that there has never been a human who has broken his word."

"Yet you twist your promises to the point that they cannot be trusted!" Jobinh snapped.

"Only those demanded of us. We twist our oaths when we are blackmailed, yes, but we keep to the letter of them even then. All our other oaths, we keep not just to the letter but also the spirit of our vows. At least, the myobu and nogitsune do."

"You are thieves. You steal from humans, or at best only pay for things with acorns and twigs disguised to look like money."

"Some of our wilder kind do, yes – especially our young," Tianhyu replied. "That comes largely from being ostracized and isolated by human society, and not truly understanding the significance of money. Those of us raised among humans – like Kieras, here – know just why it is improper to steal and how unacceptable it is to pay for things with illusory money."

Indeed, while Kieras was quite capable of acting like the thief, she would rarely – if ever – take something without paying for it with real money. That she didn't always have the right to purchase whatever it was she was buying wasn't the same thing, in her mind. As a kitsune she wouldn't even think such an act was theft, but perhaps she shouldn't mention that in front of Jobinh.

"The worst thing, though," Jobinh said, his breath quickening and face reddening as his anger rose. "Is that you combine all those things – your so-called 'human forms,' your deceitfulness, your twisting of promises, and your instincts for theft, to steal not just money, but our husbands and wives, mothers and fathers, even our children away from us! You deliberately set out to destroy our families!"

Kieras shot Ziani a wry smile, remembering their conversation about Torkki that both supported and refuted that claim, but Daneyko evidently hadn't been taught how the different breeds treated human relationships. He had heard enough. "That's not true!" A long pause from their mother, however, had him doubting himself. "Is it?"

Tianhyu sighed. "I am a myobu, and my breed of kitsune would never do such a thing. Myobu, especially, are encouraged to avoid entering into even a hint of a relationship with anyone other than another myobu. Had I not had a myobu mate prior to meeting your father, I might have been shunned for daring to breed with him."

"You had a mate prior to papa?" Kieras asked, stunned.

"Yes, dear. You have a few half-brothers and half-sisters from him that you've never met – one is even in Norre at the moment, so perhaps I'll introduce you – but my first mate died more than a hundred years before I met your father." Tianhyu turned back to Daneyko. "Nogitsune kitsune, like your father, permit relationships with other breeds of kitsune as well as with humans, with no social stigma attached. They are not vindictive, however, and would never deliberately break up a family in the way this young Elite is implying... unless it was to end some form of abuse."

Daneyko nodded slowly. "I'm sensing a 'but' here."

"Yes. Other breeds of our kind – not just the major breeds like the kumiho or the huli jeng – have been known to do such things as a lark, even if otherwise friendly with humans. They do not care that doing so could damage their human friendships, or the reputation of their brother and sister kitsune – they see it as a challenge."

Kieras frowned. She long knew that Jobinh disliked her, but never quite understood why. "Lieutenant Jobinh, if any of my kind has harmed your family in this way, you have my most sincere apologies. And my thanks for escorting me and providing me with protection in spite of your—"

"Spare me," Jobinh snapped, noticeably slurring his words. He started to stand up from the table, but couldn't seem to use his legs properly and wound up slumping back down. "I will always do my duty, no matter my personal feelings, but the apologies and thanks of a lying bunch of foxes mean nothing to me."

Even though Jobinh had ended his rant and collapsed into his chair, Torkki had finally had enough. "Jobinh! You are most definitely drunk. If you think I'm going to condone one of my officers letting himself get in this condition and launching an insubordinate tirade against both allies and—"

"Calm yourself, Torkki," Mathis called. Then chuckled slightly as he noticed Jobinh's state. "For one thing, if you haven't noticed, you're shouting at someone who has already passed out. For another, Jobinh did not 'let himself get drunk.' In fact, I think he was drugged by the very hostess you are berating him for insulting." He turned to Tianhyu. "Isn't that right? After all, it was only our food you said wasn't drugged, not our wine."

Tianhyu grinned darkly. "Indeed. I knew from my son's earlier meeting with you and Kieras that he was the one I most wanted to speak uninhibitedly, so I made the arrangements for the lieutenant to be the one to receive the tainted food and drink." She turned to Ziani. "You may go ahead and eat that pickled fruit you coveted so much, dear. I promise you that Jobinh's was the only one tampered with."

Ziani frowned, and then looked over at Kieras. The younger kitsune vixen was a bit startled to realize that the human girl was looking to her, trusting her implicitly to help deal with her mother. Parsing the promise's words carefully, Kieras could detect no loophole that she believed her mother would use. So decided, she signaled back with a nod that it was probably safe to eat the fruit, hoping she was right. She didn't want to lose that trust just because she gave poor advice.

Everyone already knew that Kieras and Ziani were friends, but this proved to everyone in the room (at least, all of those still awake) just how close they were. Hopefully this would never be used against them, but Kieras couldn't be sure with her mother and brother in the audience. Mathis looked like he wanted to give her yet another lecture on kitsune survival tips. Torkki looked relieved, and Daneyko looked amused. All emotions she was expecting – but she was surprised to read both satisfaction and pride clearly and honestly displayed in the smirk on her mother's face.

"You know," Tianhyu said, "I was a bit skeptical when I heard that you had joined a human army. Our people make great spies and assassins, but our instinct for deceit makes it hard for us to act as soldiers. It is difficult for kitsune to gain the amount of trust needed to serve in armies successfully. It seems, daughter, that your time immersed with humans has helped you in that regard. That is why we so often must rely on the aid of others such as the Eskesans, the Norrish, and the wulvers of Dahlberg rather than form armies of our own."

At the mention of Dahlberg, eyes turned to the unusually quiet Teslak, who Kieras had almost forgotten about until then. The young wulver coughed. "That is why we suggested several different oaths for the Ekholm Irregulars. Humans, wulvers, kitsune, and other mystical beings will all require different vows due to our different natures. It was our Alpha's idea, although it seemed as if Captain Mathis had already thought of the same thing, as he had several versions of the oath ready when I mentioned it."

"The oaths actually came from my mother," Mathis explained before anyone could ask. "After Kieras arrived in our village, I found all of mother's old journals. She had a number of suggestions for dealing with kitsune from her time spent with you, Lady Tianhyu, and among them was a draft of what oath she felt a kitsune would need to swear to before taking service in an army. She had to find a way to make a kitsune take orders, but to give them enough free will that they would not follow them blindly. If someone gives her an order to commit treason, we want her able to resist it. I believe your daughter was not unhappy with the results."

Kieras smiled wistfully. She had memorized the oath so that she wouldn't stumble in saying it when Mathis formally inducted her into the Ekholm Irregulars – something Ziani, Torkki, and even the Archon Savard had spent several hours helping her with. "I, the vixen kitsune Kieras, born in Kassia, do so vow for a term of one year to serve as a soldier of the city of Ekholm, to obey the lawful orders of the Archon, to take orders from my commanding officers in the Ekholm Irregulars without complaint, to resist my kitsune instincts and twist those orders only when I legitimately feel it is in their or Ekholm's best interest, to be entirely honest whenever I am on duty, and to follow the laws of Ekholm and the Tenets of the Ekholm Irregulars."

Tianhyu smirked at her while Daneyko groaned, planting his face in his hands. "You realize, daughter, that even though you were just trying to tell me of your vow, you just renewed it? A human could claim that he was just quoting himself, but you are a kitsune, magically bound to your oaths whenever they are said, whether you mean them or not. So, your service to the Ekholm Irregulars will end a year from today, and not a year from when you first made that oath."

Kieras' jaw dropped. She hadn't even thought about it, but she already could feel the magic shifting inside her. Fortunately, it wouldn't add too much time to her service, though – just a few weeks. "Er, oops? It isn't a serious problem, though."

"You must, nevertheless, be much more careful with what you say, dear. You never know what trouble you could cause yourself with an accidental, ill-timed promise."

"Yes, mother." Kieras accepted the reprimand and took it to heart.

"I've always wondered," Torkki said, changing the topic, "what happens if two promises made by a kitsune conflict? Kieras had sworn her service to Mathis before she took her oath as a soldier. If she had to disobey a lawful order given by the Archon in order to protect Mathis, say, or if she had to sacrifice my brother's life to save Ekholm from destruction, how would the magics compelling her to obey her promise resolve itself?"

Tianhyu addressed her answer to Kieras more than Torkki. This was to be a lesson for her, more than Torkki. "Usually, a kitsune will be compelled to keep as close to both promises as she can. We can use common sense and our own desires to bend a promise somewhat, even when there is no conflict – if Kieras' promise to act as Mathis guardian were to be interpreted strictly enough, she might have been forced to prevent him from becoming the Captain of the Irregulars, and would have imprisoned him for his own protection. She knows he would hate that, however, and has her own goals in mind, so she chooses to protect him in a different way – by being a soldier and staying at his side. There is enough leeway to make sensible decisions.

"The resolution of a conflict of promises works much the same way. If I were to promise to feed you a meal made entirely out of pickled plums, but had also promised to feed you a meal of anything you wanted, I would have to resolve the situation. I could try and make whatever you requested out of pickled plums if that were possible. Or I could make you a meal of pickled plums and the meal you request and only serve one of the two meals. Or, I could simply make you two different meals and serve them at two different times.

"We kitsune can be very creative in twisting our promises to avoid having them conflict. Sometimes, however, orders really do conflict in a way that cannot be resolved by simply using common sense or by bending the oath to match my desires. If the Archon that Kieras has sworn to obey gave her a lawful order to kill the man she has sworn to protect, she would have a true, irresolvable conflict of her vows."

"And what happens then?" Mathis asked. Kieras leaned in to listen, as she wasn't sure of the answer herself.

"She may choose which promise she wishes to keep and which she must break. There will always be consequences for a broken vow, no matter the reason. During its early years, one of the myobu priesthood's leaders faced a situation where they had no choice but to break a promise, to choose between saving two different people she had sworn to protect, and her *hoshi no tama* shattered when she did. It isn't usually that drastic, however – a cousin of mine claims that it was a broken promise that made it impossible for her to ever magically change her eye's shape or color, either through transformation or through illusion – it gives her human form a rather unusual appearance, but other than that is of little consequence."

Kieras must have shown some apprehension at those words, as Mathis quickly spoke to reassure her. "I will endeavor never to put you in that position."

"See that you don't," Tianhyu said, smiling fiercely. "I would hate to have to seek vengeance against you for my daughter's sake."

If Mathis was disturbed by such a casually delivered threat, Kieras couldn't tell. If anything, he made a point of how little it disturbed him by tipping his goblet of wine in Tianhyu's direction as a salute before taking another sip from it.

"Perhaps now we could get down to just why you summoned us here, Lady Tianhyu," Torkki said. He *was* visibly disturbed by the threat against his younger brother. "Surely it was for more than a simple meal."

"I suppose you wouldn't believe me if I were to claim I just wanted to meet my long lost daughter, would you?" Tianhyu asked, smirking teasingly.

"If I did, my little brother would give me a long lecture on how to see through kitsune deceptions, I'm sure," Torkki replied, chuckling.

"It wouldn't be a complete lie if I said that," the elder kitsune vixen said, looking away. "I miss my mate much as I do my children, however. I know she is here to resolve the situation that keeps me from him." Here, she did look into her daughter's eyes, a dark glint in them. "I want in."

Kieras smiled. "I may be speaking out of turn, since my quest has now been put in the hands of the Ekholm Irregulars, but I doubt Mathis will challenge me on this one. Mother, we'll be pleased to have you."

While that first breakfast in Norre had certainly been interesting, Mathis found it frustrating that he couldn't get any privacy with Kieras afterwards. Kieras accompanied him wherever he went, but her mother and brother were apparently going to stay with her as much as possible as long as they were in town. In some ways, he was grateful for their company. Kieras definitely was, since they were able to point out numerous dangers to kitsune that Jobinh was unable – or unwilling – to mention on their earlier tour. They had also been able and quite willing to identify both the good and bad shops and storekeepers as they purchased fresh supplies for their stay in Norre. However, their presence prevented him from questioning Kieras on her unusual interest in the Everflowing Fountain.

He knew she hadn't been to Norre before – that much was obvious from her behavior – but Kieras clearly had known and recognized that fountain. Given how frequently they had been together since her arrival in Ekholm, there weren't many occasions when it could have come to her attention.

He had hoped that it would finally be possible to get Kieras alone late in the day, but her relatives followed them all the way back to the Kryskow House. Even as he slept, they stayed up the whole night conversing with her, and continued their discussions through the next day's breakfast. Now the trio of kitsune were accompanying Torkki and Mathis as they made their way to the Norrish Quartermaster's headquarters.

At least they wouldn't have to deal with Jobinh that day. He had been asked to report to the Norrish Elite's command for a temporary assignment until he could rejoin his unit. Torkki could no longer ignore the tension between Jobinh and the rest of them after the drunken outburst during Tianhyu's breakfast feast and ordered the separation.

"You really should try some non-traditional sword designs," Torkki was saying as they walked. "Your unarmed hand-to-hand skills are excellent, so maybe you'd do well with a pushing sword like a kattari."

"King Kazdri used a pushing sword after losing his arm," Tianhyu said wistfully, her thoughts obviously drifting to earlier times. "It was a modified pata – a gauntlet sword – which he wielded as both sword and shield. Both are weapons which were introduced by the Skorrans, but it is not unheard of for people to wield either one in other parts of the world."

Torkki nodded. "The Skorrans have developed many exotic forms of weaponry. The Vincour Republic has as well, though most of theirs are assassins' tools. Even the wulvers have their own weapons and fighting gear, though they tend to rely on their hands and teeth when the enemy gets too close. Fortunately our quartermaster's corps has studied under and consulted with masters in many such exotic weapons in their efforts to prepare us to face them. We should be able to find you something you can use, brother."

Despite Torkki's words, Mathis was not reassured. He had never felt any affinity with any sword, spear, or staff, regardless of how much talent he had fighting bare-handed or with his bow. As most of the 'exotic' weapons Torkki mentioned tended to be simple variants of those swords, spears, and staves, he had his doubts there would be anything for him.

Mathis ignored the remaining conversation until they started heading up the steps into the quartermasters' headquarters. Not much remained to be said, however, save for the occasional word of admiration for the numerous weapons – some hundreds of years old – which had been captured as trophies and mounted on the walls. Mathis saw examples of the aforementioned kattari and pata push-style swords, as well as many other types of blades – some he knew and others of types he had never even heard of. None of them, however, called to him the way the bow had.

The most intriguing weapons he saw were mid-ranged. These included various forms of chain whips, throwing weapons like the wulver bolas, and blowguns, for the most part. Mathis felt an almost instinctive dislike of the polearms – which made sense, as his even skill with a sword, however poor, was better than his skill with a spear. So far, he had yet to see anything he thought would work for him.

Kieras, however, saw a one-sided short sword with an elegantly curved blade and a slightly thickened spine mounted on the wall. "Oh, I like this sword." The patterns of the blade's steel told of the painstaking craftsmanship that must have been employed, blending layer upon layer to form the blade, but the looping hilt was cast solid, and yet melded to the blade as if one with it. The hilt was further decorated with a fox motif, which undoubtedly was what caught the kitsune vixen's eye in the first place.

"You should," another woman said, approaching from a nearby room. "It's a kitsune blade, Lady Kieras. A falcata, or as some call it a kopis. Most falcata were simply cast in iron, thanks to the intricate single-piece hilt design, so it's an outdated design. The kitsune who fought in the First Battle of Eskesa were all armed with those blades, however, forged with a steel process we no longer understand that makes it exceptionally strong and durable. Our blacksmiths have struggled for decades trying to duplicate the process, but while our steel-makers can make steel of comparable quality, nothing we can make today shares those swords' best properties."

Tianhyu sighed. "Forged long ago, with some of the oldest surviving pieces coming from the time of Inari. Not every kitsune could learn the skills needed to make effective illusory weapons in our early days, but we all could learn how to handle a sword. The falcata was our blade of choice, and we won many battles with them. Even we no longer remember how to create this type of steel, but an Eskesan dictator, seeing the coming threat of the Erixonites approaching, insisted we give him the secret of their construction. When we insisted it had long been lost, he confiscated many of those that remained. The same dictator's arrogance and incompetent attempts at manipulation eventually led to our exile. Many friends to the kitsune suffered and died because of his stupidity, and the city of Eskesa was destroyed."

"Well I, for one, am more than willing to return this particular blade to the kitsune people," the woman said, offering her hand in greeting with a rueful smile. "I am Zadari, your guide through the quartermaster's armory today. I was a bit surprised when your messengers arrived last night to inform me that not only was the entire staff of our Arbiter's Office composed of kitsune, but that three of you would be joining me today. I am more than willing to accommodate you and your kind, however."

"I've heard of you," Tianhyu said, accepting the hand. "Few women are permitted to serve as officers in the Norrish army, and none have risen to the heights you have. Thank you for your generosity; I'm sure my daughter will appreciate it."

"We have other kitsune weaponry retrieved from the ruins of Eskesa that you might be interested in, as well," Zadari said. "Several other kitsune blades like this one, battle fans, and more." She gave the three kitsune a look of reprimand. "If I had been told that your kind were in the city earlier, I would have made arrangements long ago."

"My people will be happy for their return," Tianhyu replied, adopting the diplomatic airs of a politician. "But today should not be centered on us. Our visitor from Ekholm is in need of a weapon, and we would be grateful if you could assist him."

Zadari turned an appraising eye on Mathis, which he endured by doing the same to her. She was built much like Kieras' human form – short and slight, but with well toned muscles that only hinted at their true strength. She was more than a decade his senior in age, and scars betrayed times when she had been just a bit too slow to defend herself unscathed, but she still looked youthful and energetic. In fact, had she had red hair instead of black and her scars been less visible, she would have looked like an older Kieras.

He couldn't help himself from asking the question. "You wouldn't happen to be a kitsune yourself, would you?"

Instantly Kieras, who had been glaring at the woman suspiciously herself, started sniffing the air, as did her mother and brother. Their reaction gave Mathis the answer before Zadari could reply, but the answer was interesting anyway.

"No, but you aren't the first to ask that question." Zadari glanced at Kieras and Tianhyu, giving them the same visual appraisal she had given him. "And I'm starting to see why."

"Yes, you're clearly human," Tianhyu said, but frowned. "There's something odd, though. You were not born in Ekholm, by any chance, were you?"

"No, but I do have family there," Zadari said. "My parents lived in Eskesa, and when it fell they fled here. But my aunt and two of my uncles lived in Ekholm. And a few cousins. When you next see Uncle Savard, you might want to let him know he has a niece."

Torkki grinned wryly. "I was disappointed when I first found out she was our cousin, but my wife is probably happy about it."

Zadari snorted. "You were too young for me, anyway, boy, but I like knowing I have family out there. Maybe I'll move to Ekholm – you seem more accepting of women taking prominent roles in the army, if Kieras is any indication. It's been a struggle to be accepted in Norre."

"Eskesa long had women in the army, and Ekholm takes its traditions from them," Torkki replied. "There were several defensive units formed exclusively of women armed with naginata, though rarely were they allowed on the front line of battle. If we don't allow women to become soldiers, Ekholm will never be able to find the manpower to defend itself even from simple bandit raids. A new army is about to be formed, and I'm sure Ekholm would be very glad to have an officer of your caliber to help form that army."

Zadari grinned. "Well, my current tour of duty is up in six months. I was just going to re-enlist, but perhaps I'll go to Ekholm instead." She turned to Mathis. "In the meantime, I still have duties to perform in service to Norre, such as helping an officer in our tributary ally properly equip himself."

Over the next several hours, Mathis was given a chance to briefly try out hundreds of different weapons. First came swords of numerous types, including a falcata like Kieras' new blade as well as various types of push-blades, but Zadari quickly saw he was unsuited for them. The experiment with pole-arms ended quickly when he very nearly sliced his own foot off with a naginata. He didn't look completely incompetent with the two or three axes they tried, but Mathis didn't like that idea; a proper war axe was two-handed, which would be awkward to carry alongside his bow.

As Zadari was looking for one of the fancier one-handed axes, Tianhyu saw a kitsune war fan that caught her attention. She pulled it out and began practicing with it.

Zadari watched the lethal dance with wide eyes. The fan flicked open to become a sharp, thin blade with each swing of Tianhyu's arm, then closed with a snap on the follow-through to form a solid blocking surface. When the exercise was over, she bowed to the kitsune vixen. "An exquisite performance, my lady. I never bothered to learn much about the use of the war fan, believing it to be a mere gimmick whose main value lay in its ability to hide in plain sight. After that demonstration, however, I now wish I had studied it more. I was intending to return all the kitsune weaponry we had in the stores to your people, and that one, in particular, seems to have chosen you. Take it with my blessing."

Tianhyu returned the bow gratefully. "Thank you, Lady Zadari."

"That was fascinating," Mathis said. "Could I try them out?"

"I spent well over a century of study to learn to use a war fan that well." Tianhyu shook her head apologetically. "It took several years to reach a level of competence until I felt comfortable using it on the battlefield, and several decades to master it. I was told that I was a fast learner. While I am perfectly happy to teach you this skill, I would recommend finding something that you might be able to learn more quickly."

While that eliminated the battle fan, it inspired Zadari to look into the truly exotic weapons; the ones "so unusual even I might not know how to use them," as she put it. They varied from the seemingly basic, such as the cudgels and shillelaghs, to the extremely intricate, such as a lantern shield. Nothing felt quite right to Mathis, but it was clear they were getting close.

Mathis tested the neko-te, a set of small needle-like blades covering his fingertips that eerily resembled the Claws of Inari as Tianhyu had described them. He found there were things he liked about them and things he didn't.

"This has the right feel, but it won't work with my bow. If I wore them from the start of combat, I'd cut my bowstring on the first shot. If I waited, it would take too long to try and put them on while enemies charged down my position."

"That was an assassination tool from the Vincour Republic's ninja," Zadari said. "It originally evolved from a tool used in their fishing industry. A lot of their assassination weapons evolved from fishing tools, actually, some of which work similarly. If you like neko-te, there's a whole series of similar weapons available...."

After quickly ruling out the closest non-Vincouran equivalent (the Skorrans' bagh nakh) as too unsafe and crude of a weapon, they began a prolonged period of examining other Vincouran ninja weapons, especially the many variations of shuko – a set of bands that went around the palms of each hand (usually strapped to a metal guard that went over the backhand and was tied down at the wrist) with claw-like hooks embedded in them. In addition to being weapons, they could also (theoretically) be used for scaling walls or – as originally designed – holding slippery-skinned fish from escaping. Again, Mathis liked them, but he was uncomfortable with having those spikes on the palm of his hand, and was worried about how they would affect his grip on his bow.

Some variants he liked more. The tekkokagi, for example, moved the blades to the back of the hand, where they could be used to rip or shred his enemies... but again, like with the neko-te, Mathis was worried about the damage they could do to his bowstrings. He was beginning to despair of finding anything that worked when Kieras hit upon a solution.

"These assassins' tools you're talking about – they're a great deal like claws, aren't they?" she asked.

Mathis considered the question carefully. Like the war fan, these were weapons Zadari had no training with, but he had picked the shuko up and right away felt he might have mastered the basics with them. He could certainly see the comparison – though perhaps the neko-te were even closer analogs – but many of the shuko and tekkokagi variants were more useful defensively.

"Perhaps on the attack," he grudgingly admitted. "Though the wrist guard makes something of a shield, as well. So, perhaps you could call it a claw and shield."

Kieras nodded, but clearly wasn't concerned about the differences. "I can see that. As a kitsune, even in my human form I have claws. I can retract my claws, however, when I don't want them to be sharp. Perhaps you could find a way to retract these claw-like blades when you don't want to use them?"

Before Mathis could reply, Zadari had taken the idea and run with it. "Yes, excellent! These claws work, but they're in the way because they can't be drawn or sheathed as easily as a sword blade. If we could fix that... I'll have a runner fetch the blacksmith! And maybe we'll want someone who's skilled in the crafting of leather armor to be a part of this, too. And a clockmaker might be needed for the mechanism. And maybe a jeweler for the fine details...."

Before too long, she had people running all over town collecting the necessary tools, materials, and people she needed to invent a new weapon. The first designs didn't quite work as planned – springs that allowed the blades to extend and retract, Zadari's original concept, proved far too delicate, and several additional designs for mechanically retractable claws proved too heavy or bulky to mount into the wrist guards. Finally, however, they hammered out a concept that worked – a weapon in two parts, with a removable set of connected blades that could easily slip and lock into and out of slots on an armored wrist guard. The guard was made of armor-grade tooled leather braced with iron supports. The iron parts of the guard would act both as shield and "hilt" for the clawlike blades. Once in place, another small iron bar could be used to lock the mechanism together. The process of assembling the two parts could take a few seconds, but that was still far less time than it took to put on the neko-te, it wouldn't interfere at all with Mathis' ability to use a bow when separated, it was relatively lightweight, and it had all of the advantages of the tekkokagi.

"You might even be able to scale walls with it, like with regular shuko," Zadari said. "But I'm not sure I would want to trust those few small iron pins to hold my weight if I tried."

"They won't," said Radek, the blacksmith who had made them. He was one of the three blacksmiths initially sent to Ekholm to replace Kuralt. He had been recalled to Norre months before the Knodelians had arrived (and replaced by a large team of journeymen who would be capable of producing cheap weapons in bulk far faster than one lone master blacksmith), and had been surprised and pleased to find himself back in the service of that town. "However, it's not complete. Those are dummy blades, at the moment. You can use them for practice, if you like. I'll replace those iron dummies with sharpened blades of folded steel in a couple days, and I'll also try replacing those iron pins with hardened steel, as well, though I still wouldn't trust even steel pins to hold you long enough to do much climbing. I think we can complete the final weapon in three days or so... assuming you can wait that long?"

"We'll be staying in Norre for some time, still, so there's no great rush," Mathis said.

Tianhyu was admiring the weapons silently, but once the man said he would be replacing the blades with steel her attention was immediately caught. "With sharpened steel blades, these would be much like the fabled Claws of Inari. I am very intrigued by these designs. May we have a copy when you are done?"

The blacksmith, the clockmaker, and the leather worker all glanced at each other and nodded in assent. "Of course, my lady," Radek said. "We'll be happy to present our plans to you once we are done. And to make others, if you so desire."

"And now all we have to do is figure out if they'll work as effectively as we think they will," Zadari said. "You said these were dummy blades were fit for practice – do you need them to copy for the final set?"

"These are merely prototypes, my lady," Radek said. "All I need in order to make the final product are the measurements needed to custom-fit Mathis' wrist, which I have already written down. Feel free to practice with those as much as you want."

She grinned. "Then, put them on, Mathis. Torkki, go grab a wooden practice sword. Everyone else, clear the practice ring. I want to see what those claws can do."

Mathis carefully strapped on the new weapons, barely watching out of the corner of his eye as everyone moved to circle the practice area. He first tested his flexibility – even without the blades his wrist would be slightly constrained, though not in any way that was likely to affect his bow work. Other than that the new weapon didn't bother his hands at all.

Once his wrists were strapped down, all that was left was to attach the blades. They were held together with a metal bar that kept each of the four claws perfectly aligned – all that he needed to do was line up the tang of their blades with the slot to hold them. They went in smoothly, and once the iron pins were locked down felt as solid as they would if the iron claws and the leather armor were all one piece. He had been a bit worried about the weight of the blades being too much, but he didn't notice the weight at all – they felt like a part of him he had never known was missing. Before his first practice session was over, Mathis knew he had found the first weapon since the bow that he would enjoy wielding.

Kieras had not known how much her promise to protect Mathis would drive her instincts wild until she saw him standing across from Zadari, wielding a weapon he had never used against the human woman's wooden sword. She knew he was perfectly safe, but he was nevertheless entering into a combat situation without her at his side. It felt... wrong.

"Focus on other things, daughter," Tianhyu said. Apparently, her internal struggle was showing on her face more than she believed. "If you can keep your mind occupied, your instincts will not bother you so much."

"Like what?" Kieras asked plaintively. "There isn't that much else to focus on, here."

"So, focus on the fight, just don't focus on the danger. How about think about suggestions for how Mathis can improve as a fighter," Torkki said. "This new weapon was partly made because of your suggestions, after all. It'd be nice if you helped him figure out how to use it."

"And the more confident you are in his ability to defend himself, the calmer your instincts will be when he is in combat," Tianhyu added. "An excellent suggestion. Your instincts may make you want to interfere, but if you focus on critiquing Mathis' abilities rather than the imagined danger he might be in were this practice a real fight, it will help both you and Mathis a great deal."

Kieras wasn't sure how much sense that made, but unable to think of other options she took their advice.

The sparring session began, and she found herself lost in the fight. For someone using a weapon that didn't exist mere hours earlier, Mathis didn't handle himself too badly. Her instincts were still bothering her, though, and she wondered whether he was trying to fight too defensively for someone using what looked to her as if it should be an offense first, last, and only-type weapon.

Perhaps she was focusing too much on the fight, however. It wasn't until she felt the tug of her mother's hand on her shoulder that Kieras realized that she had started to run into the practice ring, claws extended, after a particularly nasty-looking strike of Zadari's wooden sword slipped through Mathis' defenses.

"Perhaps that wasn't the best advice I could have given, daughter," Tianhyu said, a smile betraying her amusement. "Focus, instead, on telling me why you came to Norre. I know you were unaware of my presence here, so don't try to tell me that you were looking for me. I'm also pretty sure you weren't here just because of some diplomatic mission. And if you try to tell me you came to Norre just in the *hope* that you would find something useful for your quest...."

Kieras flushed slightly as her mother's unspoken threat lingered in the air. She hadn't experienced one of her mother's punishments since she was a toddler even by human standards, but she still remembered it all too well. "My apologies, mother. I really have not been trying to keep things a secret from you. I just haven't told anyone, yet."

"Well, you can start with me, at least," Tianhyu said, smirking.

"Then I'll tell you if you really need to tell anyone else this secret."

"I will be compelled by my oaths to inform Mathis, at some point," Kieras said. "Tell me, mother... what do you know about the Everflowing Fountain?"

Mathis found himself enjoying the practice with his new "claws." They might have been developed from an assassin's tool, which would hint at an offensive nature, but he was far more interested in their defensive prowess. They were excellent tools for trapping or redirecting an oncoming sword attack, and could be quite versatile when it came to setting up a counter-attack as well.

He was still very much a beginner with the weapon – Zadari was only trying the most basic of sword attacks against him – but it wasn't like many of his opponents would know how to respond to *his* weapons, either.

Towards the end of his sparring session, however, he found himself increasingly distracted by the animated discussion Kieras and her mother were having outside of the ring. They did not appear to be arguing, but they weren't happy about whatever it was they were talking about.

His inattention was pointed out rather forcefully when Zadari managed to get in a simple sword thrust he normally would have avoided, tapping his throat to indicate a "kill." He choked briefly with the blow, raising a hand to halt the spar until his breathing return to normal. There was a rather tense moment as Kieras broke off her conversation with her mother and spun to face him, her claws out to defend him from his attacker. Fortunately, with the spar over, Zadari had lowered her weapon and was no longer presenting a threat that would set the kitsune's instincts off any further.

"Well, that's the first mistake you've made so far," the quartermaster commented wryly once she was certain that he was undamaged. "If you practice enough, we might even get to sparring at full speed in a few weeks."

Kieras had largely recovered her composure, but nevertheless stepped into the ring to prevent the spar from resuming. "What happened?"

"It was my fault," Mathis said hoarsely. "I should have been able to stop that one, but I was distracted at just the wrong moment. What were you and your mother arguing about?"

"We weren't arguing," Tianhyu said, stepping into the ring as well. "Merely talking. I am afraid I lack the authority to help with a certain task my daughter suggests is your next step, but perhaps your new teacher does."

Zadari shrugged. "I'll help if I can, of course. What is it you need?"

"Are there any openings into the catacombs beneath the city?" Tianhyu said. "I remember a few were still around when I was but a kit my daughter's age, but I haven't looked since returning to the city."

She seemed a little startled at the question, but gave it a moment of thought. "I think there are a still few unburied entrances, but they have all been sealed for generations. Why?"

"We'll have to break open a seal, then," Tianhyu said. "We're seeking an ancient power that was last seen in the city upon whose ruins Norre was built, yet we have reason to believe has never been removed. Where else do you think it would reside undetected until now?"

Zadari nodded slowly. "Well... I can get you in, but the catacombs were sealed for a reason. I'd better get my gear."

XI. Lair of the Bunyip

Finding an unguarded entrance to the catacombs beneath Norre was not that difficult, as they were places that no one – not even the criminal elements – dared to go. The entrance seal bore an artistically painted tile that Tianhyu and Kieras insisted on preserving (largely because of the fox motifs surrounding it – something which made them sure that one of Norre's resident kitsune had been the artist). This caused a slight delay – chiseling it out carefully instead of merely breaking it down took some time, but that turned out to be easier than they had expected and only set them back an hour. There was initially some concern about being observed, but a passing guardsman didn't even question them once he saw Zadari and Torkki's presence. It wasn't illegal to enter the catacombs, after all – it was just physically impossible without breaking the seals, which any member of the Norre Elite had the authority to do.

The entryway into the catacombs wasn't large enough to pass through easily. Tianhyu and Daneyko changed into their fox forms to do so more comfortably. Kieras glared at Mathis as the fresh memory that he'd seen her transform into a human – and therefore into a naked human – rose in her mind. She chose to enter the same way as he, Zadari, and Torkki were forced to – on her human hands and knees.

"Why didn't you just change into a fox?" Mathis teased when they were through the wall.

"Oh, you'd just like that, wouldn't you?" Kieras muttered, clenching her fists angrily.

"Well, it's not like there's enough light in here to see anything," Mathis muttered. She had to admit he was right. Even as a human her night vision was slightly better than his, but she couldn't see much. She wasn't totally blind, however – she could just barely make him out, fussing around with a flint and stone to light one of their lanterns. The way he was fumbling around, he couldn't even see his own hands.

Still, it was a sore spot for her. "I swear, if you think I'll put myself into the position of having to change into my naked human form while you can still see me, you are *sorely* mistaken!"

"Daughter." Tianhyu's voice was positively dripping with exasperated amusement. "Please try to remember that your promises are binding... and that you'll need to stay in fairly close proximity to this human for the next year. That oath just now was hardly your brightest idea ever."

Kieras flushed, realizing what she had just done in her anger. She wondered if she was spending too much time in the company of humans – they could afford to make meaningless promises like she had without consequence. Before her trip to Ekholm, she was always extremely careful to avoid doing things like that, but it seemed to be a mistake she was making more and more.

Before she could ask her mother whether this was a common hazard of associating with normal humans, a spark shot up from Torkki's torch, The room was suddenly filled with light, making her forget everything she was about to say.

She wasn't entirely sure what she expected from the city catacombs. The idea of dimly lit corridors with nooks carved into the walls in which coffins or mummified bodies resided was perhaps what she pictured, but so far the only resemblance between her imagined catacombs and the reality underneath Norre's streets was the "dimly lit" part... and that mostly because the torches lining the walls were unlit.

They were in a small room with polished marble walls. The floor was dusty, but appeared to be tiled with marble as well. There was a small set of stalagmites and stalactites in one corner, obviously formed from an ancient leak in the ceiling, but it showed no other signs of how old the place really was.

"Not exactly how I pictured the infamously spine-chilling

catacombs underneath the ancient and magical city of Norre," Mathis said dryly. "At the very least, I was expecting to see some caskets or dead bodies lining the walls of what is supposed to be an underground burial chamber."

"I'm not sure about bodies," Torkki added. "But I did expect to see evidence of things living down here – mouse droppings, spiderwebs, that sort of thing. All I see is dust."

"The few surviving bodies the initial survey found were removed and interred elsewhere by the Norrish government before they sealed up the catacombs," Zadari said. "I've visited the cemetery they are now buried in. It's used as a small park, now. The founders who built on top of these ruins did not want them to lie here forgotten. Even if the bodies had been left undisturbed, though, we wouldn't see any here. There was only one chamber where any were found intact, deeper in. That expedition ended when that chamber flooded, and no one ever returned to continue mapping the ruins. We might find bodies further in, but these catacombs appear to have been used as more than just a graveyard."

"If it's anything like the catacombs beneath Eskesa," Tianhyu said, "the outer chambers were probably used for safe passage between the fortified barracks and the city walls during a bombardment, with an evacuation route and additional storerooms to hold supplies in the event of a siege. Many of the survivors from Eskesa's fall escaped by using those catacombs, just as the ancients must have thousands of years before."

"But what about spiders, rats, and the like, as Torkki mentioned?" Daneyko asked. "They usually thrive in places like this, but I can't even smell them."

Zadari and Tianhyu exchanged glances. "Well," Zadari said. "As I said before we left, there are reasons the founders sealed these chambers."

"Rats and insects don't come down here," Tianhyu said. "As it is, the fox part of me is telling the human part of me to leave already. Surely you can smell why, can't you, son?"

Kieras started sniffing the air, duplicating her brother who was trying to find just what it was their mother was talking about. There was something there she couldn't quite place, buried underneath a strong scent of stagnant water. It was a much different bouquet than the cold, fresh water of the Everflowing Fountain, leading her to decide that parts of the catacombs must still be flooded. There was something... peculiar mixed in with that scent. The dander of an aquatic animal's fur, mixed with oily skin like you might find on Kassia's walruses and similar creatures.

"What is *that?*" she asked aloud, her nose wrinkling in disgust.

"We don't know for sure when or where they came from, but sometime between the ancients abandoning the catacombs and the founders of Norre re-settling the area, a colony of bunyips moved in," Tianhyu said.

Kieras didn't know what a bunyip was but everyone else seemed to, and none of them looked happy. Mathis, in particular, looked unamused.

"You expect us to believe that?" he said incredulously. "You're claiming that the leaders of one of the most powerful nations in the world sealed up the catacombs they built their most important city around just because of rumors of *bunyips?*"

Tianhyu smirked. "Well, yes. I'd come up with a better lie than that."

Mathis stared at her for a moment, then shook his head. "You're too good of a kitsune. I can't tell when you're lying or not, I guess. You can't possibly be telling me the truth."

Kieras wasn't sure what to make of the exchange between Mathis and her mother, but ignored it for a bigger question. "Wait, hold on. What's a bunyip?"

"There's no such thing, that's what," Mathis insisted. "People have been trying to prove their existence for ages and have never found anything. If Norre had ever found evidence of one – like an entire underground city infested with them – someone would have said something."

"Unless there *was* no evidence," Zadari said. "Or at least, no evidence that could be presented as proof of the existence of bunyips. Tianhyu isn't lying – or at least, she is faithfully relaying to you what our government has said is the reason for closing the catacombs."

"And the people of Norre just accept it?" Mathis said. "That there are bunyips living underneath them, even though no one has been down in these catacombs for... well, for decades, at least."

"Centuries," Tianhyu corrected. "But I'm convinced it is the truth.

I lost three siblings to them, after all."

Mathis frowned. "And how do you know they were killed by bunyips?"

"Because there are some things even a kitsune won't lie about," Tianhyu said. "A brother would never, ever lie to their little sister about how and why their other siblings were killed. He witnessed their deaths, after all."

"I believe it," Zadari said. "I've seen some of the documents the government *didn't* release to the public about it. I could believe the government lying to the people about what was in these catacombs – all sorts of reasons they might want to do that, both benevolent and malicious – but lying to themselves?" She shook her head. "No. The old tale is true. There be bunyips here!"

Mathis was stricken speechless. Kieras herself was startled, but more at what her mother revealed of her family history than the existence of some mythical creature she had never heard of before, which led to hundreds of questions running through her head.

But if the bunyips did exist, that prompted more questions she might actually get an answer on. "Okay, I'll assume you're telling the truth," she said. "How do we recognize them, so I can know how to avoid them?"

"Ask a hundred people, you'll get more than a hundred answers," Mathis said. "Part of why I find it so unbelievable that there are bunyips down here is that I don't think anyone has really described a bunyip well enough to identify one."

"The creatures that killed my brothers were supposed to be larger than a horse," Tianhyu said. "My surviving brother described the one he saw as having the face of a bulldog, the tusks of a walrus, short fur as black as night, a horse's tail, and flippers for moving in the water. I was also told they tried to kill the thing – cut its head clean off – but it grew into two different bunyips, just like a starfish can when it's cut apart... though far, far faster."

Mathis sighed. "If we really are to believe this nonsense, I should point out that they are said to be generally peaceful, but will defend their territory against intruders violently. And heaven forbid if you threaten their offspring in any way – then they will chase you for all of eternity."

"Personally, I've always thought – from the stories – that they were shape shifters," Torkki suggested. "Not as good as kitsune, by any stretch of the imagination, but good enough to change parts of their bodies into whatever they need – fangs, flippers, or anything else."

"Whatever they are, they're fierce fighters," Zadari said. "Thousands of soldiers and dozens of kitsune were lost in battle with them before the catacombs were ordered sealed."

"Well, then," Kieras said, "let's try our best to avoid them... whether they're real or not."

Mathis sighed. "Well, if they really exist, and if they really do live down here, that might be a bit difficult. We're looking for the source of the fountain – a pool of water, most likely. Bunyips are supposed to live in pools, swamps, river beds, and any other form of watering hole."

"Well, then, is there anything that might distract them – give us a chance to cross their territory safely?"

"Nothing I know of," Tianhyu said.

"Nor I," Zadari replied.

"I'd assume they might be distracted by food, but we don't know what they eat... or even *if* they eat," Mathis said. "I think I'm going to continue hoping that I'm right, and that they don't exist, because if they do...."

Well, if there really are bunyips lurking in these catacombs, they're certainly the cleanest mythical horror I've ever heard of, Mathis thought, still astonished at how polished and unsoiled the undisturbed rooms were. A few had leaks, which could erode the walls and ceilings to more resemble the surface of a cave than polished stone, but most rooms looked like they had been inhabited only weeks before at most. Every time they went from one of the limestone-encrusted rooms into one of the fresh rooms, it struck him how far beyond "unusually good conditions" the catacombs were for ruins of that age. He was starting to buy into the idea that *something* unusual inhabited the catacombs, bunyips or not.

Certainly, something had caused the Norrish government to seal these ruins. With that in mind, Mathis was on high alert for traps, hazards, and anything that might possibly be living, but so far had seen no evidence that so much as a tripwire had been laid. He was not expecting the first sign that they weren't alone to come from one of his traveling companions, however.

"There's something in front of us," Kieras said, frowning. "On the other side of that wall."

"What do you mean?" Torkki asked. He had been about to pry open a door that had been rusted shut along the wall she was pointing to, but stopped when she spoke.

"I... I don't know," Kieras said. "But... I have this really odd feeling. It doesn't quite hurt, but it feels like there's a barrier in front of me that I shouldn't pass."

Tianhyu smiled on one side of her mouth. "That sounds like the magic binding your promises coming into effect. There's something on the other side of the wall that if you encounter it, a promise will be broken."

Kieras' eyes widened. "I'm wearing illusory clothing. There were several relics from the ancient city Norre was built around that can dispel kitsune illusions. Jobinh mentioned several of them while he was giving us our tour. "

"Perhaps it's a fortunate thing, then, you made that rash promise, earlier," Tianhyu suggested. "We now have a way to detect such things, as the magic sealing your promise will warn you before you can touch them."

"Nothing to worry about, then," Torkki said, starting to pry the door open again. "Just watch where you walk and what you touch while we go through these rooms and you should be fine."

Kieras nodded slowly. "Well, that's a good thing, I guess, but... why is it moving?"

Mathis' eyes widened. "Moving? Torkki, stop!"

The warning came too late. The knife Torkki was using proved to be quite effective at breaking the lock on the door, forcing it open and making it impossible to latch closed again.

Mathis found himself being carried away from the door as Kieras picked him up and started running. Judging by her face she wasn't in complete control of her own actions, but he had only a moment to assess her behavior before something crashed through that broken door.

It was smaller than a horse, though not by much, but it did have a bulldog's face, a horse's tail, flippers, and tusks. It also had claws on the front feet that look like they belonged on a lion, porcupine-like quills covering its rear, and a great deal of bulging muscle for its size. And it seemed rather angry, charging straight at Tianhyu the moment it got through the door. That was all he was able to see before Kieras started dragging him away again.

"Let me down!" he protested.

Wild-eyed, Kieras shook her head nonsensically. "Must protect you – swore an oath!"

Mathis took a deep breath, trying to figure out how to reason with someone who was compelled by magic to be unreasonable. "I can protect myself far better if I'm on my own two feet, you know. We should be far enough away for you to let me down."

Kieras didn't seem to break free of her magically-induced haze entirely, but she did let him down to the floor. Mathis glanced over at the fight to assess the situation as best as he could from a distance.

An illusory sword Daneyko was attempting to wield dissolved on contact with the beast. Tianhyu was wounded with multiple bloody claw and tooth marks decorating her forearms. Zadari was disarmed, and Torkki was slumped unconscious against the door he had just opened.

And all that had happened in less than ten seconds.

"I know I'm the better archer," Mathis said, pulling Kieras close enough he could talk into her ear without attracting the attention of the creature. "But I don't think I've ever asked – can you use a bow and arrow?"

"I... yes," she said.

He handed her his longbow and quiver of arrows, then started to don his new "claws." He still lacked anything better than practice-grade blades for it, but it was all he had to work with.

"Well, you can't approach that thing because it disperses magic. I have to go in there—"

"No!" she snapped, her eyes getting wild again.

"But you can still protect me with that bow," Mathis continued, ignoring her outburst. "I have to do something. We cannot abandon our friends and family to that thing, and even if we could it'll start chasing us once it's finished them off. We will not be able to outrun it forever. I've got an idea, but you have to let me fight that thing." He paused. "Don't let your oaths conflict, now. The best way to protect me right now is to let me fight the thing on my own terms. Remember that, and you should have no problem maintaining your vows."

"I... okay," Kieras said.

"Good. Then here's the plan...."

Well, this isn't good, Tianhyu thought wryly. Her arms were shredded, she was dazed from when she hit the floor during the initial attack, and her kitsune magic wasn't working. Something her last surviving brother hadn't told her about the bunyip, it seemed, was that it disrupted magic completely. She could feel hers coming back, though. In a few minutes, she might even be able to use her transformative magic again, even if her illusory magic and foxfire abilities were unlikely to recover until the next morning. But she would not be able to do anything until that creature was out of the room.

Torkki was down and out, and had been from the start of the battle. He'd hit his head, but she didn't know how bad it was – he might be fine in a moment, or he might already be dead. Daneyko had tried, but he was only armed with illusory equipment that simply dissolved as it got close to the beast. His bare claws also seemed to turn into more human fingernails during the fight. Zadari had tried to wound the beast with her sword, but even her steel blade proved ineffective as the claws of the beast knocked it away. And who knew where Kieras and Mathis were – her daughter was driven by the magic of her promises to run away and take the young man with her. Usually, such a promise only affected instincts, which could be overcome if the situation was drastic enough, but it appeared even the magic in her body was compelling her on this one.

Zadari, not one to give up even after having been disarmed, was attempting to engage the beast bare-handed. Her hand was injured after throwing a punch at its head, but otherwise she was... well, surviving. She seemed fast enough and flexible enough to avoid the creature's strikes, but it was only a matter of time before she moved too slowly, or slipped, or guessed the wrong attack, and then it would be over. Tianhyu was disappointed to see that her son had frozen up when his weapons proved ineffective, unlike the human woman, but she didn't blame him. She hadn't exactly been able to put up a real defense, either, once she realized her magic was completely ineffective.

"Zadari, back!"

It was Kieras' voice. Evidently she had managed to overcome her instincts and the magical drive to keep her promises. Or at least had figured out a way around them. Or maybe had managed to get Mathis into a safe place far away, fulfilling the conditions of her promises and allowing her to return. However she managed it, she had returned to the fight.

Zadari leapt back, and immediately an arrow shot itself into the head of the beast. It pierced the creature's hide, sticking under the skin, but that seemed to be the full extent of the damage. The arrow had, however, attracted both the creature's attention and its ire.

"That's it, beastie," Mathis taunting, standing at Kieras' side. "Follow me."

Mathis had some pieces of broken rock from one of the more cave-like rooms that he must have liberated from wherever Kieras had taken him to. He started throwing them at the creature in a pattern that must have been deliberately designed to aggravate the creature. Once the beast was really mad he started running, the beast charging straight at him. He stopped, watching the beast come. Tianhyu almost couldn't watch – the way this was going, the creature would rip the boy in two before he could do anything.

A twang alerted Tianhyu to the fact that it was her daughter, not the master archer, who had sent that first arrow into the beast... and now sent a second. The creature started to change direction mid-charge, seeking out the new threat, but its momentum caused it to stumble. Mathis stepped towards it, stabbing low with his "claws" and surprisingly piercing the beast's tough hide with his iron blades. His other hand followed, stabbing at the top of the beast, with his palms upwards.

It must have taken a lot of effort. Mathis had to use his lower arm – braced by his entire body – as a lever, pulling his upper arm with all his strength and rolling himself onto the floor to allow the beast's own momentum to aid him. It still took a superhuman effort, and he probably hurt himself doing it, but Mathis managed to flip the creature over his body and send it tumbling back into the room it came from.

He rolled back to his feet, wincing as he did, but despite the inevitable injuries he moved as fast as he could to stand up and slam the door shut. He took out a knife and wedged it into the corner of the door, sealing it closed. Kieras ran in a moment later, carrying several large stones likely broken off of a stalagmite. She slammed the stones down in front of the door, bracing it shut. It didn't seem to matter –

after almost a full minute of tense waiting, it became clear that the creature would not challenge the soundness of the door.

Mathis whispered something to Kieras, who promptly went to check on Torkki while he turned towards Tianhyu. Daneyko finally came to his senses, and started rushing to her side as well. Mathis was intercepted along the way by Zadari. His older cousin asked for medical supplies before patting him on the back encouragingly and joining Kieras at Torrki's side. Zadari was the only one among them skilled with medicine, and Torkki looked to be in the worst shape after the battle.

"Good job," the weapons master said as she moved off. "That was a feat worthy of those weapons."

He merely nodded to acknowledge the compliment before continuing on to the kitsune matriarch. Mathis bent down, joining with Daneyko to help her to her feet. "Well," he said slowly. "Maybe, *just* maybe, I believe you about the bunyips now."

Tianhyu's laughter was a welcome sound, indeed.

Mathis was relieved – his brother was alive, and everyone else had survived as well – but now that the battle was over, he had some decisions to make. After Torkki regained consciousness (though he wasn't quite right even after waking up; his eyes wouldn't focus and he was having trouble with loud noises), the group of six had to decide whether to keep going or to go back and accept defeat. Kieras was adamant about going forward, but the threat of the bunyips held most of the others back. Mathis was willing to continue, despite the threat, but thought that maybe they should leave until the wounded recovered and return when they were better prepared. Daneyko just wanted to stop altogether. His sister might have a quest to complete that required a vaki, but certainly there were easier ways to get to vaki in the world. Zadari felt the others could do what they wanted, but she was planning to return home on her own. She had helped them get into the catacombs, and the adventure of exploring them initially sounded fun, but she hadn't intended to spend what might be days helping them fight their way through these seemingly invincible bunyips.

Tianhyu was still hurt, but her kitsune abilities had already dealt with the worst of the bleeding. She was the first to give full support to Kieras' position.

"There's something you all haven't considered," she said. "We now know the location of this one bunyip, but there are probably others – many others. For all we know, they're now behind us, blocking our exit. We won't survive another battle with them, and the one we did see didn't seem willing, or able, to negotiate."

"Not the best position to be in," Mathis said. He was trying to be the voice of reason, but he had to admit the battle had shaken him as much as any of the others. He was also in serious pain – his back hurt severely, as did his legs, and it felt like he had pulled both of his arms out of their sockets – but how could he complain when Tianhyu was bleeding out in front of them and Torkki appeared concussed? "Which is why I was suggesting we leave and come back later. We need to be in better shape if we want to make it through these halls alive. There's also a lot of equipment that would give us an advantage – I could get the steel blades for my claws, and you kitsune could grab real swords, like Kieras' falchion, that wouldn't dissolve on contact. We didn't come down here properly prepared for that kind of battle, but it looks like we'll need to fight our way to where we're going."

"Ah, but we do have one major advantage," Tianhyu said. "We have someone who is capable of sensing bunyips from a distance. It is only with her help that we can be certain to avoid any of the creatures. And she's the one who is insisting on going forward."

"With or without the rest of you," Kieras chimed in, smirking.

Mathis could argue the point – he could exploit at least three oaths she had taken to follow his lead and return to the surface – but he wasn't going to argue the point. The fact that no-one else had clued in on this (at least, no-one who said anything; he was sure Tianhyu would have thought about that, for one) made it his call. He still believed that the sensible thing was to retreat and resupply... but then again, the sensible thing was also to not antagonize your kitsune guardian who would be your shadow for the next year. He remained silent.

That settled the debate. With those terms, the rest of them had to keep going. Zadari, as the one who had the most familiarity with Norre and therefore the best chance of figuring out where the source of the fountain was, resumed her lead as a guide, but now Kieras joined her up front as a bunyip detector.

*

The continuing journey through the catacombs proved to be more of a maze than any of them had accounted for. It was hard to tell time underground, but Mathis estimated they had spent three days of wandering through the ruins. They often had to take significant detours to avoid bunyips before retracing their steps in an effort to head in the right direction. Once her magic had recovered sufficiently to do so, Tianhyu had transformed into a fox for the remainder of the journey – as she explained, Inari created the kitsune to give his daughter the ability to survive a lethal wound, but it came at a price. The most effective form of a kitsune's accelerated healing required a transformation into the opposite form of the one that was injured, and she had a lot of healing she needed to do for her human form.

At last, however, they finally found what Mathis believed was their goal. A large, clear pool, filled with fish (that proved to be predatory fish – Daneyko had almost lost a finger when he tried to catch one) and a curiously placed "natural" bridge to an island in the center of the grotto. This was the source of the Everlasting Fountain, they could tell... and now there was proof it was an artificial fountain – a set of large, ancient clay pipes, covered in what Mathis thought might be magical runes, proved to be the mechanism through which it functioned. The runes didn't seem to be the source of the purity of the water, however. Just by looking at the lake, Mathis could tell it was the same water as he had seen in the fountain above.

"Well, we're here," Zadari said. "Now... why are we here? I thought there was supposed to be some sort of creature of myth other than the bunyips inhabiting this place."

"There is," a soft voice said, very quiet and barely drifting over the water. "Come to my island and we shall talk."

That startled Zadari, but Mathis took the unexpected voice in stride. Mystical beings of power like the haltija were expected to be capable of hearing even the slightest of whispers. Still, it gave him enough pause to start going through everything they had said during their trip through the catacombs, making sure they had said nothing to insult the creature.

Kieras was completely unfazed. Before Mathis had even noticed her move, she was already thirty feet down the length of the bridge.

"Let's go!" he called, rounding up the others to follow. They managed to catch up with Kieras when she was halfway to the island.

By the time they had all finished crossing the bridge, the speaker made herself known.

"Hello there!" the haltija chirped.

Mathis blinked. "Well... um, I'm not sure what I was expecting, but... uh...."

Kieras looked unsurprised, but Mathis and the others certainly hadn't expected the haltija to look like this. It was just a tiny, adult human female with unnaturally colored hair – blue, in this case. Mathis had expected some sort of massive entity, worthy of a reputation as the guardians of nature, not some tiny faerie-like girl.

"I am a haltija of the water, a veden vaki as you now call us," the little blue-haired being said, giggling. "I haven't seen a living human being in almost two millennia, or anything else other than a bunyip, so I'm very happy to meet you all."

"Haltija of the water," Kieras said formally, bowing at the tiny mystical being. "The haltija formerly of the Byvald Mountain has recommended you to me. I am in need of your assistance, to heal a man of what we believe is a poison beyond my abilities to heal."

The vaki danced around slightly as it spoke. "I've been bored out of my mind for two thousand years. I'll gladly help, but could you perform a task for me first... please?"

Kieras started to reply, but Mathis got his answer in before her.

"This young woman is under my command," he said. "Before I allow anyone to commit to doing you any favors, I must know what they are."

The vaki looked at him curiously. "You look familiar. What is your name, child?"

Considering the being in front of him was, by her own admission, more than two thousand years old, Mathis did not take any offense at being called a child. He was, however, surprised that she thought she recognized him. "My name is Mathis of Ekholm," he said, sketching a clumsy bow. "And, as a human being of just two decades, not two millennia, I assure you we have never met. Your name, milady?"

The vaki giggled again. "My kind have no names, really. We are so rare that, when dealing with humans, we are usually considered the haltija of whatever we choose to be the guardian of. Two thousand years ago, however, many of the humans who lived here called me Ainali, which would be Spirit of the Water in their tongue. A foolish name, since I am no spirit, but arguing with them never worked."

"Ainali, then," Mathis said. "What boon are you asking of my kitsune retainer?"

"There it is again," the vaki insisted. "Are you sure you didn't live here, say, two thousand years ago?"

"If so, I certainly don't remember it," Mathis said, trying very hard not to annoy the creature. "It was at least nineteen hundred and eighty years before I was born."

"And I'll assure you he looked nothing like he does now just ten years ago. He was an ugly child," Torkki said, giving a teasing smirk at his younger brother. Mathis ignored it, considering Torkki still wasn't quite all there after the bunyip knocked him loopy.

"Ah, well." The vaki sighed, then laughed. "That's a good thing, I suppose. The person I'm thinking of meant well, but he was so arrogant and manipulative. He made horrible mistakes... though he did great works, as well. He had kitsune retainers, too, and wouldn't allow them to make any promises without asking him first."

"Then he was smart, since kitsune are magically bound by their promises even if they later get turned against them."

"Smart, he was," the vaki said. "I know all about magical bindings. I've been bound to this pool for two thousand years thanks to his magic. I'd really like to see the sun again, someday."

"Bound magically?" Mathis said, startled. "What did you do that would cause the people who lived here to imprison you for two thousand years?"

"Oh, I was not imprisoned – not intentionally," Ainali said. "I was being protected. Two thousand years ago, when the people of Vikstad—"

"Vikstad?" Zadari repeated. The expectant curiosity on her face was plain, and her eyes almost sparkled with enthusiasm. "Where was Vikstad?"

Ainali looked at her in bemusement. "Do humans no longer even know the name? Vikstad was this city, the capital of the nation of Viklund, which ruled these lands two thousand years ago."

"Norre was built on the ruins of Vikstad, then," Zadari said. "Although no one now knows the names of those ruins, nor that of the nation of Viklund. We respect them greatly, however – many of their ancient roads are still in use today, and several of our cities are built on their ruins." She paused. "I must admit, no one has ever thought to ask the vaki what they knew of these lands, though that could be because we haven't known where any of your kind were. Our historians would love to interview you, though, I'm sure."

"I am always glad to impart knowledge," Ainali said, a smile on her face as she bowed to the human woman. "As a young haltija, I settled into the man-made fountain that this lake feeds. The people of Vikstad worshiped my kind, and so welcomed me to their city with open arms.

"But then a great calamity came. I still do not know exactly what was happening – I paid little attention to the world of humans outside of Vikstad's walls – but whatever it was threw the entire city into a panic. The people of Vikstad feared for my safety. I could always retreat to this underground pool whenever I wanted privacy, but there were ways my fountain could be used to compel me to appear.

"I was cautioned that I needed to hide here, and they would protect me from being compelled to work for Vikstad's enemies. They had their mages create the guardian beast they named the bunyip, which they released into my waters to protect me should their enemies attempt to enter the catacombs. The last human I saw was a mage, who placed the runes that would prevent me from being able to travel to the fountain through those pipes leading to the surface, before he released the bunyips to their eternal guard. I was told they would return when the crisis was over, and I would then be released.

"When no one returned after many years, it became obvious that I was forgotten at best. As all of Viklund has faded from human memory, I must assume I wasn't the only thing forgotten in this city."

Mathis glanced at the rune-strewn pipes. "I thought those runes were simply replacing the mechanical pumps most fountains now use. I didn't realize they had nothing to do with the fountain's function..."

"Well, they aren't there only to keep me from entering my fountain," the vaki said, erupting into the giggles. "*Most* of those runes have a purpose other than for my 'protection.' Many are, in fact, to replace your mechanical pumps. You need to study your magical runes better if you didn't know that."

Mathis had a niggling feeling he knew what it was the haltija wanted to ask of them. "Ainali, there are no teachers of magical runes anymore. Knowledge of the practice of magic has left humanity." He paused. "We have no way of removing the rune imprisoning you here."

To his surprise, her smile didn't falter. "Well, that's a shame, but I'm not so worried about that. It should be easy enough for me to re-open the door to my fountain from the other side – I just can't do it from here." She turned to Kieras. "Tell me, kitsune – just what is it that you need my help doing?"

"There is a man my father has sworn service to who was poisoned," Kieras said. "My mother was able to preserve his life with our kitsune powers, but if any knew that this man was still alive they might target her. With her dead he, too, will die. So, my mother has had to flee from her home – leaving my father behind – for her own protection. If this man were healed, my mother would be able to return home. This man may be the only solution to a crisis that has affected the lives of my parents, my siblings, and myself, so I need the help of someone who is capable of healing him. It will take some travel to reach him, however, as he cannot be brought here."

Ainali nodded slowly. "You were able to pass the bunyips to reach me here, the first creature of any kind to do so in two thousand years. Yet I sense many of you were hurt in the process...." She briefly touched Tianhyu, Torkki, and finally Mathis. The aches from Mathis' dislocated shoulders and strained back vanished in an instant, while Torkki's eyes lost that concussed look. It was harder to see the change in Tianhyu, at first, because she was still in her fox form, but shortly after she was touched she skillfully transformed into her human form to examine her now scarless arms. "Do you think you may be able to leave this place safely?"

Mathis nodded, still amazed at how quickly their wounds had been healed. "We found a way to avoid the bunyips. It should be possible for us to leave safely, although it may take several days of travel and we're running low on supplies. We only intended to be down here for a day or two, at most, and it's been five days already."

"That should be okay," Ainali said. Haltija were known to be carefree, bubbly creatures, but even so her continued giggles had Mathis wondering if the thousands of years stuck underground had damaged her mind. "I don't need to eat food like you humans do, and I have more than enough water here for your needs. But if you wish my aid, then I will need your aid in ending my imprisonment. I will need you to take some of my water to the surface, and pour that water into the fountain above. If you do that, I can travel to the surface and break the magical barrier from the other side of the fountain. Then I will be free to help you as much as you desire."

Kieras looked to Mathis before answering. He appreciated that – he had asserted his authority before she could answer, earlier, in order to protect her from herself, but he had worried she would take offense to that and become obstinate. If she was now looking to him for permission, though, then she hadn't been too annoyed. He gave her a nod to let her know he would rely on her judgment in this case.

Kieras finally bowed before the vaki. "We would be honored to assist you, Ainali. And thank you."

XII. By Claw and Arrow

It felt very weird to be back in Kassia after almost a year of living in Ekholm and Norre. Kieras wondered if it felt even stranger for her mother and brother, who hadn't been back in decades, and suspected it did. Still, they were back, and much faster than she had expected.

The mission Mathis had ostensibly been sent to Norre to accomplish was completed without him even being present. While she, Tianhyu, Torkki, Mathis, Daneyko, and Zadari were crawling around the catacombs trying to reach the surface, Teslak found himself the only person available to represent Ekholm to the Norrish Court on the day of their appointment. It worked out for the best – as a wulver, he made a rather dramatic impression on what Ekholm could bring to the Hegemony.

In the long run, it turned out that Ekholm's choice of representative didn't matter. Norre's defense of its tributary powers were a significant expense, so any which felt ready to enter the Hegemony in a more proper fashion (even in stages, as Ekholm intended) were given immediate acceptance. Norre would still provide the training and the necessary support for Ekholm to build its own armies, and Ekholm's own transition plan was amended so that there would be no staged reduction of tribute as Savard originally proposed. Under the new proposal, a Norrish auditor would ensure that the funds Ekholm would have otherwise spend in tribute were instead used on building up Ekholm's defenses. After a time, Ekholm would then be required to maintain enough surplus forces to assist the allied powers in any military venture, as all full members did.

With the treaty complete, a veden vaki recruited, and her mother found, they no longer had any need to stay in Norre. After a short rest to recover from the trip through the catacombs, Mathis, Kieras, Ainali, Tianhyu, Daneyko, and the other Ekholm Irregulars left for Kassia. Neither Torkki nor Zadari could join them, as they were once again under the command of the Norrish army. They had been busy re-sealing the catacombs well enough to prevent escaping bunyips when Kieras had left.

It took some time to arrange a method for transporting Ainali. She could not move far from her waters, so they had to be brought with her. Because of her small size, she wasn't able to move very rapidly on her own even without that issue, making it quickly apparent she would need to be carried for the entire trip to Kassia. They had arranged to take her and some of her water in Daneyko's merchant cart, which also carried most of their food, camping supplies, weapons, and other equipment. It made returning to Kassia far easier for Kieras than leaving it had been, especially when they discovered the sentries that usually guarded the roads into Kassia had been withdrawn. This proved fortuitous for Kieras and her companions, though questions about where those sentries had gone lingered.

They had yet to enter the actual city. The remains of the old manor house outside of the walls, where King Kazdri was hidden, were still unguarded. That was their first destination, and would be their headquarters for a while. The ruins could still be seen by passers-by on the road, including members of the Kassian Guard, and secrecy remained paramount. They had needed to wait for nightfall, hiding in Daneyko's cart until they had slipped into the manor.

It was cold – the long winters of Kassia were running even later than normal – but they couldn't afford a large fire for fear of alerting people passing the ruins to their presence. As might be expected of long-abandoned ruins, the manor house was also dirty, wet, and, in general, uncomfortable.

They kept themselves busy, at least. Ainali's water had been carried north in a bladder, which was fine for her transport, but she needed to be in constant contact with it in order to heal – or even diagnose – Kazdri's ills. They unpacked a shallow bowl they had stored on Daneyko's cart, carefully making sure that it had not been damaged during their journey and poured Ainali's water into it. When that was done, it was decided Kazdri probably could use a good sponging down. He had been kept relatively clean over the years, but the dust and grime accumulated by such a long sleep should still be washed away before he was awakened. Not wanting to use up Ainali's limited supply of water, they had to find something else with which to wash the sleeping king. Tianhyu found an ancient well, but the stagnant water in it was unusable. Ainali's mystical abilities were able to clean it, but that took some time.

Finally, however, the vaki was ready to perform the treatment, and it would start with an overall diagnosis. Kneeling in the ceramic bowl that they had rested on Kazdri's chest, Ainali made quite the sight tracing over Kazdri's features with glowing hands. It didn't take long before she was ready to make a pronouncement.

"As you suspect, he was poisoned," she said. "I can heal him, but I will need you to awaken him, first."

Tianhyu grimaced. "While it is my magic that is keeping him in this state, I cannot awaken him alone. I need Lahti here for that."

"Someone will have to fetch him, then," Mathis said.

"He should show up on his own at some point," Kieras suggested. "Father checks Kazdri regularly to be sure he is safe... and that you are still alive, mother."

"Do you really want to camp out here for days, perhaps even weeks, until he decides to show up?" Mathis said, blowing a cloud of his breath out demonstratively to point out how cold it was.

"Not really," she admitted.

"I'll go and get him," Tianhyu said. "I know the tunnels that connect this place and Kassia just as well as he does. I can go in unseen and be back before morning."

Mathis shook his head. "Not a good idea. You are a target – if someone saw you before Kazdri is awakened...."

"They still don't know that he's alive," Tianhyu said. "And even if they did, no one is aware of my part in keeping him alive."

"You were sent away from your mate and exiled from your country for several decades solely because of the threat that someone could connect the dots if you were present. It is possible that in the intervening years someone has discovered Kazdri's body lying here, and left it to set a trap for you," Mathis said, glaring at her defiantly. "Do you really want to make all of that time and effort meaningless by rushing things in the last minute, when there are safer options out there?"

"Safer options?" Tianhyu replied. "Who would be safer? Kieras?"

Kieras blinked. "Well, why not me? I know those tunnels, too. I could do it!"

"Because they're looking for you," Mathis said. "You would be an even worse choice. The inhabitants of the city know who you are, so you can't possibly travel through these halls anonymously."

"I can use my illusory powers to make myself seem like someone else," Kieras pointed out. "Mother could, as well."

"I didn't say it wasn't possible for one of the two of you to manage this," Mathis replied. "Just that there are safer options, here."

"Who, then?"

Mathis smirked and then pointed over at Daneyko. The male kitsune was lounging underneath some heavy blankets, ignoring the brewing argument as he tried to keep warm. "I understand that the tunnel was partially blocked, so at best only a kitsune in fox form could pass through it. Well, there happens to be a kitsune who can travel through that tunnel as a fox, but who if he is recognized would have a perfect excuse for being there. He can believably claim to have no knowledge of what's been going on in Kassia. Surely Lahti would trust him at least as much as he trusts the two of you."

Kieras grinned over at her older brother. The others turned to look at him, too, until he started to notice all their stares. "What?" he said. "Oh, no. Me? I was just starting to warm up!" He sighed miserably. "I forgot how bad winter was up here."

"Go on, Daneyko," Kieras said, laughing. "You were the first of us to leave – it's only fitting that you're the first of us to see him again. And don't let the snow and ice fool you – it's springtime in Kassia."

Daneyko rolled his eyes, but with no further protest than a sigh got up and stretched out his legs. "Fine. But someone will have to show me through the tunnels."

"I'll show you to the entrance," Tianhyu said. "After that, it's all a straight line to the exit."

Mathis frowned. "Perhaps I should join you. You might be tempted to take Daneyko's place, otherwise."

"Now why would I do that?" Tianhyu said. "What you've said has made perfect sense, and—"

"Okay, now I know I need to join you." Mathis laughed, rolling his eyes. "You wouldn't be deflecting like this if you didn't have something planned. Besides, I'd like to know where this tunnel is, myself." He turned his eyes first to Kieras, frowning, then to Teslak. "You're in command until I return," he said to the wulver. "Establish a perimeter, but make sure you stay out of sight. Kieras, work with him – he may need your help to create illusions that can conceal our people."

She raised an eyebrow at him. "You aren't concerned I'll try and slip through despite your sending Daneyko?"

Mathis snorted. "You've sworn an oath that places you under my command. I know you well enough to know I can trust you to follow orders, especially when confronted with common sense. Your mother, on the other hand...."

Tianhyu harrumphed in mock disgust, getting Kieras to laugh. "If you aren't back in an hour, we'll assume mom drugged you and send a rescue party. Daneyko, if you aren't back by morning, I'll come after you whatever Mathis orders. Good luck!"

Both of them saluted mockingly, in what almost appeared to be a coordinated gesture. Kieras rolled her eyes. She hadn't been that bad, had she?

"If he's not back by morning, I'll lead a rescue mission. But that's not going to be necessary, because he knows to just get in and get out, right?" he asked, smirking at Daneyko with a warning clear in his voice.

"Uh, right," Daneyko said. "I just want to get this over with, anyway."

Mathis, Tianhyu and Daneyko all left, their teasing banter following them along the way. Kieras watched them go, and then turned to Teslak expectantly.

The young wulver glanced over at her, cocking his head. He was clearly surveying her. From his body language he was trying to decide what to do with her. Finally, he said, "Doell, Raux, come with me. Milady, we'll be back once we've figured out where along the perimeter we might most need your services."

"I'll be ready," she said.

Teslak nodded. "Good." With that, he and the other two wulvers bounded off.

Kieras headed over to her baggage that had been dropped off near Kazdri's body. Most of the illusions the wulvers might need required some element like a twig, leaf, or nut to work, but with the winter snows it would be pretty hard to find them. She had thought to pack a selection of such debris before leaving Ekholm, although she couldn't remember exactly where in her baggage she had stored them.

Ainali hopped down from her perch in the bowl of water to watch her work. "You've certainly made some interesting friends in your journey."

Kieras started, reminded of the vaki's presence for the first time since Mathis and her mother had started arguing. "I suppose so."

"Well, let's see," Ainali said, continuing to watch her. "You met my sister haltija, who sent you to me. You met the wulvers – who, let me tell you, were quite reclusive in my day...."

"They still are, today," Kieras said. "Although the ones in Dahlberg seem to be opening up somewhat."

"And then there are your brother and mother," Ainali continued. "All three of you are kitsune, but I sense significant differences among you."

"I'm a nogitsune kitsune," Kieras explained. "They are myobu."

"With your bloodlines, the difference between the two is merely in the color of your fur," Ainali snorted, putting her hands on her hips. "But if that is what you wish to believe, so be it. Even the humans you've met, though, are quite interesting. I still say young Mathis looks like someone I knew."

"He can't be," Kieras said. "You—"

"I know, it's been thousands of years." Ainali waved her off. "But he could be a descendant of the person I am thinking of."

Kieras thought about it and shrugged. "I suppose. No one really knows what happened to the... Viklunders, was it?"

"Yes, the Viklunders," Ainali said. "It's funny that your people know of Inari, but not of the Viklunders. Especially since Inari was a Viklunder."

Kieras didn't quite know what to say to that. She wanted to know more about Inari – she was enough of a myobu she could not deny that – but for some reason felt compelled to avoid any discussion of Viklund.

"So, just how is Mathis so unusual? I admit, he seems to be able to see through my deceptions pretty easily, and he has a talent with a bow, but other than that...."

"He's far more than he thinks he is," Ainali replied. "I understand from his brother that he thinks himself a poor leader and worthless soldier, but he has been in clear command since I have met you. He even seems capable of taking three kitsune under his direction, only one of which is tied to him by binding oaths... which was difficult for a human even in my day, when kitsune instincts were weaker. The first generation of kitsune weren't as heavily affected by the magic inside of them, but I can see a lot of changes have happened in the past two millennia. Your powers have grown stronger, but so have the mental changes."

"Well—"

"Oh, isn't that what you were looking for?" Ainali asked, pointing to something in the bags. It was the components Kieras needed for her illusions – she had actually had her hand on it and hadn't noticed.

"Yes," Kieras said. "I guess it is. How—"

She didn't get to finish before Mathis returned, looking disgusted. Her mother and Daneyko were in tow, as well. "That was a waste of time," he said without preamble.

"What's wrong?" she asked, watching him make his way to the middle of their camp.

"The tunnel's sealed from the other side," Tianhyu said. "It wasn't the last time I was here, so something must have happened. But there's no way any of us are getting through."

"We need another plan," Mathis said. It didn't take him long to come up with one. "I've got an idea, and I still think Daneyko is the best person for the job, but it will have to wait until morning."

"Is there anything we can do in the meantime?" Kieras asked.

Mathis grinned tiredly. "As a matter of fact...."

Daneyko supposed he should be grateful – he was the only one who got any sleep the previous night. He just wished he didn't feel quite so vulnerable.

He wasn't quite sure what to think when Mathis asked just how long he could hold an illusion without his *tama*. Kieras had explained that some of her own illusions could (and had, in the past) held for days without hers. That turned out to be considerably better than he could do – he could only hold an illusion for about eight or nine hours, at best, depending on the extent of the illusion, and that his solid illusions dissolved in seconds without his *tama* nearby.

That turned out to be long enough for Mathis' plan. Daneyko would be heading into Kassia right through the front gates, playing the part of a merchant trader. Anyone entering Kassia was being searched, however, and they could not afford for his *tama* to be discovered.

They had his merchant cart, which was the perfect disguise. Everyone had stayed up the night before searching the Manor House to find trinkets to fill the cart, making him look more like an ordinary trader. The problem came with disguising the creatures pulling his cart – while they would expect him to look like he was from out of town, they would be unlikely to allow someone from out of the country. He used a team of adaba to pull his cart – a beast of burden that looked like a bulky horse, wielding a pair of crooked horns on its head. Adaba pulled like oxen, had the stamina of a donkey, and could run like a thoroughbred racehorse. They didn't normally live anywhere close to Kassia, however, nor even in the more temperate climate of his home in Norre (though they were slowly being cultivated in the region). Such unusual creatures would draw far more attention than was desired, so an illusion to make them appear like simple draft horses was required.

So here he was having his cart (and his person, though that had already been completed) searched for contraband (or whatever it was these guards were looking for), holding an illusion over a couple pack animals without his *tama*, to enter a city he hadn't been to for decades, hoping to see his father who he hadn't set eyes on in just as long.

He glanced around him. When he had last seen the city, they hadn't even finished the keep or the castle walls – now, the place was built up almost as fully as some of the smaller cities in the Norre Hegemony he routinely visited.

"A lot has changed," he mused.

"Oh?" the guard said, taking a closer look at him. "Have you been here, before? I don't recognize you."

"A long time ago," Daneyko said, forcing a smile. He hadn't meant to say anything aloud, but now he had to make conversation to get through this checkpoint. A small blunder on his part. "I was just a kid."

The guard looked him up and down and grunted. "You still are a kid. What are you, eighteen?"

"A few years older than that," Daneyko replied, going the route of telling all half-truths. "It was more than a decade ago that I left, though – things change a lot in that time."

"Yeah, especially here." The guard sighed. "They're building this city up, adding soldiers and tradesmen and other people by the score, making things larger and taller. We need more guards to keep the peace in the streets, but instead of stationing us in the city they're constantly pulling us away to fight at one of the fronts. We're expecting someone to pull the rest of us any day now. After all, why should there be anyone left to protect this place? It's only the capital city!" He snorted, shaking his head. "Eh, never mind me. But mind your purse – like I said, there are a lot more people around here than there was when you left, and not enough guards to keep them in check. Crime is on the rise, and there's not much we can do about it anymore."

"Thanks for the warning," Daneyko said. Chuckling, he gestured to his cart. "But who'd want to steal from a junk peddler, anyway?"

"Hey, some of this is real fine stuff," the guard said. "This tea set, for instance, looks like it comes from the old kingdom. Where did you get all of this stuff?"

"I'm no thief, if that's what you're asking," Daneyko said. He had to be very careful, now. He didn't want to wind up being hauled off for interrogation before even entering the city. "Like I said, I'm a junk peddler. I go through other people's trash and find things I think could be cleaned up, repaired, and resold. Sometimes, I'll even pay for the privilege. That tea set came from Lord Belyk's trash." Daneyko had played games with Belyk when both were still children; he knew he'd been made lord shortly before he left, and that Belyk's manor was far enough away from Kassia city that it would be nearly impossible to check the story.

"Lord Belyk?" The guard laughed. "Yes, I suppose that senile old fool would have thrown out priceless treasures. Still, I'm surprised you've kept it that long, since he's been dead more than a year, now – one of those unfortunates from that incident in the Elder's Villa Lord Kobach set up."

That stung. Kitsune often outlived their human companions, but this was the first human playmate of Daneyko's youth who had died of old age. However, he couldn't afford to let that pain show to the guard – he had to school himself like a proper kitsune should.

"I don't price expensive things like that to sell. That tea set is great to display, to draw customers in, but at the price I set for it most customers ask for something cheaper. Like the bargain priced simple clay tea set you'll find in the crate right below that one – it's got a few chips on it and doesn't look nearly as fancy, but it's just as useful and costs a hundred times less."

The guard grinned. "Smart sales strategy, there. Well, everything here seems to be in order. Go on in. I'd suggest you see Madam Pletka first – she helps new merchants in town and arranges space for them in the market. Then you might want to go to the Black Kraken Inn. It's cheap, there, but they're good about helping people new to the city adjust. I know you've been here before, but things have changed a lot in the past ten years, so you'll probably need the help."

Daneyko smiled a genuine smile at the guard. This was a man who cared for the people – the sort of person who made saving Kassia from itself worthwhile. "Thanks. I'll do that."

"Any time," the guard said.

Daneyko moved on into the city, failing to notice a certain brown-haired spymaster who'd been particularly interested in the conversation.

Kobach frowned as he studied his papers. Devane truly was an incompetent idiot, as far as Kobach could tell. While it was always nice to have a useful idiot under your thumb, Devane was starting to lose his usefulness. It was one thing for him to drive the constant state of war so far that Kassia would have to pull manpower from all over ("all over," in this case, meaning the city of Kassia). That was the plan, after all: Once enough of the guards were out of Kassia and the Lords firmly on Kobach's side, they could move in their own loyal armies and manage a nearly bloodless coup.

A *bloody* coup had been possible for some time, now, but there was a far greater chance of surviving the retribution if Kassia didn't have a bunch of loyalists to the Kazdri line inside the capital city. With the city of Kassia under his control, and the Lords willing to pledge their loyalty to the first truly strong ruler in Kassia's history, the rest of the country would follow suit.

Devane, however, wasn't just pulling men from Kassia City to support multiple military campaigns – he was *losing* them. Not in numbers that would irrevocably ruin their ability to defend themselves, but he was still losing far more people than they had planned on. The current rate of expansion was unsustainable. They needed to keep the borders secure, both now and after Heshka was overthrown.

To that end, he might have to prematurely pull men from his mercenary army for Kassia's defense. It was an army he had gathered in secret, and would be using to secure Kassia City after the coup. If Devane forced him to reveal his army and ruin all their plans, Kobach had no qualms about sending Yulaev after him.

He was growing a little uncomfortable with his spymaster's antics. Kobach had pretty much guessed that Yulaev was a kitsune even before the assassination; now that the suspicion was confirmed, he started to wonder just what the huli jeng kitsune was getting out of the deal. A kitsune of his breed wouldn't be interested in money or power, and no huli jeng would be aiding any human for purely altruistic reasons, but whatever motivated Yulaev had yet to be revealed.

"My Lord," a voice called from the doorway.

Speak of the devil, Kobach thought. "Yes?"

"I was just strolling by the central gates this morning when I saw someone you might be interested in," Yulaev said, entering the room. There was an odd smile on his face that Kobach couldn't place.

"Who?" Kobach asked.

"It's not so much a 'who' as a 'what,' actually," Yulaev said. "It was another kitsune. A young one, but a kitsune nevertheless."

"The girl?" Kobach asked. If Kieras was back, they could begin their plans ahead of schedule under the cover of a royal wedding.

"No." Yulaev laughed, dashing his hopes. "I think he is another relative of our nearby nuisance, however. Kind of had that smell."

"One of his sons visiting, perhaps?" Kobach sighed, disappointed. If it was one of the sons, that would be more detrimental than anything. They had plans to account for Lahti, Kieras, and even Lahti's "mate," Tianhyu, but not for his other children.

"Almost certainly," Yulaev said, still laughing.

Even his laughter is starting to get disturbing, Kobach thought. "Just what is so funny?" Kobach banged his fist on the table impatiently.

"A kitsune's children don't just return to their father on a whim," Yulaev said, finally ending his laughter. "Once leaving home, kitsune children generally make their own path in the world. If one of the sons has come back to Kassia, it must be for a reason. Someone asked him to come – most likely the girl. This kitsune child may not be Kieras... but if he's here, she's likely here as well. Or at least he knows where to find her."

Kobach paused. "Then... then we can get to the final stage of our plan."

"Yes," Yulaev said, placing a hand on Kobach's shoulder and pulling him up. Kobach was startled to find himself pinned to the wall by one hand. "The final stage of *my* plan is about to come to fruition. Thank you for your help... it was fun working with you."

Mathis knew Teslak hadn't understood why he wanted a guard placed on the collapsed tunnel leading from the castle, but the young wulver had assigned one, anyway. That guard, Raux, had taken the seemingly unimportant duty without protest. It was undoubtedly a dull assignment, given how little he would need to do, but Raux seemed quite excited when he bounded back into their camp with something to report.

"Someone's removing the blockage in the tunnel!" the excitable wulver proclaimed. "Hurry! I don't know how long before they get through!"

Mathis was not too alarmed, but he did gather a few soldiers together to meet the intruders. The wulvers were brandishing their broadswords, bolas, and great bows, Kieras had her falcata out, and Tianhyu had her war fan, but Mathis had neither strung his bow nor clicked the blades of his claws into place. The group made it to the head of the tunnel just as the final stone blocking the exit rolled out of place. There was a brief, tense delay, which Teslak spent getting his wulvers lined up and in position to either charge or defend themselves.

It was a bit of a squeeze, but soon a large red furred fox appeared with three full grown and one half-grown tail trailing behind it.

Kieras and Tianhyu were the first to relax, joining Mathis who had never been concerned to begin with. "Your fourth tail is coming in? I always thought you were younger than that!" the elder of the two kitsune vixens said.

The fox turned into a red-haired man the wulvers and Mathis had never seen before, but who could only be Lahti. The redhead stepped forward, wrapping his arms around Tianhyu.

"It's coming in prematurely, actually," Lahti sighed, relaxing in her arm for the first time in decades. "The last year or so has been extremely stressful."

"I can imagine," Mathis said, stepping forward and offering his hand. He didn't begrudge their reunion, but he'd like to be certain that they weren't on any sort of time crunch before allowing them the luxury. "I presume you're Kieras' father, yes?"

The red-haired kitsune sighed, releasing Tianhyu, and turned to glare at Mathis. The later stood there, unflinching, until Lahti finally nodded with a grin and clasped his hand. "That I am. My son, Daneyko, has to remain in the castle until someone gets his tama to him, but he told me about you. You must be Mathis, the young man my daughter has pledged to protect, yes?"

"I am," Mathis replied, releasing the handshake. "I'm really going to need your help if we're going to be successful in this venture, so could I ask for an oath of honesty of some sort until this situation has resolved?"

Lahti frowned. "My daughter may trust you, but I don't know you at all. I'm not sure that it is in my best interest to commit to you in that way."

Tianhyu snorted, bumping her hip against him playfully. "Oh, give him the oath, Lahti. Your daughter trusts him, I trust him, and I assure you that you'll like him in time. He's smart – another one like Kazdri."

Lahti looked first to his exasperated mate, then to his daughter – who was glaring at him, arms crossed and foot tapping – and then finally to Mathis, who really hoped that he was doing a good job of keeping the amusement off his face.

"Oh, very well." Lahti sighed. "I swear that, for the next month, I will give honest answers... when you ask for honesty. Satisfied?"

"No," Mathis said, finally letting himself laugh. "But it'll do for this: Lahti, I am formally asking you for an honest assessment of the situation in Kassia. I'm here to help you, but the most recent information I have about the current crisis is several months old."

Lahti nodded. "Very well. But I know that you and Kieras have found a veden vaki willing to help heal King Kazdri, so let's talk as we head that way."

"Of course," Mathis said, gesturing. "After you."

"You have, of course, noticed that the tunnel was sealed shut," Lahti began. "What you don't know, however, is that I'm the one that sealed it. I was worried about someone finding the tunnels and exploring the place they led."

Mathis' eyebrows narrowed. "But why would... oh. You think a kitsune has joined your enemies, don't you?"

The pain Mathis saw in Lahti's face could not be feigned, even by a kitsune. "I don't just think it, I know it. A huli jeng kitsune to be precise – one who murdered a friend of mine named Gedig. Gedig lived just long enough to tell me his assassin was a huli jeng before he died."

"Gedig's dead?" Kieras said, stricken.

"I'm afraid so, daughter," Lahti said. "The discovery of a huli jeng working on behalf of the conspiracy against King Heshka has terrorized the loyalists... but it has also kept others from *joining* the conspiracy, as most people will not trust someone who would ally themselves with a huli jeng."

"And rightly so!" Tianhyu snapped. Mathis agreed with the sentiment, but had to wonder why the kitsune vixen was so adamant about it.

"Does this have anything to do with the arranged marriage of your daughter to the current heir apparent to the throne?" Mathis asked.

"I still don't quite understand that," Lahti admitted. "Czerniak is certainly not part of their conspiracy, and since Gedig's death I've become convinced that even King Heshka is blameless in this. A marriage between Kieras and Prince Czerniak would only make me more loyal to the royal line, which they seem intent on replacing, so... I'm really not sure what's going on. I just knew I couldn't let her be used in their plans."

"So, with a conspiracy against your king, a huli jeng assassinating your friends, and a plot to entrap you in service by marrying your daughter to the king's son, what is *your* plan? You must have had one when you sent your daughter away – is your plan still viable?"

"Well, the plan I had when I sent my daughter out was to preempt the coup by returning King Kazdri to health and power. He could rally the lords well enough to prevent the leaders of the coup from recruiting any additional support," Lahti said. "Even if it meant removing Heshka from power myself, at least Kassia would not be ruled by the likes of Lord Devane or Lord Kobach, the leaders of the conspiracy. A few months ago, however, my plans had to change.

"A peaceful counter-coup is no longer possible. At the very least, Lord Kobach and Lord Devane are so heavily committed that they face execution if they fail, and they will have supporters among the other lords who are just as committed. And now there's this huli jeng who must be dealt with." Lahti sighed. "So no, my plans, such as they were, are no longer possible. Going forward depends on a number of things. What sort of military support did you bring? If it's strong enough, we might try going out to seek the mercenary army Kobach is 'secretly' raising to 'replace' our regular royal guards, and stop them in the field."

"Well," Mathis began, his voice quirking in wry humor. "I have, at my disposal, the entirety of the Ekholm Irregulars, the principle offensive force of the Ekholm Republic. But, uh, the entirety of the Ekholm Irregulars consists of myself, your daughter, and a couple dozen wulvers. I suspect your mate and son would help you as well. And maybe the veden vaki, but I'm not sure she has any appreciable fighting ability despite her powers. On an individual basis, soldier to soldier, we've probably got the toughest military force in the human world, but we lack the manpower to stand against a full-sized army."

Lahti sighed. "Okay, new plan, then. Let's wake King Kazdri and see what he can come up with. At the very least, having him around won't make things any worse."

Awakening Kazdri proved to be more of a light-show than anyone but Ainali expected. While firelight was kept to a minimum, Ainali's water literally glowed as she channeled her powers. Kazdri glowed with magic, himself, as Tianhyu and Lahti removed the spell that was keeping him alive and asleep. Kieras started putting up illusions to hide the light from the outside world.

Kazdri was restored to life through the combined magic of Kieras' parents and the vaki, but he did not rise to full consciousness, and appeared to be getting rapidly ill. He was awake enough, however, to swallow the glowing water that Ainali forced down his throat. That luminous water shined through his skin, and occasionally even his clothes, as it traveled through his entire body before returning to his mouth. He vomited up what was once Ainali's water, a foul black substance leaving his body with it.

"There," the vaki said, collapsing into her little pool of water with a sigh of exhaustion. It was odd to think of a creature as mystical as one of the haltija of legend being worn out by curing a single man, but no-one would deny the evidence of their eyes that day. Kazdri was lucky to be alive. "The poison is out of his system, and the damage it did to his system is largely healed. His muscles surprisingly haven't atrophied – I did not know kitsune had such talent for preserving the living – so he should be up and around, well rested and healthy, in a minute or two. It was a terrible poison, however. It took a great deal of my strength, and I must rest."

"Then rest, friend haltija," a voice none had heard in several decades croaked. Kieras looked over at Kazdri to see him slowly rise to his feet. "Your job is done."

"King Kazdri!" Tianhyu and Lahti chorused. Kieras vaguely remembered the voice, herself, and so she joined her parents in bowing to the man she recognized as her king.

"I recognize you as my friends. Even you, Lady Kieras," Kazdri said, addressing the younger kitsune vixen, his voice growing in strength as he spoke. "But you have definitely gotten older – you were but a wee child with the cutest fox ears and tail when I last saw you. Lahti, how long have I been... asleep? It must have been years for your daughter to have grown so much."

"It's been a several decades, my king," Lahti said. "Long enough for several of your descendants to take the throne in your absence. And while I will eventually endeavor to explain everything that has happened while you slept, there is a crisis we need your immediate assistance with."

Kazdri grinned wryly. "Yes, I figured things weren't quite right. We're sitting in the ruins of my dusty old manor house, surrounded by wulvers, decades after I was given a lethal poison. If it has indeed been generations, then many of my friends are probably dead by now; many others, who were just children to me yesterday, are undoubtedly old men. But I'd already outlived most of my friends and seen people who were just children become old men in the decades before this latest attempt to take my life, so I suppose I should be getting used to it. Did you ever catch my assassin, by the way?"

"Long ago, yes, My King," Lahti said. "But the situation now is even worse than a lone assassin who slipped through my guard...."

While Kazdri ate a simple meal at Ainali's direction, Lahti spent the next hour explaining the crisis and answering questions. Finally,

Kazdri appeared to be mostly caught up with the situation. He didn't immediately offer any suggestions to remedy the situation, but it wasn't long before he started asking even more questions.

"So... Ekholm," he finally said, addressing Mathis. "A new nation built upon the remnants of Eskesa, which I still remember as my country's most powerful ally. How new?"

Mathis blinked. "What do you mean?"

"How recently was it that Ekholm formally reorganized itself into an independent nation?" Kazdri asked. "Recently enough that your people might still be sending ambassadors to neighboring countries seeking recognition?"

A twinkle appeared in Mathis' eyes. "Ah... I get where you're going with this. While Ekholm has just been recognized as a full-fledged state in the Norre Hegemony, we have yet to declare ourselves to the other great nations of the world. And, as it turns out, I am the sole Ambassador-at-Large for Ekholm, having just finished formalizing our relationship with Norre. The other great powers have yet to be informed, however, which is a job I could be expected to perform."

"The arrival of a new ambassador should be enough of an event to bring out the entire Council of Lords, as well as the King and his family," Kazdri said, shooting a conspiratorial look Mathis' way. The two sensed a kindred spirit in each other, and it showed. "Now to decide what to do when we get them there. Lahti, you must have a pretty good idea of how many of the guards are loyal to my line, and how many will betray us with this... Lord Kobach, was it? If those loyal to Kobach were removed, how serious would the lack of manpower in the castle be?"

"If none of our loyalists were killed, the walls could be held from without, I believe," Lahti replied. "However, between their personal guards, the kitsune assassin, and the lords themselves, there are enough people inside of the Royal Court to cause serious problems, nonetheless."

"How many people will remain on your side, worst case estimate?" Mathis asked before Kazdri could continue.

"A little more than a hundred for sure," Lahti said, then shrugged. "But that's just a guess. I'm hoping we actually have much more than that, but even at best we have less than a thousand."

"And our enemies, worst case?"

"Inside the castle? About the same, I'd wager."

Mathis glanced at the wulvers surrounding them and grinned. "We might not be able to take the castle for you, but we can even up the odds. We will be your protectors until reinforcements can be brought in."

"The longer we wait, however, the stronger Kobach and Devane's position grows, correct?" Kazdri asked. "Well, then, let's stop the bleeding and treat the cancer, by slitting the throats of Lords Kobach and Devane."

A few disguises were needed prior to Mathis leading his "Ambassadorial mission" through the gates of Kassia City. Unlike some kingdoms' Royal Courts, it was perfectly acceptable for visitors to the Kassian Court to wear weapons.

Each member of the Council of Lords was also expected to wear a sword. Swords were often used in ceremonies (such as ceremonial votes; the blade was placed at the lord's feet – turned away was an aye, turn in was a nay, and laying perpendicular was an abstention). A lord was expected to have several armed guardsmen with him at all times.

Ambassadors from foreign powers were typically granted the same rights as a lord, and depriving foreign envoys of the luxury of their own sword and guardsman was seen as insulting. If Mathis were to approach the Royal Court as the only ambassador from as tiny a nation as Ekholm with an escort of twenty armed wulvers, however, he would almost certainly be denied entry. A train of several ambassadors from a multi-state power like Norre, though, each accompanied by their own honor guard, might just be allowed in.

Lahti could appear as himself, of course. Tianhyu, whose position in the Arbiter's office would grant her some legitimate authority to claim Ambassadorial rights for Norre, took the position of one ambassador. Teslak could pose as a representative of the wulvers of Dahlberg – somewhat less legitimately, but the authorities in Dahlberg would most likely look the other way if it was ever brought up. He would have four of his wulvers as his honor guard – an intimidating, but still reasonable, number. The cover story was that Dahlberg, in addition to Ekholm, was entering the Norre Hegemony, and was joining the ambassadorial train to seek recognition of this fact.

The others, though, needed excuses. It was decided that Mathis having an honor guard of wulvers would make their story less plausible, so illusions were placed over the four wulvers selected to be his "honor guard," as were the four selected to escort Tianhyu.

Ainali declared she would not be joining them. She claimed she had no combat skills and didn't believe it important for her to appear, and then used her water to transport herself home to her fountain in Norre instantly.

"But make sure to take some of my water with you when you go," she said before leaving. "When you need my healing talents, simply release my water and call my name. I will come."

That left Kazdri, Kieras, and the remaining wulvers to account for, and they were running out of nations for which they could safely claim to be envoys.

"If the rest of you were girls," Kieras muttered, "We could all go in as the Ambassador's handmaidens, and no one would bother searching us for weapons."

"Well, why don't you?" Mathis suggested. "If you can cast an illusion over a wulver that makes him look human, surely it's not that much harder to make them look female, too."

Kieras flushed. "I... uh... hadn't thought of that. It's doable, definitely, but I can't change their voices – they'll have to keep quiet until we break the illusion."

"It is an excellent idea," Kazdri said. "For everyone but me. I cannot afford the potential for embarrassment. Furthermore, I cannot use kitsune illusions to disguise myself at all – I must be able to make myself instantly recognized when the situation calls for it, and relying on someone else to drop the illusion for me is not ideal."

"Then we'll need to figure out some kind of robe we can make that will hide your face and your missing arm," Lahti said. "Your portrait is found in many public locations, and it's accurate enough you'd be recognized even by those who weren't alive when you were last in the city. You'd probably just be thought of as some sort of actor or impostor, but we can't afford that kind of attention."

Mathis rubbed his forehead. "I don't suppose we have any priest's robes handy, do we?"

"I could get us some easily enough," Lahti chuckled. "Though I'm not sure it will do King Kazdri's reputation much good, impersonating a priest."

*

Lahti was surprised to hear that a full meeting of the council was already in progress when they reached the doors to the Royal Court. The Sergeant-at-Arms manning the door almost stopped him from entering until Lahti explained about the arrival of "an Ambassadorial train from Norre, demanding an immediate audience." The Sergeant-at-Arms led the entire band into the gallery, where a furious debate could be heard.

"...men at the borders are desperate. They need reinforcing!" Lord Devane was saying. He was in the middle of a loud and impassioned speech, but his words were some that Lahti had heard before, time and again, every time he asked for reinforcements on the front line. It was hard to believe he could still muster the enthusiasm for it.

"And just what are you proposing, exactly?" King Heshka asked. His son was standing by him, looking rather angry. Czerniak had been getting more and more frustrated with the corruption in the Council of Lords, and it was getting difficult to keep him from saying anything that could prematurely spark Kobach's faction into making a move.

"Our reserve forces have been depleted," Devane said. "But the line must hold! We have an abundance of soldiers available, guarding cities and castles so deep in Kassia that there is no chance of them ever seeing action. These soldiers are often redundant, as every city and town in the country has also formed a militia that operates independently of the national army. If we shifted defense of these cities to the militia, and pulled those soldiers together, we would have a massive force capable of ending these battles once and for all. In fact, we really only need to pull them from one. Kassia City, itself, has enough soldiers to turn the tide in any of the battles along the front line."

"And which front line, pray tell, do you suggest we reinforce?" Czerniak snapped, clearly unable to contain himself further. While Heshka's reputation for losing his temper had dwindled since Gedig's death, Czerniak's rose, but at least that temper was directed at his enemies rather than his friends. "You now have us engaged in wars with every single neighbor we have, save the Erixonites. Tell me, Lord Devane, as the General of our armies, just why have you forced us into so many wars knowing that we cannot possibly win them all?"

"That is a question I, too, would like to know," Kazdri said, stepping forward. It appeared to Lahti as if the only man he ever truly recognized as his liege lord was going to reveal himself earlier than he had expected.

"Who is this?" Heshka snapped, turning his attention to the gallery for the first time. "And what are all these people doing here?"

"Forgive me, My King," Lahti said, stepping in front of Kazdri with an apologetic look directed he split between both royals. "I missed the start of this meeting because I was busy checking out the credentials of our guests. I believe they may be of some relevance to the current situation, however."

"Well, introduce them, then," Heshka snapped. Lahti now knew the King's seemingly hair-triggered impatience was feigned, for the most part, but it was still a good idea to play along.

"I am privileged to present a team of ambassadors and other representatives from the Norre Hegemony and its member states. Arbiter Tianhyu of the City-State of Norre."

Tianhyu grinned, stepping forward and bowing. She made no attempt to disguise herself beyond wearing Norre's colors, so some of the older lords recognized her. "Greetings."

"Ambassador Mathis of the newly established Ekholm Republic," Lahti continued.

Mathis stepped forward. They couldn't figure out a way for him to carry a bow and arrow into the court unquestioned, so he was restricted to his unusual claw-like weapons. He was far from defenseless with Kieras was on his arm, however. She refused to be separated from the man she was responsible for protecting and so disguised herself as a lady of refinement. She was not too heavily disguised, however, and there were some growing murmurs of recognition by the court, especially from those who had earlier recognized Tianhyu.

"We look forward to a lasting and pleasant relationship between our two nations," Mathis declared, bowing.

"Teslak of the wulver city of Dahlberg...."

Teslak stepped forward and bowed, but did not say anything. He looked rather uncomfortable in this setting, but people who were not familiar with wulvers would not have been able to guess that.

Lahti stepped back, and gestured to allow Kazdri to make his own introductions.

"And I am the rightful King of Kassia, Kazdri I, newly restored to health. And I have a few questions." There were several gasps as Kazdri shucked his robes, revealing a face and figure that was known by all present. Some people looked as if they were accepting his return without question – and with relief – but they were in the minority, with most giving him skeptical looks. Undeterred, Kazdri continued, "The first is why we have a king on the throne instead of a regent when I never actually died. The second is why we are fighting so many wars of aggression simultaneously. I did not establish Kassia to be an expansionist empire, but rather a principled icon for other nations to aspire to copy. I'm guessing someone forgot that after the attempt on my life."

Devane seemed flabbergasted, but Lord Kobach stepped forward as if he had expected such a vanished legend to emerge in front of them. "Indeed. Suppose we believe you are who you say you are – which I don't, though I commend you for the accuracy of your impersonation. The real King Kazdri launched several wars of expansion in his day, sometimes more than one at a time. That strikes me as the actions of a king forging an expansionist empire."

"There are times when wars – even wars of expansion – are appropriate," Kazdri said, directing his attention more to Heshka and the other lords than to Kobach. "Taking strategic territory from hostile powers to keep it from being used against you, or freeing your people from slavery – those are causes for which a war of aggression is just. That does not make one's nation an expansionist empire. Launching so many simultaneous wars of expansion, requiring so much manpower that you cannot defend the territory you take, is more of a concern than simply whether the expansion of your territory is just or not – it is strategic lunacy."

"Perhaps all those wars were launched for the reasons you have described," Kobach replied, then pointed at Lord Devane. "Though I think the 'strategic lunacy' you describe is more likely a failing of our General, here."

Devane, caught completely off guard by such an attack coming from his ally, started blustering. His reaction gave Kazdri time to prepare a rebuttal, but it also gave Lahti time to think. Kobach was acting extremely strange. Not that he didn't frequently act somewhat suspicious, but his behavior was so unorthodox that it demanded Lahti's attention.

In Lahti's experience, Kobach preferred the role of the manipulator, working behind the scenes; not that of the agitator, confronting people in the middle of the Royal Court. Kobach was usually fairly calm, but when the unexpected happened he could be rattled. And, as one of the only things Lahti admired about the Lord Treasurer, he knew how to handle his allies well, never offending them even when he needed to reprimand them. The man now railing against Lord Devane's incompetence had none of these traits, and Lahti began to wonder if there were other differences he might be able to catch.

"...assure you, Lord Devane, that my comment was merely in the hypothetical, and not a true reflection of my feelings," the man who appeared to be Kobach was saying. "I was merely pointing out that there was no way that this person claiming to be King Kazdri could possibly know otherwise... unless he was not who he said he was."

"Hold on, now. Even if this man is who he says he is, I am still king, too," Heshka snapped. That caught everyone's attention, but the surprisingly wise comments he followed with threw everyone off guard. "Whether my predecessors were put onto the throne illegally or not, they were also Kings of Kassia after Kazdri's fall. They – and I – should not lose our title or our status, even if King Kazdri is still alive. But that does not mean that King Kazdri should lose his throne if he proves to still be alive, either. He was sometimes called Kazdri the Immortal, and for good reason – the man refused to age for many decades before he was poisoned, and no-one ever found his body. I am inclined to believe that King Kazdri may, in fact, still be alive, whether this man is he or not. I must admit that his return would force our nation to deal with the ramifications of having two kings – a prospect I do not relish – but both kings should command authority in this room, and both will receive the respect due royalty. At this point, the man purporting to be King Kazdri should not just be handed the authority of a king on his say-so, but until it is proven otherwise he should retain any other courtesies that may belong to him."

"But—" Kobach protested.

"There are many methods of determining the truthfulness of this man's identity," Heshka continued, ignoring his long-time advisor as if he hadn't spoken. "His words are often regarded with distrust among this court, but the Honorable Kitsune Lahti should be able to tell the real King Kazdri from a fake instantly. I would ask Lahti to perform an examination now, and we will accept his verdict until such a time as a more reliable test can be administered."

That was the opening Lahti needed. Before the court, he transformed into his fox form, where his nose worked best, and sniffed. A grim satisfaction grew in him as he turned back into a human – things were about to be settled, one way or another.

"Actually," Lahti said. "I already knew that King Kazdri is who he said he was. Who do you think would have hidden him, protected him, and eventually guided him back to health? I needed to acquire the assistance of many people to complete this process, but I swear that he is who he is claiming to be. However! I find it quite peculiar, 'Lord Kobach,' that you are so insistent that he is an imposter when you are one!"

There was a moment of complete silence, during which Lahti started to wonder if the imposter in front of him would deny it. A slowly growing smile, however, was only the start of the change, as the man who appeared to be Kobach lazily transformed into a man usually seen acting as Kobach's assistant, now revealed as the huli jeng kitsune assassin, Yulaev.

"I suppose I couldn't fool the vaunted kitsune guardian forever. Took you long enough, though." He laughed. "But now that you've confirmed for me that this really is King Kazdri, pulled out of hiding, I really don't need that disguise any more. Ladies and gentlemen... now!"

Doell knew he was running late. His role in the plan was to slip away from the Ambassadorial train before they reached the Royal Court, find Daneyko, give him his tama, and escort him to the throne room. The hope was that he would get to Daneyko before the expected battle started, but the sounds of the fight broke out before he'd gotten out of earshot of the Throne Room.

His nose made him a great tracker, but in this castle there were a lot of scents that he was unfamiliar with. Fortunately, Doell had a general idea of where to go. It wasn't long before he reached the room Daneyko was supposed to be in, but all he saw was darkness. He started using his other senses.

His nose picked out the strong scent of blood the moment he started sniffing, but before he could put himself on his guard the metallic ring of a blade being drawn rang out. By the time Doell realized what was going on, it was too late.

The conspiracy to usurp him was far better organized than Heshka could have imagined. The initial moments were a bloodbath. Yulaev had at least twenty of the lords and their armsmen following his command. That wasn't quite half of the council, but it was more than enough to overwhelm and slaughter many of the unprepared half before they could react. The few surviving "loyalist" nobles were running, and most of the guards – including his own armsmen – were dead or dying. The only people left to stand up to the conspirators were the new arrivals (on the other side of the room, unable to reach Heshka), Kazdri and Lahti (standing in the center of the room, surrounded), Czerniak, and Heshka himself.

There were more wulvers than he would have thought possible. The moment Yulaev acted, a cloud of illusion dissolved to unveil that the woman on one of the ambassador's arms was the long absent Kieras, and the people escorting him included almost two dozen wulvers for all to see, with everyone armed to the teeth. The wulvers leapt out to take on the disloyal lords and their associates, which may very well save Heshka's life, but he would still have to fight his way through to those protectors. Bringing a well-equipped foreign army into the throne room of the king was certainly an odd way to go about protecting him, but Heshka knew to expect that sort of thing from a kitsune protector like Lahti.

So be it, Heshka thought. As he was he couldn't fight, but with most of the enemy paying attention to the wulvers he had a chance to prepare himself. He doffed the ill-fitting crown, released the catches on his utterly useless ceremonial armor, and kicked off his painfully tight royal boots. That left him in his loincloth, some under-armor padding, and nothing else, but at least he could move.

"Well, little king," Lord Devane said, slipping through the line of combat to approach him. "It looks like you have chosen to die looking like a peasant beggar."

"No," Heshka said, smirking darkly. "I just chose to fight, and not be frozen in worthless junk while people come to kill me." With that, he grabbed a loose shoulder piece of his discarded armor and swung hard, throwing it at the old general's face. Using that as a distraction, he ducked and rolled over to the body of one of his armsmen, recovering a still undrawn sword. Heshka vaguely remembered meeting the man's family, once, and decided – if he survived this – to give his death a more heroic tale than reality could claim.

Without his armor, Heshka gained an advantage in speed, and the ceremonial armor he had been wearing would not have helped in any way, but he had to admit to himself that it *felt* safer to be wearing it. He would have to be extremely careful – without armor, misjudging just one swipe of Devane's sword could kill him.

"Do you have any actual talent with the blade, little king?" Devane asked, laughing haughtily.

"Come over here and find out!" Heshka spat.

"I will," Devane said. "But you should know that I don't like fighting battles if I don't outnumber my opponent." Three more of Devane's armsmen had also worked their way through, swords drawn. "So how are you going to beat all of us alone?"

I shouldn't be alone, though, Heshka thought, suddenly worried. He was backing his way towards a column so he could have his back covered but still have several directions for retreat, but it would have been better if he'd been able to fight back-to-back with the person he thought had been right by him. *He was here before this all started. Where the hell is Czerniak?*

Prince Czerniak recognized Kieras the moment he saw her enter the throne room. He wasn't very happy to see her on the arm of a stranger – it was something of a blow to his ego that she would run out of the country to avoid an arranged marriage with him only to return with another man – but he was glad to see her in good health, nonetheless.

When King Kazdri first announced himself – and Czerniak didn't doubt for a second that it was Kazdri, since Lahti would never have allowed someone to imposter him unchallenged – what little attention that had been on the Prince was now directed elsewhere. Czerniak took the opportunity to slip away from his father, hoping to approach Kieras and talk things over with her. He wanted to be sure she wasn't angry at him for the attempt at an arranged marriage – she was his friend first and foremost, and he wanted to keep it that way.

He hadn't quite made it to her side when the huli jeng kitsune disguised as Kobach revealed himself. Instead, he was standing by the Norrish arbiter, Tianhyu, who had a rather striking resemblance to Kieras.

"That... utter... bastard!" the Norrish woman snarled. The threat in her voice could not be produced by a normal human. Czerniak realized she was also a kitsune... and then the name clicked. This was Lahti's long-lost mate and Kieras' mother, returned to Kassia for the first time since before he was born.

"Uh, milady?" he said, turning to her. For that reason, he only heard, and didn't see, the swords being drawn behind him.

"Look out!" Tianhyu snapped, grabbing him and forcing him down. The amount of strength in her grip was surprising, as was her forcefulness. Czerniak found himself shoved down on his knees behind the woman. Claws formed in her hand, and she sliced off a sword-bearing arm that would have otherwise beheaded him.

"Let me give you a hand," a young man said, helping Czerniak to his feet. It was the man who had been on Kieras' arm – Mathis, the Ambassador out of Ekholm. His voice was calming and friendly, and he held out a sword to the prince, hilt-first. "Do you know how to use this?"

"I can," Czerniak said, but he didn't see anything the other man could defend himself with. "But I won't leave you defenseless by taking your only weapon."

"That's not my only weapon," Mathis said confidently, reaching into his robes to pull out some contraption Czerniak didn't recognize. "In fact, I'm giving it to you because I can't use it... though I am far from defenseless. You're the prince, correct?"

"How do you know who I am?" Czerniak asked.

"Lahti made sure we'd know who we could count on as allies before we got here. He tasked me with finding you and ensuring you were safe and uninjured. Which I assume you are, so please just take the sword, already – Lady Tianhyu could use our help."

Tianhyu, who was now wielding a battle fan, did seem to be struggling slightly fighting against four people at once, three of whom were fully armored veteran armsmen. Czerniak took the proffered blade and charged in, drawing off one of the armsmen and engaging him in a clash of swords. His opponent was clearly experienced, but Czerniak had been trained by the best in Lahti. It was a fairly even fight, and might have lasted some time, but the fight was interrupted when a hand, metal glinting from the tips, flashed in and slashed through a joint in the armsman's neck armor. The armsman died instantly.

Czerniak blinked, and then looked to see an oddly smirking Mathis standing at his side. "What are you – another kitsune?"

"No," Mathis said before demonstrating a metallic contraption strapped to his forearm, which mounted blades that extended over the knuckles of his hand. "I just have trouble with swords, so I fight by claw and arrow instead." He glanced over at Tianhyu, who had a snarl on her face and seemed to be looking about wildly. The humor left Mathis' face instantly. "Lady Tianhyu?"

"That kitsune!" she cried, pointing a bloody claw at Yulaev, who was fighting with Lahti. Kieras seemed to be trying to join her father, but hadn't reached him yet. "He is the murderer of my first mate, *and* of two of my children! He... he... he cannot be allowed to kill any more of my kin! He cannot!"

Mathis' eyes widened. "How do you recognize him?"

A fox-like growl emanated from her throat. "Believe me, I know!"

Yulaev disappeared from Czerniak's view, reappearing a moment later backed up against a door. He was wounded – from the look of it, the katar Kazdri had been wielding was stuck in his shoulder – and had chosen to run rather than stay and fight. Lahti and Kieras ran off in pursuit and Tianhyu started to go after him as well.

"Wait!" Mathis said. Tianhyu turned and stared a bit wildly at Mathis, but she stopped. Czerniak was somewhat surprised to see that Tianhyu listened to him – he knew, first hand, how hard it was to get an enraged kitsune to listen to you. "King Kazdri, King Heshka, and Prince Czerniak are all still here. They need your protection."

"The wulvers are here to fight them," Tianhyu snapped. "That is my mate and my daughter—"

"Who are chasing down a wounded coward," Mathis said. "Your mate has sworn to protect Kazdri and his family. If one of them dies during the pursuit of this huli jeng, you know what that will do to him."

"Lahti and Kieras cannot do it alone," Tianhyu said. "They need my help!"

"So does King Heshka! And immediately!" Mathis snapped, pointing. Czerniak was startled to see that his father was trying to fight off four men at once, one of whom was the fabled swordsman

Lord Devane. He needed to go help, but he couldn't afford to do so alone – Czerniak would be over-matched if he didn't get assistance from one of these two. "Look, I am much less of a loss to the battle here than you would be. Without my bow, I'm not really much in a fight against larger numbers like this. I'll go retrieve my bow and help Lahti hunt down the huli jeng. You are needed here, protecting Lahti from the consequences of that hunt!"

"How will you help fight off a huli jeng, the greatest warriors of the kitsune breeds there are, when you are of so little value to *this* battle?"

Mathis looked her right in the eyes. "Milady Tianhyu, I have been asking kitsune for promises since the first time I ever met one of your kind. I've made a few promises in return, and have always done my utmost to keep them. I'll make another one now: I swear that I will find a way to be sure that neither your mate nor Kieras die in battle with this huli jeng. But I need *you* to protect the royals of Kassia while I do."

Tianhyu met Mathis' unwavering gaze, and after a very long moment Czerniak felt he would have to try and rescue his father on his own. Just as he turned to head toward his father, Tianhyu nodded. "Very well. But beware my wrath if you fail!"

To Czerniak's confusion, Mathis handed her a water skin bladder before, and with a nod was gone. Tianhyu stared after him briefly before turning to the prince, though she didn't seem able to meet his eyes.

"Well, let's rescue your father. I have what you might call an *unspoken* promise to keep, as well."

As a weapon that combined sword and shield into a single implement wielded with one hand, the katar had been the ideal weapon for Kazdri since losing his arm. It was disconcerting to be without his katar, and the fact that it was lost in the shoulder of a powerful huli jeng kitsune was cold comfort when he was still in the middle of a fierce battle. It didn't help that two of his most powerful allies immediately ran off after that huli jeng. He quickly armed himself, grabbing a longsword from a fallen soldier and looking around to find his best match among the enemies.

Even with just one arm and wielding a less than ideal weapon, he was confident he could be effective in a fight. It might be his first bit of swordplay in decades, but for him it was as if mere days had passed. Before his poisoning, he was possibly the most experienced swordsman alive (outside of some kitsune). With a katar Kazdri was an exceptional warrior, the likes of which no normal humans could possibly hope to stand against; with a longsword, he was still about as good as the average elite soldier, even with his missing arm.

The wulvers were very effective, and most of the surviving humans on their side were now behind their line of protection. Prince Czerniak and Mathis were in deep conversation with Tianhyu, who could surely handle any threat the average human could bring against them. That left just one small group to assist, where King Heshka was going up against four men on his own.

Stabbing a man in the back was considered dirty fighting, but so was four on one odds, so Kazdri felt no qualms in stabbing through the back of one of the four conspirators on his way to relieve Heshka.

"Ah, you," Heshka said, his voice strained with exertion as he fended off attacks by the other swordsmen. "To be honest, I wasn't sure if you'd care whether I survived this battle or not, since I'm sure you want to reclaim the throne."

"A good king cares about his people," Kazdri said. After a quick assessment of their opponents, he drew the two lesser swordsmen to himself, allowing Heshka to turn his full skill against the strongest – the one Lahti had identified as Lord Devane. "Especially his great-great grandkids... or whatever we are to each other."

Heshka gave a breathless chuckle. Kazdri was glad to see he knew to play along. There were two schools of thought on fighting: One said that you should always maintain a calm single-mindedness, going about your battles silent and emotionless. This school of thought believed that if you broke into taunts, you would lose your concentration. Devane, Lahti had told him, was known to be an adherent to this school, though it was often said he had a temper on the battlefield.

The other, which had been favored by Lahti when training members of the Royal family in Kazdri's day, was ideal for exploiting that temper. It believed in segmenting your mind, fully focusing one part on the instincts and tactics of the battle while allowing the other to plan ahead. This school found taunting and intimidating your opponent into mistake an acceptable maneuver, even though it was sneered at by the first school. A favorite technique was using "casual" conversation to enrage an opponent into making mistakes of aggression – and Heshka was quick to demonstrate that this was a technique Lahti still taught. "Don't make me laugh," he said, dodging the swing of Devane's sword. "I'm too old to laugh and fight at the same time."

"Oh, come on," Kazdri said, parrying one of the conspirator's thrusts. "I'm at least sixty years older than you are, and I don't have a problem with it."

"Yeah, but you've been sleeping the last four decades," Heshka replied, ducking under yet another sword swing and using the follow-through to send him off balance. "You're well rested. Meanwhile, I've been out here, walking around wearing that unbearably uncomfortable ceremonial gear trying to keep this all from happening. I'm entitled to be a little tired!"

"I can't believe you're carrying on during a fight like this," Devane roared. "Are you really this unconcerned with death?"

"Oh, I don't know," a voice Kazdri recognized as Tianhyu's said, seconds before his two opponents were mauled by the claw and steel of a kitsune with a war fan. "My people always joke around in a battle. We feel bantering in the middle of a fight keeps your mind active and reduces the trauma after the battle. Our results seem to bear that out. I'd suggest you try it, but you won't live long enough. Foxfire!"

It was the first time that foxfire had been deployed during the battle, and the effect was immediate. Devane was engulfed in flames, rolling on the floor screaming as he died. His allies, their attention drawn by the call of her attack, were briefly frozen in horror by the demise of their greatest fighter. Within a moment, their resolve broke, and they started running. The wulvers started to pursue, but Kazdri called them back at once.

"Let them run!" he said. "Secure the throne room! There's not much more they can do to us outside of this room, and since we know who they are we don't have to catch them now. They won't get far, so let's first make sure we're safe."

Tianhyu frowned. "I should have done that sooner."

"You never had a clear path," Czerniak said, walking up to join them. "The fighting was almost entirely close quarters action – you couldn't send out a foxfire without hitting an ally. You'll notice even Yulaev would not risk one while he was in battle."

"Ah, him," Tianhyu repeated, growling. "Your lordships, do you need any further assistance from me here?"

"To be honest, Milady," Kazdri said, nodding to the kitsune woman. "I am surprised you're helping us at all. The oath to defend me and my kin was made by your mate, not by you."

"I don't want him to break his promise by losing the lot of you," Tianhyu said ruefully. "But I'm going after him. I won't be losing another mate to that accursed huli jeng! So, I ask again – do you need me any further?"

Heshka glanced at Kazdri, receiving a nod of agreement. "Go," they said together. And that was all she needed before flying out the door at a run.

Kieras caught up with her father almost immediately, but he was not happy to see her.

"A huli jeng of this level is far beyond your capabilities, daughter," Lahti scolded her. Yulaev was still ahead of them, but it was only a matter of time before they caught up to him. "You know that a kitsune re-doubles their power with each tail they grow, and he has more than even the four tails on me."

"Then you'll need help," Kieras insisted. "I can be that help. I've grown in several ways since I was that little troublemaker that left here."

Lahti sighed. "That was just a year ago, daughter. I seriously doubt you've improved *that* much. I would suggest something else you can do to help me, though."

"What do you mean, papa?"

"I sent one of Mathis' wulvers to find Daneyko and return his *tama* to him," Lahti explained. "He should have met us at the door before we entered the Royal Court, but he wasn't there. He still hasn't shown up, and I'm starting to get worried. Go check on Daneyko. If you can find him and see to it that he has recovered his *tama*, maybe the two of you together can come and help."

Although her father was trying to get rid of her, and was doing so out of a misguided – in her mind – effort to protect her, Kieras knew that this was the truth. She had been wondering where Dancyko was, herself. If Daneyko was hurt, or if something happened to the wulver who held his *tama*, someone needed to help him. She looked to be the only one who could.

"Very well, father," she said. "Leave enough of him for me to have some fun, will you?"

"That's my girl," Lahti laughed. Then he was gone, turning down a hall after Yulaev.

Kieras knew exactly where she was going. Daneyko was supposed to be waiting for their arrival in Lahti's suite, which she was intimately familiar with. She did get briefly turned around when entering an area that had been under renovations when she left, but she quickly figured out how to get through that patch and made her way to the suite. It had only been a year – she still knew all of the shortcuts.

The room she entered had some rather unpleasant surprises, however.

"Ah, I was wondering when someone would be coming by. This poor kitsune lad has really been waiting a long time."

Kieras' eyes widened. A wulver – Doell, if she remembered right – lay dead on the floor. Daneyko – while he was still clearly breathing – appeared to be badly wounded and unconscious. Standing over him – holding Daneyko's *tama* tauntingly – was a man who was part of an event that would be etched in her memories for quite some time: Verot, the last surviving Knodelian officer from the Battle of Ekholm.

"You!" She cried. "What are you doing here?"

Verot snorted. "I didn't have many choices when Knodel surrendered. I was a soldier for a country that no longer existed, so I offered my services to someone I thought would appreciate them. A huli jeng kitsune paid me handsomely for word of your whereabouts, and has taught me much about how to fight against your kind. While Yulaev may have intended some other use for me, I'm quite happy to have this chance to avenge my captain."

"There were six of you trying to capture me last time," Kieras snarled. "You failed then. What do you think you can do to me now?"

Verot just smirked, holding out Daneyko's *tama*. "Isn't it amazing how powerful your kind are when you have one of these things, yet how easily beaten you can be without it?"

"I won't be dropping mine this time," she snarled. She leapt forward, claws swinging, but he seemed oblivious to the danger. He brushed the blow aside, smirking, and raised his arm to show it was unwounded. Kieras looked at her hand, startled to see fingernails instead of her claws.

"Yulaev taught me how to use a *tama* to disrupt kitsune illusions... such as the one which makes your claws solid. As a human, I still cannot use it to transform or create foxfire, nor even to cast illusions, but I can use it to defend myself from them for a time." Verot drew a sword with slow, methodically intimidating precision. "You can't fight without your kitsune magic, can you?"

Kieras smirked, drawing her falcata. "I learned my lessons from our last match. I have other weapons, too, now."

Verot frowned. "Then I guess we'll be doing this the hard way."

After their initial clash, Kieras realized her falcata was at a slight disadvantage against Verot's spatha-style longsword – the falcata was shorter by almost ten inches – but she wielded her blade expertly. She would dash in to attack, take several swings, and then draw back as his longsword came into play, forced onto the defensive until she saw another opening. It was a nearly even fight – although one she knew she would win – but the question became how long it would take her to beat him. She kept thinking of her father, undoubtedly outmatched by Yulaev, fighting on his own. She and Daneyko should be there helping him. Instead she was fighting this... this... she did not have a pejorative strong enough for the man delaying her from helping her father. Worse to her eyes was her brother and his severe-looking injuries, lying on the floor bleeding. Speed was of the essence, but this fight seemed interminable.

"I don't have time for this," she insisted. "Foxfire!"

Verot raised his hand, allowing the *tama* he held to absorb her magical attack. She had counted on that, and with a quick swipe removed Verot's hand from his body, *tama* and all.

"Ah!" he cried in pain and horror, dropping his sword to clench his wounded arm's wrist. Kieras smashed his head with the butt of her sword hilt, and then kicked him to send him flying to the ground before bending over to retrieve Daneyko's *tama*.

It was a bit gruesome, picking the magical sphere from the clenched grip of the severed hand, but things were far too urgent for her to care. She noticed a slight drain on her magic when she picked the *tama* up, but that faded by the time she walked across the room to her brother.

A slight scrape of metal warned her a second too late that she needed to make sure her enemies were down permanently before moving on. She spun around, seeing a longsword swinging in her direction with no chance to stop it.

Twang. Twang. Two arrow shots less than a second apart first disarmed and then killed Verot. The first hit his hand, the second dead-on in the ear. She knew of only one person – of any race – capable of those shots.

"Mathis!" she cried, staring at him in surprise and relief. "What are you doing here?"

"Keeping a promise," he said, walking over to inspect Verot. It was the one answer he could give that stopped her from asking any further questions. "Is Daneyko...."

"Still among the living," Kieras answered before he could finish asking. "But he needs to heal, and quickly. Do you have Ainali's water?"

He shook his head. "Your mother has it. He'll have to transform into a fox and heal that way. Do you have his *tama*? I'll wake him up – you help him change. Then – together – we'll go to help your father."

Tianhyu was worried.

She was having a hard time tracking her daughter and her mate. They had split up at one juncture and she wasn't sure which to follow. In the end she picked her daughter; her mate could probably take care of himself long enough for her to catch up.

Unfortunately, Kieras' path was somewhat erratic. There was an area of construction where she had doubled back twice, ultimately going in a circle before moving on, and tracking her had been a real challenge. Finally, however, Tianhyu made her way out of that maze and went forward.

She smelled blood. If she had not already been worried, the iron tinge she smelled made her downright fearful. At the end of a long hallway was a door into a room she vaguely remembered had been her and Lahti's suite, and that was where the blood scent was strongest.

"What happened here?" she wondered aloud, surveying the damage. A wulver lay dead. She didn't remember his name, but he had been as friendly as any wulver she had met – her new friends and allies would regret his passing. Also lying dead – and freshly dead, if she was any judge – was a human she didn't know, a hand missing and arrows through his other wrist and head. It wasn't Mathis or anyone else she recognized, so she passed him by. However, what caught her attention the most was a large pool of blood up against the far wall.

Blood that she could clearly identify by scent as her son's.

His body wasn't there, but he was clearly hurt. And there were still others she had to find, as well.

Worried was an understatement – Tianhyu was in a full-on panic.

Mathis wasn't entirely sure how he had found Kieras, earlier. The terrain didn't leave most of the signs he could use to track wildlife, and he was entirely unfamiliar with the area. He wasn't even entirely sure he would have been able to find the castle entrance without a guide, but he'd gone chasing after the trio of kitsune anyway. He'd gotten only a little ways down the hall before the trail of blood he had been following vanished. Not wanting to turn back, he started running down unfamiliar hallways in the general direction that the blood drops had taken him. It was only a stroke of fortune that he found Kieras at all, much less when he did. But now he had to rely on her to do the tracking.

"This isn't going to work." Kieras glanced over at him, her glossy eyes showing her frustration. Her brother was cradled in her arms, still in his fox form and carrying his tama – they could not leave him behind, but bringing him along was clearly not the ideal way to prepare for what might be the fight of their lives. Mathis had assumed that Daneyko was the reason they were traveling so slowly, but perhaps not. "I can follow their scent, but I can't go any faster than this. They're getting farther and farther away. Their scents are fading fast, and will become untrackable before we can catch up with them."

"All right," Mathis said calmly. "In that case, let's take another tack on this. Yulaev almost certainly wants to get out of the castle – he's smart enough to know that with this many wulvers present, he will not survive long unless he makes himself scarce. He's also probably going to want to avoid the main gates of the keep; he knows that once the Royal family is made safe, loyalist forces will be sent by Kazdri or Heshka to cut off his most likely escape routes. What other, less protected ways might there be out of the city?"

Kieras paused. "Well, there are several tunnels out of the King's Keep. They lead to each redoubt, the barracks, the two residential towers, and many other city landmarks, but they all still leave you behind the city walls. Oh, except for the one leading to the old manor house, but I don't think Yulaev knows about that one – if he did, Kazdri would have been dead before I ever returned."

"Any other exits?"

"There's one through the graveyard along the western wall... or so father said. Yulaev wouldn't be able to use it, though – I don't understand how it works, but it is apparently a way only open to the royal family."

"Any ways he might be able to actually *use?*" Mathis asked impatiently.

"There might be an old shepherd's gate on the south wall," she answered after a moment's thought. "It only has a single watchman because it has been locked shut since they completed the main gate's guardhouses – all foot traffic goes through the main gate, now. If he can make an illusory key for that lock, he might be able to leave that way."

Mathis nodded slowly. "What's the fastest way to that gate?"

"The tunnel to the Retainer's Residence, out the southeast exit, and then down past the granary."

He grinned. "All right, then, lead me to that tunnel, and we'll see if we can pick up the scent from there."

Lahti was tempted to just let the huli jeng go. Yulaev had been found out already, and everyone in the castle knew his face. There was no way he could infiltrate Kassia City, long-term, when his natural human form would be so easily recognized. The conspiracy to usurp Heshka had been unmasked, Kazdri had been resurrected, and in a few short years it wouldn't matter if Yulaev tried anything, anyway, as he would be released from his oath of servitude to the Kassian royal line.

He had his pride, though. Yulaev was a menace, and had insulted him by trying to pull his tricks in the heart of Lahti's territory – in his very home, in fact. Even when two kitsune were of different breeds that were hostile to each other, it was considered taboo to run this sort of scheme in another kitsune's home.

"You won't escape, Yulaev," he called. They were empty words, and both of them knew it, but it might slow the other kitsune to respond.

"You won't survive unless I do," the huli jeng shot back. "Just how are you going to stop me without my killing you?"

They were running down the tunnel towards the Retainer's Residence. With the Council of Lords scheduled to be in session, it was practically unoccupied. Lahti was intimately familiar with that tunnel, having been a part of the process as it was designed, excavated, constructed, and finally decorated. He knew defenses that had been built into those tunnels that no other living person knew about.

These were hidden defenses, like the series of spiked portcullises meant to close off the tunnels in the event an invader made it into one of the keeps. Originally this was intended to be a well-known feature, which the soldiers and guardsmen would have to protect their city with, but after Kazdri was poisoned Lahti had hidden the knowledge and disguised the physical features with small strips of wood that looked like extra support beams and the like.

He threw a knife – a solid illusion, but it would last long enough to do the job – that flew past Yulaev. The throw caused the huli jeng to pause for a moment as he turned to stare at Lahti incredulously.

"Did you actually just miss?" he asked.

Lahti grinned. The knife hit a secret latch, releasing one of the portcullises to slam down to the ground. As long as Yulaev remained in his human form, he could not get through the bars. If he tried to change into his fox form, Lahti would be on him before he could finish the transition, and in terms of combat a kitsune's fox form was at a significant disadvantage.

"No," he said.

"I see," Yulaev said. The huli jeng flexed his wrists. Despite his wounded shoulder, he seemed in perfect control of himself and his magic as he formed a solid illusory sword that Lahti quickly duplicated. "You should have just let me pass, you know. You might have survived. Now I fear your mate will be widowed a second time."

It didn't take Lahti long into the fight before he realized he had severely miscalculated their difference in strength.

The sounds of fighting echoed down the tunnel long before they could see the battle. Explosions of foxfire let them know it was a fight between kitsune, and not just Kobach's supporters battling with the guards.

"Sounds like you were right," Kieras said.

Mathis grimaced. He had been pretty sure their logic was sound, but he'd been of two minds as to whether that was a good thing. It also sounded as if Lahti and Yulaev were already fighting. He'd gotten the definite impression from Tianhyu that Yulaev was far older and stronger than any kitsune he'd ever met, which meant Lahti was likely in over his head. "We have to hurry," he urged.

The tunnel had no splits or intersections down which they might need to search, but it wasn't straight. The designers of the castle must have remembered the classic military doctrine that said it was easier to defend a road built on a curve than one built on a straight line – though it was more a series of slight angles than an actual curve. The effect was the same – it slowed marches and severely reduced the range of projectile weapons (like Mathis' bow), and it obscured sight lines significantly. Full water barrels had been placed at every corner, intended to douse fires or as a base for quickly constructed barricades. No such barricades had been constructed, but all put together it slowed them down and prevented them from seeing how the fight was going until they were almost right on top of it. There were also some odd wooden ornamentations in various locations whose purpose was not immediately apparent... though Mathis had a pretty good guess at what they were.

What they saw as they rounded that final corner was almost sickening. Lahti wasn't just losing the battle, he had already lost it. There was no question that all he was doing, at this point, was simply trying to escape in order to survive. Yulaev was bleeding from his shoulder, but that wasn't fresh. Outside of the injury Kazdri had given him before he fled the battle in the Royal Court, he seemed unhurt. Lahti, as the blood on the floor made apparent, had needed to transform into his fox form just to survive his wounds, and was barely limping even in his fox form.

Mathis started down the passage, intending to try and delay Yulaev long enough for Lahti to escape. Before he could take more than a couple steps, however, a powerful feminine hand held him fast.

He turned to see a glassy-eyed Kieras, one tear falling down her cheek. One hand was holding on to his arm, the other was cradling her injured brother. "You... you can't rescue him. My promise... I can't let you fight him."

"Your father will die if we don't help him!" Mathis snapped. Inside he was sympathetic, but he couldn't afford sympathy at the moment. "This huli jeng killed your mother's first mate, and two of your half brothers fell at his hands long before you were born. They need vengeance. I know you are bound to your promises, and that you think you won't be able to protect me properly if we get involved in that battle, but your father needs rescuing whatever promises were made. You may need to protect me, but you have to let me fight, too."

She shook her head. "I... I can't break my promise... I... maybe I could go rescue my father while you wait here."

Mathis sighed, turning to face her. The action finally dislodged her arm, but he didn't move right away. "You know neither of us can beat him alone, right?"

"I... I know. But what else can I do?"

Mathis gave her a soft smile. "You've made many promises, and those promises can conflict sometimes. I never wanted to put you in a position where they do, but it looks like I must. I'm sorry. As the commanding officer of the army you have sworn to serve, I am giving you this order: Figure out which promise needs to be broken before it's too late."

"Wha—"

He didn't even watch the growing confusion on her face as she processed that order, instead quickly stringing his bow and shooting an arrow. He had seen some rather cleverly hidden levers hidden behind those wooden ornaments he noticed earlier, and after seeing the portcullis deduced that his guess about their function was right. The arrow struck the lever, and another gate-like portcullis dropped between him and the kitsune vixen. He backed away from the bars so she couldn't reach him.

"Sorry," he apologized again. "But I don't see any other way for this to work."

"No!" she screamed as he turned and ran to face Yulaev. The scream did not draw Yulaev's intention, but Mathis was okay with that. He stopped right behind one of the water barrels, using it as cover, and put another arrow on his bow.

Yulaev had a sword raised, ready to strike an unconscious Lahti lying on the ground. Once again, thanks to the architectural features of the tunnels – which had been designed, in part, to prevent people from using bows and arrows successfully – Mathis' only available shot was to disarm. An arrow to the wrist sent Yulaev's sword clattering to the floor.

"Who?" Yulaev snapped, spinning around to see Mathis already notch another arrow on his bowstring, stepping in closer to negate the tunnel's design. "I don't even know you. Why are you even here? Leave! This is not your affair!"

Mathis said nothing in reply, shooting out another arrow. They were only about thirty paces apart, so he had to take the opportunity to fight at a distance while he could.

Yulaev seemed unconcerned with the arrows. Now that he was aware of them coming, he could dodge them before they struck. He was fast – faster that Mathis had thought possible.

Nevertheless, Mathis continued shooting. He could fire quite rapidly when he put his mind to it. With one arrow forcing the huli jeng to dodge, he could actually string another and fire it where he anticipated Yulaev to be. The kitsune was still able to dodge them, for the most part, or to at least avoid all but a glancing blow, but it kept him busy. Mathis only had a finite number of arrows, however, so if things didn't work out soon, he was going to be in real trouble.

A shot finally made it through, hitting almost the exact same spot Kazdri's katar had struck earlier. The blow didn't seem to slow Yulaev, much, but it did anger him.

"Enough!" he screamed. "Foxfire!"

That was the moment Mathis had been waiting for. He took careful aim and fired, then started to move.

Even if this works, he thought ruefully. *This is going to hurt.*

Yulaev couldn't believe it. The ridiculous little human child had actually hit him with one of its silly little arrows, and not just a grazing blow, either. He had been going easy on the brat, and this was how the sniveling creature repaid him? It *hurt* me! he thought, astonished. *How dare it hurt me!*

He sent a powerful foxfire to end the nuisance's life. He was an eight-tailed kitsune about to reach his nine hundredth year of life. As each tail grew in, the power of his magic redoubled, including the ferocity of his foxfires. To his amazement the human confidently stayed in his position, firing another one of those silly arrows... which proved to be not so silly when it hit the precise center of his foxfire, causing it to prematurely explode in a powerful flash of heat and light.

Yulaev was blinded temporarily as he felt the heat scorch his skin.

He had briefly lost his eyesight from the premature detonation of a foxfire several times in his youth, and during those periods of inconvenience he had learned how to handle it. He immediately focused his nose to distinguish smells, and focused his ears on the surrounding echoes.

His nose could tell him nothing, except that his foxfire had been exceptionally sulphurous. With that much sulfur, there was probably enough smoke to inconvenience his enemies as well, but it buried everything else underneath that scent. His hearing proved more fruitful, but he didn't understand the noises he distinguished. Before the light of his foxfire had faded he heard a liquid splash, followed by a pair of metallic clicks.

His eyesight started to clear up after just a few seconds, but he might as well have still been blind. His foxfire was rather smoky in nature, and all he could see in front of him was a dark cloud.

Until a slight glint poked out of one part of the cloud, reflecting a set of steel blades. Yulaev barely had time to react, raising his hands defensively as the human child emerged from the smoke, wearing blades of steel around his wrists. *Are those Inari's Claws?* he wondered in awe.

Inari's or not, they were dangerous. The steel was sharp enough to pierce through the armored hands he held out to defend himself. Despite Yulaev's remarkable strength, even for a kitsune, he found his hands pinned out, away from his body. The young man's head then crashed into Yulaev's own, dazing him, followed by a knee to his gut driving the air out of his stomach. At this range, another foxfire could be lethal to them both, and Yulaev had no desire to commit suicide just to stop some idiot human child he didn't even know.

It was a valiant effort for a human – even Yulaev had to admit that. But it was pointless. "Boy," he croaked. "You've reached the limit of what you can do. You may have trapped my hands, and gotten in close enough to prevent my foxfire from being useful... but those are far from my only weapons."

Yulaev flexed his toes, and steel-like claws formed in place of his toenails. A quick kick, and the human would be dead – and surely the human knew it already. Yet the boy still seemed unfazed.

"I might have used all of my weapons to get to this point," the human said. "But I didn't come alone."

Yulaev didn't know what that meant, but then something he couldn't quite figure out started happening. At first, it seemed like someone was running shards of ice across his body, but then the pain struck. Yulaev was astonished to see a kitsune vixen transforming in front of him, standing in the impossibly small space between him and the human. She had successfully formed sharp, steel-like claws, and they were trying to split him in two from crotch to throat.

In a human, it would be a lethal blow... and still could be, even with a kitsune of Yulaev's caliber, if he didn't act quickly. He staggered back, his hands sliding out of the blades that had pinned them. There was only one way to survive, now. He transformed into a fox and started scampering away, slipping through the bars of the portcullis behind him.

As he left, he took one last glance back, trying to see if he could recognize the intruding kitsune. She vaguely resembled a myobu he knew several centuries before, but was younger... and she was completely naked save for the blood that had sprayed over her when she struck him. She was a pretty thing, a nogitsune, with astonishing flame-red hair and a gorgeous body. She was young – couldn't have been even a full century old – but that hair seemed to float around her face, resembling the nine tails that only the oldest of the elder kitsune managed to grow. His guess was that this was Kieras, the daughter of Lahti, but her name no longer mattered.

He would remember that vixen.

Epilog: The Broken Promise

There was no way to catch him. Kieras knew that much. It would have to be enough that she had wounded the huli jeng so badly that it would take months, if not years, before he could assume human form again.

Kieras turned around to check on Mathis. She had been shocked when he had closed that portcullis on her, but it didn't take long for her to figure out his intentions: She could slip through in her fox form, once she relieved herself of the burden of Daneyko, and could support Mathis secretly until he was ready for her to transform back.

It was ridiculous what she had to put up with to keep promises to that man.

By the time she had managed to wiggle her way through those bars, Yulaev had sent out his foxfire attack. She had watched on in horror, only to see Mathis detonate it with an arrow, douse himself with water, and charge headfirst into the fireball as it dispersed. By the time she had reached them, Mathis was locked in hand-to-hand combat with the huli jeng. Now that the battle was over, she had time to calm down and see just how much damage he had done to himself.

"Are you alright?" she asked, looking him up and down.

Now that the danger had passed, he seemed to be having trouble meeting her eyes. Or looking at her at all, for that matter. "Um, well, yes, I suppose I am."

She eyed the blisters on his arms incredulously. "You sure about that?"

"I'm sure," he insisted. "Not that I don't appreciate the view, but, uh, could you put some clothes on, please?"

"What? Oh!" She had completely forgotten. He had warned her that she would need to break a promise, but even as she broke it she hadn't realized what it was. She had even forgotten she was nude – something she quickly tried to remedy. Tried and failed. "Uh oh."

"What's wrong?" he asked, still not looking at her but with worry clear in his voice.

"I... I can't form clothing," she said, unable to believe it herself. She tried again, focusing even harder, and found her illusory powers were resisting her in a way they never had before. She was riding the emotions from the battle too much to start panicking, but she suspected she would be if she wasn't. "My magic is rebelling against the idea. It won't let me create the illusion of being clothed, solid or not."

Mathis shrank back. "This wouldn't be because I made you break that promise, would it? I am so sorry. I had no idea this would happen. I don't suppose you can still form solid illusions like armor, can you?"

Kieras felt strangely relieved by the idea. It should be upsetting her, but honestly she was just happy that Mathis, her father, and her brother were all alive after a battle like that, even if it meant she had to sacrifice a few minor powers. She picked up a few rocks as spell components, deciding to try Mathis' idea. She found herself capable of creating several pieces of leather armor, which she quickly donned for modesty's sake. They survived being worn, not conflicting with her magic at all, so at least she could still protect herself. "I guess I can. It's not a permanent substitute for my illusory clothes – there's no way I'm going to walk around in armor all day, every day – but at least I can protect myself. Hopefully this is only temporary."

He looked more sincerely apologetic than any time she had seen him since Dahlberg. "I didn't mean to... but it was the only way I could... I'm sorry!"

Kieras rolled her eyes. As embarrassing as this situation was, she didn't really want his apologies. She might want vengeance, later, but that could be tacked on to the prank she owed him. Honestly, she wasn't even sure she cared enough for that much. She had bigger things to worry about... like checking on her father. She started walking over to him, but decided to throw some comforting words over her shoulder.

"Don't worry. I understand exactly why you did it. And I'm grateful you did, actually – I think Papa's going to make it, if we can get treatment for him soon enough. I'm not sure we'd have saved him if you hadn't."

There was a long pause. "Let me guess. You are going to make this practical joke you owe me that much worse because of this, anyway, right?"

She smiled broadly. No, she decided. Despite the new limitation on her powers, she did not think he really deserved any added punishment. But there was no reason to let him know that. "Perhaps."

"Oh, my child!" came a cry from down the hall. Both turned to see Tianhyu standing there, cradling Daneyko to her chest. "Are you all right?"

"Mother!" Kieras cried, running down the hall. "I don't know how to open this gate, but Papa's here, and he's hurt in both forms. Daneyko's hurt, but he will be okay – he'll just have to deal with being in fox form for a while."

Tianhyu snorted, reached up, and pulled yet another hidden lever. The portcullis rose effortlessly. "Lahti sometimes forgets this, but I was around during the construction of these tunnels just as much as he was. And these portcullises were my design."

"Do you have Ainali's water with you?" Mathis asked anxiously. Kieras turned to see him examining Lahti anxiously. "He's alive, but we need her now unless you want him to live the rest of his life without a paw."

That got Tianhyu moving again. She seemed to almost be out of breath. Undoubtedly she had been running all over the castle looking for them, but she could still put on a burst of speed it seemed. She pulled a bowl from her pack, along with the skin of precious water they had collected from Norre.

"Ainali, we are in need!"

A minute passed, and all three of the conscious people present had started looking at each other anxiously, fearing they had done something wrong. Finally, however, Ainali arose out of the water.

"Sorry about that," she said, giggling slightly. "It's been so long since I was out of that underground lake, I've forgotten how some of my powers work."

"We have several wounded," Mathis said hurriedly. "Lahti, here, needs your immediate attention."

Kieras was wondering why he seemed so panicked, but her mother seemed to understand. "Relax, young Mathis," Tianhyu said. "I consider your oath to me fulfilled. All of my children and my mate are still alive, even if they *are* a little worse for wear."

Suddenly, Kieras remembered his words about "keeping a promise." It occurred to her that his insistence on acting, himself, in the battle with Yulaev, was as much him trying to keep her safe as it was his desire to defeat the huli jeng or to prove himself in battle. Going as far as he did to keep a promise was something any kitsune would instantly respect.

"Whew!" Ainali said, breaking her musings. Kieras looked to see her father healed, though still unconscious. "That took more out of me than I thought it would. I keep forgetting the dual forms of you kitsune means I have to heal you twice over. And it looks like I have other patients, too... next!"

Ainali spent time healing all of them. Even the blisters on Mathis' arms were gone by the time she was done. A brief touch refreshed Tianhyu and Kieras, too, and then she was ready to return to her fountain, with everyone perfectly healthy.

She did have some parting words for Kieras, however. "I sense there is a newly formed magical blockage inside of you," she said, her words so soft Mathis almost couldn't hear her... and the others didn't seem to hear them, at all, despite their exceptional kitsune hearing. "Were you forced to break a promise?"

"Yes," Kieras said. "But I don't regret it. It was only by breaking that promise that we all survived."

Ainali nodded as if she had expected that. "Yes, I could tell. Do not worry – this is not a permanent block. There are several ways you may remove it. And, you may wish to know, once your magic resolves the consequences of breaking a promise, you are forever released from it."

"It's such a minor thing compared to what might have happened." Kieras shrugged her off. "What does it matter if my ability to create illusory clothing is gone forever? My father is alive!"

The little vaki laughed. "In itself, perhaps it matters little. But when the block is lifted it will be a signal of great things. Keep trying to break through that block, young one – once that power is restored, you will know that the magics inside you have approved of the path you have taken."

While Kieras didn't particularly care about the minor inconvenience caused by that "magical blockage," as Ainali put it, she wanted to know what she meant. The haltija went silent, however, and soon took her leave after receiving their profuse thanks.

Now recovered from their wounds, it was time for them to return to the Royal Court, where Lahti could summon trusted guardsmen who would support Mathis' wulvers in picking up the pieces.

As they told her the whole details of their battle, Tianhyu did not look happy that Yulaev had escaped, wounded or not. She still expressed per pride that her husband and daughter had survived their battle with so powerful an enemy. Later, Kieras knew, her mother would want to see what could be done to pursue that huli jeng. But in the meantime, all of them would celebrate their reunion and survival, and put those anxieties aside....

Kazdri sighed. "This is going to be a mess to sort out." After the battle, he had found a quiet spot to rest and think, not saying another word until Lahti had called forth his most trusted guardsmen to protect him. "I'm not even sure if I *want* to continue as king, much less if I should."

"I feel the same way," Heshka said. "As king, I had to pretend I was an idiot, wear armor no sane man would wear, and lose friends I care about and time with family that I love. And honestly I'm a lousy king, even if some of the things I did were exaggerated in order to counter my enemies' plans. Nevertheless, we must work this mess out to restore our kingdom's strength and good reputation."

"I'll help," Lahti said, stepping forward to join the two kings. "Every step of the way, until it is as it was when we founded this great kingdom. There was another kitsune trespassing in my territory, in my very home! Who knows how much damage he has done. It will take years for me to fix it all, but you can count on me until that's done, I assure you." Heshka and Kazdri both looked at Lahti, understanding what an extraordinary and noble promise this was for him to make.

Czerniak finally managed to talk with Kieras alone. She and Mathis appeared inseparable, but he could not begrudge the other young man her friendship. He was worried that Kieras might hate him for the attempted marriage, but she never blamed him for any part of it. Still, she didn't approve – Kieras explained that, while she was quite fond of him as a friend, she had no romantic interest in him and no desire to be married to anyone any time soon. She was bound by oath to follow Mathis back to Ekholm, anyway, so it was just as well. Letting one's bride (or bride-to-be) travel to a foreign country with another man would have been a poor way to start a relationship, to say the least. Czerniak wasn't quite sure he was ready to give up, though, and considered asking his father for an appointment as the new Ambassador to Ekholm.

Mathis had been asked to name his reward for helping to save the royals of Kassia. He had been rather embarrassed, but then finally mentioned that – in the process of battling Yulaev – Kieras had lost the ability to create the illusory clothes she was accustomed to wearing. Funding an entire replacement wardrobe went far beyond the abilities of his meager pockets, he explained, so he wondered if the throne could arrange for this wardrobe? His request went over with much amusement for everyone, even the slightly embarrassed Kieras.

Though his injury forced him to remain in his fox form, it was almost an advantage to Yulaev as he made his way down to the tunnels toward the old manor house, following the remnants of Lahti's scent. Occasionally he caught traces of the others as well, less familiar but just as recent. He wasn't sure where he was going, but he was convinced he was on the right path.

Reaching his destination, he found what must have been Kazdri's resting place in those decades he was missing. He had wondered if the man Lahti presented before court really was the old king, or if he was an imposter brought out to disrupt Kobach's plans, but this room was evidence of the truth. Yulaev waded through the remains of the bedchamber, searching carefully but finding little. Then a trace of scent – old, faded, but oft repeated, a clear indication of its importance – led him to follow a path up and through the manor house.

Aha, he realized. *The old library.*

The cabinet door was no obstacle, despite his fox form's weakened state, and soon his paws were reaching in to grasp a small but ornate wooden case with a glass cover. It was filled with myobu jewelry, some of which – by the look of it – had been around since Inari's day. There was no lock to break, but a trick catch of some sort which resisted his claws' attempts to find and manipulate it. He settled for dragging it over a shelf ledge, where it fell to the stone floor and shattered its glass cover.

Careful to avoid further injury on the glass shards, Yulaev's claws sifted through the wreckage. He snarled quietly, discontent.

Nothing. Useless trinkets. Of interest to one of those idiot Inari worshipers, perhaps, but...

A splinter of the wooden bottom splayed out from the case, and he picked at it aimlessly with a claw. *Wait, what's this?* A trace of yellowed parchment peeked out under the corner.

Probing gingerly, he discovered the box's secret. The bottom stuck stubbornly, but eventually slid off, revealing a thin compartment barely large enough for the papers it held. He recognized the language on the papers, as old as it was, for he had seen a similar document before. He couldn't read it, himself, but he was able to pick up a few words... including one which seemed to be the name of a city he knew well. *Eskesa...*

"The ancient ruins," he muttered to himself. *I wonder if they even knew they had this. If I put this somewhere that a member of that damned myobu priesthood can find it, I bet they would do my dirty work for me. But I'll take part of it. Those priests will have to come to me if they want the rest of it.*

Discussions about the structure of Kassia's government, going forward, continued well into the evening as refugee loyalist nobles were found, reassured, and returned to the court. In the end, the seventeen surviving lords were outnumbered by the wulvers who had survived the battle. Those surviving lords who had conspired with or supported Kobach, Devane, or Yulaev were quickly being hunted down and executed. It was still unclear how many might have escaped, but they were no longer an immediate threat.

There was brief debate as to whether Kobach actually existed, or if he had been Yulaev this entire time, but too many people had seen the two of them together (as recently as earlier that day) for that thought to be taken seriously. Kobach had clearly been the head of the conspiracy against Heshka, as well, which left Yulaev's exact role unclear. Just why had Yulaev involved himself in this petty human conspiracy? What was his endgame supposed to be, anyway? And what happened to the real Kobach, anyway?

A simple guardsman brought an answer to that last question late in the evening. "My Lords," he said, bowing before the throne. With two kings, both wearing crowns (though Heshka's still fit poorly), it was difficult to say which he should bow to, but no one begrudged him his uncertainty. "I have just come from the investigation in Lord Kobach's suite."

His announcement drew silence from all present, even the most garrulous of the Lords. "What have you found?" Kazdri demanded.

"Not much," the guard admitted. "Everything in the suite had been burned, but the room had apparently been ransacked before that. Tables, the bed, and a few chairs were all broken apart in ways the fire would not have done."

"Did you find a body?" Mathis asked. He was not a royal, but his deeds had earned him enough status to ask his own questions in this investigation.

"Not as such," the guard admitted. "A few burnt bones at most, no longer intact enough to be sure they were human. But at the hottest point in the fire, I imagine anybody would have burned to ashes. It was actually so hot in places that the stone melted into glass."

Kazdri snorted. "Well, whatever happened there, it's safe to say Lord Kobach is no longer in the kingdom."

"No," Lahti said. "But Yulaev *is* a kitsune, Your Majesty. He is very wily and we should not make any assumptions. I have yet to figure out just why he targetted us in the first place."

"He won't be back for a while, at least," Czerniak said, grinning over at Kieras. "I think we can be certain of that."

"This may be true," Mathis said. "But I urge you to be on the alert nonetheless. I, for one, am going to strongly suggest to the Council in Ekholm that we learn more about the huli jeng kitsune and what we might do to protect ourselves from them. And should there be any other such creatures we ought to know more about, I hope our kitsune friends will help us prepare for them as well."

"There you are," Kobach snapped as a fox scampered over to the small abandoned farm building they had agreed to meet at. "Well? First you make me think you were going to kill me, then you gave me orders like you were *my* master, instead of the other way around. I let you take my place at the council meeting. You said that, by the end of this day, I would be king. Am I king, yet? How did it go?"

"I probably won't be able to safely transform into a human for months – maybe not even for a year, thanks to that mess," the fox snapped testily. "How well do you think it went?"

"I told you it was premature to launch the rebellion, Yulaev," Kobach laughed. "For all your vaunted kitsune trickery, you're still too impatient to make a plan of this grand a scheme succeed."

"Yes, impatience!" Yulaev growled. "Impatience beat us. It *was* impatience that led you to try that ridiculous arranged marriage scheme, correct?" One of his paws contemplatively reached over and stroked his underbelly but he continued to send his foxy stare into the now deposed lord's face.

"What do you mean?" Kobach replied, shifting uncomfortably. "That should have worked."

Yulaev shook his head. "Lahti seemed to believe you were planning to use the marriage of Czerniak to his daughter to control both him and the boy. It prompted him to train Czerniak to be a stronger man and a better king, one who wouldn't be influenced by the likes of you. That wasn't your plan at all, was it?"

"No," Kobach said. "But if you're going to tell me that Prince Czerniak foiled our plans, I refuse to believe you. The prince is a weakling and a sap – someone that you should have been able to handle easily, no matter what training Lahti has given him."

"No," Yulaev said, "Czerniak's ascendancy is but only one of many consequences of *your* impatience. In five years, Lahti would have been released from service to the line of King Kazdri, but you wanted the throne sooner than that. You would have used this marriage to drive the King and Lahti apart, then kill the last heir to the throne and remove another of us 'dangerous kitsune' from your midst. Was not that your plan?"

"Not really. Of course, you never bothered to find out what I was trying to do, but let's go with that." Kobach rolled his eyes. "You make it sound like you advised against my plan from the start. When I told you I wanted to turn Lahti and Heshka against each other, weren't you the one who suggested the arranged marriage in the first place?"

"Well, of course. But I am a kitsune, after all – I had ulterior motives." Yulaev barked a laugh. "Kobach, my friend, you no longer have any chance to claim that throne. By now, your mercenary army has heard of your 'death' at my hands, and will be scattering to the winds."

"My death?" Kobach replied, startled. "What are you talking about?"

"I faked your death for you," Yulaev explained, making it sound as if he'd done Kobach a favor. "It will throw the Kassian Guard off your trail, allowing you to make your escape that much easier. No need to thank me."

"Thank you?" Kobach cried, outraged. "Even in exile, while I still had my name I could have rallied my forces and claimed the throne. Now that my allies think me dead—"

"You've lost everything. Yes, sorry about that." Yulaev didn't sound apologetic at all. "I have my own goals which have nothing to do with your greedy desires to seize Kassia's throne. You should be grateful that I spared your life – I could not afford for the line of King Kazdri to die out, so I was preparing to betray you before you could assassinate them, anyway."

"Your own goals?" Kobach exclaimed. He was so worked up, he didn't even seem to care about Yulaev's threat to betray him – something the kitsune found quite interesting. "What nonsense are you spouting on about, now? What goals? And what does it have to do with the line of King Kazdri?"

"I am an old kitsune," Yulaev began, deciding to explain everything. There was no point in hiding anything, now. "Older than my tails would lead you to believe. I was in the first generation of the huli jeng, the last and greatest of the kitsune races. We do not get along with many of the lesser breeds, especially not the myobu, but we do share a fascination with the ancient wizard Inari. Many centuries ago, I learned that there was a powerful legacy of Inari's that would only be opened to the world again when his heirs were once again united."

"What is this treasure?" Kobach asked, his curiosity piqued.

"No one knows," Yulaev said. "That does not matter. Making sure it does not fall into the hands of the myobu priesthood's allies is vital, however. The question we should be asking is 'who are the heirs?'"

Kobach raised a single, curious eyebrow. "All right, then – who *are* these heirs?"

"Inari had two children," Yulaev began. "Both daughters. The first daughter he turned into a kitsune, the first of the myobu. Not all myobu were this daughter's children, but I believe that her bloodline has spread across the entirety of the myobu race by this time. It is the other, oft-forgotten daughter who, in my mind, is the important one."

"I know little about Inari," Kobach said. "I wasn't sure I believed the story that he'd changed one of his children into the first kitsune to begin with. I can't see how his other child would matter, though."

"Raedeke, Inari's second daughter, is perhaps the most underrated mage in all of history," Kobach continued. "She created at least one breed of kitsune of her own – the nogitsune. She worked other wonders, but many of her deeds are lost to history. I believe there is at least one other breed of kitsune, a secret fifth major breed, that she created late in her life. The important thing is that one of her own children was made into a nogitsune. Her other child remained human, however. In order to obtain this legacy of Inari's, I need to reunite through marriage or child the bloodlines of Inari's firstborn, Myobu, and his grandchildren, both the nogitsune and the bloodline founded by his lone human grandchild. I believe that Kazdri and his descendants are one of these human bloodlines, the so-called 'Heirs of Inari.'"

"And so that is why you suggested I force Kieras and Czerniak into a marriage – you wanted to 'reunite the heirs!'" Kobach exclaimed.

"I'm amazed you figured that out so quickly," Yulaev said, the dripping sarcasm only barely hidden by his fox form's animalistic accent. "Now, of course, that plan is quite impossible. She has rejected Prince Czerniak... and if Kieras is who I think she is, well, I've already decided she needs to be slaughtered for daring to harm me. A shame – she is a pretty one. We will just have to find another set of Inari's Heirs – there are still plenty of them out there!"

He looked away, his thoughts apparently drifting.

"And, there's something... something that must be found, as well. At least now at least I have an idea where someone should look." He returned his gaze to Kobach.

"And me?" Kobach asked, the realization sinking in that his goals and Yulaev's goals had never exactly matched.

Yulaev paused to assess him carefully. "Hm... well, you can be glad for your life's sake that I may still have *some* use for you...."

Also from Fennec Fox Press

The Law of Swords Series
Genre: Heroic Fantasy, New Adult

The Law of Swords: A set of laws written to prevent infighting among Svieda's Royal Heirs if the King dies unexpectedly. One of these laws has never been needed... until now.

I. In Treachery Forged
When Svieda is betrayed and invaded by a former ally, Sword Prince Maelgyn must travel to the province of Sopan to take command of his armies and help repel the invaders. Along the way he rescues a Dwarven Caravan, forges a badly needed alliance, and accidentally gets married. And then he learns about the dragons...
NOW AVAILABLE!
Ebook: $5.99 retail
Print: $18.99 retail
http://www.fennecfoxpress.com/

II. In Forgery Divided
Maelgyn may have proven himself to be a High Mage, but he's only one man. His wife is captured during a massive battle, his new King turns out to be an imposter, and the Dragons are entering the battle. Despite all this, Maelgyn has to turn his attention to a rescue mission which pits him up against an even bigger threat: The Elves.
Coming January 2015

The Inari's Children Series
Genre: Heroic Fantasy

Once magic was plentiful and the world was dominated by a singular empire whose name has long been lost to history. In its time, the great wizard Inari developed his greatest creation: The kitsune. His enemies were quick to copy him, and soon the world was populated with many different types of this remarkable creation. Two thousand years later these different breeds of kitsune are fighting amongst themselves, and the rest of the human world is about to join them.

I. The Kitsune Stratagem

To avoid being used as a political pawn against her father, a young kitsune vixen named Kieras must leave her homeland. She soon gets caught up in the fortunes of Mathis, a vagabond hunter from Ekholm, a once sleepy little town on the verge of becoming a small city. To find a way to return home, Kieras must first help Mathis save Ekholm from threats both inside and out.

Ebook: $5.99 retail

Print (Coming in August): $18.99 retail

http://www.fennecfoxpress.com/

II. By Claw and Arrow

Mathis and Kieras return to Ekholm. They don't get to stay for long, however, before the Myobu Priesthood approach them with a mission that sends them to the ancient ruins of Eskesa. Yulaev takes Kobach to Erixonite lands, while Kazdri and Heshka resolve the issue of just who the reigning King of Kassia is, anyway.

Coming 2015. For updates, please sign up for our mailing list at: https://tinyletter.com/FennecFoxPress

THE RINK OF WAR SERIES

Genre: Space Opera, Short Fiction

Former professional hockey star Alexander Zednik had a career-ending injury very early into his career. To rehab his injury, he went into space, to the "gold rush" in the Main Belt Asteroids. There, he attempted to set up a new sport: Microgravity Hockey.

Several years later, he and his plans have been largely forgotten. He is making a living running a small warehousing business for the local miners, which introduces him to Anita Condon. All she wants is warehouse space for her uncle's science lab, and a guide through this new world of the Main Belt Asteroids....

An open-ended series of novelettes and novellas.

I. TO THE RINK OF WAR

When Alexander Zednik accepts a warehousing client named Anita

Condon, he finds himself fighting off a rogue mercenary intent on destroying her cargo.
Ebook: $0.99 retail
http://www.fennecfoxpress.com/

II. TITLE TBA

Coming 2015. For updates, please sign up for our mailing list.

THE SHIELDCLADS SERIES

Genre: Space Opera

During an Academy exercise, an Earth Navy student invents a new system for energy shielding warships. This revolutionary technology is immediately put to the test when Earth is hit by a surprise attack. The new enemy reveals that they have energy shields of their own... but where did they come from, and how will Earth respond to this threat?

I. THE MERRIMACK EVENT

When a real war breaks out during a Naval Academy wargame, it falls upon a squadron of cadet-crewed warships commanded by a former Army officer to strike back, resulting in the first ever battle between shieldclads.
Coming October 2014.

Standalone Titles

This Book Cannot Possibly Make Any Money

Genre: Multi-genre Anthology, Humor

An anthology of experimental fiction, inside jokes, story fragments from the cutting room floor, and high school poetry, all of which conventional wisdom says cannot possibly make any money.
Coming Soon. For updates, please sign up for our mailing list at:
https://tinyletter.com/FennecFoxPress